BLOOD TIES

BOOK 1 OF THE CITY OF BLOOD DUOLOGY

FOX KELLY

©2025 Fox Kelly

E-book ISBN- 979-8-9989904-1-0

Paperback ISBN-979-8-9989904-0-3/979-8-9989904-2-7 B&N

Library of Congress Control Number: 2025915950

This novel is entirely a work of fiction. The names, characters, and incidents portrayed in it are the work of the author's imagination. Any resemblances to actual persons, living or dead, events, or localities are entirely coincidental.

 Formatted with Vellum

CONTENTS

For mama
Thank you for my love of books.

Author's Note and Content Warning

Reader,

Thank you, sincerely, for giving this book a chance. It is something I love dearly and is a book I genuinely would want to read.

This book is a paranormal romance, and while there are a lot of light moments of romance, complete devotion, and jokes, there are also some dark themes.

The world of Blood Ties takes place in a world where the political landscape looks very different than our own but there are moments where the people who live under the oppression of the vampire government may experience things that are disturbing to some readers.

Please be mindful of content such as:

- Sexual Blood play
- Murder
- Religious themes that may be considered offensive
- Torture- both human and non-human
- Sexual choking

- Non-consensual choking

While I have no hope or intention that any of these themes cause reader's distress, discretion is advised.

If you have any additional questions, or concerns related to the content, please contact the author at LK@foxkelly.com.

GLOSSARY

Alla salute e alla felicitá (Italian)-To health and happiness (a toast)

Amare in eternal (Italian)- To love, forever

Bokor (Haitian)- Witch, Vodou priest/ess

Bonjour (French)- Hello

Buon Compleanno (Italian)- Happy Birthday

Castello di Fenis (Italian)- Fenis Castle, Malvani family estate

Cattedrale (Italian)- cathedral

Cattedrale del Trono Notturno (Italian)- Cathedral of the Nocturnal Throne

Corvo di Sangue (Italian)- Blood Raven

Crepuscule (French)- Twilight

Crepulsculien (French)- no direct translation- means "Twilighter" or not of the light and not of the night

Fleur-de-lis (French)- lily flower, the symbol of New Orleans and the Devereaux family

Governaturno (Italian)- 'governors' for each of the districts in Ville de Sang.

Gran zanmi mwen (Haitian Creole)- My great friend

Guerra de Sang (French)- Blood War- the war between the French and Italian vampires

La Casa del Corvo di Sangue (Italian)- The House of the Blood Ravens

La Luna (Italian)- the moon

Las chiens de sang (French)- Bloodhounds/ blood dogs

La stirpe della mia famiglia (Italian)- My family lineage

La Stirpe Malvani di Vampiri (Italian)- The Malvani Vampire lineage

Legame (Italian)- Bind/Bond

Legame di Sangue (Italian) Blood Bond

Le Lien Eternal (French)- The Eternal Bond

L'Empire des Ombres Nocturnes (French)- The Kingdom of the Night Shadows aka the Shadow Kingdom

L'immortal (French)- the immortal

Mon Tresor (French)- my treasure

Nipote (Italian)- Nephew

Ombra (French)- Shadow

Perfetta (Italian)- perfect

Piazza della Luna (Italian)- Moon Square

Principe/Principessa (Italian)- Prince/Princess

Re/Regina (Italian)- King/Queen

Sanguine Nocturnus (Latin)- roughly "blood at night"- what the vampires call themselves

Si, c'erano tesori da catturare (Italian)- Yes, there were treasures to be captured

S'il vous plâit (French)- please

Società Italiana di Mutua Beneficenza (Italian)- Italian Mutual Benefit Society

Stellino (Italian)-Little star

Tesoro Mio (Italian)- My treasure

Tisaneuse (Haitian Creole)- Herbalist/ magic

Tout est parfait (French)- Everything is perfect

Tutela a mortuis (Latin) - Protection from the dead

Tet mare (Haitian) - head covering. A type of wrapped and tied head scarf worn by Haitians and Haitian Creole

Un'cuore, un'anima, un'eternità (Latin) - one heart, one soul, one eternity

Vampiro (Italian) - vampire

Ville de Sang (French) - City of Blood

Voglio stare con te fino all'ultima luna. Siamo fatti l'uno per l'altra. In eterno. (Italian) - I want to be with you until the last moon. We are made for each other. Forever.

Zio/Zia (Italian) - uncle/aunt

IN THE BEGINNING THERE WAS

S anguis.
       Blod.
         Sang.
Kan.
Sangue.
Blut.
Khun.
Sangre.
Blood.
BLOOD.
BLOOD.
BLOOD.
BLOOD.

CHAPTER 1
ELINA

When New Orleans fell, it fell as a lamb. That is to say, at the slaughter.

I'VE NEVER EVEN KNOWN this place as New Orleans. When I came screaming and bloody into the world, it had long since been Ville de Sang. The City of Blood is a dramatic name for a city but here—where the streets often run crimson with blood—there is no better name. Behind the tall walls guarded by the Shadow Court, we humans live our lives as normally as possible—if normal is even possible.

"Lilly! Get out here or I'm coming back there and dragging you out! Rian is so tired of your shit. You've got a client waiting and I'm sick of you fucking up my tips," I yell into the hallway behind me. "Ungrateful, little shit," I mumble under my breath as I push through the door behind the bar, wine glass in hand.

Wednesdays are slow in the bar, and tonight is no exception. It's almost cozy in its intimacy on a night like this. The dim lighting creates a comfortable atmosphere, with the customers spaced around the room, while the piano man plays relaxing jazz interspersed with covers. People put in requests which he puts his own blues-style twist on. The stage is not set up for dancers tonight, but rather, the three piece band that works occasionally for tips. Crooning from the stage, I hear a rendition of an old Louis Armstrong hit.

"Here you go, Lucian. Lilly will be right out," I say, smiling at the dark, broody, and quite frankly, pissed vamp sitting across the shiny wooden bar top from me. He drums his fingers against the wood, exuding aggression, his hand holding his glass tightly. There is an unusual darkness in his grey eyes. His sharp cheekbones are shadowed by the long black hair that hangs in his face. He's a regular and Lilly is his favorite. I don't blame her one bit for hiding in the back though, the bite doesn't have to hurt—it can even be pleasurable, or so I've heard—but tonight he's in a particular mood and when he's in a mood, it doesn't matter that he came to the Velvet Tomb on his own, that he's paying for her time, her blood, her body.

He won't make it easy for her.

A few hours later, as the sun rises over the Mississippi River, I slide into the backseat of a hired black sedan and lay my head back on the headrest. Trying to decompress in the twenty minute ride from the French Quarter to Little Woods is crucial if I want to get any sleep at all before it's time to start over again. The streets are quiet this early, after the *Sanguine Nocturnus* have retired to their dark windowless tombs for the day, and before the humans start to move about in the sun. It's the way things are now—humans keep the city running and moving forward in the day and the vamps prowl the streets at night, staining them red with their brutality and disregard for human life. A lot of residents of Ville de Sang have long since abandoned any hope of escape or change.

As the car pulls to the curb in front of my house, I push a $20 through the slot, thank the driver and climb out. Trudging up the path to my house, exhausted and half dead on my feet, I grab the mail from the box and place my palm on the reader on the door.

"I'm home! Grand-mere? You around?" I bellow as I enter the warm interior of my family home. We've lived here since before the Closing. These walls are our sanctuary, our protection from the monsters that go bump in the night. They are also where all my happy memories live. The smell of creole spices always permeates the air, as though its part of the very foundations of the house. The well-loved matching floral-patterned living room furniture I've gotten yelled at far too many times for jumping on, and the worn, but functional, tables and chairs make up the painting of the first 28 years of my life.

Within this safe haven, Grand-pere Jean drew his final breath, my mother took her first, and I came into the world— only to lose her too soon. Three generations of Girards, born, lived, and lost in the same place. My Grand-mere Celeste lived here with Grand-pere Jean when the walls went up sixty years ago, and my maman was born upstairs in the second room on the right. And I was born in the first room on the left twenty-eight years ago. This little house is the only place I ever fully relax or feel safe. No one has ever invited a member of the *Sanguine Nocturnus* inside and we are as safe as we could ever be.

Safety in The City of Blood is always an illusion though.

"Elina? In the kitchen dear." *Who else would it be*, I think as I roll my eyes. Grand-mere Celeste is cooking when I wander into the kitchen. It smells like cayenne and maple syrup in here as Grand-mere stands in front of an ancient stove, cast iron skillet on the fire. Her long, blue, satin night-dress clings to her wide hips and moves slightly as she sways. The deep tan of her skin never fades and is a testament to her creole heritage. The white braid all the way down her back speaks of a long life lived.

"Would you like some ho-cakes? Bacon?" She doesn't approve of the Velvet Tomb and my work within it, but she stands as my staunch supporter and her warm breakfasts help bring me back to humanity when I emerge from the darkness.

"No thanks, I just wanted to say hi before I head upstairs." I pause, rifling through my bag. "I'm putting money in the jar." I drop $200 into the family jar—not a bad take for a Wednesday night. Climbing the old creaky stairs, a few at a time, I trail my hand up the worn banister, feeling the warmth of home flow through me. Pushing my door open, I find my tiny room at the top of the stairs as I left it, bed unmade, piles of both clean and dirty clothes spread around. Memories of my childhood littering every surface, reminding me of when life was simpler. Flopping facedown on the bed, I am asleep in minutes.

BEEP. BEEP. BEEP.

Four too-short hours later, my alarm drags me from the pit of sleep. I fight against its hold though my exhaustion overwhelms me. The beeping doesn't stop. Sighing, I sit up. I'm covered in a fine sheen of sweat and my sheets are damp. I don't know if it's from the heat or from the nightmares that often plague me, it's impossible to tell. March in Louisiana is only the beginning of the heat, and its still suffocating here.

Peeling off my clothes and heading down the hall to the bathroom, I start compiling a list of things I need to do before work tonight; laundry, check on Sarah, weekly blood donation, pick up vitamins from the pharmacy.

Mundane human tasks that seem so normal if you don't think about the fact that Sarah is recovering from a vamp attack in the street, or that my weekly blood donation is for *La Casa del Corvo di Sangue*. And that my vitamins, iron supplements and B12, aren't for wellness but to keep me able to continue donating and *not* collapse from blood loss.

I stand in front of the cathedral in my tour-guide uniform in the afternoon, tugging on the hem of my black polo. I haven't slept enough but there aren't any more hours available for sleep today. The small group gathers around me, languishing in the bright sun.

Sucking in a deep breath, I prepare to begin speaking.

"We are going to begin the tour of Ville de Sang here in front of *Cattedrale del Trono Notturno* or Cathedral of the Nocturnal Throne. Formerly St. Louis Cathedral, the *Sanguine Nocturnus* renamed the historic church multiple times in the last sixty years and it has had its current name since 2006. It's been twenty-five years since *La Casa del Corvo di Sangue* overthrew *L'Empire des Ombres Nocturnes* for control of the city. The Blood Ravens currently control the city with the Malvani family sitting in court within these very walls every night. Re Marcus, as he is known, is for all intent and purposes, the King of Ville de Sang. I warn you though, humans are not safe at night so do not venture out of your hotels without an escort at any time. Questions before we move on?"

"Are there any places where humans can interact with the vampires safely?" A short, heavy, blond woman asks from the back. *Goddamned tourists.* Why they want to come here and gawk at the humans trapped within the confines of the concrete barriers and play pretend with the vamps, I will never understand. At least the forsaken tours help pay the bills.

"Safely?" I laugh. "No, but if you want to pretend for the night there are places that cater to...curiosity. Please set up safe transportation with your hotel. 21+ and over only." I hand over a card.

AT *PIAZZA DELLA LUNA*, as it's been called since the Jackson Square name was stripped away, I take in the low wall by the water and the evenly spaced guards, in their perfect black suits, one about every 25 feet. The concrete surround is only about eight feet high in this part of the city, the river on the other side. I guess the aesthetics of a water view won over the practicality of a higher fortification. Where the walls meet the highway, they tower fifteen feet off the ground, making it impossible for a human to scale them. The guards studiously ignore us, uninterested unless someone were to try to run.

"Behind me, you can see the wall blocking access to the Mississippi River and the Shadow Court guards. For those who don't know, the Shadow Court acts as the police force for the Blood Ravens and they are humans who are enthrall to the vamps. When a human blood-shares with a vamp, a bond is formed which results in humans who are loyal, even unto death, to a vampire. The humans behind me serve the Blood Ravens through blood and duty, protecting the borders of The City of Blood through force. They will prevent any human from unlawfully leaving. When the barriers went up, the human government outside of New Orleans signed a treaty agreement that the *Sanguine Nocturnus* would rule inside the borders without interference from the outside as long as they kept their bloodlust contained within the very walls they had erected. For 60 years, the vamps have run Ville de Sang with no further issue from anyone. Questions?"

"What happened when the Blood Ravens took over?" asks a young black man, probably college age.

As if this isn't history that is easily found online. I know what they want: a first-hand account, they want to know what it's really like inside the blockade. I'm not allowed to tell them the truth. The bloody awful truth of what it really means to live here. The iron fist with which the vampires control the humans.

The forced feedings, the murders, the fear.

I definitely can't tell them what I know about the takeover —not with so many Shadow Court milling around. The original Shadow Court was eradicated, along with any aggressive vamps. Anyone loyal to the Shadows were killed in the streets; humans and vamps alike.

"Well, I was only three years old when it happened, but from what I was told by my family, it didn't really affect the humans much. It was a quiet exchange of power, a few renamed buildings since the Blood Ravens prefer more Italian names as opposed to the French influence of the Kingdom of

Nocturnal Shadows. That's why the enthralled are called the Shadow Court—because the previous ruling family, the Devereaux, were the Shadow Kings." There are no more Shadow Kings.

A few people fidget nervously as they process what I said. It was more than they were prepared for: too gory, too intense. Too much. It was a sugar-coated version of the truth. A fairytale to convince outsiders they were safe during their stay here.

This isn't a horror movie or a circus performance.

This is our life.

Walking into the Velvet Tomb staff entrance on Saturday evening, as the sun turns to long shadows across the French Quarter, I take a deep breath to slow my heart. No matter how many times I cross this threshold, I still break out in a nervous sweat and my heart rate picks up. The Velvet Tomb is The City of Blood's foremost human-vamp bar and brothel, catering to whatever you want in the backrooms. Make no mistake— despite the humans usually wandering around, taking in the deep red velvet walls, the raised stages, the shiny black table tops, and the cherry wood floors stained a dark burgundy— this is the domain of the night dwellers.

There is a reason for the moody, almost romantic, decor. It's set dressing, really. The dim lighting hides the unsettling otherworldliness of the vamps. The almost black floors are dark to hide drips, splashes, and spills of any liquids. The corners are shadowy to camouflage anyone lingering, watching, or trying to find a moment's privacy.

Thick black velvet curtains hang floor to ceiling around the room, absorbing what little light there will be and creating pockets of quiet along the walls. The stage runs almost the entire length of the back of the room, and has poles for dancers and a piano in one corner. It's a multipurpose area depending on what we have planned for the night. The entire right side of the room is devoted to the long bar where we serve whatever the patrons might be looking for. Blood of all types fills the blood warmers—some drinkers have preferences, others don't care much.

We cater to all things at the Velvet Tomb.

Now, an hour before opening time, the lights are high and bright. I can see everything that's usually hidden in the dark. I clean up missed spills from last night; blood, alcohol, body fluids. I check that the bar is stocked with everyone's favorites and turn the warmers on for anyone who doesn't want to pay to bite or try and coax a human into a live donation. There are rules, of course, regarding public displays of feeding. On the street, anyone anywhere is in danger of a bite, but inside, at bars and restaurants, biting is consensual. If vamps could feed on anyone at any time, we would not have the thriving tourist industry we have. Vampires don't need to bite, but they often prefer the hunt.

I wander from themed room to themed room and check they are ready for the night. The castle with its tapestries and old world charm, standard hotel style rooms with giant comfortable beds, a bondage room with restraints and furniture made specifically for those activities, and a log cabin are some of the rooms that line the hallway of the brothel part of the building. Toys, tools, and medical supplies are stocked.

The dungeon room is my least favorite and often the messiest to clean at the end of the night. The vamps who book the dungeon are not here for sex and pleasure—they are here for torture and blood. The dark stone block wall, the concrete floor with its floor drain, the shackles, whips, chains, and blood-letting tools spread out on a stone table against the wall. No windows to bring in any moon light and only a single set of torches by the door. I suspect this reminds the night stalkers of earlier days when their victims didn't come to them so willingly.

A place built for suffering.

My favorite room is the sun room. It's a beautiful room with a large, four-poster canopy bed and glass surround with artificial sunlight streaming through. The soft bedding grants the human experience. If I close my eyes, I can almost believe it's real, which is the appeal. We all want to feel real. It looks like a greenhouse, lots of beautiful plants, and light colored rugs cover the pale wood floors. No tools of torture. This room is almost always reserved by a vampire couple or a human-vamp couple who want to pretend for a few hours that they can lie in the sun. Whatever they want, we can provide in these rooms. We also provide the humans to go with them. The humans are willing and paid incredibly well for their services.

"Elina, let me get a Long Island iced tea?"

"Bartender, blood. Warm."

"Excuse me, can I get a chardonnay and a whiskey on the rocks?"

It's only 4 hours into an almost 12 hour shift and I'm already overwhelmed, overworked, and so tired. Sarah usually works alongside me at the bar but she is still out following her attack on her way home from work last week. Which is exactly why I pay a car service everyday. You'll only catch me on the streets after dark if I'm dead—or undead. I'm by myself tonight at the bar and we are *slammed*. Humans and vampires alike line the bar, fill up the bar stools, and crowd into every available space. Music pumps through the speakers creating a club-like atmosphere, and girls, guys, vamps, and humans dance in the crowd and take turns on the stage.

Saturdays are a bit of a free-for-all in the Velvet Tomb, no scheduled dancers or entertainment, only a DJ and a big crowd. All the back rooms are booked solid until sunrise and the men and women for hire are too. It's going to be a long night.

"Hey Elina, can you pour us a couple shots of tequila?" Samantha says as she bursts through the bar door. The petite blond stands with Lilly, a raven haired girl from my neighborhood. They are both stunning in their skimpy lingerie outfits. "Me and Lilly got a client in the castle in 20 minutes and we need a little boost."

"Sure thing, babes. Can you watch the bar for a few minutes so I can take a break?" I ask in my sweetest Louisiana drawl as I pour 2 double shots and ring them in as comps.

One long dimly lit hallway later, I push open the heavy door to the restroom. Gazing at myself in the long mirror, I look over, what I consider, my uniform. Tight black leather skirt over thigh high stockings, a matching leather corset with scarlet beads making it look as though blood is dripping down the front, and tall black boots with a thick heel. My tits overflow the top just enough to create tip-worthy cleavage but not enough to be truly indecent, which would make it appear I am on the menu. And finally a ruby studded choker rings my throat. While I fix my skirt over my ass, the rhythmic thumping that I've heard from the closed stall door increases to, what I assume is, the climax, with a muffled cry and a faint growl. What seems like seconds later, a waitress, Amelie, and a tall vampire emerge from the stall. Amelie makes eye contact with me in the mirror and has the decency to flush a bright pink even as she wipes the drips of blood making their way down the side of her neck. Her unnaturally red hair is messy, as though *someone* had their hands in it. The vampire that follows her is a few inches over six foot and, honestly, kind of huge. His chest is broad and his neck thick. He looks like he would be a body-builder gym guy in another life. Her friend does not spare me much more than a grey eyed glance as he leaves the bathroom, followed closely by Amelie.

"Get to work!" I yell after her which is followed by a giggle.

Walking back out to the bar, I pass the stage and relieve Lilly and Sam of their work behind the counter, sending them on their way to their client. I clear out some of the bar orders and start restocking. I feel a prickle on the back of my neck and look around before making eye contact with the same man from the bathroom, tucked into the corner of the bar, no drink in hand. Tall even when sitting, wavy black hair swept across his brow and dark grey eyes, he watches me curiously. He looks vaguely familiar, though I can't place why. Despite knowing he just fucked my friend in the bathroom, being trapped under his gaze makes me blush and I feel the pink tinge coloring my cheeks. *Fucking vampires.* I look away, annoyed with myself. Wandering over, bar towel in hand, I approach him with a questioning lift of my brow.

"Hey, what can I get you?"

"Red wine. Something decent, if you even have that here," is his reply, his voice Italian accented and full of disinterest. One of the old ones then, if he has an accent. The younger blood-drinkers and the newly turned are Americans—or they were. Now they are simply *Sanguine Nocturnus*. Only the Malvani family and their sirelings are Blood Ravens though; the royalty and the law. Turning away, I make my way over to the wine cooler, don't find what I'm looking for, and push open the door to the wine cellar. Grabbing a bottle of 12 year old nebbiolo red, I pull the cork and pour it into the aerator before transferring it to a glass.

Stupid, fancy, demanding vampire.

"Yes, we have something decent here," I retort, sliding the glass to the vamp. "Anything else? Something warmer?"

"No," comes his curt reply and he drops a $100 on the counter before getting up and walking away, glass in hand. *No problem, Dracula.* I laugh to myself at my own joke. Slipping his huge tip into the jar, after I ring in his drink, I decide it's worth the broody presence for the extra cash.

I really needed more than a few hours of sleep this morning, I'm practically dead on my feet. Thank fuck it's well after midnight and the human crowd is slowing down—they don't tend to be able to keep up all night partying like the vamps do.

The sudden terrified scream of a woman cuts through the noise in the room, bringing everyone to a hush. The music ends abruptly. Snapping my head in the direction of the scream—a shadowed corner near the stage—I squint to try and see something.

At this exact moment, a glass shatters against the floor as the Italian vampire from the bar drops his glass and shoots like a bullet toward the corner where the scream came from. Before my brain even has time to register, there is a small flash of light over there that can only indicate one thing, I have a dead vampire and maybe a dead woman in my bar.

Great.

"Alright, everybody out! You know the rules. Out. Out. Out." I yell as I wave my hands in the general direction of the door. It's not as though I can call the police since they don't investigate murders anymore—it's safe to bet the murders are all vampire related and move on. Obviously the humans can't set out onto the street so they all huddle in the waiting area outside the bar for their transportation to wherever they are going.

"Shouldn't someone call, like, the police or something?" A tourist asks me, the fear etched in her brow contrasting her frenzied excitement. Even if we can't contact the police, we still have to make a show of doing something, anything, for the tourists. If they think we let people die, we won't have a tourist industry to profit off of anymore. They have to feel safe if we want them to return. Little lies. 'You're safe'. 'We care about you.' 'We won't let you get hurt.'

But we do. We let people die all the time. Between our lives and their's, how could we ever choose them? It's the worst part of this dark world we're trapped in.

"Go back to your hotel. We will handle everything."

Once the bar area is empty, I stand frozen, unsure what to do next. I know the Italian has killed the offending vamp. I know he is an old one. I know he is over there in the corner. What I don't know is what I am expected to do. Usually if there is an incident, we call the Blood Ravens and report it. I have no idea what happens after that. Right now though, I think the Blood Ravens are already here. At least one of them.

"Excuse me, uh, Mr. Italian guy," I whisper-shout in the general direction of the incident, knowing he can hear me either way, and feeling wrong about yelling now that it's me, him, and whatever is in the corner. "Do I need to call and report this? It's the rules."

"No," he replies again. He seems to say that word a lot. There is a harsh end to the word that makes it clear he does not intend to say anything else and does not want me to ask any additional questions. I may be trapped in this city and I may be in the bar all alone, since everyone fled, with an old vamp who is god knows who but I am not stupid. I will not be sticking around to find out what is going to happen next. I quickly close up the bar, pull the money from the tip jar and the register, and swear to the camera above me that I will clean up Monday morning.

"Ok, well, goodnight then," I say into the quiet room and push through the door into the staff hallway where the offices are, passing the door to the back rooms on the way to my tiny office. Slapping my palm onto the reader on the office door, I enter the office, set the money on the desk, and sit down onto the pink faux leather sofa. Putting my head in my hands, I allow a few solitary tears to run down my face. A few tears for that woman who is not making it home tonight. A few more for the rest of us and how helpless we are.

Standing, I pull myself together, wipe my face and exit the office, letting the door lock behind me. I make my way to the back room hallway and let Sean in the security office know what happened in the bar.

Another night in The City of Blood.

"How do you bear to watch?" I ask him as I perch on the edge of his desk, watching him flick through the various camera feeds showing the rooms. I truly don't know how he does it. Some of the stuff I encounter when I clean up is already more than I can handle.

"If me watching is the only way they stay safe, then I watch," is his stoic reply. He's older, in his fifties, certainly not busting in and taking down any bad guys but he never misses an incident in the rooms. His hair is greying at the temples and he has frown lines between his brows, but if I trust anyone in this place, it is definitely Sean. He takes his job and the safety of our workers extremely seriously. While everyone gets up to some rough shit in those rooms, no one dies. It's in the contract they sign. As far as I know, it's only happened twice and the families were well-compensated. It doesn't change what happened to those girls though.

"Thank you, Sean. It means the world to all of them, knowing you're watching—even if I can't imagine doing it. I'll be in the office when you're ready to lock up," I tell him and he barely nods, already focused on the screen again. I slide off his desk, thump the bill of his hat, and walk out of the security office back to my own.

KNOCK. KNOCK.

"Come in," I say as I press the buzzer button under my desk when I spy Lilly and Sam standing in the hallway on my camera. It's about an hour until sunrise; they must have finished up with their clients.

"Hey, Elina," Lilly says as she flops down on my sofa.

"Hey, girly," comes from Samantha at the same time.

"Ladies." I lean back in my chair. "I assume you heard about the incident in the bar."

"Yeah, and fuck Lina, I hate when shit like this happens. It makes it too...real, I guess. I can pretend it's just a normal bar out there most days but this shit? It makes me want to run and never come back. Except...there is nowhere to run too," Sam says all in a rush, ending in a whisper. She isn't afraid to say it —not really—but hearing it out loud makes the situation feel even more hopeless to think about.

"Lina, your family told you what happened when the wall went up, didn't they? My parents died in the *Guerra de Sang* and I never knew how we ended up here or why we could never leave," Lilly says from her reclined position on the couch.

"Yeah, Grand-mere Celeste told me. She and Grand-pere had been married the year before, at 19. They bought their house in Little Woods near the water in April and were enjoying being newly married. Then the city announced they were building new levees, you know, for flooding. Every inch of Ville de Sang—well, New Orleans then—that touched water suddenly had a huge levee. All the roads in and out had a fifteen foot tall watertight gate. It took 2 years and everyone was so happy it wasn't going to flood anymore. Soon, even the roads that were not near water had a gate. The city promised it was to protect us and no one was worried.

"It happened one day in June, just 2 years after the levee project began. In the early hours of the morning, before the sun came up, all the gates closed. All at once. No explanations. That morning, when people got up to go off to work and tried to drive out of town, they couldn't get through the gates. That was the only day they could have escaped, before the Shadow Court started guarding, but no one knew yet why the gates were closed. They were told to come back after dark. So, at sundown, everyone lined up to find out what was happening. That night, the vampires checked everyone's ID, and if you lived in New Orleans, you were told to return to your home. If you lived outside the city and had gotten trapped, you were allowed to leave but you couldn't return.

"Grand-pere and Grand-mere had their home here and weren't allowed to leave. They were the only Girards inside New Orleans at the time, and thus were cut off from their families. That was the beginning of the end of New Orleans. The Shadow Kings brought their own enthrall humans—I guess they knew they would need people in the daylight hours to enforce their new rules. In the days and weeks that followed, anyone who caused problems during the day were imprisoned, and after dark, they became dinner for all the newly turned vamps. New signs went up for Ville de Sang, new laws were passed, a king sat on a throne at St. Louis Cathedral, and everyone got trapped inside. And in sixty years, not a single resident of Ville de Sang has managed to escape the city and live." I blow out a breath as I finish the story, wishing, like I have a hundred times before, that it had a different ending.

"Well. Shit." Is the only reply from the couch.

CHAPTER 2
BASH

"One night! One fucking night out to try and enjoy this swamp *hell-hole* we live in. And what do I get? A baby vampire with no self-control *ruining* everything!" I bellow as I throw the *cattedrale* door wide open, startling the humans here to meet with Marcus. "My apologies," I say with a slight bow of my head, continuing my way through the antechamber of the old church. I storm through the doors at the back of the vestibule, into the office where I know Marcus and the rest of the council are meeting.

"Sebastien! What is the *meaning* of this?" Marcus responds to my sudden appearance in front of him.

"Marcus, get the *children* under control. The new *sanguine nocturnus* are creating sirelings all over the city and they are unchecked, untrained, and out of control." I storm around the room, feeling a bit like I am throwing a tantrum. "Tonight, I was at the Velvet Tomb and -"

"You were where? A brothel?" My mother interrupts from the other side of the council table.

"Mother, not now," I answer, with a dismissive wave.

"Anyway, I was having a glass of wine when a newly turned *vampiro* drew a woman into a dark corner and proceeded to feed on her with no foresight as to not draw attention to himself. He fell upon her uncontrolled, and tore her throat out, creating a scene for an entire bar full of humans. Disgusting animal." I spit. "And, being as I am a member of *Corvo di Sangue*, I have an obligation. Therefore my night was ruined and I had to extinguish his flame. Elina had to clear out the bar, which was full of tourists, by the way, and didn't know what she was supposed to do." I suck in a huge lungful of air, my monologue complete. Marcus watches me like he has never seen me before—like I am doing something decidedly unexpected. My mother tilts her head curiously, a look in her eyes I don't like.

"Elina? Who's Elina?"

"Mother, please focus," I beg, as ice blue eyes with a curiously lifted eyebrow flash in my mind.

"What do you want me to do Sebastien? Kill them all?" Marcus shouts irritably. I have no idea why he acts as though he has no power, he's the Re. The council shifts uncomfortably under this challenge of Marcus's authority.

"I don't care what you do or how you do it, but you must do something. It's going too far and it's out of control." And with that as my final contribution to the conversation, I walk through the room and out into the night air of the gardens. The sky is barely starting to lighten behind me but at my age, the early light does not bother me as much.

I head over to my loft off Pirate's Alley and climb the stairs to my windowless room. The humans like to think it's a coffin or some sort of tomb, but I am much too old and particular for anything less than a comfortable bed in a secure space. After twenty-five years in this humid buggy swamp, I fall asleep with a face in my thoughts and a need to know more.

CHAPTER 3
ELINA

After the night I had, I want nothing more than to fall into bed and sleep until Monday. Sunday is my only day off and it's the only day I get to spend with Grand-mere Celeste. For a species that lives on the death of others, vamps are surprisingly devout, or maybe it's a holdover from their European roots and old religions. Either way, Sundays are a compulsory day of rest for everyone in Ville de Sang. We do chores, we go to church, and we relax. We do not leave home after dark.

When I finally arrive home, right after sunrise, I, again, find Grand-mere in the kitchen making breakfast. This time, I join her.

"Good morning, Grand-mere Celeste. I hope you had a good night," I say by way of greeting when I enter the room.

"Oh! Yes, my dear. Yes. Sit, sit. Eat something. You're gone too much, you work too much, and don't sleep enough," she lovingly scolds me. As though we have a choice. It's me and her, like it's been almost my entire life, but now, she's 80 and needs my help more than ever.

As I start on the breakfast of eggs and bacon she piles on my plate as she takes the seat opposite me.

"Do you remember the *Guerra de Sang*?" I ask.

"Of course I remember. I lost my only child and the streets ran red with blood." She looks lost in her memories for a moment, and the memories aren't happy. "It wasn't the Blood Ravens that named it the Blood War, it was us. We were the casualties in their territory dispute. Fighting and killing in the streets for the right to feed on us. Despicable. Why do you ask?"

"I was wondering if you would tell me about it—about maman and the real story. I can't trust the history books," I say, leaning forward to hold her wrinkled hands in mine. She hesitates, but only for a moment. I've made it a general rule to skirt around this part of our history, knowing she doesn't like to talk about it.

"You were only 3 at the time, and I was still working at the hospital. One night, after 35 years of relative peaceful co-existence, the Italian vampires descended on the city. They flooded over the walls like the water used to. They attacked anyone in the streets, vampire and human alike. Blood ran in the streets like rainwater. Little flashes of light going off all over the place from the vampires being extinguished, their flames going out. Your mother was working in the French Quarter, not far from the cathedral. One evening, at dusk, she was making her way home and was attacked by someone, we aren't sure what side they were on. She died in the street. It was the greatest heartache of my life." She stops talking then, a hitch in her breath. Her bottomless brown eyes fill with tears, the same eyes my mother had. My mother's death is still an open wound 25 years later.

"Oh Grand-mere, please don't cry. I shouldn't have asked." I squeeze her trembling hands. I avoid these types of questions, they always upset her. I try to change the subject—"What time are we leaving for church?" I ask, even though I know by now —it's the same every week.

I drag myself up the stairs, my mind cloudy and confused, needing sleep. Only a few hours before the day begins.

Climbing into the shower of our only bathroom, I bow my head under the spray and let the hot water relax my muscles. When I close my eyes, I picture perfectly windswept hair and steel grey irises. There is something alluring about him and I feel heat in my belly at the thought of him. Shaking my head to clear the vision, I wonder who he is, and why he was in the bar, especially considering I've never seen him before. How old is he? He must be an old one and clearly a member of the Blood Ravens. He handled everything, including making the bodies disappear. Unlikely to get answers to any of these questions, I dress in my Sunday best and head downstairs.

During the day it's possible, easy even, to forget that we can't leave and we are little more than food that makes money for the vampires. Sitting in church, listening to another sermon about having faith and believing in salvation, I wonder if God has abandoned us as surely as everyone else. The preacher is allowed to preach whatever he likes, but he cannot outright disparage the vampires or even say the passage Deuteronomy 12:23 out loud.When he reaches the passage, he pauses momentarily, as though letting us fill in the blank.

> *Only be sure that you do not eat the blood, for the*
> *blood is the life, and you shall not eat the life*
> *with the flesh.*
> *Deuteronomy 12:23*

After church, we file out onto the street in the bright sunshine.

"Grand-mere, I'm going to head to the Quarter to go to the library—there's something I'm interested in. Do you need to go that way or are you planning to head home?"

"Go ahead, dear. I will just be resting and making supper. Don't be late!" she answers, pulling me in for a hug and a kiss on the cheek. I know she will be fine, all of her friends are gathered around chatting and laughing.

Waiting at the bus stop, I decide whether I am likely to find what I am looking for in the public library, or if I will need to go to the cathedral and visit the archives. A flyer blows across the ground and wraps around my leg. Leaning down, I pull it free, seeing what news the blue sheet of paper brings.

Deliveries into Ville de Sang are only permitted during daylight hours on Mondays and Thursday. Outgoing traffic, excepting vampire movement, is prohibited except Friday-Sunday, 24 hours a day.

Rolling my eyes, I crumble the sheet of paper up and toss it in the garbage bin inside the little covered waiting area.

I hate going to the archives. Being in the home and the seat of power of the vamps sets me on edge, way worse than being at the Velvet Tomb. Even though, I guess technically, it's perfectly safe since it's the middle of the day and everyone is asleep. The archives it is, I guess.

The archives are a small library within the cathedral that holds all the available information about the vampires, their history, and anything else they believe worthy of archiving. While the cathedral's public areas are open to the public during daylight hours, the archives are closed to tourists as no vampire information or lore is allowed outside of the city. We aren't allowed to have cellphones at all and tourists are not allowed to bring them out of their hotels—it's too difficult to control the flow of information. If they do, their phones are forfeit and they are forced to leave the city.

Checking in with the Shadow Court librarians, showing my ID, and having my picture taken, I wander through the small stacks to locate what I am looking for.

Running my fingers across old, dusty tomes bound in leather and canvas, I pause on a title that may hold what I need.

La Stirpe Malvani di Vampiri

I don't know all of the words but I recognize Malvani vampires. "Perfect," I mumble in the quiet space, pulling the book off the shelf. Cracking the old book open, I carefully flip the pages. Page after page of ego-driven descriptions of great vampires who did great deeds—both benevolent such as donating to charity and absolutely heinous such as wiping out an entire village because someone had extinguished a vampire flame. Horrified, I cover my mouth to avoid gasping aloud. Obviously, almost all of it is from Italy—since they have only been in America for 30 years or so—but there is a passage about the *Guerre de Sang*. It doesn't tell the real or whole story, much closer to the fairytale we sell the tourists about a peaceful transfer of power that benefits the humans. *They even lie in their own archives,* I think, scoffing at the text.

Finally, I find a family tree. Despite there being a vampire library, and despite having been under their rule for 25 years, humans don't know that much about the inner workings of the Blood Ravens. The new vampires, those not connected to royalty, create vampires by murdering those they have blood-shared with, and those people rising again as *Sanguine Nocturnus*, but the Blood Ravens look like a family. It looks like they breed and reproduce rather than turning others. I have never seen a vampire child though, so maybe not? I am not likely to find out the answer either since their secrets are so heavily guarded.

A notation has been added to the bottom of the family tree I've found which looks newer than the surrounding text.

Re Marcus, b. 1034 AD, to Titus and Octavia, is the eldest of four children. Two sons born together, Victor and Darius, b.1040 AD, and a daughter Vespera, b. 1044, followed behind Re Marcus. Re Marcus sired one daughter, Julia, (deceased), whose maternal parentage is not on record. Victor bonded Valentina and sired Lucien, (deceased), Gianna, and Filomena, who remain unbonded with no sirelings. Darius married Lucinda and sired Aurora and Alessandra, who remain unbonded and have no sirelings. Vespera sired Sebastien, whose paternal parentage is unknown. Sebastien is unbonded, with no sirelings. Sebastien has been named Heir Apparent.

The notation does not provide any additional information that isn't available in the family tree other than the dates of birth for Marcus's siblings. No other family members have birth dates which may or may not be supportive of my theory that they reproduce. Also, the word sirelings could be in support of or against the theory also. Basically no more than I knew before, except, I have names for other family members that I have never seen and would not recognize if I saw them on the street or in my bar. I do know for certain though, the mystery vamp from last night is most definitely on this page, but which one is he? Is he a cousin of Marcus or one of his brothers? Or maybe his nephew Sebastien, the heir apparent?

Holding the spine tightly, I study the lineage on the page. Was the heir in my bar last night? Commanding control?

Sarah should be back to work tomorrow but I don't think I can wait that long to talk to her—the bar isn't really a safe place anyway. Hopefully she is up to visitors.

"SAAAARRRAAAHHH!" I call out from the front entry of her house, a half hour later. I can unlock her house with my palm so no need to knock. I barge in and start yelling, which I have heard, from her, that she hates, so I keep doing it.

"SARAH! Love of my life! Sister of my heart! Where are you?"

"Elina, for fuck sake, please come inside like a normal human. I'm in the reading room," Sarah shouts from the back of the house. Weaving through the narrow rooms and down the hallway, I move toward the direction of her voice.

"No thanks, this is much more fun. How ya doing today? How do you feel? Ready to get back to work?" I send a barrage of questions her way as I flop down onto a green velvet chair and look over at my best friend with a huge smile on my face. Flaming red, curly hair, big green eyes, and a lot of freckles—I am so grateful she's on her feet again after last week's attack. She's sitting at her sewing table, smiling back at me, and shaking her head at my loud entrance and obvious comfort here.

"Lina, what are you up to today? You're going to see me at work tomorrow, and Sundays you usually spend at home. You're here for a reason—spill it." She lowers her brows and crosses her arms over her chest, watching me curiously.

"Ok, but listening only. No opinions until the end." I level her a look that says *I mean it, control yourself.* "I don't know if you heard about what happened at Velvet last night, but some blood-sucker killed a woman right in the bar in the middle of the night. There was a Blood Raven in the bar too—" Queue the big green eyes getting bigger. "I know! They never come into the bar. Anyway, he extinguished him and took care of the bodies. He told me I didn't need to call anyone or anything. So, I got my ass out of there. Now I can't stop thinking about him and I want to know who he was. I just came from the archives and I saw the family tree, and I have some suspicions who it could be, as well as some theories about how they make baby Malvani vamps. Oh, AND I saw him in the bathroom fucking Amelie and feeding on her before this whole thing happened. God, I wish you had been there. Did I mention how tall he was? LIKE A TREE!" I rush out in a long babbling speech and suck in a deep breath.

Sarah huffs out a laugh.

"I...I don't even know where to start. Are you ok?" I wave a dismissive hand in her direction. "Amelie, huh? In the bathroom? With a Blood Raven? Not a bit of shame in that woman's body. I wonder if she knew who he was? Probably not—in a brothel giving it away for free." She shakes her head like she can't believe it but also knows it's true. "So, he was tall like a tree was he?" More laughter from my best friend, who I fear may be seeing through the show I'm putting on.

"Was he hot?" Sarah asks, leaning forward like the answer is really important to her.

" I...he...Blood Raven, Sarah. Killer, night dweller, royalty! It doesn't matter if he was hot," I respond, stuttering a little as a blush rises to my cheeks.

"Lina, you're blushing. I'm sure his long, black hair and brown eyes didn't do it for you at all," she comments with an eye roll.

"His hair is short and wavy, and his eyes are dark grey.

Who are you...oh." I narrow my eyes at her. "Listen, I didn't pay that close attention, I only noticed. You know what, leave me alone. Ugh! Anyway, according to the family tree, there are only a few possibilities of who it could be. Lucian and Orion are cousins of Marcus, Victor and Darius are his brothers, and Sebastien is his nephew and heir. Those are the only living men in the family. We know they don't really age quickly but Marcus doesn't look at that young, like in his fifties maybe? So, it stands to reason his cousins and brothers would look similarly aged. Which leaves Sebastien. The vamp at the bar looked maybe 30? Also Marcus is over 1000 years old and looks like he's fifty. So...?"

"Seems possible. So you think the hot tree-like vampire is Sebastien, heir to the Blood Raven throne?" I nod in response to her question. "Interesting. My question is, do you think he will come back to the bar and see you? Oh, also how do you think they make Malvani babies? There are no vampire babies. Just new vampires. You've seen it yourself; family and friends turning, overtaken with bloodlust." Sarah looks sad as she finishes her thought, no doubt remembering Ethan and my heart breaks a little for her. She should be married with babies by now, not all alone here.

"I think the Malvanis reproduce. The old fashioned way. Like, yeah, there is lots of fucking and no babies, so there has to be some other part to it, I guess. The family hasn't expanded since Marcus and his siblings sired their children and *none* of those children are married. We also have no idea how old they are because the family tree didn't have birth dates for anyone at all, and only a footnote told how old Marcus and his siblings are. From what I have seen of the family, when they are in the papers or city events, they look pretty similar. I don't know. Someone has to know though." I have no idea who would know but there has to be someone.

"Your hotty vamp definitely knows. Ask him when he comes back."

"He's not coming back!" Spying the clock sitting on the shelf above Sarah's head, I realize the time. "I have to go, Grand-mere is waiting. Why don't you come over for supper? You can stay over so you don't have to travel back after dark. I have to get to Velvet in the morning to clean up from last night since I ducked out after the incident." I extend the invite, hopefully, but I already know she will decline. After Ethan was enthralled and left, and later turned, she simply isn't like she used to be.

"Next time, I promise," she whispers as I lean in to hug her.

"Love you."

"Love you too."

"Why do you think that maman didn't ever tell you who my papa was?" I ask Grand-mere Celeste over crawfish pie for supper.

"I wish I knew," she says. She fidgets and stirs her food around, as though she is suddenly not interested in eating. "After your maman died, I wish I knew so you could have a parent. She didn't have a boyfriend that I knew of. It was only me and her like it's been just me and you. She didn't stay out overly late, didn't put herself in danger, but she also never brought anyone home. She broke down crying one day and told me she was pregnant. I begged her to know who had done it, if for no reason other than to make him step up and be a part of your life. Babies need two parents. After Grand-pere Jean died when she was a teenager, you needed a man around to be a parent. Then, when we lost her, all we had was each other, Elina. But I think we did alright," she tells me while she strokes my hair out of my face, a wayward curl looping at my temple.

"I wish she had told you, too." I never let myself think of him, this mystery man. Knowing my mother cried when asked about it makes me so sad. Who was this man?

Maybe I'll add finding my father to my list of mysteries of late. An enigmatic vampire from a royal family and a poor orphan of unknown parentage. Quite the mystery indeed.

CHAPTER 4

BASH

S itting straight up in bed, ice blue eyes and wild brown
curls haunt my thoughts. The way those eyes
watched me through the mirror in that bathroom.
The slight flush to her cheeks as she made eye contact with
me across the bar. The little curls that stuck to her temples
and neck in the warmth of the room. The golden tone of her
skin, a sexy smattering of freckles across her nose, reflecting
the pulsing lights in the darkened room. The curve of her
waist, her grabbable hips taunt me in my memory. The
thought of her thick, soft-looking thighs causes a tightening
low in my abdomen. I shouldn't have even been there. I definitely should not have been in that bathroom with that
woman. I honestly don't know what I was thinking. I can't
help but wonder about her now that her face is seared into
my memory.

"Bash!" A loud banging comes from my door. "Let us in,
Baaash–it's your birthday!" Followed by more banging.

"Alright, come in, come in." I call out to the terrors outside
my door. I pull the sheet that has fallen to my waist up a little

higher, the blanket covering my lap, as my cousins throw the door open.

"Bash, I can't believe you're still in bed—it's been moonrise for almost an hour. It's going to start soon. Father said the entertainment is going to be amazing—they brought humans! Bash, come on!" Aurora almost screeches as she tries to pull my blankets off.

"Aura *let go*, I'm not dressed! Let me get ready. I'll meet you outside in 20 minutes." They disappear in a flurry of lace and silk, and slam the door behind them.

Climbing out of bed, letting the blankets fall away, I walk into my attached en-suite and go right to the shower. Stepping under the freezing spray, not patient enough to wait for it to warm up, I lean my head on the wall. Birthday parties for a 477th birthday seem so...absurd, honestly. My family will be looking for me to find a mate and sire my own family soon. At that thought, the eyes are back. I groan as the, finally, warm water runs over my back and down my legs. Why can't I get her eyes out of my head? Focus, Bash. The party, the family— this is important. Stop thinking about human women— *a human woman.*

I run my hand down my face before following the water's path down my chest. I grab my hard cock, tipping my head back, and give an impatient tug on my shaft.

"Fuck," I hiss through my teeth as I pick up speed, sliding my fist up and down my length until I feel an orgasm starting to build. Leaning my head on the wall again and feeling the water on my back, I stroke faster and faster. I grit my teeth. Eyes closed and her face in my mind, I push myself to the edge before pulling back. My skin tingles as I imagine how it would feel to wrap her legs around my waist and push into her in this shower. How it would feel to sink my teeth into her neck and her blood flow across my lips. Imagining myself thrusting into her, I pump my cock, my orgasm barreling forward before I roar through the release and take a labored breath, slowing my strokes to finish. Breaths heavy, I rinse myself, and try to rid my mind of her memory as the water washes it all away. Almost 500 years old and jerking off in the shower like an adolescent. She probably hasn't spared me a single thought. *Pathetic.*

Finishing my shower quickly, I dry off and dress. Black pants, a custom tailored black shirt, and black polished shoes complete my outfit. Running my hands through my hair to fluff it a bit, I take a look in the mirror and decide this will do. The all black ensemble really feeds the creature of darkness stereotype, but I shrug and embrace it.

Aura and Lessa are waiting at the bottom of the stairs to my loft in their party dresses—Aura in a gown of the deepest blue, embellished with what seems like millions of tiny crystals and a large skirt. Black hair flowing down her back like smoke, she looks like a princess of the night. Lessa has gone a completely different direction with a tight fitting, silk, sheath-style, floor length gown in blood-red, and her blond hair is curled and pinned like a crown.

"Beautiful as always cousins," I tell them as I extend both elbows for them to take, escorting them to the party.

"*Principe* Sebastien Malvani, Alessandra Malvani, and Aurora Malvani," announces the master of ceremonies as he gives me a nod and leads us into the cathedral. All of the catholic adornments have been removed, and tonight, a dance floor has been added. There is security scattered around all the entrances with doormen checking invitations. The strictly invite-only party is the event of the year for vampire society in Ville de Sang.

Multi colored lights bounce off the frescoes that adorn the ceilings, making the religious icons appear to writhe to the beat of the music. Jesus looks down on me from the pulpit and scantily clad human dancers swing from ribbons affixed to the balconies. A full bar is set where the confessionals used to be, complete with alcohol and warm blood on tap. Human donors also dance provocatively along the walls, available for blood or other services. Re Marcus sits upon the Nocturnal Throne, a giant gaudy gold chair, on the altar. A golden crown dripping with rubies sat upon his brow. I make my way over and sketch a bow.

"*Zio*. This is....what did the girls call this again?" I ask, quirking a brow as I look around.

"Oh, Uncle now, is it? Yesterday it was *Marcus* being yelled at me," he says. "I believe the invitations said, 'The Eternal Night Bash'," he bellows boisterously into the large space.

"Heavens save us," I say with a grin.

"I don't think they will, *Nipote*. Have a happy birthday, Sebastien. Me, your uncles, and your mother will only be here for a few hours—then you can enjoy your real celebration with the young people." He gives me a knowing smile, saluting me with his glass. Wandering the room, a glass of whiskey in my hand, I take in all the gorgeous otherworldly women gyrating on the dance floor. I make eye contact with a few, making promises for later. I don't need her—she is just a human who works at a bar. I'm not sure why I spend any time even thinking of her.

Making my way over to human blood donors, I find a woman with brown wavy hair, rich brown skin, and delightful curves.

"Neck, now." I growl at her, turning her to face the wall so I can only see her hair and the curve of her neck. My gums tingling as my fangs descend, aching for blood, I slide them into her jugular and pull deeply. She allows a small moan to escape and I wrap an arm around her waist to pull her tight against my body as my other hand holds her hip. She moans again, encouraged by the reaction she can feel in my body as I feed on her. I withdraw my fangs and lick my lips before running my tongue up the side of her neck to slow the blood flow. She lets out a little shiver.

I fantasize about the sight of a curly brown-haired girl on her knees for me. I could have this woman relieve the ache I feel but I don't. It makes me feel alive to yearn. The next few hours pass in a blur of whiskey, dirty dancing, and birthday wishes. Right before midnight, the lights brighten slightly as my mother and uncle climb the stairs to the pulpit.

"Friends, family, humans—thank you sincerely for attending this most joyous of birthdays for my nephew and heir, Sebastien!" Sounds of clapping and whistles fill the air as Marcus pauses for the noise to die down. "We are so happy we have a place to call home, here, in Ville de Sang, and love all of you for being here and supporting the Malvani family. Raise your glass in a toast to Sebastien."

"*Alla salute e alla felicity! Buon compleanno!* Happy Birthday, Bash!" my mother adds to the toasts as soon as Marcus finishes speaking. Everyone has their glasses in the air for a salute when the clocks strike midnight and the bells toll across the City of Blood.

"We will now leave you to your party. Good night!" Marcus says as a farewell before heading toward the door to the council chamber, followed by my mother, uncles, and aunts.

"Re Marcus! Re Marcus! Long live, Re Marcus!" The chorus of shouts is deafening. As soon as the door closes behind the elders, the lights dim until we are swathed in shadows. Couches, lounges, large tables, and daybeds are moved into places all around the dance floor. A large gilded cage with human women inside is wheeled into the center of the space. A woman inside makes eye contact with me—I assume she is attempting to lure me in but her eyes are lifeless, unfocused. The lingerie-clad women dance and simulate sex from inside their cage as partygoers begin to find places to sit and lie around the room. The music gets lower and sultrier, and people begin removing clothes. Naked men and women lay on the large tables, presenting themselves as a feast, available for any sort of feasting. Couples begin fucking in twos and threes and more. There is a full orgy happening on the far side of the church.

I find an empty lounge and lie back, a hand behind my head. A waiter comes over to offer me a glass of wine and a tumbler of warm blood, I take both. I don't have any interest in partaking in the physical goings-on but I will watch. The women in the cage are fully nude by this point and putting on a show for the men gathered around the perimeter. I sip my blood and enjoy the heady buzz from the alcohol and the party. Eyeing the large pile of gifts in the corner, I wonder what people brought for the prince. I don't even know most of these people—they are only here to pay homage to me.

"Happy birthday, old ass man. Shit! 477 is a little old for party balloons, don't you think?" Jack asks me as he squeezes onto the end of my lounge.

"At some point, Jack, the number doesn't matter anymore. It's just a reason for people to party—and engage in orgies, apparently," I respond, laughing.

"Right, right. You find anyone interesting tonight? The offerings are pretty good and they are all hoping for you." Jack is my oldest friend and we've been thick as thieves for over two centuries. If I can confide in anyone, it's him.

"Nah, what I want isn't at this party, and I'm pretty sure she's not ever going to be an option."

"Wait, is Sebastien Malvani, heir to the throne, smitten with someone?" He puts on a fake Italian accent, a slight mocking tilt to his words. "Who? I can't believe you've been holding out on me!" Jack scolds me, lovingly of course.

"Did you hear about the incident at the club, The Velvet Tomb?"

"Oh yeah, news travels fast. Some baby vamp made a scene and you had to do your governmental duties and snuff him out. What has that got to do with the girl?" Jack tilts his head curiously.

"She works there—was there last night." He looks at me suspiciously, like he can't believe I'm becoming obsessed with a sex worker. "She's the bartender, so fix your face. The night started out with her happening to find me in a public bathroom with a coworker and ended with me flaming out a vampire in her bar," I finish and rub my face with my hand at how stupid it all sounds when I say it out loud.

"Ok, but what happened in the middle? Surely something happened to catch your attention so thoroughly. I've never known you to not participate in parties, especially when the entertainment is so good."

Another palm to the face as I try to figure out how to explain.

"We made eye contact, she blushed, I ordered a glass of wine. Then I extinguished a vampire and she fled like she was going to be next." Every time I open my mouth, I realize how ridiculous this all sounds and I have absolutely no reason to feel the way I do.

"Ok then. So, after nearly 500 years, you're seemingly falling for a woman who...looked at you? After she already knew you had fucked someone minutes before?" His face is absolutely incredulous. "This can't be it. Bash, please that can't be it."

"That's it. She looked at me and something happened. Something changed. I can't explain it."

"Did you at least speak to her?"

"No, not really." I shake my head. "I ordered my drink, and I was kind of a dick."

"Alright, well tomorrow night, we are going to that bar and you'll order another glass of wine, and maybe you will actually speak to her this time." With those final words, Jack wanders off into my party—my party that I suddenly had no further interest in. Standing up and walking out the doors of the cathedral, I make my way toward my loft intending to find out everything I can about Elina the bartender before tomorrow night. Before I visit her again, I will know everything there is to know about her.

My kingdom stretched out before me, gilded and covered in blood, is so empty and performative. Tonight, I will find her in the dark. Tomorrow I will entrap her.

At 7:15, Jack knocks on my door, exactly four minutes after moon-rise. Seems he is as eager as I am, considering I have been dressed for 20 minutes. Throwing a black blazer over my black evening shirt, I pull the door open and step out onto the balcony outside my front door.

"Not even an offer of a drink before we leave? You must be smitten." He jokes as we descend the stairs.

"They have drinks there, it's a bar," I tell him with a side-ways glance. His blond hair is perfectly styled and his green eyes shine in the twilight glow of the setting sun. His tan suit and green button-up shirt are much lighter and more approachable than my black-on-black outfit. I take a moment to reflect and wonder if he is more her type. His boyish charm,

Irish accent, and handsome easy smile do tend to attract women more readily, even if they are more curious about me. It's kind of like seeing a golden retriever next to a cane corso. I'm taller, broader, and scarier, and even if people think I'm beautiful, they keep their distance.

Since the Velvet Tomb is only a few blocks away, and no one would dare approach us, we walk over there. We enjoy the night air, listening to the sounds of the city and people milling about. We don't even make a lot of conversation, both of us inside our own heads about what might happen tonight, and what it will mean for me. Likely nothing will happen though, especially if Jack catches her eye.

Approaching the bouncer, I flash him a fancy grin and slide a $50 in his palm, ducking through the curtains into the dark room. As soon as I get through the door, I look over at the bar and there she is, all sinful curves and a happy smile. She is wearing the same black corset with the perfect amount of cleavage, and that red drop choker that makes me think of what it would be like to taste her throat and her blood. I am only staring at her for about 10 seconds when her head snaps up and she looks me directly in the eye, like she felt my gaze on her and knew exactly where I was. She isn't alone behind the bar tonight—there is a lean woman with bright red hair in a tight black mini dress moving in perfect sync with Elina, like they are two halves of a single bartender.

"Ok, Casanova, let's find this girl and see what we can make happen," Jack says as he rubs his hands together like a movie villain. Nothing is going to happen. I just want to talk to her.

"She's behind the bar, let's go."

"Oh, is it the spunky looking red head or the short black cat? Either way, I'm fine being your wingman," he adds with a cheeky grin. I grab his arm and haul him through the space. We walk up behind two younger vampires sitting at the counter

"Move, *vampiros*" I whisper gruffly between the two of them. When they see who is talking to them, they almost fall over themselves to vacate their stools for us.

"I love that trick." Jack laughs. As we sit down, I watch Elina make eye contact with the other human working alongside her. The red head turns my direction, eyes widening dramatically before leaning over and whispering furiously in Elina's ear.

"Is that him? The mystery vamp from Saturday? I knew he was hot. You're such a liar. Wonder who the other one is? Is he a Blood Raven too?" I stop listening so closely to give them back their privacy. Superhuman hearing is great and all until people around you realize you can listen in on anything they say. I guess she did talk about me at least. I wonder what she said—it sounds like she told her friend I wasn't hot. *Rude.*

"I guess I'll take the redhead since your girl is the curvy goth." Again with the villainous hand rubbing.

"No one is taking anything. Now shut up."

"You're back. Nice to see you again. Red wine?" Elina asks with a smile, without sparing Jack even a single glance. *That's my girl.* Wait, where the hell did that come from? She's not mine, she hasn't even had a conversation with me yet.

"Hey, sorry about the other night. These things happen." She flinches a little at the mention of the incident. I wonder why. "No, not wine tonight. Can I have a whiskey on ice, same for my friend."

"Sure thing. Coming right up," she responds before quickly turning away to grab the drinks.

"Great job, Romeo, knocking it out of the park with those suave conversation starters. Talking about a murder and ordering a whiskey," Jack says, shaking his head at me.

"Here you fellas go," the redhead offers as she sets the glasses in front of us. Jack reaches out to touch her wrist before she turns away. She gasps a little at the contact.

"Sorry, love, I know it's a little cold. My name's Jack McCray and this is Bash. I'm really sorry about what happened here the other night. I've never been here before but Bash said I should check it out. Any recommendations for me?" he asks her while putting on his best golden boy smile. She slowly drags her arm away from him before answering.

"Hey y'all. I'm Sarah. If you want to look at the menu, I'll grab one for you. I'm sure you'll find something." She hands over a menu before turning away and heading to the other side of the bar. Looking down, I realize she gave him the girls-for-hire menu and I snort in amusement.

"Great job, Romeo, she thought you were looking for a good time that you have to pay for." A genuine laugh bursts from my mouth as I try to keep from smiling. Jack scowls at me.

"Fuck you, Bash," he retorts while looking over the menu with a raised eyebrow. "Do you see some of the stuff on here? I would never even think...I mean nevermind." He lays the menu back on the counter. Sarah is back whispering in Elina's ear but I don't bother listening in this time. I watch a slow smile spread across her face and pretend she's smiling at me.

I settle in more comfortably and sip from my glass. I plan to creepily watch her for the rest of the night to try and get a glimpse into her life, learn about her when she is in her element. Yes, I can admit it's creepy. From my research this morning before I went to sleep, I know a little more about her. All the information about humans is kept in an online database so we know who and what everyone is up to. Elina Celeste Girard is 28 years old and her birthday is in August. She lives in Little Woods with her Grandmother, Celeste. Her mother was killed during the *Guerra de Sang* and her father is unknown—we share that unfortunate fact in common. I did try and find anything on her mother but since the information is from before, I don't have access to the entire database of the Shadow Kingdom. Elina started working immediately after graduation from high school to contribute money to her household since it's only her and her grandmother. She is a tour guide during the day and a bartender at night. She regularly donates blood for my family so it's likely I have tasted her before, but it's a mixture so I could not identify it if I tried.

But, within the mundane uneventful information about her, I discovered that yesterday, after what happened here, she visited the archives at the *cattedrale*. I saw her picture, beautiful in her Sunday clothes, a focused look on her face, in the library's camera. I watched her peruse the shelves on the camera feed, walking around until she landed on a book with *la stirpe della mia famiglia*, flipping pages until she reached the family tree. Her fingers delicately tracing the family lines until she found my name and gently rubbed her fingertip across it on the page, a slight thoughtful tilt of her head. Curious about me too, *tesoro mio*?

I haven't spent much time around everyday humans in, at least, a hundred years, and I am fascinated watching her. The way she and Sarah move in harmony, the easy smile she has for the bar patrons, the confidence with which she does her tasks, and the strength she exercises when discouraging would-be harassers, all draw me to her. She moves around the bar effortlessly, pouring drinks and laughing. She smirks as though she has a secret and is the only one who knows it. Seeing the men in the bar, humans and vampires alike, try and paw at her and harass her for attention sets my teeth on edge and my fangs itch to eliminate the threat. I leave her alone and only watch, though. She is capable of protecting herself in the bar and the partiers respect her enough not to push their luck.

I watch her over the top of my rocks glass, as she approaches, her hips swaying.

"Bash, right? I'm Elina. We didn't really get to meet on Saturday. Amelie isn't working tonight but I can tell her you were here if you are looking for her." Elina says to me sassily, with a cock of her hip and a smirk on her face.

Rubbing the back of my neck, a bit awkwardly, *what is this?* I ask myself. I don't do awkward, what are you doing to me, Elina?

"Yes, it's Bash, and that is not necessary—I'm not here for her," I say, looking more steady than I feel.

"Ok, well if anyone else catches your eye, you let me know. I'm sure the lucky girl would love to know she's gotten your attention." She grins at me as she says this, and I realize she's teasing me.

Looking directly into those eyes that are haunting my dreams, I lift just the corner of my mouth, telling her, "Trust me, you'll be the first to know." Picking up my whiskey, I watch her as I sip my drink and blood floods up her neck and across her cheeks in a blush. She can tease me but can't handle it, I see. It's nice to know she isn't as unaffected by my presence as she is pretending to be.

"Another whiskey also, Elina." I draw her name out.

A quick tip of her chin and she spins on her heel and walks away, heart beating quickly like a hummingbird in her chest, and a little unsteady on her feet.

"Much better. Much, much better," Jack murmurs in my ear, giving a tiny clap of his hands and I duck my head and laugh.

"I don't know what it is, Jack. I can't even think straight when she's in front of me. And bringing up Amelie? Why?"

"She's trying to gauge whether you're involved with that other girl. Good thing she isn't here, it could have been more awkward, if that were even possible. Did you hear her heart pick up? She's interested, or, at the very least, really nervous around you. I have to say, after 200 years, watching you squirm from a—what, 25 year old— human has been the highlight of my year."

Rolling my eyes at him, I reply, "She's 28."

"I don't even want to know why you know that, considering I just watched you introduce yourself. It's quite stalkerish of you, Bash, tsk tsk. Don't be creepy."

Leaning over to set the fresh glass of whiskey in front of me, I get a good look at the line of her throat, pulse humming under the skin and feel my fangs push toward the surface of my gums. It's hard to figure out where the line between desire for her flesh ends and desire for her blood begins. Honestly there is far more overlap than I would like to admit.

Sitting back, I reflect on what is happening to me. I am drawn to her in a way I can't understand. I am fascinated by her. The idea of being involved with a human is far too complicated. Mother would extinguish me herself if she even suspected I was considering a serious connection to someone as fragile and mortal as a young human woman. I am duty bound to bind myself and sire a lineage. I will lead in Marcus's stead one day. I have no idea when, since he seems content on his golden chair, but eventually, it will be asked of me. I will need to have an heir of my own. A legacy, for a kingdom built on the backs of others before me.

I need to get her out of my head before I do something so incredibly stupid, I can't undo it.

CHAPTER 5
ELINA

"He's still watching," Sarah whispers to me as I pour a beer. I am well aware. So aware. More aware than I have ever been of anyone or anything. My skin tingles under his gaze. Bash has been posted up at the end of the bar with Jack for eight solid hours. They haven't danced, or had any conversations outside of talking to us, or each other. They have not so much as glanced at any women. I still have 3 more hours of work, and Bash does not seem to be in any hurry to leave.

"What can I get you, Honey?" I ask the man who has sat down at the bar. It's warm here so his outfit, including a high collar and hat, is slightly out of place. I lean over so I can hear him in the loud space. He smiles, showing me his fangs.

"Blood, warm. From the tap preferably," he says, grabbing my wrist as I try to move away from him. I attempt to yank my arm back, my breath picking up, but his grip on me is like iron. My stomach twists with panic as I look for anyone, any*thing*, to pry him off me.

"Sir, I need you to let go immediately. I am not on the

menu. Let go now!" I pull my hand harder as he gleefully pulls my arm toward his mouth. Suddenly, not only does he let go, but he is also no longer sitting on the stool in front of me. He is dangling by the neck from the outstretched arm of a 6 foot 3 inch, extraordinarily pissed off, Sebastien Malvani.

"I believe the lady told you to let go," he hisses through clenched teeth, fangs on display. I don't ever venture out after dark and I spend all of my vampire time in the bar, where vamps are generally on their good behavior, at least to and around me. Rian does not tolerate any shit, she is always watching the cameras when she is in the bar, and neither do I. That's why I have never witnessed two vampire males posture like this. In response to Bash's aggressive stance, the stranger does a combination hiss-growl, showing all of his teeth and fangs, twisting out of the hold Bash has on him. Standing at his full height, he is at least three or 4 inches shorter than Bash and significantly less broad, but the face he makes is terrifying. I can feel Sarah at my back, her warm presence making me feel a little calmer.

"Get the fuck out of my bar," I hear Rian yell as she pushes forcefully through the bar door. Security flows through behind her, as well as coming from the front of the room. It takes four quite burly security guards and a few vampires to get the stranger out of the front door, a stream of hissing and profanities following behind him.

"You *crepuscule* whore!" is the last thing I hear from him as he is yanked out the door.

"Jesus, Elina, are you alright?" Rian asks as she wraps her thin arms around my shaking body. Over her shoulder, I see Bash standing there looking every bit the terrifying heir to the vampire throne of Ville de Sang, fangs on display, face twisted in rage. His friend, Jack, stands beside him, breathing heavily, pupils dilated, as he looks around the bar-room. People have turned to look at what the commotion is about, but no one seems overly concerned.

"You!" She points her long manicured finger at Bash. "Are you making trouble in my bar? I don't care who you are—I'll throw you out on your ass if you're endangering my girls."

"No, I was trying to keep trouble from your bar." He leans a little to find me around her. "Elina, are you alright? I wouldn't have let anything happen to you, on my honor."

"I'm fine, and there is no such thing as vamp honor." Turning, I walk through the bar doors down to my office. I need to relax before I have a panic attack. Vampires are predators, and anytime they make me feel like prey, cortisol floods my body. I'm going to have a heart attack one of these days. This can't be healthy for the human body. Being in a constant state of fight or flight has to cause some sort of nervous system problem.

Storming through the door of my office, my hands shaking, I fight the urge to collapse right there on the floor.

"FUCK!" I scream as I sink back on the couch, taking a few deep breaths.

There is a tentative knock at my door. I lean over so I can see the camera feed on my desk, and in the hallway are Rian and Sebastien. Standing, I smooth down my skirt and pat my hair. I open my door, leaning casually on the frame.

"Hey, I'm coming out. I'm fine, just needed a minute"

"Bash was hoping to talk to you. You've met him right?" She says as she gives me an imploring look, trying to telepathically tell me he's important and I should let him in. I slide my eyes from her to him standing behind her, hands casually in his pockets, looking like the Italian aristocrat he surely is, and not at all like the predator he was back in the bar.

"Yes, I am well aware of him, and no thanks. I have no interest in being trapped in a windowless room behind a locked door—" sweeping my eyes from his shiny shoes to the top of his perfect wavy hair, "—with a lion." Rian inhales a quick breath of surprise at my response but I spy the hint of pride on her face. Rian is like a stand-in mother, acting as security and sentry for those of us who work in the bar. She doesn't tolerate bullshit and doesn't allow us to either. Bash's face, however, gives nothing away, no surprise or anger. He wears a quiet, almost resolute, look in his eyes. With that, I turn and walk back down the hallway, giving them my back.

Walking through to the bar, I see Sarah chatting quietly with Jack and I roll my eyes. After Ethan, the chances of a night-walker getting close to her are virtually zero. It is fun watching him lay it on thick though— he seems to be flirting pretty adamantly. Bash catches up to me then.

"Please allow me to escort you home this morning. I'm worried about your safety. I don't know who he was or why he was so aggressive, but I need to make sure you're safe," he says quietly as he herds me into a more secluded area by the door.

"Why do you need to make sure I'm safe? We have talked a total of 5 minutes before now—I'm nobody to you. I have seen you keeping women safe in the bathroom and I am not interested. Seriously, Sebastien, I don't need you to protect me." His face changes into one of confusion, as though he can't believe that I am not accepting his offer for help. It seems like he doesn't hear 'no' very often.

"I don't know why, I just do. That bathroom situation, I'm not going to apologize and it's not as though it's something unusual around here. You didn't even pay any attention to me as I walked out. You certainly did not seem scandalized so stop acting so offended by it. You may not need me to protect you, but I want to. Ok?" He reaches out to hold my hand while he makes his speech. I back away and don't let him touch me.

"I've had enough vamps touching me for one night. Go home, Sebastien." At my words, he walks around me toward the bar and takes up residence back on his stool next to Jack. I guess he doesn't intend to go home but I am not entertaining him. Sarah can handle them for now.

The remaining two hours of the night pass without incident, thankfully. I can't decide if Bash's presence in the bar is the catalyst for the incidents that keep happening or coincidence. Clearing out the bar a half hour before sunrise, I relish the quiet for a few minutes.

"You sure you don't want a ride home?" Bash's voice interrupts my first moment of peace in eleven hours.

"Certain, Bash. Go home. And stop coming here—trouble seems to follow you."

"Can't do that, Elina. I'll see you tonight," he says with a sad note in his voice before he walks out the front doors. Sarah and I spend a few more minutes gathering things up and putting the last things back in their proper place before heading out that back door as the sun lightens the sky over the river—the same view everyday. We both get into the back of the sedan this time, Sarah will be riding with me from now on, no more walking alone. As we pull away from the curb, there's Sebastien leaning against a street sign, a hint of morning light reflecting off the top of his head. *Huh, his hair isn't black at all.* It's a deep brown with a scant auburn tint in the diffuse sunlight of the early hour. Sunlight he never really sees and the thought makes me sad.

Everyone deserves the sun.

He must be much older than we thought if he can even be in the early morning light at all. I've heard the ancient ones can withstand some UV light, though only early morning, right before moon-rise or when we have complete cloud cover.

"So, Sebastien." Sarah eyes me from across the back seat.

"So, what? He is Sebastien Malvani, heir to this absurd

kingdom they carved out of the swamp and stole our lives to hold. What about him?" I ask her impatiently. "He is bathed in blood, and did you see his face tonight? Terrifying. What do you want me to say?" I'm as irritated with my reactions to him tonight as I am with her for trying to force it out of me. The shiver that went down my spine when he looked at me over his whiskey tumbler and the warmth that crept up my neck and stained my cheeks red when he made his insinuation about women he might be interested in, are shameful. I shouldn't find him attractive. I shouldn't be curious about him at all. But dammit, I haven't been able to get him out of my head since Saturday.

"Woah Lina, reserve the hostility for your vibrator," she cackles as she says it, to which I huff indignantly, before she continues. "I know you don't want to be interested in him. I'm not suggesting you marry him and have his vampire babies—if we are going with the theory that vampire babies are a thing— I'm just saying, for curiosity's sake, you could take one for the team. Find out if his big dick energy is all ego or not. That's all I'm saying."

"Why don't you find out for yourself then—Jack seemed awfully curious himself. I'm sure he would let you take him for a ride." I roll my head in her direction to see her reaction which is as delightedly shocked as I expected, and a laugh escapes me.

"Rude."

We ride in silence for a few more minutes, before stopping at the curb in front of her house, and she hops out, giving me a quick wave before heading inside.

Stopping at my house, I pay the driver, and jog up the stairs and into the house. I pop into the kitchen and give Grand-mere a kiss on the cheek, put $700 in the jar—thanks to an unquestionably generous vampire prince—and head upstairs to shower and sleep. And maybe take my irritation out on said vibrator.

I jolt upright in the early afternoon, heart hammering in my chest. My dream is vague but those eyes—the dark heavy gray—felt like a weight on my chest. I can almost taste the whiskey in the air. My heart hammers like I was running from something. Bash is always followed by a faint whiff of the whiskey he drinks too much of, the cologne he covers it with, and smoke. Or fire? I can't really tell. The men in the romance books I read, when I have time, always seem to smell like wind, snow fall, sunlight, or even flowers. In real life, the monster in my dreams smells like warm liquor, some sort of woodsy cologne, and burning. I don't know how vampires are actually killed, since I have never found myself close enough to one that is being extinguished to find out. I know it causes a flash of light and it refers to their flame going out, so maybe the fire is because Bash is a vampire? Do they all smell that way? I have no idea. I shouldn't yearn for the answer.

I have even less idea why I am thinking about the way Bash smells or why I noticed the way Bash smells. I have a few hours before work and decide to go grab some food. I'm a little more flush with cash than usual—considering the extra tips from last night—so I throw my uniform clothes in a backpack, and get dressed in a pair of skinny jeans and an oversized tee that says 'Vampires: Just goth mosquitos'.

"Bye Grand-mere! I'm going to grab some food and then head to Velvet, see you in the morning!" I yell, and head out the door.

CHAPTER 6
ELINA

After a full week of nightly vigils in my bar by Sebastien, I've had enough. I haven't spoken to him since last week except for me to greet him when he sits, give him his whiskey, and bid him goodnight at sunrise. He watches me, silently, from the end of the bar and Jack hasn't made another appearance.

"Why do you think he keeps coming?" Sarah asks me on Saturday night after I give Bash his third drink.

"I have no idea, but this is the last night he sits and watches me. I can't tell if he's trying to wear me down with his presence or if he thinks I need his protection. Whatever it is, I'm tired of him just sitting there." I walk over to him and lean across the bar.

"Hey, Bash, you're here. Again. Why have you been here every night? You're here from sundown to sun up every day. Since you're, well, *you*, I would assume you had like kingdom business or something. Instead, you sit here all night and drink whiskey after whiskey. Why are you here?"

"Why, hello, Elina. What a break from your standard

protocol of ignoring me. Am I not allowed to patronize this bar? I don't have anything going on as, you know, Re Marcus is more than capable of handling business on his own." He pauses, his face contemplative. "Listen, I will make you a deal. Tomorrow is Sunday and the bar is closed. Give me two hours tomorrow night and if you don't want me to come back, I'll never come here again. Just two hours Elina. Please." He looks at me expectantly, a small look of triumph on his face, like he can already hear my yes. He never abandons our eye contact, never even looks down, though I know he can see down my corset. It's sweet in a medieval sort of way.

"Where would we go? The streets are dangerous at night for me—" *because of your people,* I add silently.

"Not if you're with me, they aren't," he cuts in.

"Ok, but it's Sunday night. The Rest Day Law means everything in The City of Blood is closed."

"Again, not if you're with me, they aren't." I frown at him. So, the rich and powerful vamps can flout the law and the humans are trapped in their houses. Of course.

"Sunday is the only day of the week I am not working—I work day and night, 6 days a week. On my only day off, I can't do anything during the day and I am forced to stay inside at night, and you and your rich nepo-baby vampire friends are breaking the laws you set? And I am to participate in that?"

"Elina, it's my only opportunity to be with you, outside of these walls, *because* it's your only day off." His voice is a little pleading but he doesn't acknowledge my, *very valid,* points. "Will you give me a different day? I can make up for the money you'll lose by taking the night off."

"Wow Bash, you're really unbelievable. Are you trying to buy me now?" I pick up the brothel menu and slam it on the counter in front of him. "This is what you can buy. I am not for sale." With the satisfaction of having the final word, I walk away. I glance over my shoulder and see the dejected look on his face as I reach Sarah.

"Don't you think that was a little harsh, Lina? I mean, I know you're trying really hard to not like him, but it didn't sound like he was trying to offend you. It was a stupid misstep in the conversation." Sarah gives me a scolding look.

"Sarah, he and I? We are too different. That's the point I'm trying to make. I can go out on the street because he's there to protect me? I don't want his protection. I only need protection because of *his* family. I can go out and enjoy a night on the town on a Sunday night? I, *only*, can't do that now because of his family. He can't solve the problem he created that easily."

"Just give him a chance please. Maybe it will be a waste of time, but at least you'll have done something. And if it's a disaster, he won't come back. If it's not a disaster, maybe you'll find yourself in a position that matters instead of behind this bar, selling other humans to the vampires so you're not out on the street. Give him a chance." She looks at me pleadingly, having grabbed my hands at some point. I get it, I really do, this is a chance to, at the very least, have an important vampire see humans as more than entertainment or food. But, it's dangerous too, for all of us.

"Fine Sarah, I'll give him a chance. I refuse to believe that anyone who sits at the right hand of my captor is doing anything other than playing a cat and mouse game. I never even hinted at telling you to try and give Ethan a chance. Remember that." I practically spit at her and her face crumples. I immediately regret letting the thought leave my head. "Fuck. I shouldn't have said that. I shouldn't have mentioned him. I'm sorry. I love you. I'll try." Sarah hangs her head, dropping my hands and walking away. *Fuck.*

I spend the next 4 or 5 hours working the bar like my life depends on it. Pouring drinks, ordering girls for the customers, and keeping tension down through my sunny disposition alone. Ok, even I don't believe that last part. I refill Bash's glass 2 more times and pocket two $50s in tips from him without an ounce of guilt.

A few minutes before the last call, I wander over to make sure he doesn't need a refill before I shut the drinks off.

"Need anything else before I close the well?"

"No, Elina, thank you. I didn't mean to make it sound like you were for sale before. I'm not used to this ok? This is new for me"

"Yeah, it's new for me too." Appraising him, I decide how to respond to his question. "Alright Bash, you get two hours and that's it. I'll set a timer. 2 hours." I hold up two fingers in front of him, driving my point home. A slow smile spreads across his face, lighting him up in a way I haven't seen before. A special smile almost, one that is only for me. I find myself grinning in return, against my will.

"*Perfetta*. I'll pick you up at 8 and get to keep you until 10, *Tesoro mio*." The lapse into Italian is a little unexpected but it's perfect coming off his lips. Tesoro mio? I'll have to find an Italian dictionary if Bash is going to start adding Italian to our conversations.

"Alright, I'll see you at 8. Good night, Bash"

What have I done? In 13 hours I have a date with a vamp. And not just any vamp. An old, Italian, aristocratic vampire that may have been a vampire baby at some point and smells like fire. A grumpy, broody, tall heir-to-the-vampire-throne vampire. The kind of vamp you think of when you think of a stereotypical blood-drinker. Very Dracula in the modern era— Dracula if he wore coordinating black-on-black suits.

It's fine. I'm fine. I'll set a timer, I'll be home before 10:01. "*Perfetta*," I tell myself, in a mock Italian accent.

Every Sunday is the same and this one is no exception. Except there is a guillotine hanging over me, a dread in the distance. A dread that has left butterflies in its wake. I have breakfast with Grand-mere while I avoid the grey cloud hanging over 8 pm. I go to church and listen to an hour-long sermon about the dangers of giving into lust and resisting the devil. The pastor reads from 1 Peter and I am amazed at how prophetic the sermon truly is.

> *Be sober-minded; be watchful. Your adversary, the*
> *devil, prowls around like a roaring lion, seeking*
> *someone to devour.*
> *1 Peter 5:8*

I do not feel better after church.

Sitting down with Grand-mere Celeste for supper, I fidget in my chair, trying to figure out how to tell her my plans for tonight.

"What's wrong with you girl? You have ants in your pants. Stop squirming and tell me whatever it is that has you all worked up." I suck in a deep breath.

"I have a date tonight," I say quickly before I lose my nerve.

"A date? A date with who? On a Sunday night? At night?"

"Yes, tonight, at night." I hang my head, hands in my lap and mumble out, "With Sebastien Malvani," like I'm a child who broke the rules. I am genuinely worried about her reaction though. Life is hard for everyone and especially Grand-mere. The vamps are a touchy subject we generally avoid.

"Who? Speak up Elina," she tells me sternly.

"I said with Sebastien Malvani," I repeat, peeking up at her through my lashes while I wait for her response. With that, Grand-mere Celeste gasps out loud and clutches her chest with a look of horror. Something in her expression pulls at me. I can't read the emotion in her bottomless brown eyes but it's almost like a memory, one of dread. This is going as well as I had expected. After about a minute, she recovers her wits and gives me a weak smile.

"Well, if that isn't something. A Blood Raven taking you out. Are you sure that's safe?"

"No, not really. He's been coming into the bar for a few weeks and, I don't know, I feel like I need to go through with this and see what happens. Sarah thinks that if things go well, maybe I could be in a position to do something. He is the heir after all—that has to mean something, right?" Another gasp.

"The heir? Like, Marcus's heir?"

"Yes, I looked up the family tree last Sunday and he's Marcus's nephew—the only male in the family line under Marcus. Marcus has some brothers but I guess he passed them over." Maybe I could ask Bash about it one day.

"Bash? You are quite familiar with this man. I don't feel well about this but it's your choice and your life. You can't stay here with me forever." She gazes at me sadly, her mouth turned down, her hand still over her heart. She's wrong—I can and I will.

"I'm going up to get ready, he will be here soon. I promise to be careful Grand-mere, and I will be home tonight. Please don't worry about me." I drop a kiss on her cheek and head up the stairs to get ready for the date I did not want and am scared to go on.

One long, very hot shower later, I'm getting dressed. I have no idea what I'm supposed to wear since he didn't tell me where we are going, but it's probably a safe bet he is wearing black dress pants and a black button down. Pulling on black jeans with rips in the knees, I decide I need to add a jacket. I laugh softly to myself as I look at my outfit in the mirror, fluffing my curls before heading down the stairs.

At exactly 8 o'clock, a black sports car pulls up to the curb in front of the house and Bash unfolds himself from the driver seat. Interesting, he struck me as the type to have a driver.

Walking out the front door, I extend my hand as he waits at the bottom of the stairs. A feral grin on his face.

CHAPTER 7

BASH

Walking out of the Velvet Tomb on Sunday morning, the sun peeking over the horizon, I feel different. Lighter, somehow, as though something has changed—something important. Will this date actually make a difference and be a turning point? It has to, I can't go on like this. I know in my soul that she was not exaggerating when she said I only had this one date—these 2 hours to change her mind—or she will be lost to me. I overheard her argument with Sarah, I know this is a most reluctant courtship to her but I need this chance.

Now that I have *tesoro mio* committed, I have to decide what to do with her. Walking quickly toward the cathedral, I arrive in time to run into my uncles, Marcus, Victor, and Darius, who look almost identical, long black hair tied at the nape of their necks, walking with their heads bowed as they murmur amongst themselves.

"Kept it a bit late today, Nephew?" Uncle Darius calls as he watches me striding across the black-and-white checkered floor.

"*Si, c'erano tesori da catturare.* Ville de Sang has such beautiful treasures," I tell him with a roguish wink.

"What treasures have you captured, Bash? Anyone we know?" Darius follows up in an almost interrogatory way.

I smile cryptically and incline my head respectfully before heading through the chapel, toward the exit. This exit is the closest way to my loft without going through the sun lit streets. I can feel the sun's presence in the world despite being unable to see it in the windowless room. It drives me to bed, to rest.

"Keep your secrets then!" comes a shout and a laugh from behind me.

Undressing quickly once I'm in my bedroom, I brainstorm date ideas. I haven't taken anyone on a proper date since before *La Casa del Corvo di Sangue* conquered Ville de Sang, quite a few years before, if I'm being honest. Settling in for the next 12 hours, a plan starts to form in my head.

I awake right at sunset and have less than an hour before I have to pick her up. After a quick shower, I dress in a black henley and black jeans. Of course it's my traditional black outfit, but a bit more casual for her. After running my fingers through my hair a few times, I head down to the *cattedrale* for a bite.

"Good evening, *Stellino*, don't you look nice? Very relaxed. Where are you off to?" my mother says as I walk into the room. She eyes me, missing nothing, as usual. Her auburn tinged deep brown hair is pulled back in a severe bun, and she wears a designer pant suit, her usual overdressed outfit. A trait she has passed on to me. Moving toward the warm blood on the counter, I give her a secretive smile, hearing the thick liquid fill my tumbler. Sipping blood from my glass, I wonder if Elina is in it.

"Out for a few hours, I'll be back for council. And stop calling me that—I'm nearly 500 years old," I playfully scold her for my nickname.

"You may be 'nearly 500 years old', but you'll always be my little star. Have fun darling and don't get into any trouble."

Finishing my breakfast, such as it is, my appetite is suitably satisfied, but warmed blood donations are hardly what my body craves. My teeth still ache to tap into an artery. I stop to wonder what Elina would taste like, her blood flowing into my veins and filling me with life. I have to pause that train of thought before I embarrass myself. Walking toward the garage that stores my family's cars, I ponder whether a comfortable sedan, a sports car, or even a bike would be the best choice for tonight.

I decide on the Ferrari Roma—sleek, black, and fast. If tonight doesn't go well, at least I will have fun driving. And if it does go well, I can take her for a quick drive through the empty city. Does she like fast cars? Would she like a motorcycle? I'm going to ask her.

Heading east on I-10, I open up the 611 horsepower engine and top 130 miles per hour before slowing as I get into Little Woods. Pulling up to the curb in front of the small two story house Elina shares with her grandmother at exactly 8 o'clock, I reflect on how differently we grew up. I spent my childhood running the halls in the *Castello di Fenis* with my cousins and friends, and she grew up behind these walls in this modest house with only her grandmother. I want to know so much about her life here. I want to ask her everything, but more than that, I want her to want to answer me.

Climbing out of the car, I walk up the path and watch as she slowly opens the door and steps onto the porch. She's absolutely gorgeous, and taking in her outfit, I think I should have brought a bike. She is wearing worn-in Converse sneakers, black holey jeans that hug her curves like they were made for her, a lacy tank top that shows the perfect amount of cleavage, and a black, leather riding jacket. Her brown hair falls in curls around her shoulders and down her back. Her blue eyes are ringed in kohl and look glacial and inhuman contrasting her dark tawny skin in the moonlight. She's perfect.

"Stunning," I breathe as I extend my hand toward her.

A smile breaks across her face and her eyes light up as she takes me in.

"Not so bad yourself, *l'immortel*," she sasses, as she takes my hand and lets me help her down the stairs. I'm reluctant to let go on the path but she pulls her hand from mine. "Could you have picked a more excessive car?"

"Probably," I shrug. "Do you not like fast cars? Or is it this car you object to specifically?"

"It's the unnecessary flaunting of your money, Bash. Look around, read the room."

So I do. I try to look objectively at the human neighborhood. I don't spend any time in these communities. The French quarter is almost all vampires now. The homes were probably nice at some point but a lot are showing their age. They are run down or have peeling paint. I can tell that the people in this neighborhood genuinely care about their houses and lawns, but only so much can be done. Their cars are old, some rusty or with broken windows covered in plastic.

"I didn't...I don't—"

"I know Sebastien, why would you? Let's just go."

Taking her elbow I guide her around the car and open her door so she can slide into the seat. Moving quickly to the other side, I get seated and pull away from the curb. We ride in silence; I'm itching to reach over and touch her warm hand. I can see the flush of blood under her skin and she's glowing in the moonlight. She looks over at me occasionally, but doesn't say anything and I don't know where to even begin.

"Where are we going?" she asks me as we get off the highway and I don't go into the French Quarter.

I don't immediately respond as I pull over to the curb in front of the gates to St. Louis Cemetery No.1.

Her eyes widening and a smile trying to break through, she looks at me and back to the gate.

"The City of the Dead?" She looks at the closed gates of the oldest cemetery in the city, a little starry eyed. "It's been closed since, well forever. Since before I was born. Bash, this is so amazing," she says excitedly, trying to open her door. I jump out and rush around to the other side before helping her to her feet.

"Don't jump out, ok? Wait for me—it's safer that way," I say and she rolls her eyes. "I thought you might like a little history lesson, if you're up for it."

"Yes, Sebastien. A million times yes!" I can't believe how excited she is. I was hoping for something better than the disdain I usually get but this is more than I could have asked for. I reach out, take her hand in mine, and lead her to the gates.

"We've seen Marie Laveau and that pyramid that was never used, but what I really wanted to show you is over here." I pull her through the rows and rows of aged tombs. Coins and trinkets sitting outside of them for blessings and protection. "Did you know the voodoo priestesses and priests have been entombed here for far longer than Marie Laveau? Their names are lost, but practitioners still come here to clean their tombs, leave offerings, and ask for protection. Witches, too. A lot of the people who were laid to rest here are unknown. There are even tales of people being buried in the ground under the tombs—mass graves for yellow fever victims," I trail off to give Elina a chance to ask a question or offer a thought.

"What about vampires? Before the Shadow Kingdom and the Blood Ravens, I mean."

"Let me tell you a story while we walk. In 1740, a man appeared at the court of King Louis XV and began to work for the crown as a spy and a diplomat. He traveled to different courts and engaged with kings and princes across Europe. At the time, he claimed to be 100 years old. He traveled all over the world for the French throne." I look over and see her rapt attention on me, her eyes following my mouth. "He hosted parties where he neither ate, nor drank, only partaking in thick red wine. People who encountered him, years—even decades —apart claimed he was an alchemist and used magic to avoid aging. In 1784, he was reported to have died in Germany, though no one ever saw his body and the funeral observation was never completed.

"In 1810, a man matching every description—even his name—appeared in the war camps of Napoleon and talked war strategy with General François-Joseph de Saint-Hilaire, attempting to turn the tide of the Napoleonic wars. He was unsuccessful. And sometime in the 1910's, a man named Jacques St. Germain, a wealthy European aristocrat, showed up in New Orleans. A man who, supposedly, did not age despite looking decades younger than his purported age, who never ate or drank. Have you heard of him?"

A gasp. "Wait, I know this story. He threw lavish parties all night until, one day, a woman threw herself from his balcony claiming he attempted to bite her. Then, he disappeared. They later discovered wine bottles full of blood, presumably human. His house is on my tour. He was New Orleans' first vampire." She turns her wide eyes on me. "Was he actually a vampire?"

"Imagine. Vampires are real and exist right here in this very city?" I feign surprise and excitement. Elina looks at me confused for a minute before breaking out in laughter.

"Did you just make a joke?" she asks me incredulously and I'm momentarily caught off guard that she has never heard me joke. I guess it makes sense since we didn't talk much at the bar.

"Yes, *Tesoro mio*, I did. Stop looking so surprised, I'm actually quite funny. Now look, this is what I wanted to show you. St. Germain may be the reported 'first vampire' in New Orleans, but I assure you, we Italians have been here *a lot* longer than that. This is the *Società Italiana di Mutua Beneficenza* tomb. It's the largest, most elaborate tomb in the cemetery and was built specifically for the benefit of the Italians who settled in New Orleans in the mid and late 19th century. At the time, we were ostracized and pushed out of society by the French settlers. Even then, there were Malvani's here. The Black Hand mafia boss, Luciano Matranga, was not one of us, but he had *vampiro* muscle that ran the streets at night. They lie in rest here." I stop speaking to give her time to take in everything I've shared with her.

This time, she grabs my hand and drags me down Conti Alley until we reach Alley 10. Among the vaults, she stops in front of one that reads the name Girard. I realize that, because she has never been here, she has never seen this tomb before but she knew exactly where it was.

"We've been here a long time too," she whispers, leaning

against my arm and taking a breath that sounds a little like she might be crying. I don't move, for fear that she might get spooked. I want to ask her how she knew where to go, but this moment feels heavy, important, so I just stand quietly. After what seems like a long time, she lets go of my arm, steps back, and claps her hands once.

"Ok, time to go. What's next?" and the moment is officially broken.

"To the car, *Tesoro mio*," I say and I lead the way back out toward the street.

CHAPTER 8
ELINA

"Why do you keep saying that? Or calling me that? What does *'tesoro mio'* even mean?"

"It means 'my treasure'," Sebastien tells me, speaking quietly. The moment we shared in the cemetery weighs heavy on me. It felt right, standing there, leaning my head on his arm. He's probably 10 inches taller than me so I didn't quite reach his shoulder, but it still felt right. I didn't want it to but it did, and I don't know what to do about it. Now, to find out he has such an endearing nickname for me, it feels too intimate. Too personal. I don't know what to think of all of this.

"Next, we'll be making a quick stop at Nocturne Noir, a little shop for all your magical needs." His voice is playful and full of excitement. "There is magic in the soil of Ville de Sang and you seem a little short on protection." He opens my door with a bit of a flourish and bundles me inside. I giggle despite myself as he makes his way to his side of the car.

Parking his stupid flashy sports car at the end of Pirate's Alley, Bash helps me from the car yet again. Unlike at the cemetery, there are people, or rather vamps, all over the place here—having conversations and laughing, drinking, playing games like football, and relaxing on the stairs of the cathedral. Almost as though, this is when they relax. Bash catches me watching them and leans down to whisper–

"You're trapped inside on Sundays—Sundays are the only day we can relax without the stress of humanity. We don't have to think about the fragility of humans or endangering them. We don't need to defend them from baby vampires or be tempted by their blood. We simply exist."

Makes sense, I guess. We attract some looks—and some outright stares—as we walk down the alley toward the shop.

"Seriously Bash, a fucking *human child?* Out in Pirate's Alley on a Sunday night? What the actual fuck is *wrong* with you?" An absolutely stunning vampire with a deep bronze skin and thick braids in a mini skirt aggressively snaps at Bash. "Wow, for a *week* you've been skipping parties, not returning my calls —your cousins didn't even know where you were—and you show up here with a *human.*" The way she says 'human' is clearly meant to be insulting, like we are dirt beneath her. Not even worth consideration. I raise my chin in defiance of this woman and try to look menacing.

"Talia, please. I'm trying to enjoy my Sunday like everyone else. Don't make a scene. I will call you tonight when I get home." Bash tells her tensely as he carefully angles his body in front of mine.

"Sure, Bash. I can't wait to hear you explain this." And she stomps away, back toward the cathedral.

Bash puts his hand on my lower back and steers me back on track.

"Let's see about that protection I mentioned."

The shop is dark and smells strongly of incense, but it's not overwhelming—more comforting than anything. A tall woman, skin the color of deep mahogany, with a red-and-green patterned *tet mare* steps out from behind a curtain at the far end of the shop, the bells on her robe and bracelets tinkling delicately as she moves. Her headscarf and dress are adorned with a traditionally French-creole pattern.

"Bash! *Gran zanmi mwen!*" she exclaims as she comes around the counter, arms out for a hug. Bash smiles at her affectionately and hugs her close to him. I'm stunned that this creole *tisaneuse*—or even a witch—would be so friendly and welcoming to *l'immortal*, going so far as to call him her greatest friend. Simply stunned.

"Zelie, my heart smiles from such a warm greeting. How are you? How is Elodie? Do you need anything? I'm sorry I haven't been in more often. I wish I had an excuse," he says as he kisses her on both cheeks. For my part, I stand here speechless.

"I'm well—as are Elodie and the baby. They are settled in at home. And who have you brought to my shop tonight?"

"Zelie, this is *mon tresor*, Elina. Elina, this is my lovely friend, Zelie—she owns this shop. I've known her for, what, fifteen, twenty years?" He asks, before turning to her, "I want her protected." He motions to me. Bash's mention of knowing her fifteen or twenty years surprises me, Zelie doesn't look any older than thirty herself, around the same as Bash and I. I guess the difference is that I'm 28, Bash is who-knows-how old, and Zelie seems to be just as timeless. I'm certain she's human though. If she has suspended aging, she must be a bokor—a magic practitioner.

"*Tresor,* you say? Hmm. Step forward, child, let me look at you. You have a strong heart and your blood is from this land. You're as much as part of this place as I am—there is magic inside you, I can feel it." She considers briefly before speaking again. "You'll need a salt and ash pendant. I'll walk you through it. First, you take a silver pendant, as silver is resistant to supernatural powers." She pulls a plain, silver disk pendant from behind the counter. "Then, salt and charcoal made from burned sage, garlic, and rue are rubbed on the surface to imbue it with the power to repel vampires. It is left overnight for the morning dew to accumulate on the surface which gives it properties of the sunrise. An obsidian, left to bathe in the light of a full moon, is set into the silver. Finally, it is inscribed with '*tutela a mortuis*', which means 'protection from the dead'. Once I make the pendant for you, you will spill one drop of your blood, freely given, on its surface. This will bind the pendant to you and protect you from harm at the hands of a vampire as long as you are wearing it. This magic is old—sacred."

She levels me a look before continuing. "Also, illegal. You are not to tell anyone who made you this pendant, or encourage anyone to try and make it themselves. Not only is it dangerous magic, but it is also punishable by death. Being bitten by a Sanguine Nocturnus is not the only way to die in this town." She explains the entire process in hushed tones. I guess that's part of the whole it's-illegal-to-create-vampire-repelling pendant thing.

"Thank you Zelie. This is—" I stop, unable to continue speaking past the lump in my throat at the sweetness—but also the importance of the gesture that Bash is presenting to me. Like, my safety matters. I'm speechless. I feel Bash move closer and wrap a tentative arm around my midsection.

He leans down and whispers, "Your safety is the most important thing I've ever cared about, *Tesoro mio*." A shiver runs down my spine. I tell myself it is the cold interior of the shop or the magic in the air. I don't believe him, can't believe him.

I make a plan to return to Zelie's shop on Wednesday because the full moon is Tuesday night, and will be the last step in her creating my magical protection. Bash takes my hand as we exit the store, leads me up a set of stairs hidden next to Nocturne Noir, and we come out on the balcony above the shop.

"This is my loft. That's why I am so familiar with Zelie—I have lived up here since the turnover of power. She wasn't sure about me at first, but I think I won her over."

"I'm not going to fuck you, Bash. It's a waste of time to bring me to your house. Besides, I gave you two hours—we only have a half hour left." I'm irritated that he even brought me up here. I can't believe he thought I would have sex with him because he took me to a cemetery and got me a present.

Something resembling hurt flashes in his eyes, like he can't believe I would think that. "Elina, I didn't bring you up here for that. You're always so quick to assume the worst of me. I wasn't even planning to open my door. This is the quickest way to the next part of the evening, before I take you home. 28 minutes and counting." He looks hurt, like my accusation wounded him. He grabs ahold of my shoulders, touching the least surface area as possible and jumps.

"Holy mother, ahhhhhh, fuck! What the *hell*, Bash, are you trying to kill me?" I start ranting as soon as his feet touch solid ground. At some point during the jump, I buried my face into his chest. Now, I can smell his whiskey and cologne smell as well as that burning smell. I make a note to myself to ask him about it. Pulling my face out of his chest, I peer up at him and see his eyes already on mine, his head slightly tilted, and a look I can't identify on his face—wistfulness, maybe? I push off him and look around, gasping as I realize we are on top of the chapel.

"Bash, what are we doing up here?"

"I figured we could finish the night sitting up here and talking. We haven't talked much and I'm sure you have questions about or for me. I want to know you too. Can we just... talk?" He looks at me pleadingly.

"Ok. Twenty questions, it is. You know we don't really know much about you—as a species, I mean. I can ask anything and you'll tell me?" I ask him sweetly as I lie down on the roof and look up at the stars. He lies down beside me, shoulder to shoulder, the toe of my sneaker brushing his knee.

"Yes, as long as it doesn't endanger you or me. I want to be honest with you, if you'll be honest with me".

I stare up at the moon hanging in the sky above us. There are so many thoughts—so many questions—on the tip of my tongue. Everything about tonight has been perfect, Bash has been so open and vulnerable, I don't even know how to process all of this.

I launch into the first thing that pops into my head.

"I have so many questions. First, I was looking at the Malvani family tree and I saw your lineage, as well as the notation about you being the heir, not having any sirelings, and your paternal parentage being unknown. And I figured that it kind of seems like the Blood Ravens were born. Not turned. Born like babies. But I've never seen a vampire baby and I've known lots of human women who have had sex with vamps." That comment is accompanied by some side eye aimed Bash's way. "So it doesn't make a lot of sense but it seems that way. Marcus looks like you, and I have seen a few of the women from your family and they look similar too. And Marcus looks older than you, but not a lot older. And there were no birth-"

"Stop, Elina. Take a breath. I will explain. Vespera is my mother. Not my sire, my flesh and blood mother. She carried me and birthed me as a vampire. Correct, my father is unknown, but in order for me to be a born vampire, he had to have been one too. Women do not pass on their vampire genes. Human women can carry vampire babies and those will also be

Sanguine Nocturnus when they come of age. We grow up as functionally human until around the age of 30. Then the vampirism settles in and we become this. Immortal—beautiful forever. We do continue to age, but incredibly slowly. Marcus has aged about 20 years in the 1000 years he has lived. He could live another thousand or even more. We don't all age the same. I am not aging at the same rate Marcus is. My mother is only 10 human years younger and appears years younger despite also living more than 1000 years. She only looks about ten years older than me."

"How old are you? How are vampire babies made? Why aren't there more vampire babies?"

"Last Sunday I celebrated my 477th birthday. My vampirism settled 448 years ago." My mouth drops open at that. He's 477 years old—positively ancient! I giggle at the thought. "What are you giggling at, *Tesoro*? As for how vampire babies are made—they're made the same way as human babies. When a man really wants a women, he takes his-"

"Stop, stop, stop. I know how babies are made," I laugh loudly at his joke. "I was giggling because you're so old, like *ancient*. Happy birthday, by the way."

"First of all, I'm not nearly as old as my family, or any other ruling vampire family. Second, jokes aside, we do produce vampire babies the same way. The reason why you haven't seen any vampire babies is because they are, like I said, functionally human. Some are being raised by humans. I, of course, always knew what to expect since my entire family are *Sanguine Nocturnus*, as well as Blood Ravens. The final question was, why aren't there more vampire babies?"

"Yeah, ya'll are fucking all over town. No one even knows that vamps can make babies." I speak earnestly, pleased to be able to ask all the questions I have.

"Well, only bloodline male vampires can reproduce.

Malvanis are a bloodline. The Devereaux family—you know them as the Shadow Kingdom family—The Vilkas are in Croatia, The Drakos are in Greece. There are more, they are all over the planet. Only direct descendents of the original families can reproduce. Now, as for why we, the Malvanis, are not overrun with babies. We have to take a blood oath, sort of like a sanguine wedding, in order to reproduce. Even then, it's difficult sometimes. My mother only had me. My Uncle Victor and Aunt Valentina had 3 children in 200 years; Lucien, Gianna, and Filomena. Lucien died in childhood before his vampirism settled. *Zio* Darius and *Zia* Lucinda had the twins, Aurora and Alessandra, and were never able to reproduce again. Re Marcus had a daughter, Juliet, but she was extinguished more than 500 years ago." This is such a huge amount of information, information that I feel fairly sure is not meant to be told to humans, or really even people outside of the family.

"That's amazing. No one knows any of this." Excitement blooms in my chest, I can't wait to tell Sarah everything. "Ok, your comment leads me to my next question. How do you extinguish a vamp? And why do you smell like fire or smoke, something burning? Are those two things related?" I ask excitedly since this is really the question I have been wanting to know.

"I really shouldn't tell you this." He gives me a sardonic laugh. "I don't recall anyone smelling particularly like smoke so that may be a 'me' thing. Inside all vampires, whether turned or born, is their life flame. It's the light that replaces the sun. It's not a literal flame, but when we are killed, or extinguished, that flame is put out. When the flame goes out, there is a flash of light that explodes from the body as the light energy from the flame returns to the universe. I don't really know how it works—it's magic, I guess. The ways to extinguish us are decapitation or removal of the heart. I guess the easier way for humans is to decapitate us. The *vampiro* I extinguished in the bar last week? I reached into his chest and pulled out his heart."

I'm momentarily taken aback by how matter of factly he speaks of the snuffing out of his own species. I think he notices, but he doesn't comment. I glance at my watch and see that it's just after 10. Our date has run late.

"Let's go. I'll get you home," he says, standing up from the reclined position he had taken on the roof. He extends a hand and pulls me up to my feet. Bash then leads us to the edge of the roof nearest to where we parked the car and wraps me tightly in his arms. He gazes down at me, longing in his eyes. I tilt my head up to look him in the face and he leans down. I know he is going to kiss me and I want him to, I really do. I also know it's not the right thing to do. I have no idea how to trust him or if I even should. He was honest with me tonight, but that doesn't mean we have overcome all the barriers in our situation, the largest obstacle being the two completely different worlds we reside in. He leans closer and closer, very slowly, until his breath mingles with mine.

He moves at a glacial pace, like he is giving me time to stop him. And I don't. I'm going to let him kiss me. I can feel his intention, his breath. In the second before he closes the final gap and captures my lips with his, I turn my head and he kisses my cheek. When he pulls back, if he is surprised, he doesn't show it. Holding me tightly, he bends his knees and jumps off the roof onto the street near the car. This time, I know what's coming and smash my face against the hard planes of his chest. When we are back on the ground, I am in no hurry to extricate myself from his hold and he doesn't push me away. I stay holding on to him, breathing in his scent, and thinking I won't ever forget this smell for as long as I live.

Eventually, we separate and he helps me into the car. The

drive back to my house is silent but not uncomfortable, he holds my hand, enveloped in his cold one, the whole drive and I don't want to pull away. Before we pull up to the curb, he asks "What's your favorite food?"

"Crawfish etouffee," is the first thing that pops into my head and out my mouth. He smiles. He jumps out and runs around to my side and opens the door.

"Good night, Elina." He pauses. He breathes like what he says next really matters. "Should I stop? Do you want me to disappear? If not, I'll be there tomorrow."

"Good night, Bash." I lean up and plant a kiss on the outer edge of his mouth. "I'll see you tomorrow night."

CHAPTER 9
BASH

"Tonight, I am bringing the matter of the out of control, newly sired *Sanguine Nocturnus* to the council." I watch Marcus pace the council room, his voice commanding our collective attention. "Their behavior in the streets is more out of control and unrestrained than ever. The humans are terrified and almost entirely refusing to come out of their homes after dark, which is resulting in an uptick in attacks and deaths in increasingly public places. Last week, a new sireling attacked a human woman and killed her in a bar on a busy Saturday night. Sebastien happened to be there and extinguished him immediately, but this should never have occurred. Humans are our natural food source, and cultivating such terror and hysteria among them is resulting in less available food," Marcus remarks once he has called the *Sanguine Nocturnus* council to order.

The 12 men and women around the table watch him, some looking bored, others irritated. Mother watches each person intently as she usually finds the dissent amongst the members so they can be brought to heel. Marcus runs the city in such a way that council members feel like their opinions are heard, but he is the one who has the final say. I am pleased that he has brought this matter to them though. What happened at the Velvet Tomb was unnecessary, and brutal.

"What do you want us to do about it, Marcus? It isn't as though there is a vampire academy or something." Domingo Salvatore of Mid-City asks from his seat down the table.

"The humans are here to feed us. If they aren't feeding us, we don't need them at all. Order them to come out at night so that we can eat. This is stupid—the snake doesn't ask the chicken for permission to eat, why should we?" Talia chimes in from beside me. As if her absolutely out-of-line comments to Elina weren't enough, she's now sitting in this council meeting acting as though we are out of control predators.

"Talia, you're over 300 years old. Do you have so little self control that you have to attack humans in bars? Or so little respect for the humans that run this city that you would have them forced from their homes to feed us?" I say to her scathingly.

"Some of us don't care about silly little human pets, even pretty ones, or the ones you've been watching like a lovesick fool, Sebastien," she spits at me, venom in her voice. My mother's head turns to me, a questioning tilt to it.

"All of us care about human pets. In case you haven't noticed, the only reason we have any control at all is our human pets who keep the perimeter secure while we rest. So, if you don't care about the humans, you had better start or get the fuck out."

She only huffs at me before turning her head.

"Yes, we care about the humans, insofar as they feed us and do whatever needs to be done during the daylight hours, but I don't know what else we should do. The sirelings are hungry,

Sire," Henry Romano, the *governaturno* for the Garden district contributes.

"Maybe there should be less *vampiro*. Have any of you considered that? Stop turning people. There are going to be more *vampiro* than humans soon. Then what? The humans will die off and we will be really hungry and have to leave this place," Victor chimes in from his spot near Marcus.

"Ok, for now, I am putting an injunction on turning new vampires. As you know, you're required to register new sirelings, and there will be no further vampires created until the existing sirelings are under control. In each of your districts, you know who is turning, and I expect you to get them in line. Have the sires enforce order or I will personally cull them. The next time I hear a report of an out of control vampire indiscriminately killing in a club or similar establishment, I will go to the sire himself and he will answer for the insubordinate behavior of his sirelings," Marcus tells the room to a chorus of outraged gasps. "And if anyone has anything to say about this, come to me!" With that, he slams his hand down on the table and leaves the room. The council room breaks out into chaotic whispers.

"How do we stop them?"

"We need to eat!"

"This is ridiculous. Marcus oversteps."

"ENOUGH!" I bellow into the room. "Marcus does not overstep—he is Re, his word is law. You can eat from willing donors, from blood supply bars and restaurants, from the hospital, or on the streets. But stop killing people or there won't be any people left. Tell your vampires and their sirelings that this is a life or death situation, and if they don't want to be extinguished, they had better get in line. If any of you have anything to say about it," I look at Talia and Domingo, "say it now." I wait a moment and both of them avert their eyes, avoiding eye contact. I walk out of the room, Victor, Darius, and my mother trailing behind me.

"Bash, my *Stellino*, wait. I wish to talk to you." I hear my mother call from behind me.

"Yes, mother. What is it?"

"Darling boy." She puts her hand on my arm as she kisses both my cheeks. "Would you like to tell me what Talia was referring to? You know that she was hoping you would agree to an official mating courtship. She wants the *Legame di Sangue* with you. What was she talking about, a human pet?"

"Mother, I have no interest in Talia that way, you know this. She only wants *Legame di Sangue* because she thinks it will make her *regina*. She wants nothing more than to be *Principessa* Talia and I won't have it. She isn't referring to anything, she thinks she knows something about me and she doesn't. She has no respect for me, and so, I have none for her, either."

"I only want you to settle down." She brushes a stray curl off my forehead, like she did when I was a child. "You haven't had any serious courtings, ever. You should be planning for your future. Has anyone caught your eye?" I can't tell her the truth. I can't tell her how hard I am falling for a fragile, beautiful, human woman. A human who wears all black, like me. A woman whose favorite food is crawfish etouffee. A woman who makes you earn her smiles and her time. And a woman who will never be like me, and will age and get married and have little human babies.

"No, mother. I'll let you know if anything changes. Keep Talia away from me."

Since my vampirism settled, I have never felt tired. I sleep when the sun forces me from wakefulness. I awake when the moon takes over. But I have not been tired.

Today, I am tired.

After having such a perfect evening with Elina, the drama and frustration of vampire politics is too much. My focus is split between my responsibilities as heir and my desire to follow Elina around until the end of her days. Dragging my weary mind up the stairs to my loft, I lament that it will be until tomorrow night before I can get another hit of Elina. A sound catches my ear as I enter my apartment, a slight rustling.

"What the hell do you think you're doing?" I question Talia as I walk into my bedroom, the source of the noise. She is sprawled across my bed, all long bronze limbs and lingerie.

"I came to show you what you're missing with *her*." Her voice is like poison and causes me to flinch—I'm not prepared for the vitriol. "I know you didn't get anywhere with her tonight, even after your little rooftop show. You don't smell like her and you haven't showered. Let me take care of you, the way I used to. Please, Bash. Fuck me?" She lays back on my pillows, her hair fanned out behind her as she trails a finger down her throat and between her breasts. Her nipples pointed and on show for me. She continues to trail her hand down her body until she slips her finger into her panties.

"Talia," I growl, my voice low and menacing, her eyes widening at the tone. "Get the fuck out of my bed, get the fuck out of my apartment, and do not ever speak to me again or I will rip your heart from your chest and Marcus will have to find a new *governaturno* for the By-water. Get out!"

"A human, Bash?" Her voice is sweet, taunting. "I hope you don't think she will survive this?"

"That sounded really close to a threat, Talia," I accuse her as I step into her space.

She bares her fangs to me in a wicked smile. "Oh no, *Principe*. It was a promise."

"I wasn't joking, Talia. Get out. I won't have you, because all I am to you is *principe*, not a person, a man. Out. Now."

She storms out of the room, wrapping her arms around herself and slamming the apartment door behind her.

Fucking hell.

Talia isn't going to forget this. Thankfully, I have already ordered Elina's protection pendant, but I will have to watch her closely. Grabbing my jacket and a few supplies from my desk, I follow the path Talia took and slam my apartment door behind me. Watching her take off toward the By-Water, I head the other way.

Running from *Piazza della Luna* to Little Woods takes just a few minutes. I jump up to the roof of the neighbors house and settle in to guard Elina for the night.

CHAPTER 10
ELINA

I wake up on Monday morning lighter and happier than I have been, really ever. I have never truly found a pocket of my own happiness in this existence that I am trying to carve out of misery. Lying in bed, staring out at the bright April day, I'm sobered by the knowledge that I could never wake up next to Sebastien and see his face in the bright light of morning. That is only 1 of 100 reasons why falling for a 477-year-old vampire prince is a bad idea. I can't even consider all the other ramifications or issues without flinching.

Last night was perfect. If I had ever taken the time to wish for something, it would have been last night. Unfortunately, I do not have the leisure to spend nights with my vampire friend, or to form an attachment to him. I have to stop daydreaming and focus on the here-and-now. 'Here-and-now' are me and Grand-mere Celeste in this little house in this forgotten city ruled by vamps. And he is the heir to the throne. What happens now? I fall in love with him and live with him until I am old and grey and then I die? I take that blood oath thing and give him vamp babies that will one day subjugate my own people and kill us? No, I can't let this continue. He is not a good person and he does not come from a good family. I certainly do not intend to become enthralled with him or to let him change me. This little romance that seems to be happening won't work long term, and I don't envision myself hanging out with vamps or going into the cathedral to meet his vamp family.

Dressing and going downstairs, I know that Grand-mere will have questions for me, questions I don't really have an answer for. "Good morning, Grand-mere Celeste."

"Good morning, dear. I'm glad you made it home safely. Tell me about your date with the prince?"

"Don't call him prince—I don't think that's a thing they say. At least, no one has mentioned it." I don't know how to explain it in a way that doesn't feel weird or cheesy. I hold how special last night was close to my chest, and I don't want it ruined. "Well, he took me to the City of the Dead and to a little magic shop. Then we talked at the cathedral and he brought me home."

"A cemetery and a voodoo shop on a first date? Vampires." She shakes her head in disbelief.

"It was actually kind of...perfect. It felt right for our first date, I guess. He told me some ghost stories and vampire lore, and filled in the blanks for some questions I had. At Nocturne Noir, he bought me a pendant. I'll pick it up Wednesday."

"Ok, and now what? You date? Elina, I try to let you make your own choices—God knows you shouldn't have to be alone forever—but a vamp? Then what happens? You turn into one? You ravage our friends and family?" She looks so sad as she puts words to the voice in my head. This is a bad idea.

"I don't know, Grand-mere. I expected to hate him, for him to be a selfish, violent vampire, not someone who feels...right. I don't know."

Walking toward the front door I hear her half whisper, "I just worry about you. How could this make you happy?"

Opening the door, something flutters to the floor, catching my eye. Bending to pick it up, I see it's an envelope addressed to me. Tearing it open, I sit on the porch swing.

April 12

Elina,

Last night was the greatest night I have spent in, longer than I care to admit, frankly. After I dropped you off, there was a council meeting that did not go super well. Afterwards, Talia attempted to stay the night with me and because of that, I spent the night perched across the street watching your house. Admittedly, now that I've written that, I see that I come across a bit creepy. Maybe I was too big of a coward to stay in that place knowing she had propositioned me. Maybe I just wanted to be close to you.

My every waking moment is consumed with thoughts of you and I hope that you'll give me the opportunity to earn your thoughts in return. Already, you mean more to me than anyone I've given my time to in 400 years. My heart is full, knowing you gave me even a small space in your life. I know you're going to be thinking of all the things wrong with this, with us, but please don't decide to give up what we could have because you're afraid of it. Talk to me first.

So with hope that you'll let me in, I want to write to you—to share my thoughts. I'm going to see you tomorrow. Your house is quiet now and so is the street. There is no vampire presence here, too far from the action, with only residential homes, so, no people coming and going either. I asked Marcus to speak to the council about the out-of-control, new vampires and he has ruled that for now, no new vampires can be created. Spending just a few hours with you in the city made me afraid. I'm afraid for you and I never considered what it must be like to live in fear. Tell me how to help. What to do.

I need you to know that my heart is yours, all you have to do is take it.

-Bash

This man is insane.

He's known me for a week and spent two hours alone with me and now his heart is mine? Insane. I refold the letter and put it back in its envelope. Going inside, I climb the stairs to my room. Putting the envelope under my pillow, I lay down and think through everything he said. He asked Marcus to help with the vamp problem—that's good. I guess spending time with me has helped him gain some perspective on humanity.

Talia on the other hand, what *is* that? Does she love him? I decide to ask him later when he comes to the Velvet Tomb. I'm not exactly jealous, I have no claim on him, nor do I love him. It seems too convenient for her to be interested now that she has seen me, so I'm probably not the reason for her interest in Bash. Maybe they already had a thing together, and she sees me as the interloper. I might not have been nice to her when I saw her, but I am definitely a girl's girl. and if she has something with him, I am completely uninterested. He did have that whole bathroom thing with Amelie, I didn't even get to ask him about that. *Ugh!* This is already so complicated, and we have only had *one* date.

Heading off to Sarah's before I have to do a tour this afternoon, I steel myself to explain everything that has happened since yesterday.

Unlocking her door and slipping inside, I go in search of her.

"Hello, my darling," I call out, walking through the house. It's dark and unusually quiet. I check my watch—it's after 1 o'clock—so, I expect Sarah would be awake by now. Opening her closed bedroom door, I come face-to-face with Ethan. He has his sharp fangs on display and the weak light from the hallway casts him in a deep shadow, but I can make out the floppy brown hair falling in his face, the same way it has his entire life. His brown eyes shine in the dark room, almost cat-like. I let out a startled screech as I freeze by the door, trying to make sense of what I am seeing. He jumps back with a hiss, snapping his fangs at me, and I realize that her bedroom is black as night, not a single molecule of light coming in from the windows I know exist on the south side of the room. I can hear his labored breathing, his gnashing teeth.

"Elina!" Sarah jumps up from the bed and pushes me out of the room, closing the door behind her.

"What the actual *fuck*, Sarah? There is a *vampire* in your *bedroom*! And your bedroom was a *tomb*. Oh my god, how long has this been going on?"

"It's not just a vampire, it's Ethan, Elina. My Ethan. He's been here since a few days after the attack. He showed up one night and got down on his knees and begged me to forgive him." I, mentally, calculate what that means, and that he was, most assuredly, here the last time I visited. "He heard what happened to me and panicked. He said he needed to know if I was ok. We boarded up the windows so he had a safe place to rest and he has been here ever since. He heard you come inside during his rest and jumped up to defend us, he didn't realize who you were. I'm sorry, I should have told you. But you hate the vamps so much I didn't know how." Her words rush out of her like she couldn't control the flow and needed to purge it all.

I drag her into my arms and hold her tightly. "Jesus, Sarah. I could never hate them enough to not understand your desire for happiness. That's absurd. You're like a sister to me. I want nothing more than for you to be happy. I've been so worried about you since Ethan left. Oh my god—that awful thing I said to you the other night about never telling you to give Ethan a chance—when he was here the whole time. I'm sorry I made you feel like you couldn't tell me. Let's go downstairs and talk, there is a lot to talk about it seems."

Two hours and a lot of tea later, we have covered all the ground between us. I told her, in minute detail, about my date with Bash and how I felt about all the issues between us. She told me how glad she was to have Ethan home, even if he was a vampire now. I knew she was heartbroken, and I surreptitiously swipe at the tears that escape the corners of my eyes listening to the love in her voice.

"But tell me what it's like with him here, where you live in the day and he lives in the night?"

"I don't really live in the day though, do I? I work at night —all night—and I'm only off 2 nights a week. I sleep a good portion of the day anyway, so I sleep next to him. It almost feels like sleeping next to the dead, he doesn't so much as twitch in his sleep. It's disconcerting. I keep wanting to check for signs of life before I remember he is, in fact, dead. It's so bizarre though. As soon as the sun comes up, no matter what, he is so overcome with the need to sleep that he has to lie down immediately. And then as soon as the sun sets, he sits right up, wide awake."

"How is the..." and I wiggle my eyebrows at her. She blushes from her neck to the tips of her ears, her cheeks a bright crimson.

"Oh," giggling, "it's perfect. Better than before. He has more energy, there is no downtime, and he's attentive and loving. It's so much more than perfect. Update me when you find out about Bash."

Now it's my turn to blush. "I'm not sure we will get that far —everything is so confusing and it's only been a little more than a week."

"Make him work for it. You deserve the entire world, Elina, and Bash might be able to give it to you. Don't let him put you in a different cage. What you want matters the most, and you need to be willing to fight for it. Don't give in because you think you should, make sure it's the right thing for you."

"Jacques St Germain may have been the first reported vampire in New Orleans, but it's unlikely that is the whole story. It is speculated that members of the *Casa del Corvo di Sanguine* were in New Orleans before and after St. Germain, and were even part of the Black Hand mafia in the city," I say, having added a little extra vampire lore for the St. Germain house tour stop after my date. "There is even a tomb specifically for displaced vampires in St Louis Cemetery #1, though it is closed to the public."

Walking into the Velvet Tomb that night, knowing I will see Sebastien, I am both apprehensive, and a little excited. Butterflies thrum chaotically in my belly. I still haven't decided what to do about Bash and his letter. On one hand, I know how ludicrous it is that an almost 500 year old vampire prince seems to be falling in love with me after only 2 weeks and one date. On the other hand, I know that I should not be intrigued by said vampire because he is heir to the wardenship of the prison I live in, and the monster in our collective psyche. I decide to not bring up the letter or the date until I know what to do.

Eyeing the man in black walking into the bar with yet another stunningly beautiful woman is discomforting and unsettling. The blond with him laughs happily, her laugh sounding like the quiet whisper of wind chimes during a slow breeze. I feel more resolute than ever in my decision not to mention the letter or the date until I decide what I want to do about it.

"Hey guys, what can I get you?" I lean over and Bash takes a glance down my body. I can feel the flush rising up my chest under his gaze. He smirks slightly.

Their voices overlap as the beautiful girl on his arm purrs, "Just a glass of Prosecco, Elina," as Bash says, "I'll have a glass of red wine, *Tesoro*. The nebbiolo was perfect, something like that." The blond giggles when he says the nickname he seems to have claimed for me. I feel like the butt of a joke I am not in on. Embarrassment stains my cheeks this time, as I turn away before Bash can say anything else.

Setting the drinks down in front of them, a bit forcefully, several minutes later, I dismissively tell them to let Sarah know if they need anything else. Before I can turn away, Bash lightly grabs my wrist.

"Elina, this is my cousin, Lessa. Lessa, this is Elina." He waves a large hand between us. I feel my cheeks heat for the umpteenth time today, my eyes moving between them as I take in the similar features and identical smiles, only her hazel eyes act as a contrast between them. *Of course,* they are cousins. I wish a hole would open up behind the bar and swallow me up.

"Elina, I am so pleased to meet you. Bash talked about you from the minute he got home last night until sunrise. You're gorgeous. Oh my, I can't wait to get to know you and find out what has Bash so smitten!"

"Oh, hi," I say shyly. I resist the urge to give Bash a scowl, though I can see the laughter in his eyes. He knows exactly what happened. "It's nice to meet you too." I practically flee to the bathroom to try and calm myself down. I know I have made a giant fool of myself and can't help but feel like I revealed more of my hand than I was ready to.

Hearing the restroom door open, I look behind me in the mirror and see Bash. "This is the women's bathroom, Sebastien, though it doesn't seem to have bothered you before so why would it now?" He is fully laughing now as he walks closer and folds me in a hug.

"Hi," he says into my hair.

"Hi," I breathe against his chest. He holds me like this a little longer before he lets go, exiting the bathroom as quietly as he came.

By the time I return to the bar, they're gone.

On Tuesday, he comes to the bar alone. I've decided on how to address his letter—with one of my own. After serving him his second whiskey, I slowly push an envelope across the bar to him. He looks down at his name scrawled across the front, frowning a little, and puts it in the inner pocket of his coat. He drops $100 on the bar for his $30 tab, and walks out without a word. It's as though he already knows what my letter says. Later that night, the best crawfish etouffee I have ever tasted is delivered to the bar.

April 14

Sebastien,

I guess this is where we are, reviving the lost art
of letter writing. I'm not sure where to begin. I read
your letter, of course I did, and while I find it suitably
flattering that you are so interested in pursuing something between us, I am not sure it's the right decision.
I had a really good time the other night on our date
and will admit that I am intrigued by you and want to
know more. I also know where I am in life and—where
you are— and there isn't a lot of overlap in our lives. We
are in completely different places, with different dreams
and experiences. Your family is the reason we are all
trapped here, and the reason why people are dying
everyday. Even if I decided to follow through with something with you, what happens next? How would we
make it work? I know I am getting a little ahead of
myself since this thing between us is still relatively new
but you and I both are too old to not think of the
future.

That said, I had fun, and you're more than I
thought you were. I thought you were a spoiled little
vampire prince. Instead, you're smart and intuitive. A
little flashy for my taste, but that's who you are. A trip
to the City of the Dead was a perfect first date and I
wouldn't have even considered it as a possibility until
now. So, thank you for really seeing me. For knowing
what I would like and need, even after such a short
time together. For realizing that an expensive or over
the top date wasn't going to get you anywhere. And

thank you for bringing Lessa to meet me, although I'm still irritated that you didn't introduce her immediately.

I guess what I'm saying is my time with you meant something to me. I'm just not sure how to continue it. But if that were really true, I wouldn't be writing this letter.

-Elina

April 19

Elina,

This week, being around you while you work has been both a nightmare, and a dream. I want nothing more than to take you in my arms and hold you against me. I want to smell your hair. You smell the way I imagine strawberries taste. Sweet and sticky. Is it your shampoo or something...you? I appreciate that you aren't asking me to leave your life completely and are letting me exist in your universe for a little longer. It means more to me than you know.

You asked in one of your letters this week about Talia so I will share the story.

Talia is almost as old as I am. She grew up in what is now London. Her mother was a brothel worker, her father a dockhand. She was attacked in the street and turned into a vampire about 350 years ago, give or take a few years. I met her in Egypt about 100 years ago and she joined our court, earning herself a spot among the Casa del Corvo di Sangue, after proving herself to Marcus during a fight against another clan. We were friends for a long time—I helped her understand the court dynamics since she had been mostly alone her entire life as a vampire. When Marcus made his intention to try and capture Ville de Sang from L'Empire des

Ombres Nocturnes about 10 years before we actually made a move, Talia was standing by his side as a trusted member of his court. He deferred to her for advice as she had proved her prowess in battle. When the Guerre de Sang was concluded and we were the new rulers of the city, Marcus convened the family and the court, announcing his intention to name me his heir. His brothers, the other males in his line, could be his heir, but he had always favored my mother and therefore favored me. Only males can inherit, unfortunately, due to the progeny situation, but I am the eldest of my cousins anyway, so that helps.

After Marcus named me his heir, the way she looked at me changed. She started spending more time with me and we grew closer. We began getting more serious and as that happened, it became obvious that the only reason behind her sudden interest was that I was now principe. She could never be principessa on her own and she knew Marcus would approve of the match. She planned to take the Legame di Sangue with me and stake her claim. I realized this and broke things off with her. She has been pretty angry about it for 20 years. So her anger isn't toward you, it's toward me. Yours is too. Tell me how to fix this. Tell me how to keep you from slipping away.

Good night, Elina.
-Bash

April 24

Bash,

Talia sounds wonderful *queue eye roll*. I can't imagine why you didn't marry her. What did you call it, Legame di Sangue. What is that? Can you explain?

After my mother died, it was only me and Grand-mere. She's been both my mother and my father. My mother was killed during the Guerre de Sang. A 3 year old left orphaned because Re Marcus decided he wanted my city. Many children were orphaned, in fact. And what of all the deaths since then? No one ever answers for the deaths. No one in the cathedral cares that mothers and fathers, daughters and sons are being killed. Everyday I feel worse and worse about what is happening between us.

Did you know that Sarah's boyfriend is a vamp? He wasn't but he is now. They met in high school—he was her first love. Her first everything. He was her everything. Then he became enthrall to the governor guy of Treme. He was ordered to guard the wall, and eventually, he was turned. He left her. Picked up one day to serve his vampire overlord without a moment of hesitation. He was gone for a year and half. She never saw or heard from him. He was just...gone. She was attacked the week before you came into the bar for the first time. She used to take the bus home and she was waiting for the bus right before sunrise when she was ambushed from behind. He fed on her but stopped before it went too far. He left her to bleed in the street, for the other predators to find her, but the bus came before anyone else. I guess somehow Ethan heard about it, though I'm not sure how. Maybe he was keeping tabs on her. He came back and begged for her forgiveness, and I guess now, they are giving it a go.

I don't know what it means for their future but I suspect she will eventually turn for him so they can live out their days in darkness. I don't see a similar path for myself. What happens when I am no longer young? What do you think will happen here? I can't fathom falling in love if it's not going anywhere.

You asked me to tell you about my first love. What about yours, since it's obviously not Talia? My first love was Thierry. He lived across the street from me and we went through school together, though he was 2 years older. After high school, we dated for a few more years and eventually decided to call it quits when we were 22 and 24. I had obligations to Grand-mere and didn't have any plans to do anything other than what I was doing. I didn't want to go to college—why would it matter if I was stuck behind this wall forever anyway? He did not like what he called my 'defeatist attitude'. Ville de Sang is not a large city though, so I have seen him a few times over the last couple of years. He works at the hospital now. He has a wife and kids. I haven't really dated anyone since. I guess I didn't want to go through that again.

Crawfish etouffee is my favorite because it is the first thing I learned to cook on my own. Grand-mere sat me down at the kitchen counter at 12 years old and taught me to chop the vegetables and make the roux. It was something I was good at, and eating it reminds me of summer afternoons in Grand-mere's kitchen learning about creole food. Food is such an important part of creole and cajun culture. It's in the lifeblood of Ville de Sang itself, all the way back to when it was a Haitian French colony. No matter what people call it over the years, food continues to unite the people of Louisiana across time and title.

Where have you traveled? Where have you been?

Elina

April 28

Tesoro,

Watching you in your element in the bar tonight has been so entertaining. I haven't spent much time watching humans and I haven't been one in so long I don't remember it clearly. You're so confident in your ability to keep these people in line that I sometimes wish you would turn your eyes on me just to be beneath your gaze. My feelings grow every day, and I don't know how much longer I can sit by and not take you in my arms. I dream of the night I can smell you on my skin and taste your mouth. I'm sorry if that's too much, but at this point, I am making myself crazy. You are so quick witted and kind. You take care of the girls in the bar whether they are working girls or patrons. You keep a stern eye on everyone, and it makes me insane watching you knowing that you are still not mine.

I don't pretend to have the answers. I don't know what will happen now. I don't pretend to have it all figured out. I want you to be mine and we will figure out the rest. I'm almost 500 years old, I don't care about you being young. I don't care how you look, even though you are beautiful. I care about your heart, your soul. Even a small amount of time in your light is worth a lifetime of darkness. I will continue to endeavor to earn your favor, but in the meantime, can I have another 2 hours?

I have been everywhere and done everything. And you are the greatest treasure I have found. I will take you everywhere and show you everything. I will do whatever it takes.

The Legame di Sangue is like a vampire marriage ceremony. Basically we gather witnesses, usually 1 or 2 from each party. When I take the oath, Marcus will likely be the overseer of the ceremony. We recite some archaic vows and both of us cut the inside of our arms. We are then bound together with cloth signifying a bond being forged for all of eternity. Usually Legame di Sangue involves blood sharing too since it's a commitment between either 2 vampires, or a human and a vampire, a human who intends to turn eventually. Afterwards, we usually have a party. Our parties often devolve into orgies but the newly bound couple may choose not to participate. With vampires, sex isn't related to love. Vampires are pleasure seekers. We feed. We fuck. We fight. It's all the same. We don't think less of a partner who wants to have sex with someone else, especially if we are bound. There are other advantages and side effects of the bonding but I'm not allowed to write them in a letter. We can talk about it if things ever get that far. But either way we are bound together for as long as we live.

X-Bash

May 2

Bash,
Yes, you can have 2 hours. Pick me up tomorrow
at 9?
X-Elina

CHAPTER II
BASH

Nearly a month after our first 2 hours, I get another two. All I know is I need to figure out how to get *all* of her hours. She feels right. Tonight I am bringing her here, to my home. I don't have any illusions that she will want to stay here but I want a quiet place to sit and talk. She is my future, I can feel it. Now, we need to figure out what that looks like.

I decide to take a bike this time. Throwing a leg over my matte BMW R18, I push it backward onto the street. It feels like something she will like. I clip her helmet to the seat behind me and start the bike, feeling the rumble of the engine between my thighs. Shooting down I-10, I enjoy the feel of the wind in my hair, my shirt billowing around me. I feel so free this way, like it's only me in the world. I arrive at her place at exactly 9 o'clock.

"Prompt as always. And a new flashy ride. Though I must admit, I like this one better," Elina calls from the dark of her front porch. She walks across the yard toward me in black shorts and tank top that says, "I put the *'impale'* in impaler", and I snicker when I read it. I'll tell her about Vlad later.

"Jump on the back and put the helmet on."

"You don't have a helmet," she sassily responds, clipping the helmet on before wrapping her arms around my waist.

"I don't need one," I yell as I shift into second and speed down the street. Her arms tighten around me and I drop a hand down to cover hers. She feels so perfect behind me, her thighs around mine, squeezing every time I lean into a turn. She laughs giddily and sighs in my ear. The fact that she trusts me enough to put her life in my hands has to mean something. It means something to me, anyway. Changing my mind about going straight to my apartment, I spend the next half hour just cruising around the city and letting myself enjoy the feeling of Elina at my back and the open road ahead of me.

Parking at the end of Pirate's Alley, I help Elina off the bike, remove her helmet, and push a few curls out of her face. Grabbing her hand, I haul her toward the stairs, excited to spend some time alone with her. It's been a long month.

Once I get her inside, I consider what to do now. It's an odd feeling, getting what you want, and once you have it, you're not sure what you're supposed to do next. Cradling her face in my hands, I lean down and lightly press my lips to hers. She gasps an inhale, taking my air with her. I linger for a moment longer, feeling her skin under my fingers.

"Bash, hold on please. Not yet. I'm not ready yet."

I exhale sharply at her words, and I take a big step back. Am I living on borrowed time here? How do I get her to want me the way I want her?

"Of course, I'm sorry. I'm so excited to have some time alone, I wasn't thinking. Come into the kitchen, I have dinner for you." This is a gross understatement of what I have in the kitchen. I only know of one dish she enjoys, but I can't keep giving her etouffee. I have gumbo Elodie made. I have broiled oysters on the half shell, gator bites, hush puppies, bayou shrimp, beans and rice, and some collard greens. I have no idea what any of this tastes like, but the spice in the air fills my senses.

"I know it's basically a buffet, but I didn't know what else you would like and I wanted to make sure there was something you would enjoy."

"I don't eat gators, they're little swamp puppies," she says with an exasperated sigh. "Did you know they eat marshmallows? And have you ever seen a baby gator? Sweetest thing, especially their little baby death roll." Little baby death roll? I am falling in love with a woman who thinks a baby alligator practicing to kill things is sweet. There may be hope for me yet.

"Got it, no sweet baby killers. Anything else?"

"Nope, everything else looks amazing. Thank you, Bash," she says earnestly as she throws her arms around me.

After Elina eats a huge plate of gumbo, rice and beans, a few oysters, and hush puppies, we sit together on the couch. She sits leaning against me, and I put my arms around her and kiss the top of her head. I inhale her strawberry scent deeply, feeling peaceful and calm, more so than I have since the last time I sat next to her.

"Elina, I want you to know that even if we never have more than we have right now, this moment means the world to me. I am grateful to spend it with you." I turn to face her, my voice quiet in the empty room. "I know you're concerned about the future and what happens next. And I don't know. But I know that I have never felt about anyone the way I feel about you. I'll do whatever you want—you lead the way, I will follow you. Want to meet my mother? Done. Want to leave Ville de Sang? Done. Want me to give up my claim? Done. Just let me have more of you—your time, your smiles, your life."

Lifting her eyes to mine, they are slightly filled with tears. "No beautiful girl, don't cry. We will figure it out together. I promise."

She, hesitantly at first, presses her lips to mine. Gaining confidence in her kiss, she licks my lips and coaxes me to open my mouth, her tongue slipping inside. At the same time, she throws one of her legs across my lap and straddles me, leaning against me to kiss me more fully. I set my hands on her hips and her arms wrap around my shoulders to pull at the hair at the nape of my neck. She runs her tongue across the bottom of my teeth and I let my fangs descend just barely so she can feel the sharp tips. She gasps and pulls back. I grin up at her.

"You ok?" I ask her, peering into her eyes.

"I don't think I have ever been more ok in my life," she whispers as she leans down and captures my mouth again. I slide my hands under the back of her shirt and feel her soft skin beneath my palms. My hands grab onto her waist and feel how soft and pliable she is. She moves her hips slightly as she kisses me deep and slow. She's not grinding on me exactly, but my cock hardens under her anyway. She puts her hands to the front of my shirt and begins unbuttoning one button at a time. I still her hands.

"Are you sure? I can wait. I mean, I love where this is going, but I want to be sure that you are sure."

"I'm sure, Bash." And she kisses me again, this time hard and fast, like she can't get enough of me. She rips the rest of my buttons off and I huff a laugh into her mouth at her impatience. Grabbing the hem of her tank top, I lift it over her head. Right in front of my face are the most perfect nipples I have ever seen and I lean down and suck one into my mouth, before moving to the other.

She leans forwards and attaches her mouth to my neck, and suddenly, there is a searing pain on my chest. I hiss loudly and look down. Her pendant, that usually rests between her breasts, is pressed against my chest and burning me.

"Oh, shit! Oh, fuck, Bash. I'm so sorry I didn't think. Just give me a second. Hold on." Her chest heaving, she climbs off of my lap and moves up the couch, leaning against the arm, her feet pointed toward me.

I pull one of her feet into my lap, and start stroking small circles across the instep and ankle. She moans causing my cock to twitch. "It's ok, I got you that pendant for protection and I guess, it protected you—from me. It's ok, I'm ok." She reaches up and unclasps the pendant lying it atop her discarded tank top. I pull her feet toward me, causing her to slide down the couch until she is more reclined. Sitting up, I change positions a little until I am kneeling between her feet. I rub her ankles, her calves, the backs of her knees. She lays her head back and relaxes.

I reach up to the button of her shorts and raise my eyebrow in question, she nods her head slowly, looking a little dazed. I unbutton her shorts and slide them down her hips and off her legs. She is spread before me in nothing but a tiny pair of panties—black, of course.

I continue my slow massage up her legs, kneading her thighs now. "*Tesoro*, if I slide my fingers inside your panties, am I going to find your pussy all wet for me?" She blushes a deep crimson and nods her head. "Of course I am. You're so gorgeous, and going to be so wet for me. Seeing you blush while I run my hands over your body is making me want to find out what it looks like when you come for me. How easy will it be to make you come for me, baby?" Slipping my fingers inside her panties, I find she was telling the truth. "So wet, soaked for me," I murmur as my other hand brings her leg to my shoulder and I kiss the inside of her knee. She pants and moans as I run my fingertips across her clit. "So responsive. You're doing so good, baby."

Continuing to kiss the inside of her knee and her thigh, I slide a single finger inside her. It slips in easily, she's so wet. "So ready for me. Let's add a second finger." I slide my ring finger inside her and move my other hand up her thigh. Once I reach her hip, I lay my hand flat against her stomach and push down a little while I curl my fingers up inside her. I can almost feel my fingers moving. Elina gasps and starts panting harder. "Yes, *Tesoro*, that's it. Such a good girl, so good. You feel so soft and wet. I can't wait to sink my cock into you and feel you hold onto me while you come." I rub her clit in firm circles, feeling her wetness pool in my palm.

"Bash. Oh, fuck," she gasps the words out, her whimpers and moans coming closer together while she starts fluttering against my fingers inside her. Her back arches off the couch and she writhes beneath me as I use my hand on her stomach to hold her still, pressing from the inside and outside.

Leaning forward, I take a peaked nipple between my teeth and tug gently before flicking my tongue across the pebbled skin. Sucking hard, I pull her into my mouth, never slowing my fingers as I draw her closer to the edge. Her breath forces out in short pants and her thighs tremble, she's so close.

"Yes, baby, let go. Come for me, *Tesoro*. Let me feel you come on my fingers," I whisper to her as she starts to clench around my fingers, my thumb tracing her clit, my fingers rubbing her g-spot, and my palm heavy on her belly.

"Bash, Bash, Bash." My name on her lips sounds like a prayer and it lights me up from within. "Yes, Bash!" She cries my name as she comes, filling up my palm with her wetness. I continue to gently stroke her through her orgasm as I stare at the flush of blood under her skin and the thumping pulse in her neck. I can't tell if I am more hungry for her body or for her blood.

"Wait right there, don't move. I'll get something to clean you up. That was absolutely glorious, baby." Coming back and kneeling between her thighs again, I gently wipe her down. I press a single kiss to her pubic bone and look up at her to see the blush on her cheeks.

"Hi." I smile broadly at her.

"Hi," she says shyly. Shy was never something I imagined for Elina. She always seems brave and outspoken. And like this, she is radiant. "That was unbelievable, and not at all what I expected." She looks away while wrapping her arms around her midsection like she is trying to hide herself now that her head has cleared.

"Don't hide from me, *Tesoro*. You're the most perfect person I have ever encountered. Let's get you dressed so we can talk."

"What about you, I can-"

"No, you can't. This was for you, about you. I've got all the time in the world. Like I said, I am grateful for every minute I get to bask in your light."

CHAPTER 12
ELINA

Falling in love happens slowly, then all at once. You don't even realize it's happening until your heart already belongs to someone else and you can't stop it. Even if you see it like a train wreck coming your way, it's already too late to dodge it.

That's how I feel as I lay on Bash's couch. After he teased and touched me. The orgasm was unexpected, and better than I could have imagined. I feel slightly ashamed. I guess 'ashamed' isn't the right word but something similar. Like I betrayed my own humanity by giving in. Seeing him kneeling between my knees looking so earnest and open has brought my defenses down, and I can't wait to explore what happens next. I don't want to want this. But I do, and I feel safe here, with him. That's the most dangerous part of all.

Bash brings me a glass of water and I sit cross-legged on his couch facing him. This aftercare version of Bash is a new side of him that I am excited to learn more about. "Thank you. For the water, I mean. And for the other thing too." I blush.

"You're welcome, for both. God, I love this blush so much."

He brushes his fingers down my cheek. "Let me tell you about Vlad the Impaler, please."

Twenty minutes later I am almost crying from laughing so hard at his story.

"He really was a very weird, very cruel prince. My mother could tell you more, she knew him when he was merely a whiny brat in a castle. For all his cruelty though, he did inspire the greatest piece of vampire fiction in history. Vlad Dracula!" He says this with a huge flourish and a silly accent, throwing his arms out, fangs on full show. I almost fall off the couch in surprise and burst out laughing.

"Stop, stop, stop! Now I'm going to need to know about all of the famous vampires through history."

"I'll save a few steps and say there haven't been many reported vampires that were actually vampires. Obviously, there are some *now*, since the Devereaux family threw the curtain back by invading New Orleans, but generally we tend to fly under the radar. There is another clan of Italian vampires, but they aren't the bloodline variety so we don't intermingle."

"Wait, there are different kinds of vampires? You know what? Nevermind. Let me focus on what's in front of me. I guess the pendant works—good to know. Also, still sorry about that, by the way."

He laughs under his breath and gently rubs the slight red spot on his chest. "It's ok, *Tesoro*, clearly neither of us were thinking."

KNOCK.

KNOCK.

KNOCK.

Someone knocks on his door and we both turn our heads towards it, as though we would be able to see through the solid wood.

"Expecting someone?" I ask him tentatively, suddenly feeling genuinely trapped.

"No, I am not." He furrows his brows for a moment before relaxing. "Stay here, and don't freak out or anything, but it's my mother." I don't ask how he knows that, must be a vampire thing or something. The couch is somewhat hidden from view due to the direction of the door, so I hear her before I see her when he swings the door open.

"*Stellino*, my love. I heard that you were—what's that smell? It smells like human food and—" she pushes the door all the way open and looks over at me on the couch, trying to make myself as small and inconspicuous as possible. The dark grey eyes that perfectly mirror Bash's own study me for a moment. "Sex. Oh my. I see." And just like that she turns around and walks back out the door. Bash looks a little chagrined, closing the door behind her.

My face flames as he rejoins me on the couch. "What does she mean, 'it smells like sex'?"

"Oh, um." He rubs the back of his neck. "Vampires have really good senses, you know, right? Better eyesight, better hearing, better sense of smell. So, we can smell a lot of things, including when a woman is turned on." As though the levels of my embarrassment aren't deep enough, there is a new one. It's like Dante's inferno, and I keep sinking further and further.

"Well, isn't that interesting," I answer because what else am I supposed to say?

"*Tesoro*, it's nature. Don't worry about it." His response is nonchalant, as though it doesn't matter in the slightest. I think back to his letters and the way he discussed sex and vampire culture. I guess to him, it is not a big deal. "Well, that was my mother. After you go home, I will definitely have to go have a conversation about it. Shit, I did not want to have to explain all this already to her."

"You're almost 500 years old, Bash, what could you possibly need to explain?"

"I want her to like you and she hasn't seen me with anyone besides Talia in a very long time. She will have questions, and opinions. I need to pave the way carefully here."

"Ok, so pave the way. Tell me what happens now, Bash? I'm not sure what we are doing or what this all means to me, but I can't emotionally invest unless there is something here. It's already difficult enough to reconcile my feelings with what my brain thinks is the right thing. You're the villain in my story."

He stares at me seriously for a few minutes, almost as though he is just realizing something. "I don't want to be the villain in your story because you're the sun in mine." Pulling me closer so that I am tucked under his arm, he breathes in the top of my head. "I don't have all the answers Elina. All I know is that I want more—*so* much more. Stay with me tonight, I'll take you home before sunrise."

"I can't. Grand-mere already worries too much about me when I'm here, I have to go home. And I need to think about everything that's happening. We should go now, before it gets too late."

After a truly quick ride home on the back of his bike, I climb off and hand him my helmet. Walking across my lawn, I hear a whispered "*Tesoro.*" I turn back and Bash is striding across the grass, my helmet in his hand. He drops it at my feet before wrapping one arm around my waist, lifting me off the grass while his other hand holds the side of my neck. He, almost imperceptibly, presses on my pulse point with his thumb, growling in a distinctly sexy way, and kissing me like he needs my breath to live. He's kissing me in my front yard like he is yearning, dying for a taste of me, and couldn't wait another minute. I'm breathless by the time he sets me back on my feet.

I wobble unsteadily as he lets me go, making him chuckle. Pressing his lips against mine lightly, he says "Goodbye," before swiping up the helmet and going back the way he came.

"I think you better come inside now," I hear from the porch and my eyes find Grand-mere Celeste standing in the doorway. I don't think I have ever seen her look at me that way, her eyes shrouded with an emotion I don't recognize. I think it's disappointment. I can't be sure because she's never been disappointed in me before. I look back at Sebastien who watches me warily, concern etched in his brow. I give him a nod to let him know I'm ok and I trudge up the stairs, my head hanging low.

She rounds on me as soon as we step into the living room.

"You should be damn ashamed of yourself. Standing on the front lawn of the house I raised you in—the house I raised your maman in—kissing a damn *vampire*. And not any vampire, the man whose family is the reason you're an orphan. Elina, I know you're grown now, but this is too much for me to allow. I was horrified when I looked outside after I heard that motorbike. *Horrified*. What were you *thinking*?" She all but yells at me. I have never seen her so upset about something I did. I have always tried to make her proud.

What the hell am I doing? She's right, of course. I should be ashamed. I'm falling for a man responsible for so much death and destruction. I can't give him my heart, we can't be together. I'm a human. A fragile, mortal human who is being subjugated by his family. We are blood donors for the vampires, not wives and loved ones. He has no stake in whether I or my family lives or dies. If he does decide to start caring about me, how far does that concern go? How many degrees of separation are covered by Bash's umbrella of love?

"Grand-mere Celeste, I'm sorry. I like him—I care about him—but you're right. It's stupid. I can't believe I allowed myself to be drawn in by him. I let him in and I shouldn't have.

I'm sorry. Please don't be mad at me. I vow to you that you will never see again what you saw today. I swear it," I plead for her forgiveness.

She stares at me, her gaze softening as she takes in my desperate words, the hitching of my breath, and the tears welling in my eyes. "Elina, I don't want you to be unhappy, but I can't support this. Where are the human boys you could be going out with? Don't do this to our family. Please."

"I'm sorry." I leave her in the middle of the living room, grey hair in curlers, and her feet in slippers that match the robe I got her last Christmas. I drag myself up the stairs and climb into bed. Crying myself to sleep, I clutch Bash's letters like they are a lifeline I am about to drop.

Climbing Sarah's steps midmorning, I knock on the door for the first time in a while. I don't want to disturb the sleeping vampire inside. Thinking of the fact that there is a sleeping vamp on the other side of the door still feels weird, and thinking of Sarah with him is even weirder. It's still Ethan, I have gotten to spend some time with him over the last few weeks, and he seems like himself. Except he feeds on Sarah and prowls the night streets. I don't have any room to judge, considering my own vamp was inside me 12 hours ago. If anyone can understand, it's her.

She opens the door with a big smile on her face. "How was it?" she blurts before I can even greet her.

Frowning, I tell her, "The date was perfect. The after was not."

"Tell me the before and then the after."

"He took me to his apartment." I blush as she waggles her eyebrows at me and she cackles with laughter. "He had ordered basically a restaurant worth of different creole food; gumbo, oysters, and whatnot. Afterwards, we fooled around a little. I got his shirt off and his chest is covered in tattoos. Too many to even describe. He has words in Italian, animals, swirling inky patterns. I didn't stop and stare, I was busy, but I will definitely try to get a better look. Well, maybe not. Anyway, my pendant burned him which was scary, but also really interesting to see. I haven't been around any vamps except in the bar, no one has threatened me or anything. After that, I learned that Bash has magic fingers and he talks me through it."

"I swoon!" We both dissolve into giggles.

"Seriously, it was life changing. Then, I met his mother and she said she could smell sex, before she left like that wasn't the weirdest thing to say. It was an absolutely *insane* interaction."

"Holy shit, Elina! What did he say? I can't believe your first meeting with his mom was while you were in your post-orgasm afterglow."

"He said he has to talk to her now and explain the situation. Speaking of 'the situation', the after was heartbreaking and I don't know what to do. When I got home, he gave me a kiss goodbye and grand-mere saw us. Once I got inside, she lost it on me. Telling me I should be ashamed to be with him and he is the reason why I'm an orphan. What if she's right, Sarah? What if this is a mistake?" My voice is quiet as I speak, my uncertainty clear.

"Does it feel like a mistake? What do you want, Elina? I know you are so used to it being you and Celeste against the world—but what about you? What will you do for yourself? Are you in love with him?" She looks so sincere and open, waiting to hear what I have to say.

"No, it doesn't feel like a mistake. I think I want him. I don't know what my feelings mean yet; or maybe I am avoiding acknowledging them. But it doesn't feel wrong. It feels *so* right."

"Then do what is best for you."

Should I do what's best for me? Consequences be damned? I need to talk to Bash. I need to figure this out.

After I get to the club on Monday and get the bar set up for the night, I wait for opening time. We time our opening with the sunset, and tonight, ten minutes before the official sunset, Bash walks in the back door.

"Hey, *Tesoro*. I missed you while I rested. Is everything ok at home?" He leans down and steals a kiss.

"Bash? What are you doing here already? The sun doesn't set for another 10 minutes?"

"When you're my age and a bloodline, you get a little more freedom from the sun. As long as I am not in direct sunlight, I could, theoretically, be outside." I love that he is being open with me now, telling me more about vampires but I can't tell anyone, Sarah and I don't even discuss these things when we're alone. "I still need to rest when the sun is out, so if it was really cloudy, I could be outside though I don't tend to try. I need to rest, like I feel it in my body. Not tired exactly, just a drive to close my eyes. It's almost compulsive. Which also means I can come out before the sun sets as long as I am not in the sun. The shadows are long now, so there are lots of places to hide." What an interesting revelation.

"I guess that makes sense. And everything at home is ok,

mostly, but I did want to talk to you so I'm glad you're here. Grand-mere doesn't approve of us. She blames you and your family for everything that has happened to mine in the last 25 years, rightfully so. She blames you for me being an orphan. She thinks I am making a mistake."

"Look at me, in my eyes and tell me this feels like a mistake." I can't help but notice the almost-mirror to what Sarah asked me earlier.

"No, it feels like the most right thing I have ever done. And that scares the shit out of me." He sags with relief as though he was genuinely concerned about what my answer was going to be.

"We are going to figure this out—our families will have to learn to accept it." Hearing this from Bash sounds very much like his mother doesn't approve either. Maybe if everyone wants us apart, it's the right thing to do. For the first time, I realize that this isn't only about me and him, or me and grand-mere. It's about a vampire prince and his family, too. He is the heir to a throne built by blood, and what happens when he has to make a decision about me? About us?

"I guess it didn't go well with your mom." I sigh, hearing the first customer walk into the bar. "I have to get to work, but good to know we have a complete uphill battle here."

CHAPTER 13
BASH

After dropping Elina off at home and what happened with her grandmother, I want to drive around for a while and feel the wind on my face. Heading toward Lake Pontchartrain, I get on the Causeway Bridge and open up the throttle. The 24 mile long bridge over open water gives me time to think. The first thing I think about is how sad it is that Elina hasn't ever done this. She has never made this drive and felt the air from the lake blowing across her face. I want to give her the world so she can hold it in the palm of her hand. If I only get the next 30 or 40 years with her, I want her to spend every day with a smile on her face. The thought that keeps trying to invade my mind, that makes me flinch every time I fail to push it out of the way, is how will I do that given the current state of things in Ville de Sang and the world. We are left alone only because we stay put. Do I think, for even a minute, that humans would let us exist as we do if we made spectacles of ourselves on crowded American streets? *Absolutely not.*

After I ride for a few hours all over southern Louisiana, I

cross back on the Twin Span bridge so that I can pass through Little Woods, and Elina's house. I drive slowly so the engine is quiet and stop down the street. Jumping onto the roof, I quickly find the windows that belong to her. While I don't look into them or watch her sleep like a creep, I do sit and listen to her breathe while she rests. Her breathing is a little uneven—she is definitely asleep but she is restless. Perhaps she was crying or sad. Maybe it's a nightmare. Tightening a fist, I wish I could be there with her, holding her, calming whatever is causing her turmoil. One day, but not yet.

Finally admitting to myself that I have put off talking to mother as long as I can, I head back to the Quarter.

"Mother," I greet her as I walk into her apartment across the gardens of *Cattedrale del Trono Notturno*, down Pere Antoine Alley.

Looking up from where she is perched on a chair—her back ramrod straight, not a single muscle relaxed—she levels me with a scathing look of reproval. "Sebastien Enrique." I am really in trouble if she's using my full name. "Nice of you to stop by. Would you like a glass of blood or did you get it from your pet?"

"Yes, thank you. I have not drank today." I refuse to rise to her bait. If she wants to know something, she is going to have to ask.

"Interesting that I stumble upon you, loft reeking of pheromones, with a human, and you have not drank? What exactly do you think you're doing with a human woman if you aren't feeding from her, especially if you're fucking her."

I flinch at the vulgarity and disgust in her tone. "She's... she's Elina. Just Elina."

"*Just Elina*," she sneers in a mocking tone. "Who the hell is Elina? The woman from the brothel?"

"She's everything, Mother." I drop onto the chair opposite

her. "She's the light in my darkness. She fills the void in my soul. She makes me hope, she makes me want to dream again. She is everything."

"It sounds to me like you love this human? Have you even considered what this will mean? Would she give up the light for you? Forsake her humanity?" Her tone has not even softened, she asks all of these questions with a rough edge to them.

"I don't have answers to any of that right now. It's new— we are figuring it out." I don't seem to have answers to a lot of things lately.

"New? Figuring it out? *You're kidding*. Are you saying you love this human? Is this why you've been spending all your time at that brothel? Is she a whore?"

"The correct term is 'sex worker', Mother." She sends me a steely glare and I roll my eyes. "No, she isn't a sex worker, she is a bartender and a tour guide."

She scoffs as though Elina is not even worthy of her attention due to some classist bullshit. "A bartender for my son, the HEIR!" She yells at me. "Get out, I am disgraced. Disgusted. Get out, Sebastien. I don't even want to look at you."

"Mother, please, you're being really dramatic. I'm not making any decisions right now." I lean against her knee. "Just trust me. When the time is right, I'll know, and then you'll know too."

"Get out," she whispers. I stand on shaky legs and walk toward the door. I don't even realize what I'm doing until my fist is buried in the sheetrock next to it. I will leave, and I don't want to return.

As I feel the sun pulling me to rest, I lay in bed thinking about her face. How stunning she looked as she laid underneath me and came on my fingers. My cock hardens as I think of the way she looked, felt, and smelled as she came apart.

Gripping myself, I stroke my length until I am completely pulled under.

I sit upright as the sun moves toward the horizon and begins to release its hold on me. Dressing quickly in a solid black polo, black slacks, and matching lace up boots, I peek out the window to ensure the sun is no longer shining on my balcony so I can escape before the sun sets. My door faces northeast, so as the shadows lengthen across the French Quarter, I head out toward Rue Bourbon and have a clear path of shadows all the way.

Walking through the doors of the Velvet Tomb, I lean against the door frame, catching Elina's eye a moment later.

"Hey, *Tesoro*. I missed you while I rested. Is everything ok at home?" I ask her as I lean in for a kiss. After witnessing her restless sleep, I'm worried about what may be going on in her head.

With her voice full of confusion, she asks me about my appearance before the sun has set. I spend a few minutes filling her in on the inner workings of the vampire sleep cycle. Nothing exciting but she seems interested in this information, I don't blame her. There isn't really much available about bloodline vamps.

Her conversation with her grand-mere after I left is a bad development, especially now that I have finally convinced her to give me a chance. It feels like we've been having the same conversation on opposite sides of the city. I refuse to allow regret to cloud my thoughts. This is right, I can feel it. She says all of these things openly and without hesitation. I can see it in her eyes—she blames me for it too—the orphans, the widows, the graves. I want to tell her I will take her far away from this place. I will burn the whole city down for her, except, I feel like that would make things worse and she would hate me more.

"Look at me, in my eyes, and tell me this feels like a mistake." I study her eyes, her face, her body language. I know she is trying to figure out what to say. If she asked the same of me, I know I wouldn't even be able to form the sentence.

"No, it feels like the most right thing I have ever done. And that scares the shit out of me." This uncharacteristic admission of feelings gives me hope that I am not failing at this.

"We are going to figure this out—our families will have to learn to accept it," I tell her, hoping she can hear the sincerity in my voice, and she doesn't let this keep us from trying to be together. Neither of us are children who need permission to fall in love. I can only hope she feels the way I do.

We stare at each other, the weight of this thing between us. It's not casual. We won't fade away. She looks like she is considering something. Instead of saying it, she smirks.

"I guess it didn't go well with your mom. I have to get to work, but good to know we have a complete uphill battle here."

I sit and watch her work for a few more hours, Sarah alongside her. Sipping my whiskey, I catch sight of another man seated at the bar watching them work. And another. And another. I guess they are quite the draw—my feisty goth-girl Elina, with her long, curly, brown hair that nearly reaches her waist, her short leather skirt wrapped around her full squeezable hips, and her black corset with gemstone blood drops holding the most beautiful breasts I have ever held in my hands. She is curvy and soft in the perfect places, and I can't wait for my next opportunity to feel her skin. Nestled in her cleavage is my pendant, which can even protect her from me. Beside her, Sarah wears a similar outfit of a slightly longer leather skirt and black corset, except she is taller and slimmer than Elina, so her outfit fits differently. She has recently added Elina's blood-drop choker to her throat, since the pendant has replaced it as a part of Elina's everyday outfits. Sarah has fiery red hair that curls out and away from her face and across her shoulders.

Looking closer at each man, I notice a man paying particular attention to Sarah. I decide to approach him and see if he's a friend of hers. I would like to connect with some people from *Tesoro*'s life. It will make it easier for us.

"Hi, I'm Bash. Do you know the girls?" I point with my whiskey glass as I take the empty barstool next to him. Both Sarah and Elina's eyes widen almost comically. The vampire sitting next to me does the same. *Ok, then.*

"Hey, man. I'm Ethan Grady. I, uh, I'm Sarah's boyfriend. Or fiancé. I don't know, it's kind of weird right now. I was gone for a while but I came back, and I don't know exactly what's happening. And can vampires even get married? Oh, dear god —I'm rambling about marriage to Sebastien Malvani."

I smile broadly at him, fangs on display but obvious mirth on my face.

"Hey, Ethan. I'm just Bash. Don't worry about the rest. I'm Elina's...You know what? I also don't know what I am, so we have that in common. Hopefully, I'm something, I guess. I figured we could get to know each other, since it seems our girls are two halves of a whole."

"Yeah, they've been friends since practically diapers, I

think. I've never known Sarah without Lina. I'm glad she finally told her I was staying with her. Sarah was afraid of how Lina would react, but they worked it out like they always do. Though, considering who is sitting next to me, I understand why Lina was suddenly so accepting of human/vamp relationships." He laughs and sips his drink. I think he's drinking tequila. We can drink alcohol but not really mixed with anything except blood, so if we want to drink, we have to adjust to the taste. I don't make it a habit to feed in public from the bar blood warmers, I prefer to drink at home.

This insight into Elina's previous dislike of human-vampire relationships offers some perspective on why I feel like I am battling the tide on her affections. Her feelings for me seem to ebb and flow depending on how long it is between spending time with her. Maybe befriending Sarah and Ethan will be the catalyst to get her more committed to this, so we can begin something real here.

I hear the soft click-clack of heels behind me before a hand lands on my shoulder.

"Oh, hey. I haven't seen you in a while."

I sit up, all amusement leaving my body instantly. Amelie. *Shit.*

"Hello, Amelie." I try to avoid looking at her. Shame colors my demeanor.

"Hey, I'm Ethan." The vamp next to me extends his hand to her for her to shake.

"Hey, Ethan. Nice to meet you. I'm Amelie. You're Sarah's boyfriend, right?" Elina watches us, a curious tilt to her head.

"That's right." He puffs his chest out proudly and I long for the day I can do that for my relationship with Elina.

"Hey, Amelie. Ethan. Bash." Elina gives us each a short nod. "Amelie, you have an order for me or something?" She has made her way over, I guess she decided on her course of action with Amelie talking to me.

"No, I was coming to see Bash. I haven't seen him in a while." She leans casually, a bit possessively, against my arm. Leaning in, she whispers, "Hey, baby, wanna repeat?"

Clearing my throat, I lean away from her which means I am halfway on top of Ethan's lap. He's watching all of this calmly while obviously trying to figure out what dynamic is at play here. Elina narrows her eyes at Amelie.

As soon as she opens her mouth to say something to Amelie I jump in. "Amelie, thanks for stopping by. We have no further business together."

She looks at me suspiciously then at Elina.

"You got to be kidding me. Seriously, Elina?"

"Seriously *what*, Amelie? You let him fuck and feed one time, 2 months ago. You haven't even noticed he's been in the bar multiple nights a week since. It's not like you have a claim on him," Sarah chimes in. This is quickly getting out of hand. I have to do something but I can't figure out what.

"You saw him for the first time while his cum was still running down my leg, you bitch," Amelie spits in Elina's direction. Her mouth drops open at the vulgar outburst.

Her words hit me like a knife to the chest. Elina still doesn't say anything—she only narrows her eyes at Amelie, cold and calculating. Amelie flinches a little under the hard gaze.

"Amelie, that is enough." I say. She swings her gaze to me. "We both knew what it was then and you know what it is now. Nothing. Do not ever speak to Elina like that again."

At that exact moment, before anyone else can do anything, Rian comes through the bar door. She is slight, and weighs, maybe, 120 pounds, but her face is determined.

"Get back to the floor, Amelie. If you're going to make a habit of giving away for free what I sell to vamps, you have to deal with the consequences. Back to work. Elina, if you can't control things at the bar, your boyfriend has to stay home." Turning around she storms back out.

Boyfriend. The sound of those words makes me giddy and I don't want to burst that bubble of happiness by looking over at Elina.

I'm nervous, and I swing my eyes to Elina. She doesn't look angry or jealous. She's just watching me, the way she has been this entire time.

"Well, she knows how to break up a party," Ethan remarks, I assume, in an attempt to lighten the mood. Sarah giggles. Elina does not.

CHAPTER 14
ELINA

"Elina, *Tesoro*, wait, please." Bash comes up behind me, as I turn away from my friends and walk toward the door to the back. "I haven't even seen her since that night and that was the first time I had laid eyes on her."

"Laid," I snort in derision. "Nice choice of words, Bash. Listen, who you fucked up until Sunday night is no concern of mine. But she works in my bar, and now, I have to look at her face and think about your cum running down her leg." I say half angry, half disgusted. He visibly flinches at the venom in my tone. I don't want him to feel shame—I want him to be mine, and I have to face the evidence of him when he wasn't, every day. "I let you inside my body, and that means something to me. I had forgotten, until this moment, that you don't have any qualms about having sex on a public toilet with a woman you met an hour prior. We are not the same." This is too much. The Amelie situation had left my mind. The way he had walked out of the stall without so much as a backward glance while there was still blood seeping from the wounds he left on Amelie's neck. Her skirt a little askew, her cheeks still flushed.

"Elina, I haven't so much as looked at another woman since I saw you in that bathroom. I will get down on my knees right now and confess all of my sins in front of the entire bar, but believe me when I tell you, we are the same. I can't even imagine looking at, or being with, another person. You are my sun, my moon, my everything."

The man in the bathroom is a completely different man than the one who kissed my knee tenderly as I came down from my orgasm, and got a damp towel to clean me up before helping me dress.

Which is the real Sebastien Malvani? The brute who has been around for over 400 years, who fucks waitresses in bathroom stalls—or the gentle, sensitive man who does aftercare and genuinely cares about me.

Sarah comes up and lays a hand on Bash's shoulder. "Let me have a minute, Bash. Ethan is still at the bar if you want to join him." He walks away without a word and I don't know if I'm happy or upset about that. "Lina, are you actually mad at him for what happened before he even knew you existed?"

"No, of course not. I don't care who he slept with before me. It's the way it happened, I guess. Like, who is fucking randos in the bathroom? Him. I mean, I'm not so prudish that I think there is anything wrong with casual sex but it's just not me, you know? But it seems like it is him. And I gave him a piece of myself the other night. I wanted that to mean something to him too."

"Sweetie, if you look at that man and tell me he is anything but absolutely head over heels for you, you're blind. You know what? I was thinking, what if ya'll did like a double-date thing with me and Ethan. The four of us could get something to eat, hang out, and get to know each other. I think it will help you guys to spend some time having some fun with other people around. Your—whatever this is—isn't something to be ashamed of." She looks so hopeful that I realize this is probably something she needs too. It's always been the two of us and Ethan. Then it was just us. Now there is a new person.

"Ok. I need to talk to Rian, can you cover the bar?"

"Of course." And she disappears after a quick embrace.

Knocking on Rian's door a few minutes later, I wait for her to press the buzzer to let me in.

"Come in, Elina."

I find her sitting behind her large desk, piles of paperwork surrounding her. Seven years ago, I walked in the front doors of the bar and begged the rail-thin black woman manning the bar to take a chance on me, and her support and patronage has been a lifeline for my family.

"Hey, Rian. Can I talk to you for a few minutes?"

"Sure." She sounds suspicious. "What's up, Elina?"

"So, I've been working here for 7 years, 6 days a week. But I think I need to cut back a little bit. I want to have some more time for other things, and I am here all the time."

"Mmmhmm. I'm sure this has nothing to do with a tall, dark, and handsome vamp sitting at my bar right now does it? Only a few weeks ago you were all 'I will not be trapped in a room with a lion'." She puts on a falsetto tone that sounds nothing like me, and I laugh. "Now you're cutting back on work and money to spend more time with him? Elina, you're like a daughter to me. If you need some time off, it's yours. Just don't disappear on me. What would you like to do? 5 days a week? 4?"

"It's not only that. I guess I need some time to figure me out, ya know? I've given a lot to this bar—I am thankful you took a chance on me. Now I need to do the same."

"Elina, honey, you are like the daughter I never had; a

daughter of my heart. If you need some time off to find your-self, or if you need time to hang out with your friends, life is hard enough around here. Your job isn't going anywhere." She looks at me with pride shining through her eyes and I feel like I have another ally in this. She doesn't pass judgement on my relationship with Bash. She wants me to do whatever is right for me.

"Let's do Sunday and Monday off for now. It gives me time and I don't miss any of our busy days. Sarah is off Thursdays, so you will have a bartender even when I'm not here."

"Ok, Sundays and Mondays. Got it. Hey, Elina? No brawling over dudes in my bar. If you and Amelie can't make up and get over it, we will have a problem, whether I love you or not."

"Thanks, Rian! Love you!"

Walking back out toward the bar, I stop just inside the door and watch them. Sarah, Ethan, and Bash, smiling and laugh-ing. Telling jokes and relaxing. I feel like I'm looking into my future, my family. One day, Grand-mere will be gone, and it will just be me and Sarah. Why couldn't it be Sarah and Ethan, me and Bash. We could be our own family. I don't want to give up a chance at having something for me because other people don't want me to have it.

"Guess what?" I do a little dance, spinning in a circle. "I changed my schedule so now I'm off on Sundays and Mondays. And Sarah thinks we should have a double date. Since she works Mondays, we have to do it on Sunday, but are you inter-ested?" I bombard Bash with all this as soon as I am within earshot.

A huge grin spreads across his face. "I know you aren't for sale, but I would gladly do whatever it takes for you to take as many days off as you want. And, yeah, Ethan's cool, for a baby vamp."

"Hey! I'm 29!" Ethan says from beside him, bumping him with his shoulder.

"Yeah, in human years. In vampire years, you're like, 3 months old." We all laugh together and my heart almost explodes with joy at how easy this feels. I have got to stop sabotaging my own happiness. Whether it's because I don't think I'm good enough, or because I'm worried what other people will say or think of me, I have always changed myself for other people. And I'm exhausted. I want to live for myself and do what is best for me.

"Hey, Bash? Will you take me home this morning?" I ask, my mind made up.

"Anything for you, *Tesoro.*" I wish he didn't have to go away when the sun comes up, like a vampire Cinderella. "Do you mind if I have a driver take us though, so we can get in the tinted backseat? A little extra sun protection."

"Mmmhmm, that might actually work out better anyway." He pops an eyebrow up at my comment and I give him a sly smile.

A few hours later, Bash leaves to go get the car and the driver. I am nearing last call when the mysterious man who yelled at me as he was dragged from the bar sits down in front of me.

"Chardonnay, s'il vous plaît." He has a French accent—not in the way that cajuns do—like a from-France French accent. I set the glass down in front of him and walk away. I feel his gaze on me as I finish up my work.

"That is a very nice necklace you have there."

"Thank you, it was a gift," I tell him, though why I am talking to him, I don't know.

"It must be quite special." He puts some money on the counter and he is gone as quickly as he appeared.

Not half a minute later, Bash walks in the door, tall and

intimidating. He has unbuttoned the buttons of his polo shirt and I can glimpse a black swirl up toward his neck. With his hair looking windswept from him running his hands through it, I'm struck by how scary he could look if he wanted. But like this, he looks like the best thing I can imagine.

"Ready, *Tesoro?*"

"Ready."

In the back of the blacked-out SUV, I look over and smile in his direction. It feels calm and peaceful in this little dark cocoon. Sliding off the seat onto the floor, I look up at him, a mischievous smile playing around my lips. He studies me intently as I move into the space between his spread knees. Suspiciously, but not unhappily, he says down to me, "What are you doing, baby?"

Grabbing his belt buckle, I pull his belt loose and unbutton his pants. Slowly, pulling the zipper down, I reach inside and palm his cock through his underwear. He leans his head back, exhaling slowly as he begins to harden in my hand.

"Fuck," he hisses through his clenched teeth, as I pull his hard length from his pants. Stroking him slowly from base to tip, I follow my hand with my tongue and he shivers. Wrapping my lips fully around the head, I slide him into my mouth and down my throat until I gag a little. His hands run up the sides of my neck and twine into my hair, guiding me slowly down until I have as much of him in my mouth as I can. I swallow and suck until his hands start to shake. His cock fills my mouth and throat completely, and I'm forced to choose between him and oxygen, so I hold my breath, choking on him.

Letting go, I take over sliding my mouth up and down, creating suction and trying to push him as far into my throat as I can. Pulling him completely out of my mouth, drool runs down my chin. Lowering my head, I tighten my hand and twist it while sucking his head between my lips, using his foreskin to create the friction I know he is looking for. His hips buck slightly up from the seat.

"Baby, that is the hottest fucking thing I have ever seen. Can you take more of me? How far can you go? Yes, fuck, just like that." The words stream from his mouth like he can't control them. Pushing myself to the limit, I gag around him until tears run down my face.

"Don't stop baby. I'm going to come, fuck, fuck." His cock swells in my mouth as I use my hand and mouth in tandem, my spit soaking both of us. With a growl, he pushes my head all the way down and comes down my throat. He breathes loud and fast, head pressed against the headrest.

Looking down at me again, a blissful look on his face, he grabs me under my arms and hauls me into his lap. He hugs me to his chest, murmuring contently. We pull up to the curb in front of the house as he runs his fingers under my eyes to clean up my tears and mascara. He kisses each eyelid.

Grabbing my face with both hands, he says, "How do you do it?"

"Do what?"

"Make me love you?" I drop my head, inhaling sharply, a blush creeping up my cheeks. "Don't worry *Tesoro*, I loved you before the best blow job I've ever had—I know you're the perfect girl for me. But I know you might not be there yet. That's ok, I can wait."

"Bash I-" My voice falters, my heart is cracking open and I know he can see it in my eyes. My heart almost explodes with the love and sincerity I find when he looks at me, how open he looks. I know that Sarah is right. I feel it in my heart that this is right.

"Shhh, beautiful girl, come here. Say whatever you need to say, or don't, but do not hide from me." He pulls my head to his chest and holds me for a few moments. "Go home, go to sleep. I will be there tonight." He gives me a light slap on my ass, which is completely out of my skirt and I yelp.

Inside the house, Grand-mere is waiting for me.

"So, you promise not to make a spectacle of yourself on my front lawn with that blood-sucker, and instead you, what? Fool around in the car? In front of the house?"

"Grand-mere, we were only talking. Why are you being like this? I'm not a child—why are you treating me like one?"

"Do you think this is love? He doesn't love you, you are just a toy to play with while he's bored of immortality. You're weak for believing him. Do you think for one minute that he won't throw you away and move on with his life?"

"I'm not weak," I whisper. "Why are you saying these things?"

"Because you're acting like it. You're disregarding my request to stop 'dating' that vampire. You won't listen to me. You're putting yourself in danger and acting like none of it matters. If you want to keep up this vampire romance, you need to do it elsewhere. Otherwise, act like an almost 30 year old woman and *knock it off*."

She's right about one thing.

I am almost 30 and still living at home, no husband, barely a, what? Boyfriend? Is Bash my boyfriend? No plans for the future. Once Grand-mere is gone, what then? I'll be here in this house, alone? Sarah will have Ethan, for better or worse. I will just be here, alone. I never wanted children—this is a terribly dangerous place to raise children. I wonder how Bash feels about children? He will have babies one day, with his bound wife. The idea of him binding himself to someone else for all of eternity and having children with them makes me flinch to myself. Is that his future? What is our future?

Walking back out the front door, I head toward Sarah's house. I know she just got home, and Ethan would have been home an hour ago since he can't be out at all once the sun starts rising.

"Sarah," I call out as I walk through the front door, tears running down my cheeks. Every time I am happy, something happens to ruin it.

"What's up Lina? Why aren't you—Why are you *crying*? Did Bash do something? I'll kill him. I don't know how, but I will. He was shit anyway. Fuck him." I start laughing through the tears at her sudden defense of me even though she knows everything she said is a lie.

"No," sob, "it's not," sob, "Bash," hiccough and sob. Recounting what happened with Grand-mere today and on Sunday breaks my heart even further. I always considered my relationship with Grand-mere as strong and unconditional. I am beginning to realize that what I thought was unconditional love was me always doing what she wanted and expected. I had never gone against her or done anything different and so, she never had a reason to voice her displeasure with me. I'm so heart sick that she refuses to understand this. I don't know what she has been through but there has to be room for under-standing, doesn't there?

Today I realized that Bash is my future. That I am falling in love with him. I want to choose him—my heart is so full of him. And with that, I realize that I may have to sacrifice my relationship with the person who means the world to me if I want him. How is it possible for your heart to be perfect and broken at the same time?

"Stay here today," Sarah says as she leads me to the guest room and we curl up together while I cry. I try to think logically through everything, but all I see is him. His face. His smell. His love that surrounds me.

Make me love you?

I think I already do.

CHAPTER 15
BASH

My girl is mind-blowing. I am absolutely in love with her and I couldn't hold it in if I tried. I don't know if telling her I love her was the right choice or not, but it's out there now and I simply couldn't hold back. After what happened on the ride there, I'm overwhelmed with how I feel. What she said in the bar, about sex meaning something to her, makes that incredible act of service feel an awful lot like love. The sun is forcing me to rest too soon. I just want to be near her. Maybe now that she is off on Mondays, we can spend the night and the day together. Even knowing that she is changing her schedule seems like she is making a sacrifice for me—I know how important working and taking care of her grand-mere are to her.

Approaching my door, ready to succumb to sleep, I find a note tacked to it.

Sebastien,
Come meet me when you rise.
-Mother

I roll my eyes. This could either be very good or *very bad*. My money is on bad.

"Mother." I incline my head as I walk into her office at moon-rise.

"Sebastien." Ok, still upset with me then. "Thank you for coming. You were out all night last night, *again,* so I assume you were with that woman. How long do we have to wait for you to get over her? Get her out of your system?"

"Mother, I advise you now to get used to her. She isn't going anywhere as long as she wants to keep coming around. Please listen to me. Elina is what I've been looking for."

She gasps and looks at me in shock. "Bash, do you intend to offer her the *Legame di Sangue*? A fragile, aging human. Have you discussed her turning?"

"Again, the dramatics, mother. You have got to be the most dramatic thousand year old vampire I have ever encountered. We have not discussed the *legame* beyond me telling her what it is and why it's necessary to continue the bloodline. I do not know her feelings on it. I don't believe, at this time, she intends to turn." I watch her look at me doubtfully as I try to explain. "It's only been a few weeks, and humans are easily spooked. She isn't ready for these discussions yet. Would I offer her the *legame*? In an instant. Would she accept it? I'm not sure. Right now, she believes its entire purpose is to sire the next bloodline children. I haven't explained the rest. She isn't ready." I can tell she isn't satisfied with my answer.

"The *problem*, Bash, is while you wait for her to 'get ready', she is aging. You don't have a decade or a century to convince her. She is young now, but she won't be for long. Time moves differently for us. A year for her is a long time. A year for us is nothing. Bash, I want nothing more than for you to be happy, but you can't be running all over Ville de Sang with a mortal woman who isn't going to stay with you for eternity."

"Why can't I, Mother? Even if she decides she never wants the *legame*. That she never wants to turn. If she wants to stay with me the way she is, then, in less than 100 years she will be dust in the wind. Why do you begrudge me even 50 years of happiness? You want me to bind to someone else in 50 years? Fine. I'll say the words—I'll spill the blood. But I will never love another the way I love Elina."

"Fifty years." She concedes. "Take your time with your human. And in fifty years, you'll kneel before me, a man in mourning, and accept who I choose. And I will tell you I told you so. Go get something to drink before you head out tonight. I haven't seen you feed in days. Unless-"

"No unless. I'm not feeding on her. Good night, Mother."

Pulling my phone from my pocket, I send Jack a quick text, inviting him to meet me at the bar.

Walking into the bar, a half hour later, her head snaps up as soon as I am visible. A look of obvious relief on her face. *Did you think I wasn't coming, Tesoro?* I smile at her and get a bright one in return. Just like that, the tension from the meeting with my mother eases. She is my center, my home, my sun. Sitting at the bar, a whiskey appears in front of me immediately.

"You're late, Prince."

"Sorry, Beautiful. Had to visit my mother." I roll my eyes at her and she laughs. Studying her face, I notice her eyes are red and a little swollen, like she has been crying for a long time. "What's wrong, Elina? What happened?"

"It's nothing," she tells me while tears well up in her eyes.

"Tequila!" Sarah shoves a shot glass in her hand, holding the other herself, and they both drink them back, quickly. Oh, well isn't this a revelation.

"Well, well. Drinking on the job, Elina? That's dangerous." She laughs tearfully. I don't mention the tears. I drink my whiskey and watch in amusement as she gets tipsy while trying, mostly successfully, to tend to a full bar on a Tuesday night.

"What's up, Bash?" Jack says as he takes the empty stool next to me. "Hey, little black cat," he says to Elina, leaning across the bar to kiss her on the cheek. "And Sunshine, good to see you," to Sarah.

"Hey, Jack," Sarah looks at him indulgently.

He leans over, saying, "What are we doing?"

"Elina's drinking...a lot," I whisper.

"Now listen, King Bash." She uses a shot glass to gesticulate to me—its contents sloshing over the sides as she continues to wave it—the words and actions causing Jack to snort out a laugh at her. "I like you a lot. So, no going off with a pretty bronze vampire. K? K." A pretty bronze vampire? *Talia.*

"You're the only one for me, pretty girl. Even drunk."

She laughs, loudly, which causes me, Jack, and Sarah to erupt with laughter too.

"I think I love you Bash."

"Well now," Jack responds, whistling low.

"Awe!" Sarah squeals behind her, pantomiming a swoon.

"Why don't you reserve declarations of love for sober Elina?" I kiss her forehead and she pulls me against her, half across the bar.

"Ok, but I'll still love you in the morning!" And she dances away, swaying provocatively to the music in the bar. I hope she does still love me tomorrow.

She dances back to me, spinning a little. "I forgot, we have a datal dub...no a dating dub...no a *double-date* on Sunday with Sarah and Ethan." With that, she's gone again. I am so entertained by this version of her, this new twist on Elina that I am excited to try and bring it out of her when she's sober. I see her talking to a man with a hat and coat on, handing him a glass of chardonnay. He is speaking quietly and seriously. I intentionally start to listen in.

He has a French accent.

"You're in a good mood tonight, *crepuscule*." Twilight. Why is he calling my girl a nickname?

"I am." She smiles at him and he leans in, like he is trying to get closer to her light. I don't want to overstep when I'm not invited.

"And that's a beautiful pendant you have on," he tells her, pointing to the protection pendant I gave her.

"Who the fuck is this guy?" Jack asks me, eyeing the stranger.

"I'm not sure, but it's not the first time he's been here."

"You're the second Frenchman this week to comment on it. Isn't it gorgeous? My boyfriend got it for me. He's over there." She waves in my general direction. Second Frenchman? Boyfriend? I'm so distracted by this new title that I forget everything else. I spiral into hope. Maybe she *will* have me.

"Is that so?" He doesn't look in my direction. "See you soon, little *crepuscule*."

What the hell is going on?

"Elina, get away from my customers. I can't believe you're drunk behind my bar," Rian tells her lovingly, putting a steady hand on her back. "Sebastien, can you take Elina home—I can't have her here like this."

"Oh no, we're in trouble." Jack laughs at Rian's interruption, looking like an innocent choir boy.

"Of course, Rian. Come along *Tesoro*. Let's sober you up." Since it is still early in the night, right after midnight, we have most of the next six hours to ourselves. I intend to make the most of them. "Do you want to come to the loft or go somewhere else?"

"Let's go dance, Prince!" And off she dances into the night.

"Bash, you realize you're one lucky man," Jack tells me, watching Elina's ass bounce in her skirt. Despite the fact that vampires are pretty free with our sexual encounters, I would normally be pretty defensive, jealous even. But Jack is different. If she wanted him, I don't think I would stop her. I know his commentary is harmless unless she indicates otherwise.

I throw an arm over his shoulders, "That I do, my friend, that I do."

"Well, I'm going to go find some sort of trouble to get into tonight, since you're busy and I don't think you're going to share."

"You know I don't make the rules, brother. And I don't think she's interested."

"Bye, Elina! You look gorgeous baby!" And Jack disappears into the night. Her laughter at his parting words fills the space around us.

Following behind her, I feel spellbound by this precious human. In the distance, there is a roll of thunder as lightning illuminates the sky above us. Just ahead of me, Elina squeaks in surprise, then laughs. A sudden downpour soaks us in minutes but instead of running for cover, Elina runs to me, taking my hand and tugging me into the street.

"Dance with me!" she yells over the rain.

Wrapping my arms around her waist, I pull her against my body until we feel like one person. We dance to the rhythm of the rain and I feel her heartbeat hammer against my chest. Looking down, I capture her lips with mine and kiss her with all of the feeling I have in my body. Her kiss is like electricity surging through me. It's love. It's summer rains and dancing in the street. It's warm nights and home. I surrender myself to her mercy and give her all there is of me. If this were the last moment of my life, I would gladly flame out in her arms.

As the rain subsides, our dancing slows and our clinging arms relax. I feel like there is a shift between us—like we just crossed the point of no return. Spinning her slowly to hear a little more of her laughter, my senses sharpen. A shadow in the dark alley shifts and my head snaps up. My entire body tenses.

"What is it, Bash?"

"We need to go. Now." I take off, walking quickly, practically dragging Elina behind me. I don't know who that was but I don't intend to find out, not with her here. The rain covered more than our laughter tonight and I should have known sooner.

Climbing the stairs to my loft, Elina follows me quietly. Once inside, I turn and hold her close. "You must be freezing."

"I'm fine, Bash." She swats my hands away. "What was that?"

"I'm not sure. There was someone in the alley. It was probably nothing but I didn't like that they were watching us. I'm sorry if I scared you. Let's get you warmed up."

I walk through my bedroom into my bathroom with its large shower that takes up a whole wall, with multiple shower heads.

Gesturing to her necklace, I ask, "Can you remove that?"

Pulling my shirt over my head and kicking off my shoes, I

walk toward her and unzip her leather skirt, letting it fall to the floor.

Circling around behind her, I begin to unlace her corset until I can slide it from her body. Walking in front of her again, I study her standing in nothing but knee-high boots and tiny black panties with vampire fangs that say 'bite me'. I chuckle and she shoots me a wide smile. Grabbing the material at her hips, I draw them down her legs and off her booted feet. Her boots follow quickly behind her clothes, and she is a goddess standing in front of me, with me kneeling at her feet like a man at worship. Pressing my face against her stomach, I lay a kiss on her belly button, followed by her pelvic bone, and finally on her clit just visible between her thighs. Standing, I usher her to the shower and turn the water on high.

Staring into her eyes as she stands under the spray, I unbutton my pants and slide them down my thighs, taking my socks with them. Not moving my eyes from hers, I grab my cock through my boxers and rub it. Her lips part and I can faintly hear her quick inhale. Grinning, I put my thumbs in my boxers at my hips and push them down until I am standing there, my erection standing proudly between us. She cocks a sassy eyebrow at me and beckons me into the shower where I press my body against her back, my cock between us. Leaning down, I kiss and suckle at her pulse point, rocking my hips into her back. She moans deeply when I reach around and tweak one of her peaked nipples.

Spinning her, I wrap a hand around her throat and back her up against the wall murmuring, "What do you want, baby? Tell me."

"I want you, Bash. So much it hurts." I push my hard cock against her hip, her skin slick from the water.

CHAPTER 16
ELINA

"I'm yours." Bash whispers as he tightens his grip on my throat ever so slightly. I can feel my pulse rapid under his thumb. He rubs it reverently. Looking at his face, I catch sight of his fangs on display, causing me to shiver. In return, he throws me a feral grin that shows almost all of his teeth. Kissing me roughly, so hard my lips feel bruised, he grabs my knee and wraps it around his hip so only my toes touch the ground. He's holding me up by my neck and leg, and I have never been more wet in my entire life.

Trying to take in as much of him as I can, I run my fingertips over his tattoos. A large black bird spreads its wide wings from shoulder to shoulder, covering most of his chest. Swirls of black come over his collarbone and up the sides of his neck from his back. His arms are covered from almost top to bottom in symbols, swirls, and a full sleeve of a city. I kiss a few of the dark marks, deciding to ask him about them later.

Dropping to his knees in front of me again, he takes a nipple in his mouth, sucking hard and biting me, laving it with his tongue to soothe the sting. Kissing a burning path down my body, he relaxes himself to the floor and puts the knee that was on his hip across his shoulder so I am bared to him. He runs the tips of his fingers across the soft skin between my thighs, all the way through to the back. I can hear him humming appreciatively at the wetness he finds there.

"Such a pretty pussy, so perfect."

Dipping his head, his tongue darts out and lands pointedly on my clit. The leg holding all my weight threatens to buckle but Bash lifts that one to his shoulder also, using the shower wall and his hands to hold me in place with my legs wrapped around his head. He licks me smoothly, from opening to pubic bone, burying his face in me. I throw my head back and moan. *Fuck*.

"Fuck," I gasp out.

I feel his chuckle against me and buck my hips. He wraps his arms tighter around me so I can't move, and starts licking, sucking, and biting my pussy like a man starving. I feel the pressure of my impending orgasm start to build low in my belly. It feels like I could come apart at any moment. After another minute of his constant pressure on my clit, he slides 2 fingers deep inside me, touching that spot inside that only he can seem to magically find, like my body is a musical instrument and he's its master. Fucking me slowly with his fingers, I can feel my muscles starting to quiver under his ministrations. I stay suspended right on the edge, feeling his worshipful movements.

My abdomen quivers in anticipation of my impending release, the need to come coursing through my veins as surely as my blood. I writhe and wiggle beneath his tongue, whimpering for release.

"Please, Bash!"

Releasing the torturous suction on my clit, he tilts his head back, gazing up at me from his worshipful position on his knees.

"Please, what? Tell me what you want, *Tesoro?*"

"I want to come, Bash. Please," I keen, leaning my head back against the tiles, feeling him adjust a little before diving back between my thighs. His fingers moving inside me become more insistent and set a steady pace of pressing against me, him attaching his mouth to my clit again, sucking hard while pressing the tip of his tongue against me. My legs shakes where they are wrapped around his ears.

"Yes, baby, come for me. Let me taste it. I can't wait." His words are enough to push me right to the edge. I start panting and moving my hips so he fucks me faster. He slides a 3rd finger into me, I'm so wet that I can feel it dripping out of me. He suctions his lips to my clit and hums, and I explode. I can barely breathe, I'm lucky I am not trying to stand on my feet. He laps contentedly at my lips and my opening, withdrawing his fingers as I hiss. Sucking his fingers into his mouth, he slowly removes my legs, one at a time, and sets me on my feet. He wraps his arms around my waist to hold me up and kisses me. I can taste myself on his tongue and I moan into his mouth, causing him to buck his hips into my stomach. Kissing down my throat, he sucks on my pulse point, hard.

"Bite me," I say, tilting my head. He freezes, not a single muscle moving.

"No," he speaks into my throat. His arms shake a little with his restraint. "If you want me to bite you, baby, I want to be balls deep in your cunt at the time." I gasp at the tightness in my belly at his words. He sucks again and nips at my skin, licking it after. I wonder if he broke the skin at all, or if it's simply a habit.

"So, take me to bed, Bash." He moves so fast I barely register it. He's outside the shower holding a fluffy robe before

I can even move. He wraps me in it and picks me up, my legs wrapping around his waist and he kisses me deeply as he walks me back into his bedroom.

Laying me on the bed, he lays on top of me and kisses me like he is trying to memorize every inch. Flipping me over onto my stomach, he moves my hair from my back and begins a slow descent down my body, leaving wet kisses the whole way.

When he gets to my ass, he sits up on his knees, the head of his cock nestled just at the top of my thighs. He rocks his hips against my ass and I whimper. He chuckles a little and starts rubbing me down. All the way to the backs of my calves and the bottoms of my feet. He lays a kiss on each instep and makes his way back up. He kisses the crease under my butt cheek, the small of my back, my spine on each vertebrae, my shoulder blades, the back of my neck. I have never felt so worshipped and loved in my entire life. It's like he needs to know my entire body.

Turning me on my back again, he repeats his process. He has a knee on either side of my thighs so I can't open my legs. This time, when he gets near my hips, he nocks the head of his dick right where my thighs meet, so close to sliding into me that I'm sure if I wiggle a little, he will slip inside. But I know that isn't what he wants. He leans down and plants a kiss on my belly button, each of my hip bones, my pubic bone. A tiny flutter of his tongue across my clit makes me suck in a quick breath. Down my thighs and on my knees, my shins and the tops of my feet.

By the time he comes back up to meet me at the head of the bed, I am already shaking with need. He slides a hand flat against my body, between my breasts, and rests it lightly against my throat, thumb on my pulse. He settles his body between my thighs and lays heavy against me.

"Do you want me to fuck you, *Tesoro?* I have already worshiped at your altar, are you not satisfied?"

"Bash, please."

Tightening his hand on my throat, he whispers, "Beg."

"Bash, please. Please fuck me. I need to feel you inside me. I'm aching for you."

Growling with pleasure, Bash takes his other hand and snakes it between our bodies and runs his fingers between my wet thighs. "Baby, you're so fucking wet for me. Fuck, I can't wait to feel you."

Sitting up, he opens my thighs wide and gazes down at my exposed body, an awestruck look on his face. He grabs his cock as it juts out between us and rubs his dripping precum between my lips. Pulling my legs up around his waist, he looks me in my eyes as he positions his cock at my entrance.

Grabbing my hips and never breaking eye contact, he slowly—so slowly—starts to push into me. The further into me he goes, the harder it is for him to control his movements and keep his eyes on me. Finally, he relents, groans under his breath, looks down at where we are joined, and throws his head back as he slides all the way in until our bodies are pressed together. I feel so deliciously full, his dick the perfect size to fill every available space inside me, lighting me up with pleasure. Pulling out slowly, he slams back in. One hand on my hip the other wrapped around my throat, he starts fucking me harder and deeper until I can't breathe around him. Bringing the hand that was on my hip to my pussy, he rubs small circles around my clit as he squeezes my throat.

"How you doing, baby? God, you take my cock so well. You feel so fucking good. Your pussy is so pretty, stretching around my cock." I can see the veins in his throat and his tendons on display as he fights whatever he is feeling, holding himself back. Looking down, he watches his cock piston into me over and over and his chest lifts rapidly as he breathes through his pleasure.

"Slow down, just a little. I want to feel you." I whisper. He moves his eyes to mine and slows his pace, pulling almost completely out of me before slipping his head back into me and strokes, slow and deep, sliding against me, rubbing my clit every time he bottoms out. Bowing my back off the bed, I moan and writhe beneath him as he rubs his hands over every inch of skin he can touch.

Wrapping my legs around his hips, I pull him into me, a little faster and he matches the pace, pumping into me deep, so deep it aches. His thumb finds my clit again and he rubs gently, pushing me closer to my orgasm, my muscles quivering and my thighs shaking.

"Good girl. Come for me. Can you come for me?" The circles get smaller and harder until he is thrumming my clit in rhythm with his hips, pushing me closer and closer to the edge. He tightens his hold on my neck a little more every minute I get closer to my orgasm. I feel myself start to fall over the edge and his hand squeezes tighter and tighter, slowing the blood flow and granting me euphoria as I come on his cock.

"Fuck, baby, thats it. You're so wet. You feel so good wrapped around me, squeezing me. This is perfect, you're perfect." His hip thrusts become a little more erratic as he continues to fuck me, touching a glorious spot deep inside me that elicits a moan everytime he hits it.

"Yes, baby, I'm going to come. Do you want me to bite you? Elina, do you want it?" He looks at me seriously like he is trying to concentrate despite being on the edge of oblivion.

"Yes, Bash, bite me."

He falls on my body, still thrusting inside me and starts rubbing my clit again. Before I can even catch my breath, I am on the edge with him. His breath is ragged against my pulse, his limbs shaking with restraint. I can't tell if it's need for my body or for my blood. "Yes, *Tesoro*, come with me. I want to feel you squeeze my cock when I fill you up and my teeth are inside you. Come on, baby, it's time." I fall over the edge and scream his name as I feel a prickle in my neck. Something snaps between us, and I feel whole and perfect, but vulnerable. I feel him drawing my blood out of my throat while I continue to pulse around him and he thrusts deeply inside me. He twitches inside me and his back tenses beneath my fingertips grasping onto him. Finally, he stills and starts licking the side of my neck.

Lifting his head, I see the pupils in his grey eyes blown wide. There is a faint pink tinge to his lips. "What...that was...*fuck!*" He rolls over to lay next to me, panting.

"Yeah," is all I can say. He rolls a little bit and grabs hold of me, fitting us together like two puzzle pieces, my back to his front. He feels so perfect and right pressed against me, and I don't know if I ever want to leave this bed. Laying my head on his arm, I fall asleep.

I wake up some time later and we haven't moved. I know Bash isn't asleep, it's sometime in early morning hours. His erection is pressing into my ass and he tightens his hold on my waist as he kisses my neck. "Hey, Beautiful. Did you know you do this cute little snoring thing that sounds like a chipmunk." He does this mortifying impression of me and I want to disappear. I can feel him laughing against my back. Reaching down, he slides his hand between my thighs and starts rubbing me. Pulling his hand back, he licks his fingers and dives back in, sliding them gently into me. "Are you sore, *Tesoro*? I didn't get to clean you up after, you fell asleep so fast."

"A little, but it's ok. It makes me think of you," I whisper into the dark. He is moving his fingers slowly in and out of me, loosening me up and getting me wetter by the second. He pulls his hips away from me and repositions himself until he is lined up with my opening and slides inside me. I hiss at the intrusion.

"Shh, baby." He smooths my hair and kisses my neck. Soon, we are in a calm rhythm, moving together, the pleasure building between us. I moan every time he thrusts, his breathing heavy against my neck. He uses his fingers to pull me to the edge and I feel him start to swell inside me. "God, you're perfect. I love you so fucking much. I would gladly spend the rest of eternity inside you. This is where I belong. Fuck, baby, good girl. Come for me, I know you're almost there. I want to feel you grab onto my cock." His words murmured low in my ear turn to Italian. "*Voglio stare con te fino all'ultima luna. Siamo fatti l'uno per l'altro. In eterno.*" I come, shuddering and crying out, followed by him burying his head into my shoulder as he pushes as deep inside me as he can.

He slides out of bed, leaving me panting, and goes into the bathroom. I fall back asleep before he returns.

A few hours later, I awake again. This time, he is resting beside me. He lays flat on his back. Breathing slow and shallow. He doesn't move a single muscle. It is exactly as Sarah said —it looks as though he is dead. I take a few moments to study his still form. He's only wearing tight black boxer briefs and I can see all of his tattoos clearly for the first time. Across his pecs and over his shoulders is a giant raven, wings as black as night. The one eye I can see is blood red. The black swirls on his neck are actually smoke and I wish I could roll him over and see the back. I don't know the city he has tattooed on his arm, but it's old. A few Italian words jump out at me 'in eterno', 'Corvo', 'Sangue'.

Rolling over to the edge, on the bedside table I find a glass of water, a bottle of pain relievers, and a note.

> My love, tesoro mio,
>   I have gone to my rest as you have no doubt noticed. The pain relievers are for if you're sore. In the bathroom, you will find your pendant where you left it on the counter. You will also find a pile of clothing. They are a little big, but I adore the idea of you going home smelling of me, in my clothes. I left you something else. It's for you and Sarah. The sun is stealing me from you today but my dreams are yours. Your smell and taste consume my body, and thoughts of you consume my soul. I am yours in eterno.
>   Love, truly yours, Bash

Walking into the bathroom, I find the things he left for me. My pendant is exactly where I put it, along with a pair of workout shorts, that are passable if I pull the string tight and roll them up, and a black t-shirt. I've never seen Bash in a t-shirt but since it is his, he must wear them sometimes. I am stuck wearing my own boots. I gather my dirty clothes and put them in the bag he left me. I can't find my panties though.

There is an envelope on the counter and inside is a stack of $100s with a sticky note that says, "Have fun." I laugh. That must be what he meant by something for me and Sarah. I'm not for sale, but it's hard to turn down an order like that from the man you love. Walking back into his room, I set my bag down and pick up his note, turning it over to jot on the back.

> Bash,
> I meant what I said when I was drunk.
> x-Elina

Grabbing my stuff I head out the front door and nearly run right into a large man in a suit.

"Oh, excuse me," I say as I try to side step him.

"Ms. Girard, I was told to wait for you and to drive you wherever you want to go this morning." *Of course,* this is my ride to Sarah's. And so, off we go to get my best friend.

"Hey Lina, what are you doing here and who's the suit?" She looks behind me at a man standing by the black SUV on the curb.

I push her through the door into her house. "He's enthrall, I think. Or maybe the hired help? Hard to say. Bash gave him to me for the day, so I'm here to take you out. Bash wants us to have a little fun today, his treat, so whatever you want to do, let's do it."

"Did you stay with him last night? How was it?"

"Get ready, I'll tell you in the car," I tease, wagging my eyebrows suggestively. She snorts with laughter.

In the afternoon, Sarah and I have full stomachs, mani-cured nails, new clothes, and are ready for work. I didn't know I needed a day for us to reconnect and relax, but it was so nice to not worry about everything for a while. Last night was the most perfect night of my life and I can't wait to see Bash again.

When he walks into the bar about a half an hour after sunset, I greet him with a huge smile and come around the bar to hug him. He lifts me off my feet and kisses me gently before taking up his usual spot at the bar. I bring over his customary whiskey. "Hey, Bash."

"Hey, *Tesoro*. Did you have a good day?" He watches me knowingly over the top of his whiskey.

"You know I did. We went to brunch and had mimosas. We went shopping and I got some new stuff for you to laugh at when I wear it. I also got my fingers and toes painted. Thank you, Bash. It means a lot that you did that for us."

"Your toes, huh? I'll have to check them out. I can't wait to see what new panties you have in store for me."

Blushing, I level him a look. "Speaking of panties, mine seemed to be missing from the pile of clothes this morning. Do you know anything about that?"

"Hmm, that is very odd. Perhaps you left them somewhere —or someone took them."

"That's naughty naughty of you, Bash."

He laughs at me. "I'm sure. But they had a little message only for me," and he winks. Winks! My stomach flutters a little and he takes a big inhale through his nose and gives me a knowing look.

"I know that we have plans with Sarah and Ethan on Sunday, but after, we have been invited to meet with my mother." I stiffen where I lean against the bar. "I know it's a little soon, but she makes the rules and I follow them—or so I'm told. Don't be intimidated though, she will be on her best behavior."

"If you say so." I sigh as I walk away. All my relaxed feelings from earlier, gone.

CHAPTER 17

BASH

Rising with the moon on Sunday night, I'm so excited for the first half of the night, although a little worried about the second half. Mother has requested I bring Elina to her, and I have no idea what is going to happen. I want her to love Elina like I do, but I am not sure she will. She has never had another relationship after my father, and she hasn't told anyone who he was either. Taking the *legame* in secret isn't unheard of and she had to have. I don't want to keep Elina a secret though. If she ever gave me enough of herself to bind with me, I want to shout it from the rooftops of Ville de Sang.

I dress in a black button down shirt—with a subtle grey pinstripe, rolling the sleeves to my elbows— and relaxed black jeans. Black boots are on my feet. Spraying myself with my favorite Penhaligon's cologne, I head out to the SUV with a driver I arranged for tonight. I want to give Sarah, Ethan, and Elina my undivided attention. I've planned another first for her.

"Where are we going, Bash? And a driver tonight, fancy." Elina smiles as soon as she climbs into the backseat with me.

161

She blushes a little as she notices I'm in the same seat I was in the last time we were in here. Stunning as always, she is wearing a long black skirt covered in lace, sandals, and a pale-purple crop top. Her pendant hangs low on her chest. It pleases me that it's hanging around her neck even if I have to ask her to remove it when we are together. She is followed into the car by Ethan in dark wash jeans and a green polo, and Sarah in a sundress covered in yellow flowers. It's obvious that with Sarah and Elina, Elina is the moon. But with me, she is the golden sun.

"It's a surprise, *Tesoro*. Something you've never done before." Heading into the Bywater area, we drive toward the river. This is where the gates open and we unload cargo ships. It's also where we have a riverboat docked.

There is a collective gasp from the other occupants of the car as they realize where we are going. "The river, Bash? You're taking us out into the river?" Elina exclaims, excitement in her voice. She presses her face to the window like an excited kid. I can't help but be caught up in her excitement.

"Woah, man! This is so awesome. I've never been out there. I've unloaded stuff from the ships, but out on the river? Amazing." I really like Ethan, and we have developed a friendship in the recent weeks. He's relaxing, and makes me feel younger and more excited for life.

"Bash, thank you!" Sarah chimes in.

"Ok, ok, enough of the fawning, let's go. *La luna* awaits."

The moon glimmers off the still waters of the Mississippi River, silvery and seductive. The deck of the boat is set for an intimate evening with friends and loves, a small table is set with fruit and cheese, and champagne already in glasses. The girls sit and begin snacking, giggling the entire time while they sip champagne.

Heading over to the bar, I call out, "Would anyone like

anything to drink other than champagne?" Ethan requests whatever I'm having, which is whiskey as usual. As the boat is pushed out onto the river by the crew, a gentle breeze stirs Elina's hair, a wide smile on her face. Her pulse is racing and I can hear her heart hammering in her chest, full of excitement. More food is set out around the table and the girls eat slowly, relaxed, the low chairs with their crimson cushions comfortable for lounging.

After the food has been cleared away, we all sit together at the bow and look out over the river.

"Here's to food and friends, and forever," Ethan lifts his glass in a toast.

"And to riverboats and love," Sarah responds.

"And to families you create yourself," Elina adds. It's my turn.

"*Amare in eterno,*" I proclaim, and we all clink our glasses and smile to one another. I will be happy here for as long as Elina will have me. I suspect it won't be long before Ethan is asking for permission for Sarah to turn. Maybe I could do it myself, as a way to bind us all together. Once Sarah is turned, my love for her and her love for Sarah will help Elina view our situation as more permanent. Every minute I spend with her, I am more resolved that she is my future.

The moon is like a silvery thread on the water, casting the entire night into black and white. Elina sits between my legs, wrapped in my arms, relaxed against my chest. Leaning forward into the darkness of the bow, I begin to tell a tale in a hushed whisper.

"In 1882, on this river, the steamboat, Iron Mountain, was sailing out for a routine supply run when it hit something under the surface. The boat began to take on water and the crew tried to escape, what they considered, certain death. That night, the Iron Mountain disappeared without a trace. There was no wreck. The next morning, the body of a woman was found floating near where the surviving crew claimed the ship went down, but again there was no shipwreck. For months after, pieces of wreckage reported to belong to the Iron Mountain were found up and down the Mississippi, some many miles away." The fog rolling over the river sets a spooky ambience for my story.

"Months after that, in a field, 20 miles away from the spot it supposedly sank and nowhere near the river, the shipwrecked Iron Mountain re-appeared. The investigators were unable to offer a good explanation for how it got there. Louisianan's believe it was a supernatural occurrence. Since that day, there have been many unexplained sightings of a ghost steamboat on the river, believed to be the Iron Mountain continuing on its duties, a full crew on its deck and a sorrowful woman standing as a living figurehead, leading the way." I run my fingertips down the side of Elina's neck causing her to shiver. The water laps against the ship causing us to sway slightly. Elina grips one of my hands tightly, clearly enjoying the ghost story. "If you look out that way in the moonlight, you can just barely glimpse the outline of the misty hull." I start tickling her causing her to shriek and laugh which results in Sarah screaming. Ethan and I dissolve into laughter with them.

Rolling her eyes at us and grinning, Sarah announces, "Alright, I need another drink," rising from the cushions and heading to the bar. "Who needs a refill?"

"Champagne for me!" from Elina

"More whiskey!" as Ethan holds his glass aloft.

"And for me!" my glass in the air.

The next few hours pass quickly, full of ghost stories, quiet reflections, and a lot of laughter. I have always had a life full of people. My family, the other Blood Ravens, friends like Jack, lovers like Talia, but in over 400 years, I have never felt the completeness that I feel on this steamy evening on a riverboat with them. It feels like I didn't only find Elina, I found much more than that.

Approaching the dock, my arms around the woman I love, our friends beside us, I steel myself for what happens next.

"Sarah, Michel is going to drive you both home, Elina and I have an appointment."

"Oh yeah, the mommy meet and greet. Have fun!" She does not say it like she believes it will actually be fun but I laugh at her comment anyway.

"Thanks Sarah, love you! I'll see you tomorrow!" Elina hugs her and Ethan and we go our separate ways. Grabbing her hand I lead her toward the car waiting for us.

She walks slowly, hesitantly. She squeezes my arm tightly and looks back at the riverboat one last time.

"Bash," tears fill her eyes and my heart seizes in panic. Does she not want to go? Does she regret this; us? "Thank you for tonight. No matter what happens now or in the future, what you gave us tonight is something I will never forget. I have never felt how I did out there, beyond the walls." I am absolutely gutted by this statement. She is trapped here because of us. We are why she has to stay here. I want to fix it for her but I don't know how.

My own breath hitches in my throat and I hold her against my chest, breathing in her scent. "Elina, I love you. The sun rises just for you. You are the sun in my sky—the moon that holds me close. Every moment I existed before you I was waiting, I didn't know for what, but it was this. It was you in my arms. You hold my heart in your hand and only you have the power to destroy me. I want to spend eternity making up for the first 28 years of your life and I promise I will do whatever I can. I swear it." We spend the drive to my mother wrapped in each other's arms, occasionally sharing a slow deep kiss. It could be a goodbye or it could be coming home after a long time apart. What happens next will determine the path we take forward.

Walking into my mother's office—Elina at my side and holding my hand, looking small and fragile in this place of vampires—I am afraid. I don't often admit when I am afraid. I do not think my mother will hurt her, at least not physically, but that doesn't mean she can't wound her all the same. I have finally gotten Elina comfortable with the idea of us, I don't want my family to scare her away.

"Mother." I bow my head respectfully, she does the same in return. "This is Elina. Elina, this is my mother, Vespera. You requested our presence?"

"Vespera, it's wonderful to meet you." Elina extends her hand toward my mother, who does not move or offer her own in return. Vespera watches Elina, assessing every nervous breath and uncertain movement. Elina lowers her hand but refuses to allow embarrassment to affect her demeanor. I swell with pride, watching her. The quickest way to get through my mother's defenses is to stand tall and confident in the face of her scrutiny.

"So, you are the woman my son has forsaken all reason for?" Her tone has a mocking edge to it, though her question is kind enough.

"She is." I move closer to Elina, offering her the comfort of my presence, prepared to shield her if necessary—if only from my mother's glare. Her heartbeat accelerates in the quiet of the office and I know my mother can hear it too.

"Bash speaks so highly of you. Thank you for having me."

Gesturing to the seats across from her she commands, "Sit."

I exhale a loud breath, we have passed the first hurdle. She has decided, however begrudgingly, that Elina has earned a seat, a conversation.

"Elina, do you love my son?" She starts her interrogation as soon as we sit. "Do you know what it means to love my son, the heir? It is his nature to covet treasures, to feed, to love *so strongly* it may hurt. You are young and mortal—how do you intend to stand at his side?" I wonder if she connects my mother's taunt about treasures to the nickname I gave her weeks ago. Is it a coincidence or has my mother learned that, too?

"My life may be fragile and short—fleeting—but my love is not. *In eterno.*" She raises her chin so that she appears to look down at my mother despite my mother having the advantage in this room. I want to take her in my arms and never let her go.

Mother watches her, something in her eyes, approval, perhaps? She is interested, at least. It is a battle of wills and I hope, more than anything, that Elina is winning. A long, quiet moment stretches out, tension hanging like fog in the air. Elina's and my mother's eyes never break contact. My mother has a look of consideration on her face..

"Hmmm, ok." She leans back in her chair, relaxing slightly. "I want nothing more than for my son to be happy in his existence, and it is a long existence. If you are making him happy, then I want to believe in that. I am not here to be your enemy, Elina, but you have not yet made yourself an ally. I will be watching. Once you have proven you are worthy to stand by his side, for however long you do, I will be at your back. But I will not allow weakness to affect this family. *Prove* you are worthy of him."

Elena holds my hand tightly in her lap, palm sweaty with nerves, but her voice does not waver. "I will."

With that, mother smiles, fangs on display. It is not a warm smile, but it is not cruel either. We may not have yet won the war, but a battle was fought this night, and Elina has gained a little bit of ground.

"Let us begin," mother exclaims as she snaps her fingers. The door behind her large mahogany desk swings open and three vampires enter the room, holding trays. Elina tenses beside me, gripping my fingers so hard, it might have hurt if I were not a vampire.

"It's a meal service," I lean in and murmur in her ear. "I'm so proud of you. You were glorious. Perfect." She preens under my praise and I am reminded of her in my bed, coming for me when I praise her. It seems my girl has a praise kink. I can smell her on the air in the room, and I know she is remembering too. I clear my throat and she blushes.

On the desk, the team sets two teapots—one close to my mother and one closer to Elina. I can smell the metallic blood in the air mingling with the scent of oranges and black tea. Presumably, my mother's teapot has blood and this is all for show. Each teapot is picked up along with a cup and saucer and filled from its respective pot. A cup is placed in front of me, full of tea. The fact that my teacup is full of tea and came from my mother's pot means that—I turn my head quickly in Elina's direction as she smiles up at the man pouring her tea, ready to accept his offering.

"Thank you," she whispers.

"Mother!" I growl quietly under my breath. She only smiles serenely, excitement lighting her eyes at what is unfolding. My fingers twitch against my knee, I want to reach out and stop this from happening, but I know that mother has set the stage and now I must watch the show. Elina takes her cup and looks down, seeing the cup full of blood, and blanches. She freezes and I watch her intently, unsure of what to do but knowing this is some kind of fucked up test.

Elina gazes at the cup and looks up at my mother, no

emotion on her face, and says, "I wonder if any of my own blood is in this cup?" She stares into my mother's face for a heartbeat before setting it down on the desk, the porcelain tinkling delicately. I hand her my cup of tea, which she takes gladly and sips from slowly, her eye contact with my mother over the rim challenging. Mother smiles again, this time with a bit more warmth, as though she has finally found a worthy opponent.

We walk in silence back to my apartment after we finish the meeting with my mother. I'm not sure what to even say. She did a phenomenal job, handling my mother and her games. The only problem is I don't know what she's thinking and now doesn't seem like the right time to break the silence. I would rather she let me know when she is ready.

CHAPTER 18
ELINA

L ying in bed next to Bash, I spend a few minutes in self reflection. He is resting now, which means the sun must be coming up, though his room is as dark as any tomb in the City of the Dead. Yesterday was beyond anything I could have imagined. The riverboat with Bash, Sarah, and Ethan felt like, for the first time in my life, I have done something for myself. No expectations. No need to be met or people to care for. Something for only me.

Being with Sarah and Ethan again, after all the time apart, was like fitting puzzle pieces back into place. The grief that yawned between us when Ethan left was almost too much to bear, and we couldn't even discuss the raw emotion of it. Ethan wasn't gone—he left. When our trio went from three to two, it left a wound that didn't heal.

Now, we are a four-some, and it feels as comfortable as breathing. Bash slid right in and filled a hole we didn't know we had. He is quickly becoming friends with Ethan, and he seems to care about and understand my co-dependent relationship with Sarah.

But today, I have to go home. I have been caught up in the lure of love, and wrapped in Bash so thoroughly, that I am forgetting that I have a home. I haven't been back since Grand-mere told me to go if I was going to continue having a relationship with Bash, I needed to do it elsewhere. Now that the last few days have solidified my feelings for Bash, I have to face Grand-mere Celeste.

I realized yesterday that I do love Bash. Not a little, not for now. I love Bash like I love to breathe, without even thinking about it. I love him the way the stars love the night sky, timeless, inevitable, and forever. I am hopelessly in love, my love is not a weakness and neither is my humanity. I refuse to let the people around us control the narrative of our relationship any longer.

I stood up to a vampire *principessa,* and I will stand up to my grandmother. I chose Bash. I choose him now, in the next life, and in the one after that. I don't stop to consider what that means for my humanity just yet. I'm not ready, but I know there is no other option for me right now than to stay by his side. We need to figure out how the rest of it fits together.

The carefree feeling of the riverboat still lingers in my mind. My lips are still swollen from kissing Bash last night while he worshipped me in a way that I did not think possible. The reverence in his actions are breathtaking. There is a heaviness amongst the happiness though, a fear for what today will bring. How will things change moving forward? I don't yet fully understand what is going to happen, but I know it will be the right thing, for all of us.

Walking into the only place I have ever called home is like walking into a memory, it feels the same but far away. This house has always been my refuge, my safe place, and now, in an apartment across town is an anchor I never knew I needed, and the light that calls me back. My soul aches to be back next to his. I steel myself for the confrontation.

"Elina?"

One word full of sadness and defeat cracks my already tender heart open.

"Yes, Grand-mere Celeste, it's me." I walk into the kitchen where I know I will find her. She sits at the table, a cup of coffee in front of her, looking older than I remember. Maybe it was spending a week away, after a lifetime of seeing her every-day, or maybe she has always looked this way and I am only just noticing.

She looks at me with love and concern, as though she can't figure out why I am here but glad all the same. "Sit, I'll get you a cup." She moves comfortably around her small kitchen as she has for sixty years. Everything is the same here—it has never changed, even as things change around us. I think I under-stand now, that Grand-mere loves me fiercely and worries for me. She has deep rooted, but righteous, anger at the way things have happened here but I am not one of them. The vampires deserve her ire, but I deserve her understanding and support.

"Have you been well? Are you staying with Sarah?" Her tone softens to one filled with her love for me. "I've missed you, Elina." She is trying to figure out what is happening, but is refusing to acknowledge the obstacle between us. Bash is like a bomb in the room that she is tiptoeing around, and I decide to rip the band-aid off.

"I'm really good. I stay with Sarah sometimes, but I also stay with Bash a lot, too." She flinches when I mention his name and I realize she was hoping that I was here because I had gotten over whatever it was with him.

I set my coffee cup down. "Grand-mere, he's it for me."

She goes completely still and her breath hitches.

"He is my future. I know this isn't easy for you to hear, or maybe you don't want to but I am choosing him." I sit up straighter in my resolution. "I need to be by his side. I don't know what that will look like yet or how it will play out over the foreseeable and unforeseeable future. All I know is, he is it."

"I can't lose you too." She takes a shuddering breath, clearly overcome and remembering something. I assume it's my mother. I reach for her hand, and after a brief pause, she lets me take it. "I want you to be happy. And if Bash makes you happy, then I guess you had better introduce us."

A sharp exhale leaves my lips, a half breath, half laugh as the tension drains from my body. I envelop her in my arms, squeezing her aged frame against mine.

"Thank you, Grand-mere. This means more to me than you know. Would you like to meet at Sarah's? I'm off work today so we could do it tonight." I know she is still hesitating, the idea of sitting in a room with a vampire is almost too scary for her to fathom, but I think it's better if we try and get it over with so we can figure out what happens next.

"Yes, I will come over before sun-down. Will someone bring me home?"

"Of course!"

After talking to Grand-mere, I head over to Sarah's house.

"Sarah!" I bellow as I walk through the front door. Wandering through the house, I find her at her kitchen table, coffee in hand.

"Hey Lina. Please tell me all about mommy dearest—I can't take the suspense any longer." She laughs at, what I assume is, the horrified look on my face. "That bad?"

"Jesus, that fucking bad." A sigh and run my hand through my hair. "After she interrogated me about what a big responsibility being with her baby boy is, she gave me a teacup full of blood to watch my reaction." In all my introspection today, I haven't stopped to even think about Vespera Malvani and what all of that means. It's too much for one day, for one person.

"Blood? What the hell for?"

"She set up this elaborate macabre tea party, and instead of tea she served me blood. I thought Bash was going to lose it. He always lets me handle things though. I kind of love that about him. This time, though, I felt so outside of my depth. I think by the end though, I had earned at least begrudging respect from her."

She pours me a cup of coffee and pushes it toward me, followed by the cream and sugar. "Well, thank goodness for that, or otherwise Bash might have realized his girlfriend wasn't worth it," she says with an eye roll so excessive, she rolls her head too.

"I didn't say it mattered to him...it's just that, I feel like it did. He told me we would be fine without her approval but she's his mother, you know? There is no way that wasn't important. Having her as an ally in the Malvani house feels like a turning point in our relationship. Like we could never be what we wanted or deserved without it." I take a deep breath. "And so, we cleared the first big hurdle and are on to the next."

"What's that?"

"Grand-mere. I went and saw her today."

"And what did our Celeste have to say for herself? After kicking her granddaughter out on the street because she didn't like her boyfriend."

"It wasn't that simple and you know it. I explained. I told her that Bash is it for me. She has agreed to meet him."

Sarah looks confused, unsure, and a little apprehensive. In short, she looks exactly how I feel.

"I was hoping they could meet here? She doesn't want him in her house and she doesn't travel to the Quarter after dark. This is close enough that she can walk here and be escorted back safely. Is that ok? I know I should have asked first but-"

"Of course it's ok. As long as it's ok with her that there will be 2 vampires here tonight. I have work but I'll call Rian and let her know." Oh yeah, Ethan. I had not even thought to mention that Ethan is living here now. I'm not sure how she will take it, but at this point, I need to focus on what is happening with her and Bash. I don't have the energy to deal with Ethan's presence too.

"I don't care." I shrug. "I guess she has to get used to it." There has to be some lesson here about how the further away from a tragedy you are, the less impactful it is. Sixty years after the Closing, and 25 years after the *Guerra de Sang*, and people my age are co-mingling with vampires like it is normal.

Yes, the damage to our collective psyche is still there. But fear fades with distance. I hope that I can make Bash see humanity as something worth saving. Not only mine and Sarahs, but all of ours. Yes, vampires need to eat—that isn't going to change—but humans deserve to live.

We don't need to die to sustain the vampires, so why do we?

I get back to Bash's apartment about an hour before sunset, and climb into bed with him. I'm wearing a tank top and black panties that say, "Midnight Snack", with a little blood drop. He always finds my themed panties funny. Bash is so stoic some-times, so reserved, but the relaxed playful Bash that I experi-ence when we are with Sarah and Ethan or—alone in bed—are when I love him the most. He's special, funny, and so clever, but he takes life categorically seriously. I often find myself wondering if he's forgotten what youth is like and only remembers when he is with us, or if we bring out the parts of his personality he keeps hidden.

About 15 minutes before moon-rise, he sits straight up in bed. It's the most unnerving and weirdly movie-accurate thing about vampires. They seem to rise from the dead as soon as they awake, sitting up like they were pulled from the grave. He looks over at me, relaxed, taking in my outfit, and laughs.

Pouncing on me, he peels my snarky underwear down my thighs and licks my pussy from opening to clit, sucking on me. He spends the first 20 minutes of the night buried between my thighs and I have to hunt for my underwear again. It might be his favorite game. Kissing him deeply, I can taste myself on his lips, and I hum appreciatively before he climbs out of bed and covers his stunning olive skin.

"Hey, *Tesoro*. Did you miss me?"

"Yes. It's weird sitting next to you while you rest, you look so unnervingly dead." Taking a deep breath, I sigh. "I went and saw Grand-mere today. This is sort of a could-be-good-news, could-be-bad-news thing, but we are short on time. She has agreed to meet you, to hear us out. And she is going to meet us at Sarah's. We should probably get going so they aren't waiting for us. I'm sorry to spring this on you, but you were resting."

He looks me up and down, lying in bed, hair mussed, missing my underwear, and wearing only a small black tank top. "I don't believe I'm the one that needs to be told to get dressed, Beautiful." Smirking, he walks into the bathroom.

Throwing on my Marie Laveau voodoo t-shirt and ripped jeans, I grab my hair into a high ponytail, fasten my pendant around my neck, and am ready to go by the time Bash comes out of the bathroom. Perfectly vampire-esque in his standard black-on-black, except he is dressed casually tonight in a black t-shirt, jeans, and boots.

"Let's go, Prince." I haul him out the door.

Fifteen minutes later, it's full dark and we pull up in front of Sarah's house. This is the first time Bash has been here, so Sarah will need to invite him in. He will be the first member of the Blood Ravens to come inside either of our homes, and only the second vampire ever, Ethan being the first.

We knock on the door and Sarah quickly pulls it open, giving me a look that says a thousand things, before smiling. "Prince Sebastien Malvani, won't you please come in," she says with a bow and a flourish of her arm.

Bash snorts a laugh at her and steps inside. Once inside, Ethan greets him with one of those man-hugs men always do. I lead the way into the house, with Sarah beside me and the men trailing behind us.

We find Grand-mere perched uncomfortably on a chair in the sitting room. I walk over and kiss her cheek, murmuring in her ear, "Thank you for coming."

"Grand-mere Celeste, may I introduce you to Sebastien Malvani. Bash, this is my grandmother, Celeste Girard."

"Mrs. Girard, it is my sincerest honor to finally meet you." He gives her a half bow—not quite a bow, but something resembling the show of respect. "I have heard so many things about you, about your strength and your resilience. I appreciate you taking the time to meet me."

She watches him wearily, and I can't tell if she is afraid of him or generally uncomfortable with this entire situation.

"Elina, dear, I brought you Shrimp Creole. Sarah put it in the kitchen. Sarah, would you like to eat? I know you don't eat, Sebastien, but the women do." It feels like a pointed remark to bring contrast to our humanity. It is also incredibly disrespectful for her to ignore Bash's greeting.

Bash gives her a pleasant smile. "That was incredibly thoughtful, Mrs. Girard. I'm sure Elina is hungry by now. I already *ate* this evening," he says with laughter in his tone, and my head whips in his direction, taken aback by his naughty joke. Sarah covers a laugh with her hand as though she is in on the joke also. Ethan raises his eyebrows and smirks.

"Hmmpph. Well, Sarah? Get the food, dear." Sarah jumps up and leaves the room. Grand-mere levels Bash with a very serious look. "Sebastien, please tell me what your intentions are for my granddaughter? I refuse to ask for forgiveness for my anger at the fact that your people have killed a significant number of mine, and I can not forgive it." Bash watches her intently, deciding how to respond. "I want Elina to be happy and cared for, but not at the expense of her safety, and as I understand it and have experienced it, vampires are not safe company."

"Mrs. Girard, not only do I not deserve forgiveness for those sins, but I would not dare ask for it. I have not personally committed any crimes against you, and I am not my people, but I do bear the responsibility of my name and of my Re." He takes my hand and envelops it with his, presenting us as a united front. "I can assure you, with the certainty of my love for Elina, that her safety is paramount above all else, up to and including, against my own family. Should any harm befall her, it will be because I have befallen the same. She is the sun that shines in the night for me. I only wish to remain by her side for as long as she will allow me to. *In eterno*."

We sit in silence until Sarah returns with bowls of food for me and Grand-mere. The warm shrimp dish smells so much like home that it makes my heart ache to hold it in my hands.

Grand-mere speaks with the clarity of someone who has been here before and knows the ending. "Well, Sebastien, I hope that you can hold yourself to that vow. It isn't as though I could threaten you or coerce you into keeping Elina safe, I have to trust that you mean what you say."

I lean forward, waiting for a verdict, for permission, for hope.

"I don't trust you yet, but I am willing to try. Elina is all I have left—the only family I have. Seeing her content among her friends and loved ones is all I want from my life before it ends. Do not disappoint me."

CHAPTER 19

BASH

Something feels different now. Like our future is stretched out before us and we can't veer from the course. Not that we would want to, anyway. The change in Elina since she met my mother is stark. Gone is the reluctant woman I held gently, unsure if she wanted this life I was offering her.

In her place is a strong woman, resolute.

She is enthusiastically all in. She seems to have come to some decision about herself, or our future, and is determined to follow the path she chose.

I am eternally grateful to fall asleep with her in my arms and to rise to her waiting in my bed. I hope this change is permanent.

Meeting her grandmother feels like an important step in a very slow march in our journey together. I didn't just want Elina to love me, I needed her to choose me, and Celeste was an important catalyst for that decision. I can't help but draw the parallels between our meetings with the respective parents. My mother cares about me the way Celeste cares about Elina, and they both threatened us not to disappoint them. I will protect Elina.

Meeting my mother forced her to make some hard choices, and decide on the spot whether she was going to put in the fight necessary for us. Once she made that decision, she quickly made plans for the rest of the pieces to be in the right place. She is prepared to stand by my side and face whatever comes next.

I love her more everyday.

I hope beyond hope that she will let me spend eternity by her side.

We no longer measure time between us in minutes and days, but in moments.

In May, Ethan and I laughed while Sarah and Elina danced giddily in rain-slicked streets. Their heated bodies full of red wine and joy. The two of us watching them as though they were the embodiment of summer—of freedom—with love etched in our features.

In June, Celeste Girard laughed—truly laughed—at a joke Ethan made, over a cozy night at Sarah's house where we laughed until we cried, played board games, and the humans ate home-cooked creole food until they couldn't move.

In July, while at a small jazz club, we danced under the lights and I spun Elina's back to my front, holding her close. I lifted her arm to my neck and took a deep inhale of the inside of her wrist, laying a gentle kiss there in a silent vow.

In August, when the summer heat was at the peak of its suffocating wetness, we sought refuge on the shores of Lake

Pontchartrain and laid in the gently lapping water, under the light of the full moon.

We laughed. We languished in our bodies moving together, covered in sweat. I tasted Elina's neck, her wrists, her thighs, and fell more in love everyday.

I read from centuries old books, turning the thin pages carefully, sharing history and lore with my rapt audience.

I held Elina while she cried after Celeste asked her what she planned to do when Sarah finally turned.

Sarah and Elina spent hours sparring with Ethan under the stars, learning not only to fight, but to win. To be able to take on predators who prowl the streets but also the monsters who pretend to be men.

There are whispers that get louder everyday. *"L'Empire des Ombres Nocturnus,"* said in hushed voices that cut off when I get close.

A quick and rough *fleur-de-lis* carved into the brick of an alley. A message.

Could it be possible? The Shadow Kingdom, thought lost and broken, has found a way to grow within our very city?

The shadows are pressing in.

I have to keep Elina safe. And Ethan and Sarah. Celeste. Our family.

"Re Marcus. Mother." I incline my head respectfully toward Marcus, and the other council members in turn.

"Sebastien, thank you for joining us tonight." Marcus reminds me subtly that I have been more than a little absent during the summer. "We need to discuss this *Ombra* problem. We can't wait any longer."

"The *Ombra* problem is a pretty casual way to describe a coup happening right under our noses," Samson Kitteridge of the Lower 9th barks.

"It's not a coup," Evan Rocher of St Roch cuts in. "It's an insidious growth invading the streets."

"These dramatics are actually quite ridiculous. It's not a coup or invasion. It's a pocket of resistance from before. We will find them, extinguish them, and be done with it." Henry sighs, wearied by this. Seemingly the only voice of reason within this absolutely chaotic and paranoid council.

"I think we should focus our efforts on locating them. Having the enthrall do it during the day seems the best course of action, locating the nest while they rest." Amelia Moreau of Uptown, this time.

"We have to do something quickly!" Michael Thomas of the Warehouse district intones. "The shadows rise every day, gaining a foothold for the masses. I don't understand how they are wandering undetected around *our* city!"

"I agree," says his brother Kellan, from Algiers Point.

"We have to keep a more level head about this. We are the council and he is our Re." I raise my voice above the growing panic. "We can't be here yelling and frantic like school children. Whatever this is, we will get to the bottom of it. We will extinguish it and move on." I plead with them to control themselves. "You are not in need of parenting, start acting as though we have thousands of years of military and strategic history between us and cut the hysterics down to a minimum. Honestly, I have never met more dramatic people than the lot of you."

An outraged gasp escapes a few council members. I look

around me and find the faces of those who still haven't spoken, trying to get a read on their thoughts.

Talia sits contemplatively, her hands steepled under her chin.

Victor and Darius, stoic, flank Marcus.

Mother watches everything unfold with a supernatural stillness, the kind of stillness that makes you nervous.

Celina Fallon of the Treme, and Domingo from Mid-City, are the only others who haven't said anything. Their silence feels weighty.

"I will decide our course of action," Marcus finally cuts through the quiet that has descended after my scolding. "Sebastien is right, of course. We need to keep a level head and do what is best for our city, and our lives."

Talia mumbles under her breath.

"Something to add Talia, or are you disrespecting me for entertainment?" Marcus demands of her.

"No, Re, I was remarking to myself that of course the *principe* is right, he always is." The disdain in her voice isn't veiled, it is outright hostile. "It would have been helpful if he had added anything meaningful during the last couple of months, but we are all surely grateful he has graced us with his esteemed presence today."

"Alright, that's enough. You're all dismissed." Marcus waves his hand. "Except you, *nipote*, you'll stay," he adds, as he levels me a look that brooks no argument. I keep my seat. I notice my mother has also kept hers.

"Bash, what the hell is happening with you. You've been absent from nearly every meeting since May. There have been multiple reports of you lying on beaches and hanging out in clubs with human women. You are permitted to do whatever you want, with whoever you want obviously," he studies me, "but to completely disappear into the human world as soon as you arise is distinctly out of character for you. We gave you the summer to 'sow your wild oats' or whatever it is that you're doing, but you are a member of the *Casa del Corvo di Sangue* and you have responsibilities to us. You can not continue to act as though you are not an important member of the leadership. You're not human. Stop pretending to be."

I glance over at my mother, expecting her to step in. She does not look pleased by the reprimand being leveled on me. I thought we had come to an understanding that Elina is my now, and if she is ever to be my future, I need to devote time to cultivating this relationship. It appears she has not passed that information along to Marcus.

I sit back in my chair, my posture relaxed. I'm not a threat but I am also not threatened.

"Uncle, I have found someone." He looks at me incredulously, as though he knows what is coming but refuses to believe it. "A human woman. Mother knows all about her, has even met with her a few times in the last couple of months."

He swings his head in mother's direction and she has the good sense to stay quiet while looking sufficiently contrite.

"What do you mean you 'have found someone'? Someone what? She's a human? Her life is as easily snuffed out as a candle flame. She is growing old by the minute. What do you mean, Sebastien?" He questions me with the authority of his office, not as my uncle. "I am Re. Anyone you are considering as a partner, or to take the *legame*, must be discussed with and approved by, me."

Mother sits up. "Marcus, human emotions are different from ours. Less driven by instinctual need and slower to develop. He has been courting her since April, but only in the last month or so is he drawing her closer to being serious about their future. He means to spend the rest of her life by her side." Mother tells him, doubt coloring her tone, like she can't believe I am doing this either. "I didn't tell you as there-"

"Stop, Vespera. I don't want excuses why you didn't tell me. I don't want droning monologues about their love or whatever it is you are telling me. I should have been informed if there was anything going on besides you fucking and feeding on some human whore from the Quarter."

I flinch, not only at his tone, but that he has reduced Elina to something she is not, and never will be.

"She isn't a whore and it isn't that simple. I'm in love with her. I am choosing her. She *is* my future, Marcus."

"The hell you are! Not without my approval you're not!" He roars at me, the glass trembling in the windows. "I make the rules, you don't choose, I do! If you want her, you will present her to me. Friday night. You will bring her here and you will present her to the court. I will decide." His voice rings with finality, fury, and I have no choice but to comply. "Get out."

CHAPTER 20
ELINA

Monday.

The September morning dawns with a coolness in the air, a promise of relief from the sweltering heat of summer. There are still plenty of sweaty days ahead but there is hope.

Friday looms like a yawning monster on the horizon, fear taking root in my chest at the thought of being presented to court and council for judgement. Judgement of whether our love is worthy. I have long since earned approval from Vespera and I was stupid enough to feel secure in that knowledge. I never considered that the stakes were actually a lot higher.

I still haven't decided what happens when Sarah joins Ethan in the world ruled by moonlight. I haven't decided if I want that for my life. Basking under the stars with the family we are creating for ourselves this summer was more than I could have ever dreamed of. A sense of rightness in my soul.

I know that Marcus will demand an answer to that question. I decide to spend today in the sun. I need to reflect on what it will mean for me to leave it behind. I dress slowly, perusing the expanse of black clothes and decide on a pair of black biker shorts and a t-shirt that says, "I bite back."

The warm, late summer sun burns my face. Having spent most of the summer living by the light of the moon, the days are overly bright, my skin sensitive. I don't miss the irony of that, considering the question that weighs so heavily on me today.

Bash is my forever—I can't ever picture someone else by my side. I turned 29 in August and it was the most perfect birthday I have ever had, because I was surrounded by love I never thought was possible in this place. Bash showed me, through deed and word, that he intends to spend my life beside me. Now, I need to decide if I can spend his life beside him.

In eterno only means something if I believe it.

TUESDAY.

Every day closer to Friday, more fear curls in my stomach, an ever present reminder that we are living on borrowed time, both, in our relationship and with my life. Falling asleep next to the man who has consumed my entire world is as easy as breathing. Waking up and being haunted by the contrast between the warmth of him under the sheets of our bed, and the coldness of his unmoving body, helps hammer home the fact that he lives in the darkness while I pretend it's possible to straddle two worlds.

Am I prepared to give up everything in the light? To allow the love I have for Bash and our life together to be the sun in my sky? Bash tells me daily that while he does not get to live in the sun, he gets to watch the sun rise each night when he rises and sees my smiling face. His devotion both fills me and breaks me.

I've officially moved into his loft. I've brought warmth, color, chaos. I cook in his kitchen. I clutter his once-empty bathroom counter. His space is ours now. Our home. And I don't want to lose that. I won't.

Walking through the Garden District, the streets steeped in history and memory, I wander into Lafayette Cemetery No. 1. I run my fingertips across the tombs of my ancestors and friends. I contemplate my name never being on one of these tombs. If I could live forever, would I take the chance?

I can, but should I?

WEDNESDAY.

Only two more sunrises. I don't think this is the end—I don't believe that Marcus will ask for me to be turned on Friday though I do believe he will force my hand on my decision. Force me to speak it into existence, that I am willing to sacrifice it all. The decision to give up my humanity for Bash. Lose the rush of blood under my skin as Bash moves inside me. The feeling of him sucking my life's essence from my throat, my thighs, my wrist. His teeth biting into my breast, lapping each drop up like a prayer and a promise.

Will turning take the need, the passion, we have? Is it a part of my humanity? I can't help but consider the possibility that Bash is just as attracted to my human heat as he is to my heart.

What of the dark side?

The idea of taking the life of another person, stealing their future to feed my hunger, makes me nauseous. It's a horrifying thought that if I make this decision, then soon, *I* will be the monster in someone else's story.

When Marcus makes me declare my choice, why would I delay the inevitable. I should go through with the change right

189

there, in front of the king and council. Show them what I am willing to do for love.

I want nothing more than to bind myself to Bash, take the *legame*. Leap off the bridge of uncertainty I have built for myself and let myself descend into the shadows.

Bash has left me to my brooding this week, awaiting my verdict similarly to how I await my own judgement. In our nights together, we enjoy each other and dance around the subject he knows I spend my days on. I know there is fear in his eyes reflected back at me, not fear that Marcus will deny me, but that I will deny him. The only thing I know for certain is I refuse to give Bash up.

THURSDAY.

One more day.

One more sunrise.

One more day that I get to walk amongst the humanity that thrums through Ville de Sang and pretend I am the same. That I haven't decided to forsake everything I have believed in order to chase down a new future. Forge a new path. Orchestrate a new life.

Accepting, what I know will be offered tomorrow night, will make me *principessa*. It will crown me with new enemies and new family. New responsibilities to the kingdom, things that will require me to consider the good of the night dwellers, the blood-drinkers over the humans. The innocent children, the grandparents. The food and the fodder in wars.

I feel sick sitting on the steps of the cathedral, considering that soon, this will be my home. The modest house in Little Woods that my grandparents bought as a newly married couple, the home where they brought their little baby girl into the world, the house where that little girl became a woman and had her own little girl, won't be for me anymore.

I won't be able to go inside.

I will be a Blood Raven.

I will be the enemy.

I am afraid.

I am resolute, I think.

Being loved with the devotion of immortality is like a drug. I am addicted. Bash worships at my altar like a man who has been starving for centuries.

I am ready, I think.

The possibility of forever is a path into the unknown, and I will not be afraid.

FRIDAY.

This is the day. I will not be afraid.

Tonight, when the sun slides beneath the horizon, I will stand in front of some of the most powerful vampires in existence—not as prey.

Not as a lamb.

I will not go to slaughter.

I will become a lion.

Bash is my now, but he is also my future.

Walking into my childhood home, I inhale the comforting smell of spices and Grand-mere. I walk slowly through the house, touching everything. Remembering Saturday mornings on the old comfy couch, curled up, reading a book. Dinners with friends and neighbors gathered around the dining table, good food being shared by everyone. The worn cupboards in the kitchen, the weathered boards on the back porch. I watch a memory in my mind, a little girl running barefoot through the grass, being sprayed by the garden sprinkler. This is the place where my past lives.

I wipe away the tears and go into my bedroom. The room that was all mine, my entire life. I sit on the edge of the small twin bed and take in the creaking floorboards, the small vanity, and bookshelf. The mementos of my life before, pictures of school friends, trinkets, and drawings. My entire life in one small room. I lie back and stare at the ceiling that I looked at almost every night for 28 years. I let the tears run down my cheeks and land on the pillow that is no longer mine.

Walking through the streets that were my life, the path I walked every day to school, fills my chest with joy and heartbreak simultaneously. Taking off my shoes and walking barefoot in the grass of the park, laying down to feel the sun burn my cheeks, I appreciate the work that went into ensuring that my life was full and happy despite how desperate our lives have been. I watch a few clouds move slowly across the sky, unconcerned with the matters of humans. I imagine they are animals and balloons and toys, like I did as a child.

Knowing it's time to head back into the Quarter, I decide to have a meal in a little restaurant with a balcony, where I can watch the people mill around and go about their lives in the only way they know how.

I walk slowly on the sidewalk, savoring the warm sun on my face, people walking past me. I hear someone come up to me, a hand lightly brushing my shoulder.

And everything goes black.

There is something over my head, something heavy...

I can't see.

I can't breathe.

Sound is warped in my ears.

I flail my arms around and hit the bodies standing close to me.

Who would attack me? What's going on?

A sting in my neck disrupts my panic. For just a second.

Then.

Nothing.

CHAPTER 21

BASH

Sitting straight up in bed—like rising from the dead, as Elina likes to tell me—I look around and notice my sun is missing.

"*Tesoro?*" I call out, but I can feel that she isn't here. *Where is she?*

Climbing out of bed, I wander around the apartment, looking for a note or a clue. Tonight is Friday, we have to appear at the court tonight. Panic fills my chest.

Did you leave me?

Are you done with us?

Have you decided I'm not worth it? I feel my heart cracking.

Throwing on whatever I find nearby, a pair of shorts and a black t-shirt, I head to my bike. The first place I decide to check is the Velvet Tomb. She shouldn't be there, we have an appointment. Maybe she needed a little longer. Maybe she needed a little air, a little space.

Walking in, I find Sarah behind the bar.

She looks at me in surprise. "Bash, what are you doing

here? Where's Elina? I thought you guys had some princely things to do tonight?"

"Have you seen Elina today?" Panic bleeds into every word.

Sarah adopts a very serious look. "What do you mean? I haven't heard from her since yesterday, she took the day off."

"When you saw her, did she say anything?" My voice shakes with the effort to keep calm. "About us?"

"What? No. Yesterday, she made a decision, *the decision*." She looks stricken. "She planned to tell you tonight, with Marcus." She pales. "Do you think she is...leaving you?"

"I don't know, Sarah. I can't think. I can't find her. She wasn't there when I arose. There was no note. She isn't here. Where else could she be?"

"Maybe she went to Little Woods? To Celeste's?"

"Ok, I gotta go. If you see her...send her home and tell her to wait for me. Ask her to give me a chance to talk to her before she makes a choice," I beg Sarah. I have never begged anyone for anything in my entire life.

"Of course, Bash. She probably just got held up somewhere." I run out of the bar into the night.

I almost leave my bike behind, running there would be faster. I'll need the bike to bring her home when I find her though. Climbing on, I shoot into the night like a bullet.

Jogging up the steps of Celeste's house, I can smell Elina. She was here today. I feel my panic start to subside. Ok, she's here. I have her. *Ok.*

I knock lightly on the door, hoping I'm not interrupting a moment between them. Celeste swings the door open, looking surprised by my appearance.

"Good evening, Mrs. Girard. Can I speak to Elina, please?"

She shakes her head slightly. "Elina isn't here. I haven't seen her today."

The rush of dread that immediately floods my system must show on my face.

"Where is my granddaughter, Sebastien?" Her voice trembles.

"I don't know," I whisper. Turning around and walking heavily down the stairs, I do not turn back even though I can hear Celeste's heart rate pick up and the gasp she lets out.

Walking slowly down the street trying to feel her, smell her, I catch a very faint bit of her essence on the wind. I follow my senses to a park down the street. She is more concentrated here. She was here for a while. I reach down and run my fingers across the grass. I follow her scent in the air until it ends. On the sidewalk, her scent so strong before is now intermingled with other humans, maybe 3 or 4. Strangers. I look around me.

I turn and shoot toward the *cattedrale*. I need help.

"Mother." I storm into her office and she looks up, startled at my sudden appearance.

"Bash, what are you doing here? You and Elina are supposed to be presented to Marcus in—" she looks at the wall clock "—15 minutes. Where's Elina?"

"That's why I'm here." I can hear the terror in my own voice. My mother's eyes immediately narrow and she waits for what I am about to say. "She's gone." My voice breaks and my breath heaves like I am having a panic attack. Vampires don't have panic attacks. *What the hell is happening to me?*

Maybe I am dying.

Standing up, she looks at me. "What do you mean 'gone'? She can't go anywhere. The city is closed. She is here."

"'Gone' like someone took her." Collapsing to my knees on her carpet, I cover my face with my hands. Mother kneels in front of me, removes my hands from my face, and slaps me—hard—across the cheek.

"*For God's sake*, Sebastien. Get up!" Her eyes are cold, calculating. "I need you to tell me what happened. Stop falling apart."

"She wasn't home when I arose and I knew we had the thing with Marcus." I wave my hand in the direction of the church. "I went to the Velvet Tomb and she wasn't there. I went to her house and she had been there but she wasn't there anymore." I suck in a ragged breath. "I followed her scent to the park and I found strangers wrapped around her essence, 3 or 4 of them. And it didn't go anywhere else. So I came here." I choke back a sob. "Someone took her."

"Sebastien, you are nearly *500* years old. Act like it. I know you're upset, but you need to get it together so we can figure out what is happening. Do you think you can help Elina like this? Do you?"

She's right.

I stand up, pulling my shoulders back, and take a few breaths to compose myself. I close my eyes and Elina's blue eyes are there.

I'm trying.

"Now, let's go talk to Marcus," she says before sweeping from the room.

"What do you mean *missing*?" Marcus questions my mother as we stand in front of him, sitting comfortably in his golden chair. She recounts what I told her in her office as I look around the vestibule. I take stock of who is and is not in attendance.

He drums his fingers once, twice, on the arm of his chair.

Everyone knew that we were supposed to present her

197

today. All 12 members of the council are here. Amongst their faces I see concern, disbelief, uncertainty, empathy, apathy, and, on one face, disdain. Talia. She watches me closely the way I watch everyone else. I stand tall, not letting the tightness in my chest, the fury below the surface, the *devastation*, show on my face.

"What do you want us to do, Sebastien?" Marcus uses his Re voice.

I look at him and bow my head. "I want permission to use whatever resources are available and necessary to find her. She is the future *principessa* and she is important."

"She is not *principessa* yet, she has not been presented. She is a human, Sebastien. One *mortal* woman. I can not risk soldiers for sentiment." He answers me dismissively like my entire world is not on the brink of collapse.

"I will find her and I will take the sirelings with me. You don't like it? Stop me, Uncle." I look at him challengingly. Turning to the gathered council, "Any who have sirelings they would volunteer, let me know. I will find her and I won't forget those who help me." I look directly at Talia. "And those who don't."

"Marcus, please, this is going to divide the family. He's your heir, your *nipote*." My cousins file into the room, as my mother finishes her plea.

Alessandra, Filomena, Gianna, and Aurora line up behind me, clearly declaring their side. My uncles, Darius and Victor— their fathers—look at them, slack-jawed. Surprised by this show of solidarity, I believe. They shouldn't be. I have been close to them all since they were born. They are my blood, my family.

The mood in the hall subtly shifts, vampires move around each other in a slow, quiet dance, those who are clearly with Marcus moving his way. Those who are clearly with me, moving mine. Those who are torn, loiter in the middle.

The silence is deafening.

I sketch an almost mocking bow, and I turn on my heel to leave.

With my supporters in my wake, I see that we have split the court, almost evenly.

Entering an empty office, I lean against the desk while everyone files in. My mother comes in last.

"First steps," I begin as soon as everyone is in and the door shut. "Does everyone know what Elina looks and smells like?" I open my wallet and remove the photo from her visit to the archives all those months ago, before she changed my life. I set it on the desk for reference, sadness permeating the air.

"We can smell her on you." Michael says and I hiss at him. He puts his hands up in a placating gesture. "Sorry, but it's true".

"Bash, it's too early to already be alienating your allies. You'll need all the support you can get," my mother scolds me.

She's right of course. "No, I'm sorry, Michael. That was incredibly rude. Now, back to what I was saying, since you're all aware of who she is. Anyone have any ideas of where we should start?" I look around for a miracle. "The last place I could track her to was a park near the house where she grew up, in Ville de Sang East, before she was surrounded by 3 or 4 human strangers. That is where the trail dies. They should still be in the city."

I stop and wait. Wanting to hear anything, something, to go on. My allies look around, realizing no one has anything to offer. I sigh wearily and sit down on the desk. *Fuck*.

Lessa looks up, her eyes bright like she has something. "We need to start with Elina's enemies, then Bash's. We can work through our enemies, see if there is anything that would make sense for this. We need a starting point. Our list of enemies is long, but I bet Elina's isn't."

I take a sheet of paper from the desk drawer and we start brainstorming.

Elina	Bash	Corvo
Amelie	Talia	Devereaux
Talia	Kandis	Sire Vamps
	Lucian	Voodoo Queens
	Devereaux	Drakes
		Chi

It's not an all inclusive list, but we can try and start narrowing it down based on what we have.

"It's likely not any of the other bloodline families. They may want to take our territory, but one mortal girl won't get them that," Amelia says, looking over my shoulder.

"It's probably not a human either," Lessa adds.

"Or the witches. They abhor the way humans are pawns in this war. Plus, they could have subdued *you* if they wanted a hostage," Gianna contributes. One-by-one, I strike-through the names, pen scratching on paper, louder than it should be.

Elina	Bash	Corvo
~~Annette~~	Talia	Devereaux
Talia	~~Hardis~~	Sire Vamps
	Lucian	~~Voodoo Queens~~
	Devereaux	~~Drakes~~
		~~Chi~~

"Who are the most likely suspects for vampires who are mad about not being able to create sirelings?" I ask the group.

"I don't think it's them, either. No offense, Bash, but one mortal girl doesn't really matter enough to Marcus for it to be a worthwhile hostage," Filomena says, flinching like she believes I'll be mad at her statement. I know she is right though.

"Well, me and Lucian don't exactly get along but I don't think he would betray the family simply to annoy me. I don't think he has a death wish."

I update the list again.

Elina	Bash	Corvo
~~Annette~~	Talia	~~Devereaux~~
Talia	~~Harulis~~	~~Fire Vamps~~
	~~Lucian~~	~~Voodoo Queens~~
	Devereaux	~~Drakes~~
		~~Chi~~

There are only 2 suspects left on the list. Talia and the Devereaux family. Both have very compelling reasons to do this. "Talia has threatened Elina before. When I brought her here for the first time. She called it a promise. I thought Elina would be safe with me..." I trail off, lost in the knowledge that this might be my fault.

"She was uncharacteristically quiet today. We will keep her on the list," my mother says, contemplatively.

"That just leaves the Devereaux," Aurora says, stating the most obvious possibility. We haven't been able to find anything about them at all. We know they are in the city, but we can't find them.

"But again, why would they take Bash's human girlfriend?" Samson asks. It's a good question—we have eliminated other suspects on the grounds that they wouldn't have any interest in a human girl.

"I don't know. Maybe they didn't," I say. "I think the best option we have right now is Talia. Can we have her followed?"

"Yes," mother says. "I will take care of that."

CHAPTER 22

ELINA

Drip.

    Drip.

    Drip.

Sitting in the dark, I can hear water dripping close to me. It's cold here.

The air is wet but not like it is outside. Not humid. Wet like a puddle. The ground is stone, rough against my legs. I have no idea if it's day or night.

How long have I been in this dark place? There is no light. I can't see my hands in front of my face.

Not even eating gives me any indication of time. I can't track the frequency of meals. I don't know if it's breakfast or dinner. It's the same every meal. Water. Sandwich. Apple. Every single meal. I have had 3 of them. I eat them everytime.

I lay on the cold floor and sleep.

I think about Bash.

Please find me.

CHAPTER 23

BASH

"Mother, tell me you have something, *anything*," I ask her desperately, a note of pleading in my voice. "It's been more than a day since she was taken." It's Saturday night. She disappeared sometime Friday.

"Maybe. I have been having some trusted members of my enthrall and my sirelings track Talia's movements around the city. She went to a nightclub last night after the meeting with Marcus, while we were here. She stayed inside until right before dawn." She watches me. I fidget nervously, stilling myself when I realize. Vampires do not fidget. "She went back to the club tonight as soon as the moon rose. If she follows the same pattern today, of not emerging until sunrise, I am ordering the enthrall to search the building tomorrow."

"What? Why would you wait until tomorrow? You'll go now! She is my entire life and it's been stolen!"

"If we burst into a club full of humans and vampires to search the building, not only will we draw attention to ourselves, we will alert Talia to something. If she disappears, we won't have anything to go on. I know you're worried, but you need to be patient."

"Patience." I shake my head and walk out.

Knowing that I am about to walk into my loft and find Sarah and Ethan waiting for news makes me feel sick. I don't want to tell them that they trusted me with the most important thing in their lives, except each other, and I lost her. I failed to keep her safe.

Jumping up onto the roof of the cathedral, I crouch like a predator in shadow. I watch the vampires move through the Quarter below. Looking for anything that will help. Anything that will lead us to her.

I watch Talia approach. Mother just said she was at the club. Now she is here. Maybe the club is a dead end. Mother was right, we need to be patient.

I watch her. She seems unusually light, happy even. Happy while my world is falling apart around me. What have I done to deserve this?

I stay perched on the roof like the night stalker I am masquerading as. She enters the church and I wait.

And wait.

She finally emerges and I run across the roof to keep her in my line of vision. She turns a corner and I take chase, jumping across rooftops as quietly as I can while I track her on the ground. A few blocks away, she turns ahead of me and before I am back on her tail, she disappears. Like, actually *gone* in thin air. Seems to be an epidemic in this city.

I jump down from the roof, landing heavily on the empty street, looking around for any traces of where she may have left behind. I don't see anywhere she could have gone. Nothing is even open on this street—it's all human businesses.

I swing hard at the support post for the balcony above me —crack—splintering the wood.

"Bash!" Sarah runs to me as soon as I enter the apartment. "Anything? Any news?" Dropping my head down, I feel myself start to shake. My knees give out from under me and I hit the carpet.

Kneeling, I think about all the times I knelt at Elina's feet, trying to show her the depth of my devotion to her. How priceless she is to me. I ache to cry.

Ethan kneels beside me and puts his arms around me as Sarah hits her knees next. We collapse into each other, limbs tangled, breaths shared, our grief held tight between us.

Elina was the magnet that drew us together and we need her here—our glue. We have to find her. My shoulders shake, my breathing ragged, as grief suffocates me. Sarah cries against my shoulder and Ethan holds us both while we lay our wounds open for each other to see.

"We will find her, Bash. We have to." Sarah sucks in a lungful of air, sounding as though it is a tremendous effort. "I've been thinking."

I raise my eyes to her. "Something to help Elina?"

She hesitates for a minute. "Maybe? Kind of. I think I am ready to turn. I want to help. I don't want to be stuck here like a useless human."

I shake my head at her. "No, Sarah. You would be a baby vampire—weaker, volatile, driven by blood. If Elina found out I did this only because you wanted to help, she would extinguish me, herself."

She balls her fists and pushes her shoulders back, taking in a few deep breaths.

"No! You don't get to hide behind what Elina would want

or what Elina would do." Her outburst surprises me and I look at her appraisingly. "Elina was mine before she was yours. She is the other half of my soul too." A sob escapes her. "And I am broken without her. I need to help. I'm ready. Just like she is."

"Ok, Sarah. If you're serious and truly understand what is going to happen now, then I'll do it."

"I'm ready."

Something about her, one of the only other people in this city as committed to finding Elina as I am, deciding she is done wallowing in grief steels my spine. I take a few more deep breaths and tell myself that I am done being upset, done falling into a black hole of terror and anguish. I will find her, I will bring her home, and I will make her mine, *in eterno*.

"Let's do it," I say. Excitement and love fills Ethan's eyes. I'm impressed that he was able to hold his opinions to himself and let Sarah stand on her own. I wouldn't have listened to him either way, this is and should be Sarah's decision, but I'm surprised nonetheless.

Sarah and Ethan stayed here last night, and plan to for the foreseeable future, they want to be here in case there is any news, so my loft seems the perfect place to turn her. I lead them into the guest room, already prepared for vampire guests with a large comfortable bed, ensuite bath, luxurious linens, and most importantly, no windows.

Not only will this transform Sarah into a predator of the night, but draining her completely will give me more power, more strength. The enhanced senses that accompany the blood of a dying heartbeat are addictive to a vampire. We don't even discuss it with other vampires because we do not want to encourage feeding until death. I am excited, though, because I will be able to use them for the hunt that is coming.

"Sarah, what has Ethan told you about the turning process?" I question her as I lay her back onto the duvet.

She sighs. "Nothing. He has never done it to anyone and he says he doesn't remember."

"Don't worry, I will explain everything. The process of turning someone can feel quite intimate and, more often than not, vampires feel bound to their sire because of it. You will have a thread of me. This process will bind us more closely together as a family." I breathe in deeply, preparing to explain the simple process that will no doubt be awkward. "Feeding is often accompanied by sex, as you may already know." She blushes a deep crimson, her entire face alight and I chuckle. "This process will not feel much different, and because of that, a certain amount of...arousal is not unusual, but trust that it is simply biological and nothing more. Have you ever fed from Ethan?"

"No. No blood sharing. I'm afraid of the enthrall and didn't want to feel like I'm losing myself in him, obeying him."

"Ok, well, I apologize since you don't know, but the process involves you feeding from me while I feed from you. That's the intimate part of it. It is a pleasurable process. I will open my arm for you, and you will drink from me while I drink from your neck. I will continue to drink until your heart slows and eventually stops. You will continue to drink until you lose consciousness. After, you will be dead. Tomorrow, at moon-rise, you will rise as Ethan does, and be a member of *Sanguine Nocturnus*. You will be a member of my personal household as a sireling of mine. The only other member of my household is Jack. I haven't turned anyone since before we came into power here."

I pause and watch her. It's a lot of information—life ending information. Heavy, important information. She seems to be considering everything I have shared.

"I'm ready. Tell me what to do."

Ethan climbs onto the bed next to her and holds her hand, supporting her. I give him a nod of approval.

"Lie down on the bed, on your side, facing Ethan." God, this is so awkward. "I am going to lie behind you, close enough to reach your neck. You will drink from me and I, you. Just like that." I slide into the bed behind her, close but not touching her. This is awkward enough without my erection, that will be appearing soon, poking her. It's not even sexual, it's pleasure and adrenaline.

I extend my fangs and bite into my arm letting the blood flow freely. I put my wrist to her lips and feel her first tentative pulls against my flesh. Biting into her neck, I suck deeply and flood my body with her fresh blood. The pull of my blood out of my body, and the flow of hers back into mine, is so intimate I feel overwhelmed with emotion. I can't wait until Elina is in my arms this way.

I watch Ethan and Sarah as they make eye contact, forcing their love through their connection, knowing this is the right choice for them. I am thrumming with energy, power flooding my veins as Sarah's heart rate slows, her body pulling all the available blood inward in an attempt to preserve her life. Her pull against my wrist begins to fade before stopping all together.

Ethan sighs and closes his eyes, pained. I can imagine the pain he is feeling as he watches his beloved slip into unconsciousness, knowing her life will soon fade altogether.

There is very little blood flowing through her now, her heart beating so slowly, trying to force every remaining drop of blood through her body, trying to fight death.

She gives one twitch, then another

Her heart thumps. Once. Twice.

And then it stops. Everything goes still.

"It is done."

"Thank you," Ethan whispers as I exit the room, shutting the door behind me.

Sending a summons into my bond with Jack, I wait for him to show up. Our bond isn't quite that literal—it's not a magic telephone—but he will feel it. Like static in his mind. He will know I am calling to him. He doesn't have to come, but he will. I never summon him.

I send a single word, via text—

loft.

It isn't even 5 minutes later and there is a knock at my door.

"Come in, Jack."

"What's up, brother? You called?" He has a very serious, concerned look on his face.

"Elina has been taken. It's been 36 hours and we haven't seen or heard a single thing that can help us locate her. I didn't want to call in reinforcements until I knew I couldn't handle it alone. Now, I am calling on you."

He stops moving, surprise on his face. At that exact moment, Ethan comes into the room.

"Hey, I heard a knock-" He also freezes. In a single heartbeat Jack is crouched down in front of me, growling, low and aggressive. I lay a hand on his shoulder. He instantly straightens.

"Jack, this is Ethan. Ethan, Jack. Ethan is one of Elina's best friends. He's engaged to Sarah, from the bar. Sarah is in the guest room, turning."

"I haven't seen you all summer and now that you summon me, there is another vampire here, someone is in the process of turning, and your girlfriend is *missing*. What the hell, Bash? Am I suddenly not in your inner circle?" He sounds hurt, rightfully so. It's been me and Jack for a really long time. I didn't want to build myself an army like so many vampires do. I do not have any interest in turning a bunch of soldier slaves. Jack is my best friend and I seem to have abandoned him for a new family I am creating.

"It's been me and you for decades, and suddenly you're playing house, building your own little family, and I don't even get a warning. An invitation?"

"Fuck, Jack. I'm sorry. You're right. I didn't want to admit I needed help. Please help me, help us, find her. There will be time for the rest later."

"Of course, brother, but you owe me one *hell* of an explanation later."

I spot Ethan in the back watching wearily, unsure if he should leave or not.

"Hey, man. It's nice to meet you, even under these awful circumstances." Ethan extends his hand to Jack, a peace offering, and hopefully a way to diffuse the uncomfortable tension in the room.

"Hey." He takes Ethan's hand and squeezes it, based on the slight wrinkling around Ethan's eyes, quite tightly. I roll my eyes. *Yes, Jack, you're still my number one.*

"Alright, lay out the facts, Bash. I need to figure out how I can help." I give him a quick recap of the last 2 days, which only takes a few minutes because we have absolutely nothing to go on.

"Here's what I need you to do, Bash. Ethan will stay here and guard Sarah, since she is still down. You will walk the Quarter in a grid and see if you can catch even a hint of Elina anywhere. She has to be in the city so we will start with the most likely location. Who are your allies in the court?"

"Lessa, Gia, Minnie, and Aurora. Mother, obviously.

Michael and Kellan. Amelia from Uptown, Celina from the Treme, and Samson."

"Have Michael, Kellan, Samson, Amelia, and Celina do the same walk through their respective districts. No one will pay them any attention, they're *governaturno*. Have your cousins check out Mid-City and Bywater. In groups of 2, like they are out for a stroll. Bywater belongs to Talia, so it seems like another likely spot. I am going underground. I'll listen and watch, and try to discover if anyone anywhere is talking about this, and what they are saying."

My anxiety immediately lessens, knowing we have come up with some sort of plan. I should have called Jack yesterday. He's always been far more military and strategically minded than I am on any given day.

"Thank you, Jack. Let's go. Ethan, I'll be back before sunrise."

CHAPTER 24
ELINA

Four more meals. The same.

The darkness. The same.

Drip.

Drip.

Drip.

What day is it? Is it day or is it night?

Find me, Bash. Find me. Find me.

I sleep in short, fitful naps.

I lay on the cold stone floor and let silent tears run down my cheeks.

I stand and walk the perimeter of the room. Stone walls. A single door.

Not a sliver of light.

I sleep.

Bright light bursts against my eyelids. I am temporarily blinded. I shield my eyes looking toward the source and find that the door is open, a tall body, silhouetted in the harsh brightness, behind it.

"Bash?" I croak, my throat dry and unused.

A cruel laugh.

"Of course it isn't Bash, you fool."

I'm thrown into a memory- *"Seriously, Bash? A fucking* human *child? Out in Pirate's Alley, on a Sunday night? What the* actual fuck *is wrong with you."*

I gasp. "Talia?"

"Time to wake up, little human," she says, her voice as sweet as poison. "Much to do today." More people stream into the room. There is another prickle on my neck and everything goes dark once more.

CHAPTER 25
BASH

Starting at one end of the French Quarter, I walk every single street and check every single alley. I touch and smell every surface. I find nothing.

Fuck.

FUCK!

I lash out and strike the crumbling brick wall surrounding someone's home. It tips sideways and lands in a pile of rubble, leaving a hole in their perimeter. The fresh blood of life is feeding me and I am stronger than usual.

Entering my apartment right before sunrise, I find Minnie and Gia sitting in the living room with Ethan. This meeting seems to have gone better than the one with Jack. They are discussing Sarah and Elina when I walk in.

"Bash!" They come and give me a quick hug. "We were worried you wouldn't make it home in time. We were only here for like 10 minutes or whatever, but we have to get to our rest. Listen, a few minutes ago in the Bywater, on Chartres St., where the tracks meet the docks, we smelled something."

"Was it Elina?" I ask, hope infusing my voice.

"It smelled like her, a little diluted, I guess? I've never smelled her separate from you," Gia replies.

"Wait," I run into my room and grab something from the laundry. I hand it to Gia. "Like this?"

"Yeah, that was definitely it. It was her—her smell, at least. It wasn't fresh, like it had been a few hours, but it was definitely her. There were a few different vamps with her and I think I smelled Talia," Gia says after smelling the shirt.

"We can't be sure, there were quite a few different people, but I think it was her. It was the same, a few hours old." Minnie adds.

That scheming traitor. She is a member of this court and one of my oldest friends. Well, not friend.

"I'm going to kill her." My voice is deadly lethal. Even my cousins, who I wouldn't ever consider harming, take a few steps back. The look on my face must be absolutely feral.

"Listen, we have to go, the sun is rising, but tomorrow night, we will find her." They leave as soon as they finish talking.

Reluctantly, I go to rest. This morning, I am angry and resentful that the sun is forcing me to my bed. I need to find her. I *will* find her. The time for sadness is past. We have a clue and I will extinguish anyone that gets between me and her. I will burn this city to the ground and pull her from the ashes before I allow us to be kept apart any longer.

When I rise on Sunday night, it is with a renewed determination. I refuse to allow her to be separated from me any longer. However, before I can even begin formulating a plan, I have to get to Sarah. Her first evening rise will be difficult and confusing. Stepping out of my bedroom, I approach the guest room and listen at the door. I don't want to startle her but there is the off chance that she will not immediately recognize Ethan and think he is a threat. Her instincts will be wild at first.

I hear rustling around that I assume is Ethan and I knock lightly on the door.

"Ethan? It's Bash. I need to come in for Sarah."

"Come in." It's Sarah. That is unexpected. But I am pleased to hear her. It means she rose and is cognizant.

"Good night, Sarah. How are you feeling?" I ask her, standing in the doorway. As her sire, the chances of her attacking me are virtually zero, but I don't know where her thoughts are as far as her transformation and Ethan are concerned.

She sits up in bed and watches me carefully. She smells the air in the room, no doubt trying to glean any information about my intentions from it. I take a few steps closer and she hisses, her instincts taking over before she figures out who I am.

"Bash." She says it matter of factly, stating a piece of information into the world.

I smile at her, sheathing my fangs so I don't appear threatening. "Can you feel me in your head?" I give a little push down our sire bond. When I do, she looks immediately startled by it.

Before I get to ask her anymore questions, she asks me one of her own. "Elina?" I do not yet have an answer for her, but maybe I have a plan.

"While you rested, we got some news about her potential whereabouts. Her scent was found in the Bywater district. Talia's district. Before we can do anything though, we have to take you to be presented to Marcus, register you, and feed you.

Your transformation won't be complete until you have fed for the first time"

Walking in tandem with her, we cut through the *cattedrale*, directly to Mother's office.

Pushing her door open, we realize she is meeting with some of her own sirelings, hopefully with news. "Good evening, Mother. I have news, but first, I need to present Sarah to Marcus." I gesture to her.

Mother regards me with interest before looking Sarah over appraisingly. "On Friday, you were to present your 'everything' to Marcus, and 2 days later you appear in my office with another woman you wish to present?" I can't tell if she is making a joke or honestly believes that I would move on from Elina in only a few days of her being missing.

Sarah hisses beside me, likely as offended by what my mother said as I am. Mother snaps her fangs at Sarah before looking at me questioningly. "Why is your companion expressing hostility toward me? This is a downgrade, to be sure." This comment does not help.

"Mother, please. First, Sarah is not a replacement for Elina. She is betrothed. Second, she is only an hour old—you're lucky she hasn't attacked you yet." She appears surprised by this revelation, tapping her fingers on her desk and tilting her head slightly in contemplation. "Third, she is Elina's family. She is here because she wants to help."

"Your sireling? Fascinating. It's been at least a hundred years since you deemed anyone worthy of joining you. Elina really has done a number on you. Marcus is in the receiving hall, let's go." As the *governaturno* of the French Quarter, I, technically, fall under her jurisdiction, and therefore, when I create a sireling, I must present them to mother first. She will present them to Marcus.

"There is a prohibition on turning, as you may well remember, Sebastien," she reminds me as we follow behind her, her heels clicking rhythmically on the tiles.

"I have not forgotten. I am sure you can convince Marcus considering the circumstances." The circumstances in question being his refusal to provide any help to my search, as well as the splintering of his court.

She doesn't miss a step. "I'm sure."

"Do you seek to create your own army since I won't give you mine?" Marcus asks me, fury lacing his tone once my mother has finished her presentation.

"Of course not, Re. This is a special circumstance. She has a vested interest in finding Elina, and she is betrothed to a vampire. She is also the only vampire I have ever created within Ville de Sang. I hardly have an army—I do not believe Sarah to be an army of one."

"I forbid the creation of new vampires, after *you* asked me. Now, you defy my order in my own court. You are the heir, Bash, you can't do whatever you want." He's frustrated with me, and in this case, I can't really blame him but it was necessary.

"Re, please allow me to register her so we can continue hunting for Elina." He looks around the room at the few members of the court who are loitering.

"Everyone out!" He orders them and they retreat hastily. "Give me whatever information you have on the hunt for Elina while you fill out Sarah's paperwork."

"I actually have an update I have not even gotten a chance to give Mother yet. Yesterday, right at dawn, Gia and Minnie caught Elina's scent in the Bywater district. Near the docks."

"That's Talia's domain. Have you told her yet?"

"We have not, considering her scent was found alongside Elina's."

My mother gasps and Marcus looks at me, digesting this information. "I assume Talia is a suspect then?"

"She always was. In April, she threatened Elina's life. She called it a promise. It was the first time I had ever brought Elina here. After she left, Talia snuck into my apartment, seemingly to seduce me, and when I turned her down, she promised Elina would not survive this." I watch him absorb this information, for any indication that he believes me.

"Talia is a member of the Court. This is quite the accusation."

"I'm not accusing anyone of anything. I am gathering information and trying to find the woman I love. I will deal with the rest later."

"Well, I won't. I may be unwilling to sacrifice my soldiers for this but I am not without sympathy. And if this situation can be cleared up by having a discussion with Talia, then a meeting is in order." The anger in his tone makes me momentarily concerned about what this conversation will consist of, until I remember she may have stolen the only woman I have ever loved right from under me. "Now, to the other matter. Sarah, step forward. I would speak to you."

Sarah steps up to my side. I can feel her shaking inconspicuously, from fear or nerves, I don't know.

"Bow," I whisper under my breath, loud enough for Sarah to hear but sounding like an exhale to the rest of the room. Sarah executes a small but respectable bow.

"Sarah, did you ask Sebastien to turn you?"

"Yes."

"Did you do so willingly or were you enthrall?"

"Yes, willingly."

The answers to these questions don't affect anything. Vampires are added to the ranks of the *Sanguine Nocturnus* under duress all the time. It is not nearly as pleasant as the way Sarah was turned.

"Do you understand that you are now a part of Sebastien's household and under the jurisdiction of Vespera, the *governaturno* of the French Quarter?"

"Yes."

"You may sign the register. Bash, I will be bringing Talia in for questioning. Should I send for you when she arrives?"

"Yes, please do." I feel the sting of anger, deep in my chest, burning for release.

Recounting the events for Ethan and Jack later that evening, I feel like we have finally made a sliver of progress. Now, we wait. Marcus should have Talia in his grip soon and I can only hope his interrogation yields some sort of information for our search.

CHAPTER 26
ELINA

When I awake this time, I catch a glimpse of the night sky outside the window. A window? I fling myself from the bed I'm in and run to it.

Discovering that it is locked tight, I peer out, hoping to at least orient myself so I know where I am. Looking out the window, I recognize St. Phillip Street. The old Hotel Royal. I'm only a block away from The Velvet Tomb. Right under the nose of the Blood Ravens, we are only three or so blocks away from the cathedral. Taking in the room I'm in, I find I have much more comfortable accommodations than I did before. There is a small table with a chair in the corner. A fireplace, though there is no fire. A large canopy bed laid with soft, pale-pink linens and a mountain of pillows. I am in an old New Orleans-style mansion, the sort that is appropriate for the Garden District.

Grabbing a chair from beside the small table, I swing it as hard as I can into the glass of the window. The window rattles in its frame but does not shatter—it does not even crack.

Raising a brow, I stare at it contemplatively. *What kind of magical window...?*

Behind one of the three doors, I find an empty closet. The next door does not open when I twist the knob and pull. Behind the third door is an ensuite bathroom, containing a large walk-in shower, an antique freestanding clawfoot tub, and a vanity laid with various products.

I also find a duffel bag in the bathroom containing clothing. None of it belongs to me but all of it is my size. Finding a pair of black leggings and a pullover sweatshirt, I decide to take a shower and get out of the clothes I have been wearing for—I don't know how long honestly. Too long.

I allow myself a few moments of weakness in the shower where I cry, pity for my situation saturating me as surely as the water does. After that though, I refuse to give into the temptation to wallow in a pit of self doubt, not wanting my captors to win by letting my own fear defeat me.

Once I am clean and wearing the clothes supplied for me, I sit at the small table and wait. Surely something is going to happen, they brought me from the dark stone room for a reason, now I need to find out why.

It doesn't take long before the locked door clicks open and a man I recognize from the bar walks in, with a woman walking behind him.

"*Crepulsculien*, good evening." He addresses me by the name he has called me multiple times in the bar. It sounds almost like twilight but not quite. I resist the urge to ask him about the nickname.

"Good evening," is my only answer. I've seen enough movies, and read enough books, to know there is no point in asking what I am doing here or who he is. He is going to tell me what he wants to tell me in due time, without me prompting.

I watch him wearily from the table I am sitting at, waiting.

He also appears to be waiting. After a few more moments the woman says, "Hi Elina, my name is Genevieve and this is Claudel. I believe you may have met him before, in the Velvet Tomb?" Looking around Claudel, I see that she is quite diminutive—shorter than me by a few inches—has a short blond bob haircut, and is wearing a designer-looking pant suit of deepest red. She is stunning, standing there, and very much a vampire based on her preternatural stillness and otherworldly beauty.

"Um, hi," I start, unsure of the kindness in her tone considering where the last few days have been spent. "What day is it?" I ask, hoping her kindness extends to a little bit of information.

"It's Sunday night," Claudel answers my query. I was taken on Friday afternoon so just over two days ago. Bash, Sarah, and Ethan must be going out of their minds looking for me. Where would they even start? "Come, you are to eat and be presented."

"Presented? To whom?"

"Come," he says as he spins on his heel and leaves the room, Genevieve beckoning me to follow.

Walking down the hall, I study the lush furnishings and antique rugs covering the floors. The walls have no exterior windows, so I have no idea where I am in the house. I pass door after door in the hallway, nothing setting one apart from the last.

"It's a little confusing at first but you'll catch on quickly which rooms to steer clear of." Genevieve tells me as I walk. *Why would I need to know which doors are safe or not?*

We make our way down a large, dark wood carved staircase and I can make out the front door from here. I am under no illusions that I could escape before Claudel or Genevieve would catch me. There is a beautiful floral arrangement on the hall table. Dark wood floors and paneling topped with baroque style wallpaper. The curtains on this floor are open to reveal the night outside. My soul cries knowing the people I love are out there looking for me, they have to be, and I am over here in this mansion, walking around like there's nothing wrong with this situation.

The house is richly furnished and appointed, but feels oddly juxtaposed to the fact that I am a hostage here.

"Through here." Genevieve gestures to a set of large, closed doors as Claudel pushes them open to reveal a dining room. The table is laden with various foods. It makes my eyes prickle with tears thinking back to when Bash presented me with a similarly large spread of food on our second date. I am the only person in the room besides my vampire escorts. "Sit wherever you want, and eat. When you're done, we will go meet with him."

"With who?" I ask, but by the time I glance around, I realize I am alone. I go straight to the windows that line one wall of the room, and learn they face out to a courtyard completely surrounded on all sides by the rest of the house. The courtyard has people walking all around—10 or 15 people coming and going. Vampires coming and going. I could try and get out but, like the front door, I know I won't get far. Defeated, I walk back over to the table and sit at the head, grabbing the closest food to me and bringing it to my mouth.

I don't even taste the food in front of me, I eat simply to fuel my body for whatever horror awaits me. I fill up on rice and beans, roasted chicken, and peas. I wash it down with fresh water from the jug on the table. Sitting back, full of food and nerves, I wait.

My survival depends on keeping myself calm. I might die anyway, but it won't be because I was reckless and made a stupid decision. The best thing I can do is to take in whatever information is given to me and try to glean what it might imply.

The doors are opened a while later and Claudel appears again, without Genevieve this time. "Come now." I stand and follow him from the room, my hands sweating and my heart beating a rough rhythm in my chest.

I follow behind him, my head held high. I may be quiet and compliant, but I refuse to look afraid or weak. I know every vampire in this place can hear my erratic heart but I will not let it affect the way I show myself to them. We make a left turn in the corridor after a bit of a walk and I, now, know we are walking around the courtyard perimeter.

We approach a pair of almost identical wooden double-doors as the dining room, and stop. Claudel turns to me. "Once we enter, you are the least important thing in the room, act accordingly. You will exhibit the appropriate respect to Prince Nicolas." Prince Nicolas? I've never heard that name before. Who are these vampires and why am I here? Claudel has a French accent—could this be the Shadow King's court? Or what remains of it?

We step into the room before I can ask any questions.

"Sir, may I present, Elina Girard, as requested," Claudel introduces me, bending deeply at the waist in reverence to the man sitting on the raised dais in a large wooden chair, his throne, I presume. He has pale hair, pulled back into a ponytail at the nape of his neck, and hazel eyes that are currently boring into me. He appears relaxed on this throne, in a black suit, with his jacket hanging open over a crisp, white shirt.

I incline my head slightly, refusing to bow. He is not my prince. *Principe* Sebastien Malvani is the only prince I recognize, and only because I'm madly in love with him, his family has not earned my respect.

"Elina, good evening. It is so lovely to finally meet you. I have been watching you, of course, but seeing you in my home? *Tout est parfait!*" I do not respond. I don't believe he even requires a response. I watch him carefully, looking for anything to tell me who he is or why he has brought me here. "You are much more subdued than I expected. Having watched you for some time, as well as reports from Claudel and others, I expected a much more exuberant response to being a guest in my home."

"A guest? I was not invited, nor was I permitted to decline. You might call me a guest but we both know I am a prisoner." I inject as much venom into my tone as I can. Claudel hisses beside me before grabbing the back of my neck and pushing me to my knees on the floor.

"Sir, the disrespect from the *crepuscule* whore exceeds reasonable bounds. Should I remove her?" Claudel asks his prince.

I stare directly into the eyes of the monster pretending to be a man sitting in front of me. He stares back, a slow feline smile spreading across his face, his fangs on full display. He waves his hand at Claudel who immediately releases me.

"No, Claudel. I would like to hear what she has to say to me. We are to be bound after all."

I feel my mouth drop open in shock. I twist my face into a sneer. "Over my dead fucking body will I bind myself to you."

"You'll come around." With those ominously final words, he throws me a wink and Claudel drags me to my feet. "Take her to her room. Maybe by tomorrow tonight she will be more willing to discuss our future."

Tomorrow night? How long does he intend to keep me here? I allow Claudel to pull me down the hallway and up the stairs. Pushing my bedroom door open, he shoves me in, causing me to fall to my knees. Slamming the door behind me, I hear him turn his key in the lock.

I lie on the floor and cry until my body gives out and I fall asleep.

CHAPTER 27
BASH

KNOCK. KNOCK.

At 8 o'clock, on Monday night, I am sitting in my apartment surrounded by the family I am creating for myself, taking for myself. Sarah and Ethan sit together on one end of the sofa, wrapped in each other's arms, and Jack sits at the other end, relaxed but weary.

"Come in," I call out and the door swings open. My cousin Lucian stands there, looking severe, as usual. "What is it?" I sit up straighter in my chair and every face turns in his direction.

"Re Marcus has requested you come to his office in an hour. He has something to share with you."

"Is it about Elina?"

He looks at me full of disdain and turns to leave.

"9 o'clock Sebastien. Don't be late." His voice is rife with loathing.

"What do you think he wants?" Jack asks when we are alone again. Sarah and Ethan are both watching me now.

"I'm not sure. Maybe he has Talia? He said he would call for me when he got her. Maybe he has news? I'm not sure."

"Do we need to come with you?" Sarah asks from her spot on the sofa.

"No, not this time. You can walk over with me though, all of you, you need to feed anyway."

"What's with that guy?" Sarah says, while we walk.

"Who? Lucian?" I give her a sidelong glance.

"Yes, he seems like a grade-A asshole. What's his deal?"

"Lucian is my cousin, he's a Malvani. He's actually my mother's cousin. He's been a trusted member of the court for Marcus for almost 700 years..." I try to explain the complicated relationships—it's as frustrating to me as it is to him. "He's older than me but not a direct threat to Marcus's seat. When Marcus took Ville de Sang, Lucian was...slighted. Marcus uses Lucian as his executioner and enforcer, but passed him over for any meaningful position within the court. He's been pretty pissed about it for a long time. There is a lot of bad blood between us."

Walking into the *cattedrale* a half hour later, my family following me, we go to the blood bar, finding warm blood on tap. Jack doesn't usually drink this way, but right now, we need to present a united front to the court—my sirelings and friends at my back. There is a power struggle happening with Marcus, and I need to show the court that I am as strong as I have always been.

Sarah gets us all tumblers full of warm blood and we sit at a table in the middle of the room. Others who are seated around watch us interestedly, curiosity warring with loyalty to Marcus. There isn't any reason for it, Marcus and I are fine.

I may be vulnerable right now, but I'm still going to Re one day and I will be respected.

Walking into Marcus's office right at 9, I am greeted by the seated man looking very like the cat who ate the canary, a small knowing smirk on his face. Mother sits in the corner exuding pleasure.

"Uncle," I greet him, inclining my head respectfully. "Any news? You two look suspicious today."

"*Nipote*." He reaches out and grasps my hands in greeting. "I do. Talia is below. She was brought in this morning before sunrise. Hopefully we will get a lead on Elina tonight. I was hoping you would like to visit her with me. I'm certain it will be fun attempting to get some answers from her." The raw, exposed excitement in his face while discussing torturing someone who has been in his court for a century gives me pause. Is it anger toward her for her potential part in this plot or is it bloodlust, plain and simple?

"Yes, of course I will come down. Has she said anything yet?"

"Lucian has been with her tonight but we haven't heard anything yet." My mother chimes in from her seat.

If Lucian is doing the interrogation, it is going to be difficult for her. Lucian and I may not get along as much in the last few decades, but he is by far the most ruthless investigator we have and is completely devoted to Marcus.

Marcus leads the way to the interrogation room below the altar of the church. It's not a large space, but large enough to allow Marcus, mother, and I to spread out around the wide, raised stone table on which Talia is stretched out, Lucian standing at her side. The walls and floor are also stone, the room looking as though it has been in this place since the *cattedrale* was built, maybe longer. Large lighted torches line the interior, there doesn't seem to be any electricity. There are puddles of blood gathered around the base of the stones below Talia.

Lucian has already started working on her, it seems. My cousin has pulled a steel table alongside himself, on which lay various metal tools, knives, and pliers. They are all covered in wet blood, slowly dripping onto the floor. I've known Talia for a hundred years, and yet, looking upon her in this place, knowing she had a hand in Elina's kidnapping, I feel nothing. No remorse. No concern.

"Talia," Marcus says, drawing her name out long and sensuously, like a lover. "It appears you have gotten yourself into quite the predicament." Marcus's face turns to a sneer of disgust as he scents the air and smells the blood. It's all a game meant to confuse her.

"Re Marcus, please, why am I here? Please. Please." She sobs to him, fear and panic increasing her respirations, nostrils flaring and eyes widened almost comically. Her entire body pleading with Marcus to help her.

"Dear Talia, I believe you know why you are here. Don't you?" She visibly flinches at the malice in his tone. "I think you do. Why don't you save us more of this unpleasantness and tell us what we want to know."

He doesn't specify what we are looking for. That's his way. He won't ask her outright for information about Elina's kidnapping yet, there is a chance she will reveal more of her hand than she plans to, and provide Marcus with information he wasn't even looking for. While I watch quietly, Lucian, ever the executioner, picks up a silver dagger from the table and quickly, effectively, drives it into her exposed sternum. It won't extinguish her but a silver dagger to the heart will make her wish it did.

The scream that erupts from Talia shatters the quiet of the room. Blood surges around the edges of the knife as she screams and screams, thrashing in a futile attempt to escape the blade. As quickly as he plunged it through her bone and heart, he pulls it out. The blood spurts, then stops as her body knits back together, her healing kicking in.

It's why torturing vampires is so effective—the pain lingers long after the wounds heal, and he can wound her over and over, with no reprieve, until she breaks.

"Marcus." Sobbing, she attempts to catch her breath. "Marcus, please. Re, Re, what do you want? What have I done?"

"You tell us what you did, you traitor!" My mother screams from her spot on the other side of the space. Marcus gives a small wave of his hand, an order to my mother to calm down.

"I..." Her voice breaks. "I didn't do anything. I didn't!"

This time, Lucian draws a vile of blood from his pocket and dribbles it kindly across her lips. She gasps in surprise before opening her mouth fully. It will heal her quicker, ease her pain. I watch, silent, to gauge what he intends to do. Her fangs descend, desperate to feed, the need for blood overriding everything else. Her face becomes the face of a bloodthirsty monster while she tries to capture as much blood as possible.

Lucian grabs her chin, holding her in place. In a strike as fast as a cobra, he discards the vial and grabs the pliers. Grabbing hold of one her fangs, he yanks it directly from her mouth, blood beginning to pour down her chin. Her scream is visceral, wet, primal. She whimpers and sobs.

Fang removal is incredibly painful, but more than that, it's removing something that is intrinsically vampire. Talia can't feed without fangs. Fang removal is permanent—it's a torture reserved for traitors of the vampire race, and a surprising choice for the torture relating to a missing human. Eyeing Marcus, I wonder how far he has authorized this to go.

I can't help but wonder if this is a show specifically for me, or if he knows something he isn't sharing.

"Re, I've been beside you for a hundred years." Her breath hitches before she adds, "I love you." Blood continues to pour from her mouth, it will heal but it will take a little longer. It is already beginning to slow. Marcus approaches the table and extends a hand. Gently, so gently, he runs his fingers down the side of her face. She leans into the touch, whimpering softly.

He roughly grabs her cheeks. "Then tell us what you did and this will all end." I am again struck by the violence and indifference in his tone, his stance.

"I'm sorry, please, I'm sorry. Re Marcus, I don't know what they want. They just wanted the girl." Finally, something.

Stepping forward, I walk over to the table and peer down at her. "Who, Talia? Who wanted her?"

Trembling, she says quietly, *"L'Empire des Ombres Nocturnes*, I think. They were French. I'm sorry. She doesn't matter! She's just a human!" Talia tells us, frantically, sounding as though she is trying to convince us of what she is already convinced of.

Marcus growls loudly and grabs her neck, squeezing mercilessly. "She may be a human, Talia, but the *Ombres Nocturnes* are our enemies and you were plotting against this kingdom with them." He spits at her. "You are a traitor to me." With that, he turns, walking out of the room, slamming the door behind him.

"You have made a grave mistake. Enjoy the fruits of that decision." I pause leaning over her for a moment, her eyes searching for a hint of sympathy where she will find none. I weigh the options on the metal table before picking up a shining knife.

"See, the thing is, Talia, you shouldn't make promises you can't keep. I will find her and she will rise to power beside me." She flinches at my words. "Unfortunately, you picked the wrong side." I jam the knife into the junction of her neck and shoulder, knowing the tip of the knife has sunk into her heart, blood pooling in her collarbone. Leaving through the door following Marcus, mother behind me, I hear Talia start screaming before the door closes, silence in its wake.

Storming into Marcus's office, I throw myself into a chair in front of his desk and rub my hands over my face.

"Fuck!" I yell. "What the fuck are we going to do now? Besides the fact that the Shadows have Elina, there are fucking *Shadows* in the city, infiltrating the court. You can't extinguish her yet, we need to know who she met, where, and if she knows where they are." I am so utterly furious that I can hardly breathe.

"We will find her, Bash. Now, we have a starting point, we have to find this nest of Frenchmen and flush them out. We will destroy them all. Lucian will extract any additional information. You may go." I am dismissed. My world has completely fallen apart, my family is being threatened, we are potentially on the *verge of war* with the Devereaux, and I am being *dismissed*.

"Uncle," I start, my voice tight, "you will let me know once you know any sliver of information. I will hunt them myself." I take my leave, quickly. I need to report back to my family so we can decide our next steps. War may be at our doorstep and Elina will not be the first casualty.

CHAPTER 28

ELINA

O n Monday night, I sit quietly at my small table waiting for something, anything, to happen. After I was sent to my room like a naughty child yesterday, I inspected this space from top to bottom. There is nothing anywhere that tells me what they want or helps me in any way. I pulled more clothes from the bag, today is another pair of black leggings and a solid black t-shirt. There are no socks or shoes. This choice feels intentional, like they are disarming me.

A knock on the door interrupts my internal reflection. Genevieve pushes the door open before slipping a key into her pocket. Today, she is wearing a flowing dress in a shade of pale green which brings out the green color of her hazel eyes.

"Good evening, Elina. So good to find that you are well," she says to me pleasantly. I narrow my eyes at her. Claudel makes it obvious what he is thinking and what he thinks of me, he is not a fan of mine. Genevieve confuses me, she was missing from the meeting with Nicolas yesterday, so I don't know what role she even occupies in this place. "How did you sleep?" she asks as she sits opposite me.

"Fine," I answer her wearily. We sit together, both of us watching the other, her head tilted curiously as she studies me.

"I'm sure you have a lot of questions, would you like to ask them before you meet with Nic?"

"Who are you?" I ask her, bluntly.

She gives me a small smile. "I'm Genevieve Laurent. Nic is my brother. We are a branch of the Devereaux family." She pauses theatrically, waiting for me to digest and react to the knowledge that she is, somehow, a member of the Shadow Kingdom. "Not closely enough related to hold the court," her eyes shine with excitement, "but close enough to have a tenuous claim. That's where you come in."

I give her a slow blink. "What do you mean?"

"That's why Nic wants you, so he can take over the family." She says that like it should mean something to me.

"I don't know what you're talking about," I tell her, hoping she will elaborate and fill in some of the gaps. Something is going on but I can't figure out what it is.

She gives me a conspiratorial smile, like we are sharing a joke but I missed the punchline. "That's ok, Elina. You'll figure it out. Anything else?"

"Yes, actually. What's the deal with the windows?"

She laughs, the sound light and breezy. "Magic, of course," she says, matter-of-factly, as though magic is something I deal with on a daily basis, vampires aside. She studies my face before laughing again, more boisterously this time. "It's reinforced. Like the bullet-proof kind. Nothing magical at all but made to withstand humans. A vampire could break it though. And in case you were wondering, they are reflective on the outside so no one can see in."

She shrugs before standing and beckoning me to follow her from the room.

What the hell is happening?

A short time later, I have eaten and been pushed through the double wooden doors again. This time, when I am presented to Nicolas, I have Genevieve at my side.

"Sister! Wonderful to see you as always," Nicolas greets Genevieve. He doesn't even spare me a glance, his eyes passing over me.

Genevieve moves forward, bending into a bow, then extending her hands, she kisses both of his cheeks, warmly murmuring to him, "*Bonjour* Prince." Moving back to my side, we stand and wait. I do not bow.

"No show of respect for your prince, Elina?" He asks me. He doesn't appear to be angry, only inquisitive.

"You aren't my prince," I say insolently. "I do not intend to bow to you. Not now. Not ever."

His jaw tightens the smallest amount. He seems to be working really hard to not rise to my disrespect of his perceived title.

Steepling his fingers under his chin, he asks me, "And do you intend to consent to the *Le Lien Eternel*?"

"I do not. I am well aware that the *Legame di Sangue* can not be completed without me agreeing and I do not agree. Ever."

Slamming his hand down onto the arm of his chair, cracking the wood, his temper finally explodes. "It is not *Legame di Sangue*," he mocks, the Italian words accompanied with a thick fake accent. "It is *Le Lien Eternel* and you will consent. Eventually." Standing, he approaches me. I fight the urge to shrink away from him.

I stand up straight and steel my spine in the face of his anger and approach. Reaching out, he drops to a knee in front of me. I watch him carefully as he grabs my hand. His touch is gentle, caressing even.

"Elina, give me time to prove to you why binding to me is right. That I deserve your affections. Please?"

"No." I pull my hand from his. "You are holding me hostage in this mansion full of vampires, I am being manhandled by your servants, and locked in my room all day. Why would I want to even speak to you?"

"I apologize for Claudel, he is...enthusiastic in his loyalty to me. You are only locked in for your safety; it is too dangerous for you to roam around the house. I do not wish any harm to come to you. You are precious to me." He reaches up to touch my face, his fingertips outstretched, from his place on his knee. I jerk my head away from him. "I don't want you to be a prisoner here. I want you to walk these halls with your head held high as my princess. I want you to want to be here. I want you beside me, why can't you understand that?"

I stare into his hazel eyes, the same color as Genevieve's and try and find the trick. There has to be a trick but... Last week, I was considering turning for the love of my life, spending eternity bound to Bash. Now there is a different vampire prince kneeling before me, begging for my affection. I don't speak, don't offer a response.

His eager, hopeful face falls. He stands to his full height, an inch or two shorter than Bash.

"Sister, please escort our guest back to her room. Perhaps, she would like to get a book from the library on the way? Elina, we will have dinner together tomorrow." I feel the blood drain from my face. *Is this a threat?* He laughs, easily. "You will eat dinner; I will sit and enjoy your company. You are not in danger."

Somehow, Nicolas's assurance of my safety made me feel anything but. He's more like a wolf in sheep's clothing than any other vampire I have ever met. His feigned kindness, his outreach in an attempt to sway me strikes me as genuine. But coupled with my prisoner-status and how quick he is to anger? I can't help but feel uneasy.

"Should we stop by the library? We have the most accurate archive available in Ville de Sang. I know *las chiens de sang* have an archive, but it's full of artifice." Genevieve floats peacefully along the hallway lined with doors, until she reaches one at the end. Throwing the door wide, she exclaims with a flourish, "If there's something you want to know, there's no better place to be."

I stand awestruck in the doorway of, what Nicolas called, the library. It's a room on one corner of the house, a full wall of glass windows that wrap around hung with heavy, red, velvet drapes. The floors are covered with different rugs in various sizes and patterns, covering the worn and shiny wood. There are a few desks with large comfortable chairs pulled up to them, and a large fireplace with leather armchairs in front. The bookshelves tower above me as I move further into the large room, with ladders spread around for the high shelves. There is heavy dark wood everywhere, and easily a couple thousand books. I wouldn't even know where to begin.

Smiling at me, Genevieve gestures to the left side of the library. "These are the complete records of the Devereaux family—you may find something interesting over there. Beyond that, there is a section on the other vampire families of Europe, including the Malvanis. Closer to the windows, there are fiction books with a large collection of vampire novels." She points to the selection, some with half-naked men on the covers. "Please. Feel free to browse. I'll wait for you outside to escort you back when you're done." She drifts out of the room, shutting the door behind her.

Wandering over to the European vampire section, I follow the alphabetized tomes until I find 'Malvani' and pull it from the shelf. I put it on one of the desks. Heading back, I look for a book similar to the one I found in the Malvani archive—a family tree. I want to find out exactly where Genevieve and Nicolas fit. Once I find a book that looks promising, I also pick a romance to bring back with me.

"Genevieve, I'm ready," I call out and she pops her head through the door almost immediately.

Settled back in my gilded prison cell, I sit at my little table and lay the books in front of me. First, I peruse the Malvani book. I don't find much else than what I already knew from their own archives. The slant is obvious—history is written by the victors—but the story is basically the same. The Devereaux books report that the Blood Ravens invaded Ville de Sang because they are *las chiens de sang*—blood dogs—driven by their bloodlust, and incapable of humanity.

All vampires give that impression to me, even those I care about. My goodwill only extends so far.

Cracking open the old spine of a Devereaux family reference, I flip the pages, skimming for anything useful. Locating the family tree, I study the lines connecting everyone. I find an entry explaining the bloodlines, but still, no mention of Nicolas.

Noe and Sabine Devereaux sired 2 children, Seraphine and Timothee. Timothee was bound to Violette in 1604 and they sired a set of twins, Noe and Jean; Jean was killed before his vampire nature matured and Noe went on to bind himself to Delphine in 1864. Their bond led to a single sireling, a son, Ezekiel. Ezekiel served as sovereign to the *L'Empire des Ombres Nocturnes* before he was extinguished when Ville De Sang was captured by the Italians through invasion in 2006. Ezekiel was bound to an unknown woman and sired a lost child in the years leading up to the *Guerra de Sang*. The exact birthdate of the child is unknown, though it is believed to have been between 2002 and 2005. The child, presumed to be a daughter, is believed to have been lost during the war. There is no further information. In the absence of a Devereaux heir, *L'Empire des Ombres Nocturnes* attempted to rebuild through Saraphine's bloodline.

A lost child?

I sit back in my chair and consider the young vampire who was swallowed up in the bloodshed, as were so many casualties in this turf war. I'm sad for the little family that disappeared. That little baby was the heir and now there is a gaping hole where they would have stood. Suddenly, the room feels too small, too closed up. An entire family line snuffed out so easily, she could have been in this house, maybe in this chair. Leaning in close to study the family tree, I locate Sabine's two children, Seraphine and Timothee, but Seraphine's family is missing. Maybe there is another page.

Flipping a few pages further, I find what I am looking for— tucked in the corner of the page is a smaller tree where Seraphine's line is stretched out. Seraphine was bound to Mathis and they sired Genevieve, but not the one I met, I don't think. This Genevieve was an only child. She was bound to Armand, and together, they sired Genevieve and Nicolas. *Found them.* They are distant, second cousins, maybe once removed, of the lost child. A far off branch of the family making a play for the throne. A throne that hasn't existed in twenty-five years. There aren't any other options though, the Guerra de Sang resulted in the extinguishing of almost the entire Devereaux line.

Rubbing my temples, a loud sigh echoing in the space, I rest my head on the back of the chair and wish I were anywhere but here. I don't want to be a part of this.

I can't figure out why I am.

Exasperated by this line of research, and feeling apathetic about the whole thing, I grab the romance I brought with me and curl up by the window to read.

Tomorrow is a new day, with new challenges.

In my heart, I hope that Bash is getting close. But in my head, I know this is far from over.

CHAPTER 29
ELINA

The moon rises over the French Quarter on Tuesday night, the night walkers starting to roam around the streets below my window. Laughter filters up to me from the street as I watch longingly. I would even walk the streets alone tonight if I could figure out how to escape this prison.

Bash, where are you?

A light tap comes from the locked door, startling me out of my reverie and reminding me that I have a dinner date. Whoever is at the door appears to be waiting for me to grant them entry, odd since no one else has extended the courtesy.

"Come in?" I tell them, ending on a questioning note. A small woman, dressed in an old-style servants uniform comes in, her brown hair pinned neatly below a white cap, and a long black dress with white apron on top.

She smiles shyly. I have no way of knowing for sure, but she seems like a human. "Hello miss. I have a gown for you— for dinner with Prince Nicolas." Blushing, she looks down at the floor.

The interactions I have had in this house have been a bizarre mix of fearful reverence, love, and flirtation. I am completely confused about half of the time and this is no different.

"I'm Elina." I extend a hand to her, maybe that will give me a clue as to whether she is human or not. She moves her hands behind her back and inclines her head respectfully.

"Of course, I know who you are. I'm Cindy, your chambermaid. I will lay your clothing here on the bed and go start the shower for you." Chambermaid? Have I been sent back in time to this place? I get the feeling the Shadow Kingdom wishes for a time when the ruling class had unlimited power and everyone bowed at their feet. Well, I won't be playing along with this performance.

Walking over to inspect the clothes Cindy brought, I find a floor-length, blood-red gown, red-soled stilettos, and a jeweled choker, not unlike the one I gave to Sarah when I began wearing my pendant. I snort in derision. *Yeah, right.* Undressing, I walk into the bathroom and straight into the shower, without even looking at Cindy.

After showering, I go into the closet to find the small cache of clothes I have and pull on the jeans I was wearing when I was taken, and my black t-shirt that says 'Team Werewolf' across the chest. The only shoes available to me are the heels that came with the dinner dress, so barefoot it is.

Sauntering out of the closet, confidently and in my own clothes, I watch in satisfaction as Cindy gasps at my outfit.

"Oh no, Miss Elina, you must wear the outfit that Prince Nicolas has sent for you. It would offend him otherwise." Her voice trembles a little and I wonder if she will be punished for my inability to follow directions. I will make it clear that I am in-charge of myself, if nothing else is within my control.

I roll my eyes at her, putting my hands on my hips. "No, I

don't think I will, Cindy. Nicky doesn't like it? He can go fuck himself."

There is another gasp from Cindy before she scurries out of the room, and I follow. I still can't tell if she's enthralled or terrified.

I find Claudel leaning against the wall outside my door, stoic and silent. If he has an opinion on my outfit, the only indication is a slight tightening of his jaw before he jerks his head in silent order for me to follow.

This time, we stop in front of a different set of doors than the ones I have dined behind the last two days. Shoving the doors open, Claudel bows slightly toward the interior of the room before introducing me. "Miss Elina Girard, sir." I can't see around him but I assume he's speaking to Nicolas.

He steps aside and there he is—Nicolas—seated on a balcony overlooking the courtyard which is empty tonight. He sits at an intimate table, set for two, with comfortable looking plush chairs. There are fairy lights twinkling overhead and long climbing vines hanging all over the railings for the balconies that surround the courtyard. It's a dream setting for a dinner date, if only the company wasn't my prison warden.

We watch each other in silence. Tonight, he has opted for deep green suit pants, polished black shoes, and a button down black shirt with a very subtle green stripe. The first two buttons are unbuttoned. He seems to have gone for a casually effortless look, but he is too stiff, too perfectly put together for the sentiment to resonate.

He peruses my own outfit, looking from the top of my head, my hair a little scraggly from lack of care, to the tips of my bare feet. He clearly disapproves, based on his frown and narrowing of his eyes, but he doesn't comment.

Standing, he indicates for me to take my seat as a small army of servants, all dressed in identical suits, crowd onto the balcony. A glass of red wine is placed down in front of me followed by a plate of boeuf bourguignon that smells rich and herbaceous, buttery mashed potatoes, and asparagus. The warm comfort of the French meal makes my mouth water and my stomach gives a loud rumble. A small smile of triumph tilts up the corner of Nicolas's mouth. The table, the food, the setting, it all feels too intimate, too close to something real.

In front of Nicolas sits a glass of wine to match mine, as well as a tumbler of dark liquid which I assume is his dinner. *I wonder who it is.*

"Good evening, Elina. How are you today?" Nicolas's voice comes out rough, as though he hasn't spoken much this evening.

"I'm fine." I take a sip of my wine, unwilling to give him any details and not interested in asking him the same. Pleasantries are not something I've given much thought to during my stay here. I am simply a prisoner—why pretend otherwise?.

"Did the dress not fit?" He looks inquisitive, like he is genuinely curious as to why I wouldn't wear his gift. "I thought it would go beautifully with your skin—and those bright blue eyes. Did you know my grandmother, Seraphine, had eyes almost exactly like yours? So striking." In the back of my mind, I wonder briefly about his comment. Where did I get my eyes from? I don't know enough about any of my ancestors to answer my question.

"I would not know, I didn't even try it on. I have no interest in extravagant gifts. You know—" I take a bite of the rich meat, chewing for a moment before continuing, "—comparing me to your old dead grandma isn't exactly a flattering comparison for a courtship." I punctuate my words with a little wave of my fork and stare at him boldly as I respond to his flattery.

A laugh explodes out of him. I can't tell if he thinks I'm entertaining, or if people usually don't respond to him with biting remarks, but whatever it is, it has momentarily disarmed him, a lock of blond hair falling across his forehead. It makes him look younger, the laughter making him less harsh.

I try and fail to hide a smile, and the one I get in return from him is blinding. It unsettles me in a way I was not prepared for. I school my features into something serious, and watch him relax back in his chair. He takes a sip from his tumbler of blood, and I can barely see the sharp tips of his fangs everytime he brings the glass to his lips.

The food is delicious and we eat in silence. It's not uncomfortable, but not pleasant either—we're like two strangers forced to sit together when the cafe runs out of tables.

I wonder if he will break the silence. I am not afraid of him but the desire to know his motives is bothering me. Why did he bring me here?

What am I missing?

"Elina, have you given any more thought to *Le lien eternel?*" he asks me casually, as though it's not one of the most important things I will ever consider. "I won't even ask you to turn if you don't want to. You can produce Devereaux heirs as a human."

"Laurent," I respond.

"What?"

"They wouldn't be Devereaux heirs, they would be Laurent," I tell him, defiance in my tone. "You aren't a Devereaux—that name came from the male line. You have your father's name. I saw the family tree."

"Ah, but won't they?" He smirks at me, a secretive smirk, one I very much don't like. I saw the bloodlines, he isn't a Devereaux. Noe and Sabine Devereaux gave that name to their children, and when Seraphina was bound to Mathis, her line became Laurent.

"I'm tired of these games, Nicolas. Say what you want plainly or let me go."

"I want you, dear Elina." He stares at me intently. "But for tonight, you may go. I would implore you to consider my offer though, my kindness only holds out for so long."

When we arrive back at my room, there is a file lying on top of the books I left open on the desk. In bold black letters, across the front, it says 'Baby Girl Devereaux'. Opening the file slowly, I look at the first page and gasp.

CHAPTER 30
BASH

Wednesday's moon-rise is as bleak and hopeless as everyday since Elina disappeared. It's been 6 nights since I saw her and held her in my arms. I find, with every passing day, that I am more desperate to know she is safe, and so angry at what remains of the Devereaux clan, that I feel that I could tear their ancestral lands apart with my bare hands if it would bring Elina back to me.

My family fears for me—for my sanity and for the safety of those around me—with every passing minute that stretches between Elina and myself.

Talia, despite Lucian's best efforts, yielded nothing other than a first name and a description. Claudel. The same man, based on how Talia described him, that called Elina *'crepulsculien'* in the bar a few weeks ago. With only that to go on, we have hit dead end after dead end. We have searched and inquired of everyone we can think of, who may know *something,* and we haven't so much as found a single clue or piece of evidence that leads us to anything.

I refuse to believe that the woman I love does not exist in the world any longer. Talia could also not expand on what the Frenchman wanted with Elina, just that he was willing to do whatever was necessary to get his hands on her.

Sarah and Ethan wander around, despondent and sad. Jack is always trying to come up with a plan. My other allies are combing the streets, night after night. I don't wander too far from the cathedral in case something happens and I need to be found.

It's been almost a week and we are no closer to finding her than we were when she first went missing. I feel in my heart, in my mind, in my body, that if my sun were gone, the world would dim.

As fearful as I may be for what I must do tonight, I can not avoid it any longer. Throwing on pants of black denim, and a black cotton t-shirt, I check myself in the mirror, steeling myself for tonight. I run my fingers through my hair and lean close, trying to identify some evidence of the last week, some physical toll on my body. I look the same as I have since I was 29. I wish there were dark circles under my eyes, or creases in my brow to belie my concern, my stress.

"Sarah?" I call out as I exit my bedroom.

"Yeah, Bash, what's up?" She walks into the room wearing the same sadness I have seen everyday since her and Ethan began staying here.

I rub a hand over my face. "We have to go to Little Woods tonight. It's time to talk to Celeste." She has no way to reach me, but I know she must be sick with worry. I was hoping we would find Elina quickly and I wouldn't have to return to her place – not after telling her on Friday that her only grand-daughter was missing..

Sarah's eyes widen with concern and apprehension, but

she nods her head in understanding all the same. "Ok. Let me get my stuff and we can head over."

A short trip later, we pull up to the curb in front of the house—Ethan and Sarah tumbling out of the backseat, and me climbing out of the passenger seat, the driver settles in to wait. Marching up the front steps, ahead of Ethan and I, Sarah raises her hand to knock. Before she can make contact, Celeste rips the door open. This trip is long overdue, evidenced by the deep lines of worry Celeste wears on her face and her hunched shoulders. The same signs I studied my own reflection for.

"Sarah? Where's Elina? What is going on?" I watch Sarah and she opens her mouth to speak and no words come out.

"Mrs. Girard, Elina is missing. She has been since Friday, when I asked if you'd seen her." Tears immediately begin streaking down her face, her breath coming out in short gasps. "I would have come back sooner, but I was hoping we would have news before we did. But unfortunately, we don't. We don't know anything. We have done everything we can. We aren't giving up, I will never give up. But right now, we don't have anything to go on."

Clutching her apron tightly, fear and concern written in her very bones, she beckons us forward. "You had better come inside and tell me what's going on. Maybe I can—I don't know what I can do but..." she trails off, turning to go into the house.

Sarah looks at me, mouth hanging open. "Bash, Celeste just invited us in. I mean, she's known me my entire life and may not realize what happened yet, but she *knows* you and Ethan are vamps."

"Well, we better not keep her waiting then."

A few minutes later, we are sitting in the parlor with Celeste, her clutching a teacup that is more whiskey than tea, and the rest of us sipping whiskey from tumbler glasses. Ethan is looking around, studying the house while he tries to appear more comfortable than he feels.

"You have a lovely home, Mrs. Girard," He tells her and she smiles at him.

She watches me, uneasily, as I also take-in her home. The older house is soaked in all things Elina. The smell of Elina's skin is so concentrated here that, although it's been a week since she was in this place, the scent almost brings me to my knees with need. The wooden fireplace that hasn't burned wood in so long it no longer smells of fire and ash. The mantle is covered in evidence of a childhood steeped in summers in the sprinkler and snaggle-toothed smiles in school pictures. A lifetime of laughter and sadness exists within these walls. It's humbling to me and makes me miss the castle I grew up in, more than that though, it makes me miss the home I am creating within Elina. Her heart, her light, have been sucked from my life.

"Sebastien, tell me what happened to my granddaughter," she asks of me, imploringly, wanting comfort or information. I'm not certain, but what I do know is she deserves our honesty. So, I recant everything that has happened in the last 6 nights and where we are now. I try to keep emotion from taking over my story, I don't want her to know how absolutely destroyed I am by Elina's absence, nor do I want her to think I have abandoned hope. I have not. I refuse to let them win. I refuse to allow doubt to seep into me, I will not let anyone take her from me, forever.

Celeste stands from her perch in the flowered armchair she occupies. She sets her teacup on the table and walks out of the room, wordlessly. I make eye contact with Sarah, tilting my head in question. She shrugs, confused like me.

Celeste re-enters the room, a large envelope—the kind that holds legal documents—in her hand. "I've never shared this with anyone, not even Elina. If she finds out I knew all this time, I doubt she will ever forgive me." She pulls a folder from the envelope, and across the front, in bold letters, are the words 'Baby Girl Devereaux'.

Laying it on the table and flipping it open, I look down at the contents and freeze momentarily. Sarah inhales audibly next to me. Ethan leans over, muttering, "Wha-what is it?" None of us replies.

"So, you see, I couldn't tell her," Celeste whispers into the silence of the room.

"Celeste, are you serious? You've known who her father was all this time?" Sarah almost yells at the older woman, stunned by this revelation.

"He was dead! He died before even Elina's mother. She was destroyed when she found out her husband was dead, then she died within days of him. Both lost in the *Guerra de Sang*. Elina didn't remember him after a few months. There was no reason to bring it all up and open the wound left by her mother's death." She sucks in breath, trying to figure out how to say what she means without seeming to make excuses. "He was dead—there was no point."

Does she know what happens to half-vampire, hybrid babies? She can't know. "She just turned 29, do you know what will happen soon, Celeste? Did Ezekiel ever tell you what would happen to his vampire-hybrid daughter?" I stare her down.

"Nothing happens, she never knew him, so she doesn't have to know he was a vampire. She will live her life, as a human," she answers, tilting her chin up in defiance.

"*Of course something happens!*" I explode at her. "She's a vampire, Celeste, and you've not told her. I guess you didn't know the implications but this is *insane*. She will be a vampire within the next year. It will happen, her vampire genes don't disappear because her father isn't here to help her."

"She won't be a vampire unless you turn her into one! I was trying to keep her away from you so this wouldn't happen. Now they have her and she loves you." She takes a broken breath, her fisted hands trembling in her lap. "I was trying to protect her."

"Celeste, you don't understand. She's a hybrid. Her father was the King and a bloodline vampire. She would have become a vampire even if she never met me," I try to explain. "When bloodline children are around 30, they mature into vampires. All on their own. Not telling her means she's completely unprepared for what *is* going to happen, and soon."

CHAPTER 31
ELINA

W*hat the hell is this?* I stare down at the birth certificate.

Elianore Celeste Girard Devereaux
   Father: Ezekiel Devereaux
   Mother: Nora Cecilia Girard
   Date of Birth: August 17, 2003

This is obviously me but I've never seen this document before in my life. I was born at home, my birth wasn't registered with the *L'Empire des Ombres Nocturnes*—there would have been no reason to. This disputes that fact, and a lot of other facts I know about myself. My maman took *Le lien eternel* with the King of Ville de Sang? I sit in stunned silence, trying to absorb all of this. None of it makes any sense.

If grand-mere knew, why had she lied to me for twenty-five years? If she didn't know, how had maman kept this a secret?

Based on what Sebastien told me, the only way they could have conceived is if they were bound.

I'm suddenly struck by a thought. *Oh my god—I'm a bloodline vampire.* Bash explained this to me, he did this himself. Any time now, I should begin the transformation to vampire. It was never a matter of me choosing this life or consenting to turn for Bash. It was my destiny the entire time.

I take stock of what I know. I'm in love with Sebastien and I want to bind with him. I am being held captive by a branch of my own family. Nicolas, my cousin, is attempting to get me to bind with him. Based on the information from Sebastien, I can't inherit since I am a woman, but it seems that Nicolas needs me for something. That something *definitely* has to do with who I am.

I mourn the fact that I finally learned who my father was, and, in the same instant, learned he is dead. I am just as much an orphan as I was before I had this information.

Everything has changed, and yet, nothing has changed at all. I was going to give up my humanity and walk in the moonlight for Bash, this proves to me that it was the right choice.

I know that Nicolas has left this information for me, but why? What does he want me to do with it? My trust for him has plummeted to a new low, he knew something earth shattering about me which he weaponized for himself.

Knocking on my door to get the attention of whomever is lurking out there, I yell, "I need to see Nicolas." I hope someone's out there to hear me.

The lock clicks and the door pushes open, revealing a vampire I don't recognize.

"I would like to see Nicolas," I repeat.

"No. He has already dismissed you for the evening."

"Please just ask if I can meet with him?" I all but beg in front of this stranger.

He pulls the door shut in my face and the tumbler of the lock falls back into place.

Dammit!

Lying flat on my back on the bed, I stare up at the coffered ceiling, reflecting on the absurdity of this situation. I'm Ezekiel Devereaux's daughter, a princess, if they are still observing the laws. I am being treated as a hostile intruder in this place when I suspect it should belong to me. I have to be weary and watch my back, I do not have friends in this court.

The door swings open and the stranger stands there. "Nicolas says you may attend him, he is in his private quarters," he tells me with an obvious smirk on his face. Gripping my arm tightly, he hauls me down the hall and around the corner. We enter into a new wing, past the staircase, and there are significantly less doors lining this walkway.

He pauses in front of a set of double doors. "Here you go. He's inside. Good luck." He laughs joylessly as he pivots and stands at the end of the hall.

I grab the handle, twisting it, and push the door open. As soon as my eyes take in the scene awaiting me, I understand what the vampire found so entertaining. There is a very large —larger than I've ever seen—bed in the center of the spacious room. It is heavy and dark. Surrounding it are chairs and lounges full of naked people. In the center of the bed is Nicolas, completely naked and lost in the body of a lithe woman who is sitting astride him, gyrating her hips. I can't see her face but I can hear her exclamations of pleasure. There are five other naked women in the bed in various states of sex—touching, kissing, performing sex acts on one another.

I am immediately sickened by what is happening.

"Hello, Elina. What brings you to visit this evening? Care to join?" Nicolas pats the bed beside him before returning his hand to the hips of the woman he is engaged with. He watches me, his eyes boring into mine before he flips her over onto all fours and begins to roughly pound into her body, her cries drowning out all the other noise coming from the bed.

Nicolas's movements become faster and more erratic as he stares straight into my eyes before he cries out and collapses across the woman's back. I tear my gaze away, feeling sick from the sight.

Nicolas begins to laugh. "See something you like, princess, or did you have another reason for stopping by?" His words and mocking tone are such a sharp contrast to the man who was clearly trying to charm me earlier. Him calling me princess cuts deep, knowing the truth.

"I-uh-I wanted to talk about the folder, but clearly I have interrupted–" I wave my hand in the general direction of the debauchery "–something."

He laughs again, this time with more mirth and less cruelty. "We are vampires, Elina. This is what we do. It's our nature. It will be yours soon." His fangs drop from his gums and he roughly bites the neck of the woman he is still buried inside. I still can not see her face, but he sucks deeply and she shudders under his touch.

Pulling his teeth from her neck and climbing off the bed, he comes to stand in front of me, his cock jutting out ahead of him. He gives me a slow perusal, lingering on my lips, before looking into my eyes, and I refuse to give into his trap by looking at his naked body.

"Come with me, we will talk in my office." Wrapping his arm around my shoulder, he steers me toward a door in the corner. I glance back over our shoulders and spy Cindy climb off the bed before making eye contact with me. Guilt and shame color her cheeks.

Another person who is not a friend in this mansion-prison.

The inside of Nicolas's office is exactly what I expect from the psychopathic vampire I have come to understand he is. The paintings lining the dark walls are macabre in their scenes of bloody massacre, fang-toothed cherubs, and monsters dragging people into the pit. The floors are covered with plush black carpeting, an aggressively large mahogany desk fills the entire center of the room, and dark leather chairs and a sofa create a sitting area near a black marble fireplace. There are floor to 10-foot tall, floor-to-ceiling windows behind his desk, overlooking the courtyard, showing vampires milling around. There is a tall painting above the fireplace showing Nicolas and Genevieve on a country estate, rolling hills behind them, a dog at their feet. They are wearing regency era clothing, a small tiara on Genevieve's head. The moon hangs heavy behind them.

I tear my eyes away. While I quickly surveyed the office, Nicolas has gotten dressed in dark wash, distressed, denim jeans, with a grey evening shirt he leaves unbuttoned. Sitting behind the grandiose desk, he gestures for me to take one of the chairs stationed in front of it. I sit, my bare feet sinking into the carpet.

"So, Elina, I guess you saw the gift I left for you?"

The word 'gift' is such a manipulation of the circumstances. Leaving me a file that exposes every lie that I have been told my entire life, a file that changes everything I know about myself and my future, was never about kindness or benevolence, it was always about control. He is parsing information out to me as he sees fit, on his own timeline to keep control of me and our situation.

"I did," I agree genially. It's too soon to reveal how unsettled I am. How unsteady he has made me. "How did you know about this?"

"Do you think that half-breeds are not recorded in the archives, like everyone else? Ezekiel decided to take a human to bed," he says *human* with a level of hatred I was unprepared for, "but that doesn't mean we wouldn't keep track of the offspring. Just because your sire was extinguished like the coward he was, doesn't mean we would never find you."

What does he have against human-vampire bonds?

"I meant, the archives say the child was lost in the war. Why? If you, and the rest of the remaining Devereaux, knew this whole time, why does it say that?"

"Because, *crepulsculien*, the rest of them don't know. Only Genevieve and I do, we discovered the record of your birth while looking through old paperwork buried in Ezekiel's belongings. It wasn't widely known who your mother was, or your name, so it was easy to lose you." He watches me, his eyes alight with an emotion I don't quite recognize. Almost excitement, but more frenzied somehow, like he has it all figured out and the rest of us are along for the ride.

Tilting my head, I ask him, "What is that? *Crepulsculien*? Claudel has been calling me that."

"It means 'twilighter' essentially, there isn't a translation. It means someone born between. Not of the light. Not of the night. A hybrid." He says the last bit bitingly as though I am somehow to blame for my own existence. "Now, back to the question at hand. Bond with me. You will be queen. It seems you have a thing for vampire princes." He laughs at me as I narrow my eyes.

"No." I will not bow to him and I will not tie my eternity to him.

"Have it your way." He snaps his fingers and two large vampires in black suits enter the room behind me. One of them grabs me by my arms and lifts me to my feet while the other one tilts my head back and bites me, pain searing through my body at the point of contact. I whimper as my knees buckle and he rears his head back, screaming, as the man holding me tightens his grips on my arms, yelling to figure out what happened to his partner.

"What the hell is happening?" I hear Nicolas exclaim as he rounds the desk. I can feel the blood running down my neck.

"The bitch has some sort of protection charm," the man on the floor tells them as he claws at his throat. Nicolas turns his hazel eyes on me, and drops them to my neck, to the pendant hanging between my breasts.

"Oh, he loves you does he? He must, to have gotten you such strong protection. We will get rid of that." He calls out for someone named Stephan who enters the room through the door from the sex room. "Remove that from her," he tells him pointing at my neck.

I thrash and scream in the iron grip of the vampire holding me. "No, don't touch me! I'll take it off, don't touch it!" I twist to try and get free. The man holding me only tightens his hold until I feel bones grinding under my skin, threatening to break under the pressure.

Stephan reaches up and grabs the pendant in his fist, yanking until the chain gives way.

"Toss it in the fireplace," comes Nicolas's order.

"No, Nicolas, please. Just give it to me," I beg.

"Sorry, little princess." He rubs his hand down my cheek. "The time for you to ask me for anything has passed, you had your chance. Take her away." Turning from me, he walks over to his desk and relaxes back into his chair.

The man holding me drags me from the room, defeat starting to truly infiltrate my soul. Instead of taking me back to what I have come to accept as my room, I am taken to a different room altogether. The type of room that makes me shudder in fear, my heart races as we enter and a trickle of sweat runs down my back.

It looks too much like the dungeon room at the Velvet Tomb. It's not so archaic—no stone walls but the cement floor with the drain, the shackles mounted into the concrete, and the metallic smell in the air all indicate exactly what this room is. Fear strikes me, raw and electric, and I feel my heart rate accelerate, forcing the blood through my veins and drawing the attention of the vampires in the room.

My captor pulls me toward the wall, circling my ankles and wrist in manacles, holding me in place, at the mercy of the four vampires, three men and one woman, who line the room. I'm trembling and can feel my knees weakening. I sag against my restraints, too tired and overwhelmed to stand any longer.

"The prince says you belong to us, little princess." All of the vamps gathered in the room bare their teeth at me, long fangs on display, as they stalk toward me slowly. Tears stream down my cheeks even as I try to remain strong.

"Let's see if you have any signs of your vampire nature peeking through, shall we? Jon, how should we test her?"

A man I have never come across before, with long black hair and disheveled clothing, hisses and responds, "I think we should test her healing first." My breath comes in sharp pants, my adrenaline kicking into high gear.

Snapping his finger and smiling, my captor tells him, "Excellent idea. Perfect. Bring me the scalpel. That's a good place to start."

The lone woman in the room steps forward, holding a scalpel, handle side out, handing it to my would-be torturer.

"Please, please, help me. Don't do this. It was a mistake. Please." I'm disgusted at myself for begging for anything from these vamps but the danger in this room is so potent, I can almost feel it coating my skin.

"Watch it, princess. I will gag you if you can't be quiet. Nobody likes a mouthy woman." He grabs the back of my hair and pulls my head back, bringing the blade to my collarbone and sliding the sharp edge against my skin. I feel the knife slide into my flesh, can feel it in my teeth, like nails on a chalkboard. The blood drips down my chest and into the valley of my breasts.

The vampires press closer at the sight of the spilled blood, and he starts to lap at my skin like a dog.

"Marc! Fucking share." Jon scolds my torturer, Marc.

"Shut the fuck up. You'll get your turn." He rubs his fingers into the blood, smearing it around before he rips my shirt down the middle, exposing more tender flesh to his hands. Grabbing my thigh and pushing my legs apart, he steps into the space he created, pressing his body against me. I'm trembling, praying he doesn't press his advantage and cross from torturer to heinous monster.

"So pure and clean. Not a scar, a tattoo, or a blemish. So creamy," he tells me as he rubs his bloody hands across my stomach. "Look at that, Anna, the blood is already stopping. I can't tell if it's fast healing or a shallow cut. We better try again." Backing away from me, he beckons her closer.

This time Anna approaches, almost wearily. She looks curious but not as blatant in her excitement or enjoyment of the torture happening in front of her.

I try again. "Anna, you don't have to do this. I'm like you, don't let these men do this. Help me, please, don't do this."

Quicker than I can even follow, Anna snaps her arm out and cuts my arm deeply from elbow to wrist, the blood flowing freely and dripping onto the floor. She leans forward and licks the blood from my arm and sucks at the artery which is spilling my life onto the concrete.

"You idiot! She's a human, you're going to kill her. Fuck!"

Marc pushes her out of the way as he wraps his hand tightly around the wound. The edges of my vision begin to blur and I feel my head drop against the cold wall behind me. "Fuck, Nicolas is going to kill us. He needs—" I don't hear anything else as I lose consciousness.

CHAPTER 32
ELINA

I awake in my bed, in the Hotel Royal, on a steamy evening, a week after I was taken. My arm has a thick bandage from wrist to elbow and I am more exhausted than I have ever been. I roll over and find a glass of water and two pills neatly set out on my bedside table. Picking them up I smell them and immediately know one of them is iron and the other is most likely a multivitamin for the blood loss. My arm is significantly less sore than I would expect, considering my last memory is my life's blood pouring out of me, and a punctured artery spurting blood across the concrete floor before it dribbled into the drain.

I begin unraveling the white gauze, layer by layer, and under what seems like a hundred wrappings, I find a slim puckered scar where a huge cut should be. The remnants of stitches on the padding are evidence that I was cared for, but they aren't holding the wound together. It's as though the wound is weeks, even months old, rather than just a day.

Is the transformation beginning? Bash and I never went into the details of how it happens, the settling in of vampirism for bloodline vampires, only that it happens around this age. Marc mentioned increased healing as a possible indicator, so that may actually be true. It sends a thrill through me, knowing that while I may be human and relatively helpless in this place of the blood-drinkers, I am not without some supernatural assistance.

Feeling bolstered by some good news, I swallow down the pills, drink the entire glass of water, and step into the shower. Once I'm clean, I wander into the closet and find the leggings and t-shirt combo I am most fond of. I settle in to wait for whatever fresh hell Nicky has dreamed up for me tonight. If I thought my cortisol levels were spiking at the Velvet Tomb, it's nothing compared to the nonstop adrenaline of being in this house.

Sitting at my little table, in the room that has become my only source of calm and safety, however false, I stare at the information laid out before me. I can't help but wonder who doctored me. Was Nicolas as mad as Jon and Marc believed he would be? Who was the fourth man who never approached me or participated in the torture? What happens now? I don't know exactly what Nicolas wants with me but I feel certain he does not want me to die. Or perhaps, he can't kill me.

A quick rap on the door brings me out of my musings. I rise to approach the door as it swings open and reveals Genevieve on the other side, tonight very casual in a rose colored tank top, jeans, and nude stilettos. She smiles widely, like we are the best of friends, and loops her arm through mine.

"Sister! You look so well! I heard about the unfortunate accident you had yesterday—Anna has been sufficiently chastened, don't you worry!" She tells me in a sing-song voice.

It is so contradictory to the events she is referring to, where I was tortured and drained. "Nic can't wait for dinner tonight, and this time, he said I can join you. Won't that be so wonderful?" I study her earnest face, trying to figure out her role, again. I know she is Nicolas's sister but how does she fit into the story.

She begins hauling me toward the door, her heels tap tap tap down the hallway while I walk silently in my bare feet. Last night, I was chained to a dungeon wall being bled and fed on, and tonight I am arm-in-arm with my warden's sister, off to, I am sure, an over the top dinner where I am the only one who eats.

I don't know how the pieces fit together yet but I am starting to line them up. Nicolas is pathologic—he jumps from one extreme to the other, being charming and attempting to disarm me one minute, mocking me and throwing me to the wolves the next. Genevieve, I think, is here to befriend me, to earn some trust and make me feel like I have an ally. I will not be convinced to operate against my best interests in this place, and my best interest is getting the hell out of here as soon as possible.

I plead again. *Bash, please find me.* I send it like a prayer to whoever will listen.

Padding down the hallway, we pass door after door. My room is behind a door that is identical to a dozen others. Behind a door is the torture chamber I spent last evening in. I wonder briefly what is behind the others. Another identical door is cracked every so slightly, a sliver of light spilling into the windowless hallway, the raucous laughter tumbling through the crack feels out of place in this silent mansion. I try not to flinch at the sound.

Pausing in front of the last identical door in this wing, Genevieve grasps the large crystal knob and pushes the door open. She leads the way, and inside, I find a lounge of sorts. Old world charm, large comfy chairs, low lighting coming from chandeliers, the walls covered in tapestries of deep forest green and royal blue. It feels like a men's reception room in an old country manor—warm, inviting, and undeniably masculine. It smells richly of bergamot and brandy, mixing with the crackling fire. The room is almost stiflingly hot considering, it's only September and probably 80 degrees outside, but the fire really helps highlight the ambience Nicolas seems to be chasing.

Nicolas, himself, sits in an oversized leather chair with his feet propped on an upholstered ottoman, a glass of dark liquor in his hand. A table in the center of the room is laden with finger-foods: meats and cheeses, petit fours, small quiches, and glossy fruits.

Nicolas smiles at me, his wide confident grin does not betray any malice, and motions to the food. "Help yourself."

I've come to terms with this nightly feeding ritual and have resolved to eat whenever food is presented. I have taken to sleeping most of the day as I am expected to participate in vampire life in the evening. I am usually only offered food once a day, at moon-rise, so I eat when it is available. It's another means of control from Nicolas, but it's also necessary if I am going to help myself at all.

"I'm so pleased you ladies have joined me for dinner this evening. It is always lovely to have beauty at the dinner table." He sends a wolfish grin my way. He gives me whiplash, toggling between absolutely pathological behavior and this kind, charming host who seems to genuinely want to impress me.

I sit on the sofa adjacent to him while Genevieve perches on the arm of his chair, wine glass in hand. Neither of them have blood, currently, and there are no fangs on display tonight.

"Good evening, Nicolas." I incline my head in a mock bow, if only to push off the switch flipping that turns him feral. I'm not ready for what comes after the genial attitude, and I would like to finish eating.

He focuses on me, narrowing his eyes, assessing me. His gaze falls to my arm which should be red and angry, stitched closed, and finds a scar. His mouth tips up infinitesimally, with a contemplative smile, before he nods his head slightly. "Elina, I see that you're healing well from your ordeal yesterday. Anna went too far, I will apologize on her behalf, but she will also apologize." He claps his hand and the door opens.

In comes Anna, her shoulders folded inward as if in shame. Approaching Nicolas, she kneels at his feet and lays her head on his knee, in return he strokes her hair away from her face. "Go ahead, Anna."

She faces me, still on her knees. "Elina, I apologize for my rude and dangerous behavior yesterday." She says this with a tremble of sincerity in her voice, before glancing up at Nicolas, who gives her an accepting nod.

"Show her." She turns back to me at his command and gives me a teeth-baring grimace as I locate only one fang and a gaping hole where the other one is missing. I inhale a sharp breath and my eyes shoot to Nicolas's. Satisfied with his display, he taps her shoulder and she retreats from the room. "Elina, you look surprised. Did you know that the ultimate punishment for one of us is a fang extraction? It's incredibly painful and it will never grow back. It's very shameful. I can't believe anyone would expect anything less for the punishment of putting my betrothed in danger."

My mouth opens in surprise at his words, both the explanation of punishment, and him framing it as an attempt at protecting me when he was the one who put me in danger.

"Are you expecting me to thank you?" I ask him sassily. He can't possibly believe I would be grateful for this.

"Yes, Elina," he answers dryly, "I do. You should be grateful.

I will always protect you. You will come to know this. Your safety is of the utmost importance to me." I fight the urge to roll my eyes.

"Thanks, I guess." It grates at me to even say this, but I know I need to preserve his goodwill a little longer. Long enough to get through this meeting and get back to the relative safety of my room.

"Good," Nicolas purrs. "I knew you would appreciate what I am willing to do for you." Genevieve nods her head enthusiastically at his words, the crystal of her wine glass catching the light at the movement.

"He really is so protective, Elina. He is such a good man." She rubs his shoulder, possessively, and I tilt my head. Curious development, Genevieve seems to have some complex feelings about her brother-prince. "Nic, would you like to feed now? I can bring her in."

Her? He's intending to feed in front of me?

"Not yet, Gen," he responds, his voice dipped in honey and something darker. "Let's allow Elina to finish her food first. She isn't ready to feed together, and food is important for humans–" he gives me a disdainful glance "–and hybrids." More whiplash. *What is his problem with hybrids?*

"No, I'm finished." I stand, taking my plate, still half full, to the table and leave it there. Suddenly I am not as hungry as I thought. "I'll return to my room."

"Not yet, sit." When I don't move back to the sofa, he gives me an angry look. "SIT!" Startled by his outburst, I move back to my seat. "Good. Go ahead, Gen, bring her in." My hands tremble where they are placed in my lap.

Hearing the door open behind me, I turn and Amelie is walking in, her arm gripped by Marc. Her entire body is shaking, wrists circled by bruises. She also has a ring of bruises around her neck. She makes eye contact with me and her eyes widen—tears fill my own eyes at the sight of her. I cover my mouth to avoid crying out, hoping beyond hope that he only feeds and lets her go even though, I know in my heart, that isn't the case.

"Elina, I heard you had a bit of a problem with this worker at your place of employment. I believe a bit of a spat in regards to that Italian you're attached too." He looks at me for confirmation, which I refuse to give him. "I do not agree with the silliness of fighting over a man, there should never be a reason too. Honestly, any man worth fighting over wouldn't need to be fought for. Still, I will not allow anyone to insult you, my love."

I have no words for how insane this situation feels.

"I've already shown you today how far I am willing to go to protect you, but with this, I want to show you that I will also seek revenge on your behalf."

"I-I do not- Nicolas, please, I don't need revenge. Amelie is my friend." Tears are running down my face now.

Shaking his head, he smiles. "She *was* your friend, now she is not. You will be queen darling. Insulting you is insulting the throne you will sit on, and that is unacceptable." He almost manages to look sad as he says this, but the excited gleam in his eye gives too much away. Amelie stares at me, pleading with her eyes for me to do something. I wish I could.

"I'm so sorry, Amelie," I mutter as I look away. Her shoulders fall and tears begin to coat her cheeks.

Nicolas slowly stands and approaches her, the tears falling heavier now, her breath coming out in gasps and shudders. Grabbing a hand full of her hair tightly, he yanks her head back and she cries out.

"Apologize to her!" he snaps at her, turning her face to me.

"I- I- I'm sorry," she stutters through her sobs. "Please, I'm sorry. Let me go, I'm sorry."

"Should have thought about that before you insulted my love." Tipping his head back, his fangs descend and he plunges them roughly into her exposed neck. She screams out. Genevieve approaches and latches onto the other side of her neck and she starts to collapse into their collective hold. I watch through tear-filled eyes. A few short moments later, they both release her and she tumbles into a pile on the floor, discarded, now that she has served her purpose.

I fight wave after wave of nausea, before I fail and vomit my entire dinner onto the floor, heaving over and over until there is nothing left.

For the second time in as many days, my vision goes black and I lose consciousness. The last thing I hear is unhinged laughter.

CHAPTER 33

BASH

Every day that passes, it becomes easier to let defeat creep into my heart.

We spend every night scouring this wretched city and in 2 weeks, we have not found a single thing to indicate Elina is still in the city, or even still alive.

Sarah has withdrawn into herself and rarely speaks to us about anything but our next plan. A week ago, Rian called and let us know that Amelie hadn't been to work and no one is able to locate her.

"Amelie is missing, Bash," Sarah tells me as she hangs up the phone. It was Rian—I recognized her voice on the other end of the phone.

"What do you mean? Since when?" I ask. Jack looks at me questioningly. "Amelie is the waitress I was with the night I met Elina."

His eyes widen with recognition. "Seems you may be the target after all, Bash. That is definitely personal."

Ethan spends every night trying to draw Sarah out of her misery and encourage her to live in her immortality.

Jack strategizes with our allies and walks the streets of the French Quarter from dusk til dawn every night.

And me? I do everything in between. I search. I strategize. I plan. I have almost worn a path in the streets. I have stopped at the door of every house and business in the quarter. Everyone else mimics my movements in the other parts of the city. I try to lighten the mood. I lash out in fury and take my anger out on the streets. On more than one occasion, I have antagonized someone until we've come to trading blows, even Jack wasn't spared my wrath. Standing, our chests heaving, covered in blood, I finally gain some mental clarity.

Every French-speaking vampire in the city is seen as a potential suspect—too many have fallen by my own hand. There is no such thing as innocence when the other half of my soul is missing.

"Where is she?" I ask the tall man hanging from my outstretched arm by his neck.

"I- I don't- Sebastien, I have no idea," he says, sobbing through his words.

"Well, you have about thirty seconds to tell me anything you know about her disappearance before I rip your head off."

"I don't know who has her, I don't even know her!"

His words fuel the anger that is residing in my chest as I squeeze his throat, tighter and tighter. I feel blood start to seep between my fingers wrapped around his neck. Giving my arm a twist, I hear the thunk of his head landing next to my foot as his light flares before going out. Dropping his body, I draw my foot back and kick his severed head into the brick wall ahead of me.

It smashes hard and bounces, hitting the ground, blood splattering me.

We are falling apart without the glue for our family.

I know she is alive, she has to be. If she isn't, there is nothing left for me. I will find her, and if I don't, I will burn down every single building in this city until I know what happened to her.

Sometimes, I feel her like a phantom at my back, but when I turn—she's gone.

"Fuck. I wish I knew where to go from here," Jack speaks quietly as we walk the streets, listening for even a whisper of a clue.

It's the 5th night in a row we have started from the outside edges of the city and worked our way to the Velvet Tomb where we end the night in commiseration with a glass of whiskey. The City of Blood feels hushed, like a blanket has been thrown over it. The humans have retreated into their safe places—the increased presence of vampires walking around, searching and inquiring, has made everyone jumpy. It feels as though even the air in the French Quarter is full of angst, the very stones that hold up the city are aware that something is wrong. Zelie told her all those months ago, that her blood is in the land and she is a part of this place, and now, I find it a little easier to believe that's true.

Marcus has granted me a progressively larger army as the days wear on. He didn't want his soldiers involved, but once Talia told us who has Elina, he knew he could no longer wait on the side-lines. The French gaining a foothold in our territory is a threat to us all, even if we didn't know who she was at the time. He still won't allow me to pull people from their homes, or destroy the city, in my search but every day that passes is one day closer to me snapping and embracing the darkest parts of my nature.

Telling my family and the council that Elina is the lost daughter of Ezekiel Devereaux was the turning point.

I think back to the night as my feet walk down the familiar path, recalling the stunned faces of everyone in the room.

"Mother, Marcus, I have some news to share."

"Did you find her? Do you have anything?" Mother asks me inquisitively.

"No. And yes. We haven't found her but we have found some-thing." I pause and take a deep breath. Marcus notices my hesitance and narrows his eyes. "I met with Elina's grandmother tonight. She revealed something she has not even told Elina." Curiosity turned to hunger in my mother's eyes, ravenous for information.

"She is...Ezekiel Devereaux's daughter." I say it plainly, letting it drop into the room like a bomb. Marcus looks slightly stunned and my mother's mouth gapes open.

"That is news indeed," Marcus responds, excitement evident on his face.

Ever since that day, mother has stars in her eyes at the thought that I will finally settle down, with a bloodline vampire of my own. Marcus, always the strategist, believes that uniting Elina and myself through a bond will bring an end to any potential war.

Whatever their motivations, I am grateful to have their support in the search.

As we walk, side-by-side down Royal Street toward St Phillip, we keep our heads down and our senses on high alert. We are making our way toward the bar—I like to finish my nights there, if only to feel slightly closer to my heart, which feels as if it has been ripped from my chest.

"Do you- do you smell that?" Jack's whisper breaks through my concentration. My head snaps up and I breath-in deeply as we reach the corner.

It's her. I know it's her. It's so faint I might have missed it if not for Jack, but it's definitely her. I freeze in the middle of the road. My head swims with the realization that she is here somewhere. After weeks of nothing, she's here. I don't know where but I know it's her.

"Yes," I answer in a hushed whisper. "Where? Where is it coming from?"

He prowls around in larger and larger circles, starting in the middle of the empty street and moving outwards, until he reaches the sidewalk. He stops atop the sewer opening and scents the air. We are at the intersection surrounded by buildings. Hotel Royal is across the intersection with its mirrored windows and a retail shop with apartments above it is on my left. A restaurant with tables overlooking the street on my right, and an empty parking lot. I scan the windows and balconies around us, trying to see or hear anything. I tilt my head curiously toward the mirrored windows. Something that appeared so innocuous before is fairly suspicious now. We have knocked on these doors before but I never got the feeling she was here and we've never smelled her despite walking here, every day, for two weeks.

Leaning down, he puts his face closer to a grate set into the curb. "Here. I can smell her here."

I walk closer and follow his movements—her scent gets stronger the closer I get to the opening. There are dozens of other scents emanating from the sewer but I can tell it's her mixed in. "Get it open." I point to a manhole cover in the sidewalk as I pull a phone from my pocket. "Meet us at the corner of Royal and St Phillip. Hurry. We found something."

I hang up before I get a response, as Jack lifts the sewer cover and jumps into the hole. I peer down at him, watching him scent the fetid air before I drop in next to him.

"This way." He points to his left and starts moving, me following closely on his heels. We walk, maybe 10 feet, before I hear splashes behind me. I immediately crouch in a defensive position until I recognize Sarah and Ethan's presence.

Standing upright, I press a finger to my lips and motion them to follow.

Jack leans up and rubs his fingers across a pipe draining into the sewer, pulling them back; bloodied. He holds them out to me and I inhale a lungful of a familiar scent, the first in weeks—Elina. And it's coming from the blood on his fingertips. The pipe that is dripping Elina's blood into the sewer disappears into the concrete ceiling.

That's her blood. Her life dripping from a disgusting sewer pipe into dark dirty water flowing over my shins. I feel relief at knowing she's here, but the idea that someone is hurting her, making her bleed, fills my chest with an emotion so far beyond rage that I can't think straight.

Red clouds my vision as I lose control.

I scream out in frustration before ripping a pipe that is hanging over my head out of the ceiling. I smash it into the wall, rage lashing out of me like a whip.

"I will kill them all," I whisper, my wrath like a living creature inside me, writhing around, trying to find an outlet and building up to an explosion.

CHAPTER 34
ELINA

I lose track of the days and nights that pass.

Sleeping when they sleep, waking when they wake, I am fully immersed in Nicolas's household.

The nights blur together, flashing between evenings of decadent parties and moonlit dinners, and those that are marked by blood dripping into floor drains and pain.

Two weeks at the mercy of Nicolas. I never know which version of him I will get. He has never laid a hand on me or hurt me, he reserves that for his henchmen. He uses control and manipulation to twist the knife of captivity deep inside me.

Last week, he brought me to him for another meal where he fed from and killed another person—a man this time. He overpowered him, pressing his flesh against the man, forcing a moan from his lips. I wasn't able to tell if it was sensual or merely fear. It doesn't matter either way, the man died all the same.

On another evening, he sent someone to my room for a 'donation', where I was forced, under Marc's watchful eye, to fill a bag with my blood. I, then, had to sit across from Nic as he sipped my warm blood from a wine glass. I was expected to not only sit there, but also to eat the bloody, rare steak that was served to me.

I currently sit, attired in my black, sheath dress and barefoot, waiting for the knock that will bring me to Nicolas for the evening. I know when I awake what sort of night to anticipate based on the clothing he provides. Cindy has taken all of my other clothes, piece-by-piece, over the last few days, until I have no choice but to wear what she brings. Tonight, a tight-fitting, silk, floor-length gown appeared in the wardrobe while I slept.

A party it is. Whether it's the sort of party that involves me trying to placate Nicolas in private chambers, or the sort where I put on a show in front of the court, I do not yet know.

Not a single sound infiltrates my bedroom. It's a sensory deprivation chamber—I sit in complete silence.

A sharp knock on the door brings me to awareness. I know, based on the harshness of the sound, that Claudel has been sent to fetch me. There will be no allies, not even of the pseudo kind, tonight.

Standing, I approach the door just as he flings it open, the door knob banging into the wall, causing me to startle and flinch away from the jarring sound. Claudel wears a smug smile tonight as he takes in my outfit.

I am not provided with underclothes so my breasts are on display and I feel disgustingly exposed to his roving eyes. The expedited healing that has been developing also means that my skin does not betray the scars and bruises my soul bears from these weeks in prison.

"Prince Nicolas awaits." His clipped tone, followed by his quick retreat, unnerves me as I rush to follow. The hallway outside my room is dimly lit this evening, and unusually cold. I cross my arms over my chest, rubbing them for warmth while trying to hide within myself.

I rush, on silent steps, behind his retreating figure. We make our way down the stairs into the courtyard where there is a party already underway. As we enter the open space, there are vampires everywhere. They hang over the balconies and are framed and backlit in the doorways. Sitting on the lounges and at the tables. Humans, carrying trays of wine glasses and blood, intermingle with the vamps—the occasional feeding happening against a wall, or in the cleared space meant to be a dance floor in the middle of the room.

I follow Claudel closely. I am in danger here. We approach Nicolas sitting in the large chair, with a high back, red velvet upholstery and a gilt inlay. We pause and Claudel bows deeply and I affect a curtsey. Nicolas smiles indulgently at me, love shining in his eyes. I smile in return, doing my best to inject it with happiness I do not feel.

"Attention! Attention, everyone!" Nicolas calls out to the room as he stands, raising a goblet of red liquid—I can not yet tell if it's wine or blood. "My beautiful love, Elina, has arrived. Please all, pay her the deference she deserves." A champagne glass is thrust into my hand and I am spun to face the crowd as they all lift their glasses in my direction.

"To Elina!" comes a chorus of cheers as I raise my glass in return, my cheeks pinking with embarrassment and anger at this display. The bubbles in my champagne tickle my nose as I take a sip, immediately being warmed by the alcohol. I would like something stronger, though, if I am to perform for the crowd. I know what Nicolas expects now, and disrespect and flippancy will only result in more pain.

Turning back to Nicolas, I peer at him and he is gracing me with one of his rare proud looks, as though I am playing my part so well he genuinely believes the show he is directing is real. I stand in front of him, somewhat awkwardly, unsure of what I am to do now. I stare at him as he watches me.

"Sister!" I hear Genevieve at the exact moment she wraps her arms around me from behind, burying her face in my neck and inhaling deeply. "You smell lovely this evening." I feel the tiniest scrape of her teeth against my throat as Nicolas hisses in his chair. "I was only smelling her, Nic. Calm down."

"You aren't feeding from her, have some respect." He gives her a disdainful look. "Soon she will be a vampire and we can all share if you want." He wears an indulgent smile at this thought, as though that is something I would be interested in. I know from Bash that blood sharing between vampire couples is used to deepen emotional and sensual connections, and is often a hallmark of sex between bound partners. Offering this...ritual to his sister leads me to believe my previous instincts about the unusual relationship they have may be close to correct. I do not respond to his leading statement.

He does not need me to participate in the conversation.

"Sit, my love." He gestures to the stool next to his chair, low to the ground, at his feet. His casual use of the word 'love' as a term of endearment pisses me off, and I am further degraded by the subservient position at his feet. But I sit anyway. Sitting at his feet is the best case scenario in this situation.

Once I am uncomfortably perched, he rests a hand on the side of neck, a silent declaration of ownership to the room. A line of vampires begins to form in front of us. I watch, wearily. What is this party celebrating?

A tall, lean, dark skinned vampire, with even darker hair, is the first to approach. He drops to a single knee in front of Nicolas.

"Sire." He addresses him with a light French lilt to the word. "I've come to report on the progress in Ville de Sang this week. We have recruited seven vampires who are unhappy under their current leadership and want to join our army. I have provided a list to Jon."

"Thank you. Please continue to swell our ranks." Nicolas waves a hand in dismissal.

Next up is a short brunette wearing a red dress so tiny, I am unconvinced it is a dress at all. She also drops to the floor but on both knees this time. She widens her knees, sitting back on her heels. I look toward Nicolas and there is a pleased smile on his face as he watches her from his chair.

Leaning back slightly, she exposes herself to him, running her hands down her body provocatively.

"Prince." She draws the word out suggestively, Nicolas's hand tightening ever so slightly around the back of my neck as he watches her. "I was hoping for the opportunity to meet with you to discuss some issues." As she speaks, she runs her hands up the inside of her thigh, her sex on full display.

Glancing at Nicolas again, I see that his pleasure has turned to hunger. He tears his eyes away from her body, her thighs, and looks at me. Running his eyes down the column of my throat to my breasts, clearly outlined in the tight fabric, his hunger intensifies. I shrink beneath his gaze, willing him to look at her, not me.

"Come here." He motions to her with two fingers. She approaches him slowly and he pats his lap, never removing his hand from me. He relaxes back in his chair and indicates to her to straddle him. She climbs onto him, pressed tight against the bulge at his zipper. He wraps his free hand around her hip and she slowly begins to grind against him, throwing her head back and exposing her neck.

The hand he has around my neck tightens again until I can feel the flow of blood slow, a slight haziness clouding my vision, as she continues to gyrate and press herself against him. Her breaths come faster and he releases the pressure on my neck, allowing the blood to return to my brain. He rubs soothing circles against my racing pulse. Planting her hands on his chest, she moves faster, her breaths coming out in pants and moans. He resumes his squeezing of my neck, and the unfocused quality of my vision returns.

I can hear Genevieve breathing heavily from behind me, and feel her swaying slightly as her leg brushes against my back.

It's erotic and overwhelming, but also terrifying and violating. This display feels like a specially designed torture by Nicolas to keep me on edge, uncomfortable. I have grown used to, however uneasily, the free sexual nature of this court but this feels like I am exposed, and the entire room is watching me. The woman's ministrations start to become erratic as she gets closer to orgasm, Nicolas giving every indication of being unaffected, but I can feel the slight tremble in his fingers on my neck and see the erection under the woman humping him. I drift somewhere outside my body, watching it all from above, where nothing can touch me. Where I am still whole.

She climaxes on his lap with a shout, calling out his name as though he were God. He wraps his hand all the way around my neck to the front and tilts my head back, forcing me to make eye contact while the woman grinds through her orgasm. As soon as she stops moving, he pushes her off his lap with a look of dissatisfaction.

"That's the only audience you'll get from me."

I fight the revulsion I feel in my body, the need to vomit almost overtaking me, but I force it down. I can not show any more weakness than I already have.

"How are you feeling, love? Did you enjoy the show?" I know he is trying to goad a response from me and I can't bring myself to formulate anything to say. This has crossed a line tonight and I feel dirty and used. His methods, his manipulations and psychological torture have gotten more painful to endure with every passing day. He must catch sight of the hate written on my face, despite my placating attitude. His own face morphs into a terrifying look, one I have come to recognize.

I try to fix my response to something he will accept, but I fear the damage is done. He releases my neck suddenly, my skin cold from his missing touch. I loathe the feeling of his skin on mine, but it brings a certain amount of comfort knowing his wrath is hidden away when he is trying to be kind. He can't keep it hidden for long.

"Nic-Nicolas, please. I'm sorry." I beg him because I can feel the disappointment and coldness rolling off him and I know my night is going to get worse.

Casting me a glare that makes my knees tremble, he raises his hand for Claudel who immediately appears from the crowd. "You may take her now," he tells him quietly before standing again. "Please wish my lovely Elina a pleasant evening, everyone." Fifty eyes turn in my direction, but the only one I see is Marc's as he looks at me knowingly. Claudel grips my arms and leads me from the room and down the hall, to the room with the concrete floor and the shackles. I hang my head and cry.

It could be minutes or hours later. I stand tethered as I watch my blood drip from my body into the floor drain. Today, I think I last longer, I don't collapse as quickly. My vision doesn't blur as easily. The blood slows faster. I feel stronger.

Marc, Jon, and Stephan gather around to watch me, restraints at my hands and feet. My dress has been removed and I stand naked and exposed, chained to the wall for them to watch. The nudity is more mental torture, the vulnerability, the helplessness of being unclothed. The same way that my shoes being taken was in the beginning. Stripped down, I can't cover myself. I can't protect myself.

Breathing heavily, my chin resting on my chest, my arms above my head, I allow myself a moment of escape. I focus on my breathing, on my heart pumping, and know that this is not the end. He can't win. The room is silent except for the drip drip of my blood and the breath whooshing from my lungs. Tonight, I can hear the blood as it drains away, the water below the drain rushing by. I can smell the metallic scent and the dirty mixture flowing through the drain below us. Marc has left me alone, killing the lights on his way out. It's an extra layer to his torture—the silence of the soundproof room. The absolute darkness of no windows.

The silence is so profound that I think I can hear the blood pumping in my heart, moving through my body, feeding my muscles.

Faintly, I hear a rustle and a whisper. I perk my ears, turning my head to try and listen harder. Something below me —beneath the floor—rips loose followed by a scream. Raw. Furious. Agonized. I catch a faint wisp of whiskey and smoke before I am alone again, in silence.

Bash?

CHAPTER 35
BASH

"It's her! We found her!" I exclaim as I burst through the office door. Disregarding the assembled council, I go directly to Marcus. "She's here, in the Quarter."

Jack is hot on my heels, his hand still stained with Elina's blood. He holds it out to Marcus who inhales deeply and his eyes shoot to mine.

"Where? How did you get this?" His urgent questions fill me with the hope that we can get her back.

"Is she alive?" my mother adds.

"St Phillip and Royal—I caught her scent and followed it into the sewer," Jack explains, his voice tight. "Her blood was dripping from a drain pipe." My mother hisses at this news. She may not have been Elina's biggest supporter but she has seen the effect this has had on me and my family. She is as ready for war as the rest of us.

"I don't know where the blood came from, but she was alive when it spilled from her," I add in. "She is around there somewhere, in a house most likely. We need to search them."

"If they won't let us in and have human protection, we

288

can't search them." Marcus looks at me as he answers, a look of pity on his face.

"Then we will burn them down, I don't fucking care. We will find her and I will kill them all!" I growl in reply.

"Sebastien, stop. We will find her but it's late to do any–"

"No! Marcus, she's bleeding. Do you understand? Her blood was dripping from a drain pipe!"

"Yes, I heard you. But it's almost morning, so we can't do anything tonight. We can't send humans to investigate, it's too dangerous to send humans into a potential hive of vampires. Tomorrow, we will take a force and go door-to-door. If she is behind one of those doors, we will know by sunrise." Marcus uses his Re voice, a tone I am not capable of arguing against.

"I will be here at moon-rise tomorrow and we will go. Select your army and I'll bring mine." I look at my mother, give her a nod, and sweep out of the room.

Sarah and Ethan are waiting for me outside the door, disappointed understanding on their faces.

I immediately request my allies meet at my loft, before the sun rises, so I can explain the plan.

Within 10 minutes, there are close to twenty vampires milling around my living room, listening to me recount, again, what happened.

"Be here tomorrow at moon-rise exactly. Don't be late. We will meet Marcus's force and find Elina. Bring whoever you can, whatever you need. I don't know what we are walking into, but this is your future queen and the future of our kingdom." I look at each person in turn—they wear varying degrees of excitement, pity, sadness, anger, and hope.

Assembled in the chapel, ten minutes after moonrise, I am flanked first by my family, Sarah on my left, Jack on my right. Ethan stands beside Sarah, my mother beside Jack. Gia, Lessa, Aura, and Minnie in a line behind them. Our friends and allies creating a phalanx at my back. We are a blockade of might, even without Marcus's men.

Marcus enters from the council rooms, leading his party in a precise triangular formation. He takes the point, with Darius and Victor directly behind him. Lucian and the remaining council members follow, flanked by a dozen more vampires.

"Are you ready, *Nipote*?" This is my uncle today, not the man in charge of all of us.

"Yes, I will do everything I can to bring everyone back, including Elina." I reach for him, pulling him into a grateful embrace.

"That's great to hear, but I intend to lead the search. We will bring my future niece home." My mouth drops open at his words. Marcus hasn't marched into battle in centuries. When we flooded into the city and took it from the French, Marcus didn't march. When we conquered territory in Greece, Marcus didn't march. When we fought the Russians? He. Didn't. March.

My knees weaken under the weight of his gesture. I nearly fall at his feet—not from exhaustion or grief this time, but gratitude.

"Thank you, Marcus. This means everything," My mother tells him, clearly seeing my distress and inability to respond.

"Yes, thank you, Re Marcus," Sarah tells him, dropping to her knees and bowing in front of him. I believe it's the first words she has ever spoken to him unprompted. Her voice is broken with emotion and I know what it means to her, knowing that we all want to save Elina.

Pulling her to her feet by her upper arms, Marcus looks her in the eyes. "Sarah, we will save her." Looking over at the rest of us, he adds, "Has everyone fed tonight? We've got blood prepared, if not." We all nod together but go to the tap anyway, we all want to be our strongest for what lies ahead.

I can only hope it's enough. I feel as though I could tear the world apart with my bare hands. Tonight, I will hold Elina in my arms.

Walking out through the tall doors at the front of the *cattedrale*, we walk in formation. Marcus and I at the head, with Jack, Victor, Darius, and Lucian directly behind us. Mother, Sarah, Ethan, and my cousins are next, followed by a long march of vampire soldiers and allies. We march through the French Quarter, and all of the people in the windows and on the street watch our progression.

They whisper behind their hands, some add their ranks to the back of our line. Our numbers increase as we move through the streets. Humans lock up doors tight to hotels, bars, and homes.

As we approach the cross road where I know Elina is, Marcus nods his head and his vampires spread out, a soldier in front of every door up and down the two intersecting streets, and knock simultaneously.

Door after door swings open to reveal humans and vampires, or both. The men at the doors ask various questions. Some step inside to search or smell. Our core group of family members stands in the street, near the hole where we found the blood, waiting.

Jack approaches the door of the old Hotel Royal and knocks. A woman of short stature, a human, opens the doors.

"Can I help you?"

Jack takes a sharp inhale as soon as the door opens and

growls, low in his throat, capturing my attention. We all turn in his direction.

"She's here. This is it," he says, low and deadly. The woman's eyes widen and the door smashes closed. I can hear the tumblers and locks engaging. A sudden rattling draws my eyes upward. One by one, metal shutters slam down over the windows. A fortress sealing itself shut. A trap—or a challenge.

Everyone falls silent, the air thick with tension and anticipation.

"Get ready everyone," I growl. "They can't keep us *all* out." And we proceed to surround the building.

The assembled vampires jump onto the higher levels of the building, a person at every point of entry. Windows have vampires clinging to them. Marcus is working to destroy the metal shutter covering the front door. I approach him and slam my fists into the metal. I feel the flesh on my knuckles give way, splattering blood across my shirt. They heal quickly, only to re-split with every punch I lay against the metal.

The sound of tearing metal and banging fills the street. Vampires from the surrounding homes empty into the street, the humans barring their doors to avoid being caught in the melee. All of the windows are reflective, showing me, like a mirror, what is happening on the street. I can't see into the building at all, I only know of the shutters covering the windows because I heard them close. And I can hear people running back and forth from behind the barricaded walls.

Marcus and my combined efforts finally result in a puncture straight through the metal of the door, and through the wooden door behind it. Tearing through the opening like men possessed, we finally breach the entryway. Walking at a fast pace, we each begin entering any rooms we come across.

In a billiards room to the left, I find two men waiting. They attack me simultaneously as soon as I clear the threshold.

Throwing a blood covered fist in the first man's direction, I hear his jaw break under my hand. As he stumbles back, I grab the second man. Holding his face between my hands, I twist his head until I separate it from his body, letting him fall in a heap at my feet. I put a hand out to stop the other man from advancing, punching through his chest cavity and pulling out his heart—the flash of light temporarily blinding me. I drop the heart with a thump and exit the room.

This pattern repeats until I have lost count of the amount of vampires that fall by my hand. They are strong and ruthless, but they are not prepared for the lethal brutality of my anger. My Elina is in this house somewhere and I *will* find her. If the people here want to get in my way, then let death be their lesson.

CHAPTER 36
ELINA

After another night in the dungeon room, I am emotionally exhausted and beaten down when I awake the following night. My wounds have healed but I am still broken.

I know I felt Bash's presence last night—he was close by, I could feel it.

Tonight, I awoke right at moon-rise, as though the need to sleep fell away when the sun slid below the horizon. Sitting up in bed, a metallic tang is in the air. Blood. Whipping my head around, I see a half-full glass of crimson sitting on my table. Taking a deep inhale, I realize I can smell the liquid all the way over here. My gums start to tingle and my mouth floods with saliva at the smell.

I stand and approach the inoffensive glass. Next to it is a bowl of gumbo. I lean down and smell it, it smells rich and delicious, but nothing like the way the blood smells, the way it calls to me.

I lift the glass to my nose. I breathe it in like it is life itself. My entire being reacts. My hands start to shake, my stomach feels as though it is collapsing, hollow and needy. The tingling in my gums becomes a sharp pain. Something beyond my control seems to be happening to me. Something biological, uncontrollable. I bring the bright red liquid to my lips and dart my tongue out to taste.

The lifeblood immediately fuels a frenzy the second it touches my tongue. Newly emerged fangs descend, slicing into my lips causing my own blood to join the feast. My body convulses with need.

Aching, I take a gulp of blood and electricity shoots through me, like the force of the sun inside me. My chest burns with the realization of what is happening.

This is it. My fate, fulfilled.

I moan, a sensual, arousing sound of pleasure erupting between my blood covered lips. Strength invades my limbs, making me stronger and empowered in a way I have never even imagined was possible. I feel every nerve-ending being set on fire. I can hear more than I have ever heard before, the creaking of the floors, the electricity in the walls. And banging. The entire building is filled with the sounds of banging.

Just as quickly as I realize what has happened, I realize the fear and hopelessness I felt yesterday is replaced with a fury that burns as brightly as my love.

Today is the last day I allow Nicolas to make the rules. I am done being a victim. Today, I will devise my own salvation.

I glance down. My camisole and sleep shorts are soaked in blood, clinging to me like second skin. No one brought me clothes. No one came at all.

Blood. I need more. I need blood. The need is acute and eats at me. It pulls my focus from anything but feeding. I yearn for life to flow into my veins. The small glass was not nearly enough to quench my need, the hunger growing within me with every passing second.

I try to listen to anything happening in the hallway, someone usually comes to get me after I wake up, I can't hear anything beyond the banging. Walking over to the door, I put my ear to the wood. It's muffled but I can hear what sounds like feet pounding across the floor. As I strain to listen, I hear a grating noise behind me and I spin around, looking at the large windows that face out to the street, in time to watch a solid metal shutter slam into place covering the entire window.

What the hell is going on?

Going back to the door, I listen harder, and I definitely hear feet running now. I try the doorknob, locked, of course.

Stepping back, I grab the handle and pull as hard as I can. The door creaks slightly but the locks hold. Lifting my foot, I slam into the door with all my might. The door swings into my room which makes pushing through it almost impossible, but I refuse to stay here at the mercy of whatever is happening, without at least trying to save myself.

Kicking the door again and again, I can hear the wood giving way under my foot. When they locked me in here with the tools for my transition, they didn't consider that they may have provided for my salvation. I am not the same person they left in this room.

Kick.

KICK.

KICK.

The door cracks down the center as the building shudders under me. I refuse to wait for death to find me.

Pushing the splintered wood out of the way, I climb through the broken door into the hallway. There are vampires running toward the front of the house, others flowing deeper into the labyrinth of hallways. I follow them. I can smell humans everywhere. I know who they are, where they are. I can smell the vampires too, but I instinctively know they aren't going to feed me.

I need to drink. I need to bite. I need to escape. Feeding is a visceral call from my deepest consciousness. I search for food —I smell the humanity and look for the source. Following my body, I emerge into a kitchen, a room I have never been in, and see a human man huddled in the corner, fear etched into his body.

Flashing to his side, I grab him, lifting him to his feet, using his hair to hold him in place and bring his neck to my mouth.

I bite and feel the hot, salty blood flood my system with power. The fire that burns inside me flares in response. I feed and feed, filling my body with raw power. His blood is everything. More than everything. I have never wanted anything, *needed* anything, the way I need this liquid of life. I feel the lightning he houses in his body flow into me. As his heart beat slows, I know I need to stop—he's going to die—but I can't. I can not let him go.

I suck at his neck, draining him as the flow slows down, his heart beating slowly, pumping his blood to his brain, right past my lips. He has lost consciousness now, and is limp in my arms, dying. I continue feeding until the blood stops and I drop him.

Tilting my head back, covered in blood, I open my mouth and scream. A loud, long, feral scream of anguish, of power, of fury.

Falling to my knees, next to the dead man, I wrap my arms around him and sob. No tears come but the heartbreak is real. I killed a man. I fed from him until he died. I've become the monster I loathed to be.

A crash from across the house causes my head to snap up and look in that direction. Picking myself up from the floor, I tiptoe to the kitchen door. I spy a crisp white apron hanging on a peg and snatch it down, putting it over my torn, bloodied pajamas.

'*Michael*', the embroidered name across my breast reads. I glance back at the man. I'm sorry, Michael. A sob works its way up my throat as I look at the dead man on the floor. I'm now the villain in someone's story.

Silently, I enter the hallway from the kitchen. I listen and hear banging noises coming from all around the house. No one is in this part of the building anymore, so I set off to try and figure out what is going on.

Coming upon a set of doors I recognize, I turn the knob to the library and enter the cavernous space. There is an identical set of metal shutters covering the large corner windows of this room too. Something large and strong bangs against the shutters, causing them to shake and bend. They are no longer perfectly covering the window. The banging doesn't let up. I don't know what's happening but if whatever is out there comes in here, I'm escaping through that window.

Is this my rescue? Is this for me?

The relentless banging and smashing continues, the shutter becoming more and more mangled as the minutes pass. I duck behind a bookshelf, peeking around it, watching the progress. Waiting for whoever is on the other side to crawl through.

More yelling and banging comes from other parts of the house. Nicolas's court of nightmares is under siege. The doors of the library swing closed behind me, and muffle the sounds considerably but I can hear the fear in the human voices and the war cries of the vampires.

A few more loud bangs on the library shutters, and a large pale hand reaches around the side of the shutter, wrenching it back, with strength that only comes from an old vampire.

Slinking back further behind the shelf, I try to make myself invisible. I don't recognize the hand clawing its way into the room.

After a few minutes, the shutter is crushed enough that a blond head pops around the side of it. His long body coils up, his muscled forearms straining to hold the metal out of the way as he squeezes through the opening he made. His heavy boots land on a plush antique rug, his long sleeved grey henley ripped across his stomach. His chest is heaving with exertion, a look of triumph on his face. He turns back toward the window, leaning out, and giving a quick whistle.

"Jack," I breathe out, almost silently from my hiding place. His head whips in my direction as he tries to locate the source of the noise he undoubtedly heard.

"Who's there? Come out and I might not kill you," He whispers into the space, trying not to draw attention of anyone outside the library.

"Jack?" I repeat, a sob breaking my voice. They came for me. *He's here for me.*

His mouth pops open in surprise as he walks slowly in the direction of the bookshelf I am peeking out from behind.

"Elina?" he murmurs, coming closer. "Hey, baby, we've been looking for you." He speaks slowly, like he is speaking to a wounded animal backed into a corner, something unpredictable and scared. He isn't wrong in his assessment of the situation.

I stand up and fly out from behind the shelves, barreling into his arms so suddenly I almost knock him to the floor. He wraps his arms around me and holds me tight to his chest. I was expecting Bash but Jack will do. He's Bash's best friend and he will do.

He strokes my hair and lands a kiss on the top of my head.

"Hey, how are you doing? You ok?" He stretches his arms out, holding me away from his body. My blood covered face and body pulls his attention and he gasps, searching me for wounds.

I smile, widely, fangs on display, relief filling my body. "Perfect, now that y'all are here. Where is he? I'm so happy you came, I was so worried." I ask him desperately. He reaches out and presses his finger to my tooth, puncturing it. I taste the blood before he withdrawals his hand and sticks his finger in his mouth. His smile is pleased.

"He's looking for you. You're damned right we came, Bash hasn't breathed since you disappeared." He gives me another once over to make sure I am all in one piece and drags me toward the window. "Let's get you outside and then we will try and find Bash. God, he's going to lose it when he sees you."

I stop smiling, suddenly afraid of him finding me like this, covered in blood, fanged. Not his Elina anymore. Not the same woman he's been looking for.

Lifting me up, he helps me stand on the sill. I look out at the carnage and wreckage outside the window. There are dead bodies everywhere, vampires fallen, hearts ripped from their chests. Broken glass, splintered wood, and bent and mangled shutters protruding from the windows act as evidence of the battle that is still ongoing. I jump down, followed quickly by Jack who grabs me around my waist and hauls me away from the house. Pulling a phone from his pocket, he presses 1 and brings it to his ear.

"What is it, Jack?" I hear the clipped tone from Bash on the other end. I let out a gasping breath, a breath I feel like I've been holding for weeks. I sag against Jack's chest from hearing his voice.

"I've got her, Bash. Outside."

There is a loaded pause.

"Don't take your eyes off her, I'm coming."

"Never, brother."

He hangs up and we wait, side-by-side, for Bash to emerge.

CHAPTER 37
BASH

Hanging up after hearing the relief and confirmation in Jack's voice, I feel lighter than I have in weeks. I have no idea what I am walking into with her, what has happened to her or what will become of us now, but I feel as though I can breathe again.

My sun has returned.

Before I can get to her though, I promised I would kill them all and I intend to do just that. Jack will keep her safe. A man approaches me as I walk through the house, his posture submissive, his movements weary. I bare my fangs at him, a show of intimidation, not that he needs it. He shows me his throat, an attempt to surrender. I grab him by the neck, lifting him off the ground and bring his face level with mine.

"You took something that was mine and now you'll die for it," I tell him, so close I am almost breathing into his mouth, his toes skimming the floor.

"I- I didn't. Nicolas did. He wanted her."

"Well, now you'll all die for him." Placing my hand against his chest, I claw my fingers, and slowly press into his chest cavity, wrapping my hand around his heart. He hisses out in pain as I squeeze the organ pumping blood through him. Squeezing tighter and tighter, his eyes bulge before I finally pull my hand out, blood dripping, holding his heart, his light flaring into the room around us. I drop both, his body and his heart, to the floor at my feet.

Walking down the deserted hallway, I throw the door open at the end and find a lone woman with short blond hair cowering behind a large desk.

"Hello, darling. Why don't you come out from back there," I say to her as I shut and latch the door behind me. I know I am a terrifying sight, the devil himself, covered in bright red blood, my fangs dripping. The sounds that erupt from my throat are inhuman.

Shaking her head, she slides backward across the carpet until her back hits the paneling. I approach her slowly, prepared for attack.

"Don't do this, please. Sebastien, right? You're here for her, aren't you?" She looks up at me from the floor, her eyes pleading. "I'm her friend, I tried to help her. Don't do this."

I laugh cruelly in her face. "I'm not sure friend is the correct word for holding someone hostage." Reaching down, I grab her by the collar and lift her feet off the ground, holding her at arm's length. "Who are you?"

"Nobody. I'm nobody." She trembles with fear.

"I don't believe you. Who took her, and why?"

"I don't know, I don't know," she repeats over and over.

"Ok, well, if you aren't going to be useful." I lift my hand and plunge it into her chest. Her eyes widen momentarily before the light flares from the hole I created. I drop her body, her heart still clutched in my fist. It hits the carpet with a wet *thunk*.

Turning, I walk out of the room, shutting the door behind me.

I open door after door until I reach a room that smells so much like Elina it damn near brings me to my knees. The room is empty but I prowl inside anyway, closing the door behind me. There is a stainless table full of tools and implements, all covered in blood, not unlike the one in the dungeon of the cathedral covered in Talia's blood. Elina's blood covers this one. The wrist and ankle restraints are stained red, and there are blood droplets everywhere—the entire room is drenched in Elina's blood.

The fire of fury in my chest reignites with a power I have never experienced. I storm out of the room, freezing to listen for any sounds from inside the house. I hear nothing but muted fighting somewhere far off. I continue my room-by-room inspection and don't find any other vampires. On the second floor, I find another strong hit of her. Behind a splintered and broken door that looks the same as all the others, I find a bedroom. The bed is unmade and smells so strongly of her that I want to roll around in the sheets.

On the small table in the corner there is a bowl of gumbo, uneaten, and spilled blood. Most of it is from the glass that is on the floor with some droplets of Elina.

What happened here, Tesoro?

Satisfied that I have found everyone there is to find, I make my way down the stairs and out the front door.

I am coated from head to toe in blood—it's in my hair, dripping from my brow, seeping into my clothing. I leave bloody footprints in my wake. I am a distorted version of the man Elina last saw and I am afraid of seeing her, of her reaction to me.

Walking into the street, I see her standing under a streetlamp, leaning heavily on Jack. His arms are around her as he murmurs in her ear.

The air around me disappears, the street beneath my feet fades into nothing. A spotlight shines on the brown hair hanging down her back and on her drawn, exhausted face. She's lost weight, but she is still soft and I want to squeeze her tight to me. My heart cracks at the sight of her.

She looks up and her eyes find mine. The happiness that breaks across her face causes the air to crackle around me. I can feel her happiness in my body like blood, flowing through me with relief.

She breaks out of Jack's arms and runs to me as I open my arms to her. She flies at me, inhumanly fast, and slams into me, wrapping her arms and legs around me. Enveloping her in my hold, I sink to my knees and we both sob.

"Fuck, baby, I was so fucking worried about you." I breathe into her hair, not wanting to let her put even an inch of space between us. "Are you ok? Please tell me you're ok? I killed as many of them as I could, I'll kill them all. *Tesoro*, fuck, I couldn't breath with you gone."

"Bash, I love you. I love you so much. I knew you would come." She sobs into my neck. "Bash." I can feel her reluctance, her hesitance. Something is weighing on her.

"No, *Tesoro*, we have time later. Reunion now." I squeeze her as tight as I safely can. I hear people filling the streets and I release her, quickly, pushing her behind me, crouching and growling at the vampires approaching.

"Sarah!" She runs out from behind me and jumps into the arms of her friend. She takes a big inhale and widens her eyes comically. "You're...you're a vampire." Sarah startles as the sentence, confused.

"How do you know that?"

"I can smell it on you," Elina tells her, hesitantly. "I can smell Bash on you."

I gasp at the same time as Sarah.

"Elina, are you–"

She hangs her head, in shame, I think. "Yes."

Walking up behind her, I wrap my arms around her and take a deep breath of her essence, realization dawning for the first time that she is different now. "I love you so much, *Tesoro*. I can't wait to spend forever with you. No one will ever come between us again. Never. *In eterno*."

She spins in my arms, looking at me before giving me the biggest grin I think I have ever seen, beautiful fangs on full display for me before latching her mouth to mine forcefully.

It's raw. It's pure emotion, something I never thought I could claim for myself. It's bloody and it's perfect.

I can't think of a moment I have ever been happier in my life.

CHAPTER 38
ELINA

"As sweet as this long overdue reunion is, we need to go." I turn my head toward the voice and Marcus is standing beside Jack. I turn in Bash's arms, bowing my head slightly to my new king.

"Re Marcus. Thank you so much for coming here, for helping rescue me." I'm so overwhelmed with how quickly everything has happened. I went from helpless human captive to rescued vampire in only a few hours. My head is swimming with everything I need to absorb and adjust to.

Stepping forward, he takes my trembling hands in his large steady ones. "You are our family now. Let's go. We didn't get everyone and I need to hear what has happened." He gives me a steadying look. "You're safe."

None of the men and women surrounding me in the street, the army that came to rescue me, can fathom how impactful those words are, how crucial they are now.

I reach out and grab Bash's hand as we start the procession back to the cathedral, feeling better than I have in weeks but also terrified that Nicolas is still out there somewhere, ready to regroup and come back for me.

A few hours later, I have told Marcus, Bash, Sarah, and Jack everything that happened in that house. The fury radiating off of my friends is like a physical presence in the room with us. The deep well of sadness that I can feel from Bash makes me wish I could shield him from the details, but I know that this information may be valuable later.

Wrapping his arms around me, Bash whispers in my ear, "I will find him and I will rip his heart out for you, if that's what you need. But I will not allow you to walk around, afraid." Lying my head on his shoulder, I nod affirmatively.

"Can you take me home?"

"Do you need to feed first?" he asks me, stroking my face gently.

"Just take me home, Sebastien."

Sweeping me up into his arms, he carries me out of the church, across the courtyard and up the stairs to his loft.

"I hope it's ok, but Sarah and Ethan have been living here," he tells me as we enter the apartment.

I hold him tighter. I love this man more than I thought my soul was capable of. Knowing that he has embraced my friends so completely, created a family for us, overwhelms me with emotion. It's been a very emotional day.

Carrying me directly into his ensuite bathroom, he sets me on my feet and begins to remove my bloody clothes, stiff now that they are dry. Peeling the camisole over my head, he runs his hands soothingly up and down my arms. Hooking his thumbs into the waistband of my shorts, he pulls them straight down my legs. Kneeling in front of me, he lays his head against my stomach, his shoulders shaking with silent sobs.

Looking up at me, he implores. "Did he do anything to you? Violate you? Beyond what you told everyone?" His face is almost enough to bring me to my knees next to him. "Nothing he could have done would ever affect how I feel about you— but I want, more than anything in the world, to wrap myself around you, sink into you, and love you until I pass out. But I won't do anything you don't feel comfortable with."

Leaning down, I press my lips to his and try to pour as much of my affection, longing, and love into it as I possibly can.

He stands, never breaking our kiss and wraps his arms around my waist, lifting me to bring my face level with his. He slides his tongue into my mouth, tasting me, sucking on my tongue in turn. Cupping the back of my neck, he walks us to the shower, turning the knob. I can feel his reluctance to break our kiss. Pulling away from him, I step into the shower under the spray, beginning to clean my red stained skin of the night's evidence. Stepping in behind me, Bash molds his body to my flesh, comforting me, soothing my raw edges with his presence.

Taking the washcloth from the rack, he pours my favorite strawberry soap on it and runs it across my skin, starting with my shoulders, down my arms, and around my torso. I look down and watch the blood swirl down the drain. My blood, Michael's blood, the unknown blood from the tumbler. The worst parts of my nature, disappearing.

Stooping behind me, he lays a gentle kiss at the base of my spine as he rubs the soap and cloth down my legs, lifting each foot and scrubbing it before kissing the arch. Reaching around he swipes the washcloth between my thighs, rubbing gently my most delicate skin, his fingers pressing into my clit through the washcloth. The warm water, the rough cloth, and his gentle hands working together to heat my skin and light a fire low in my belly.

Leaning my head back, I moan out loud. Licking the top of my tailbone while he works my clit, wetness flooding my pussy, I arch into him, silently asking for more. Feeling his worshipping caress makes me feel cherished—not disgusted the way I felt in that house. Turning me around and sitting me on the shower bench, he kneels in front of me, his thumb finding my wet skin and making firm circles around my clit, while he takes one of my nipples in his mouth. I lie back exposing more of myself to him.

Pulling the showerhead down from the wall, he adjusts the spray to the pulsing massage and aims it directly at my center while he kisses and sucks my neck, causing a shudder to run through my body. I move my hips in time with the movements of the sprayer, feeling my orgasm building low and hot. As I get closer, he slides his fingers inside of me, rubbing and massaging that special spot inside me that makes me squirm. The warm water pulses against me, pushing me closer to the edge as I revel in the worshipful movements of Bash's mouth on my skin.

I moan his name, and it feels like a prayer and a plea all at once. My thighs tremble and my stomach flexes as my body prepares to fall into oblivion.

"That's it, baby, come for me," he whispers against my neck as I am right on the edge, my skin hypersensitive. Falling into oblivion, I pulse around his fingers as he sucks, hard, on my pulse point. "So beautiful when you come for me, so perfect. I've missed this so fucking much." He continues to murmur against my overheated skin as I slowly come down from the high. Nothing feels more real than this moment, post orgasm, my body flooded with endorphins, the man I love kneeling in front of me, reverently. This is my home.

We make love until sunrise, rediscovering each other, reshaping what we were into what we are now. Everything has changed, and yet—our love has only deepened. As the first light touches the sky, we collapse into each other, tangled and whole, letting sleep take us away.

I experienced my first moon rise as the new vampire I am, that Sunday night. It's an unusual feeling, the way the need to rest falls away, as if by magic. Actually, it is by magic. When I sit up, I look over and Bash is sitting crossed-legged, a huge smile on his face.

"What are you smiling at?" I ask him, grinning back.

"It's so weird rising and seeing you laying there. Usually, you're up and around well before I am, so it was fun watching you. Although, you sleep a little differently now." He gathers me up, wrapping my legs around his waist and peppering my face with kisses. I giggle and swat him away.

Sobering, I look into his eyes from my perch on his lap. I grab his face and look at him nose to nose.

"Thank you for coming for me," I whisper, my breath catching in my throat.

"I will never not come for you, *Tesoro*. There isn't a world in which I exist if you don't." He holds me tight against his chest, his own emotion making his chest rise and fall rapidly. "But, based on what Jack said, you were pretty damn close to rescuing yourself. He said you looked like the angel of death standing in your pajamas, coated from head to toe in blood, fangs out. And I saw your room, where they kept you—the broken door. You were ready to fight for yourself." He stops for a minute, holding my cheeks and his eyes boring into mine. "I am so fucking proud of you."

"Can we go to grand-mere tonight? She must be so worried." I look at him, trepidation in my face. "What will she think of me now?" I gesture to my new vampire body.

Inhaling a wearied breath, he darts his eyes away.

"What is it, Bash? Did something happen to Grand-mere?"

"No." A giant sigh escapes him. "While you were gone, Sarah and I visited her, you know, to update her. Anyway, she invited me inside." I feel my eyes widening in surprise. That was a giant leap of trust. But he looks almost—scared. "She told us about your mother and Ezekiel. Things she has known from the beginning and should have told you. Sarah is really pissed at her actually."

"Are you kidding?" I climb out of bed, pissed-off myself. Grabbing a pair of leggings and another of my signature shirts —'Ask me about my blood type'—I storm around the room. "She knew this *whole* time who I was and what I was going to be?" I resist the urge to put my fist through the wall, knowing the anger is a side effect of my vampire nature. It's difficult to control.

"I mean," he starts, rubbing the back of his neck, looking concerned, "she definitely knew who you were, but I asked her if she knew what this meant and she genuinely didn't appear to have any idea what would happen. She thought if you didn't know it would help you, you would stay a human."

"But she knew...so much. Not just who I am, but vampire

secrets. You know, about the bloodline vampires. And she had to know about the binding, since they would have done that." Slamming my hand down on top of the dresser, I take a deep breath. I'm spiraling. I can feel the emotions filling me like a tidal wave. Anxiety and anger lead the charge in my brain. "I asked her so many times. *So many.* This is *bullshit.* Get dressed, we are going over there."

Walking up the front steps of my childhood home, I can't help but think it feels tainted and wrong. I am so different now than I was the last time I was here, but this house is different too. I walked up these steps three weeks ago, preparing to say goodbye, to let the last remnants of my humanity fall away to spend forever with Bash. Now, I am changed. I have been bled out and reforged into something better, something stronger. A woman I may not have recognized.

I was always strong but I was jaded, and didn't truly understand what it was like to live before I was no longer alive.

Taking a steeling breath, I stand up straight, my shoulder blades drawn together—a false sense of bravery sliding over me like a shield—and knock on the door. I hear Grand-mere moving quickly our way, Bash's hand landing on my back in silent support.

"Elina! Oh my god, my girl." Grand-mere emerges from the house as quickly as she can, wrapping her thin, frail arms around me and hugging me tightly. I let her hold me, and I hesitantly return the embrace.

Looking at her as she steps back, she looks older, more worn-down than the last time I saw her. Is it, again, because of how long it has been since I saw her, or is it the stress of my disappearance that forced her to age?

"Grand-mere Celeste," I reply to her coolly. She looks at me, guilt written on her face as plain as day. I love her still, but the betrayal I feel right now is a living creature inside me, one I am not sure how to address.

"Come in, please." She looks over my shoulder at Bash, her eyes pleading. "Let me explain." She turns and goes back inside, Bash and I following her across the threshold.

"Grand-mere, it's time you tell me the whole truth, the *real* truth this time." I give her a hard look. "You've lied to me long enough."

"I will tell you everything I know, everything that was told to me. But first, I need to know, are you ok?"

"Yes," I answer in a clipped tone. I know she's worried, but I can't care about her feelings right now. "I'm fine. I've been through hell the last few weeks, literal hell. But I am still here, so let's get to the story. We can talk more after."

She looks at me with regret, her voice turning sad as she starts her tale. "Thirty-one years ago, your mother had just turned 25. She had lived her entire life behind these walls, like you have. She was working at the Vampyre Boutique in the quarter and met a man. He was a kind man, compassionate, and a vampire. He begged her to go out with him. Like you, she was skeptical of what he wanted or whether she should go, but she finally relented." This feels a little too parallel, like we were already on our destined paths. "He took her out, courted her religiously for weeks before she brought him home to meet me. Over wine and whiskey, we talked, we learned about him. I found out who he was and I was equally horrified and stunned by the revelation."

"He was so handsome—icy blue eyes, almost identical to yours, but with a more auburn color to his hair. He was olive-skinned and tall, not as tall as Sebastien, but tall enough to tower over your maman. So charming and sophisticated, he won me over instantly. It was hard to not love him. The way he looked at Nora, it was like the sun rose for her, he couldn't stop looking at her. The love in his eyes was staggering. And she, of course, loved him all the same. They told me they wished to be married, to be bound together for all of eternity. I knew what that would mean, she would become one of his kind. And she would be Queen one day. So they took the binding oath, out on the balcony of the Hotel Royal while we all watched from the courtyard below, basking in their happiness." The mention of the Hotel Royal brings a flood of memories back, Nicolas reducing the place where my parents had their first moments of happiness to something dirty and perverse.

Grand-mere fidgets in her seat, seeming reluctant to tell the remaining story. Picking up my glass of wine, I drink deeply, grateful she offered the drink before we got to the confession part of the evening.

"Go on. You lived an entire life you've lied about, don't stop now." I know my words are cruel, but the depth of pain I am feeling can't be expressed any other way.

"They got pregnant almost immediately, something Ezekiel said was a miracle. Vampire pregnancies are not easy to come by," she says. Bash nods his head, absently beside me, as though he is lost in the story. "Once you were born—*God,* Elina, you were their entire world in a little pink blanket. Ezekiel doted on you like you were the moon hung in the sky. His family embraced us, and watching the joy and wonder in their eyes as you laid in the courtyard, laughing and kicking your feet, transitioning into a laughing, running toddler, wandering around your father's kingdom, was everything I could have ever wanted. You loved laying on the rug in the library, holding your dolls, going from shelf to shelf. As you grew, it was more and more obvious this was your place in the world. Your mother was deliriously happy, there was never a day where she was not pleased beyond measure. I would catch her looking wistfully out the windows or watching you play on the floor of your father's office, a peaceful smile on her face."

I am again struck by how Nic perverted that perfect little island of peace my parents enjoyed in their home. Disgusted, I drink down the remaining wine in my glass and pour myself another. Bash lifts an eyebrow at me, I dismiss him and his concern tonight—this is my history, my story.

"When you were three, growing into a gorgeous little curly-haired girl, the Italians flooded the city." I eye Bash consideringly, knowing this wasn't his fault, how could he have known? Would he have cared, if he did? He, at least, looks contrite. "Ezekiel was killed that day, but you and your mother had fled to this house, where you were sheltered from the fighting, the war. Your mother's heart shattered right here in this very room as soon as she felt your father's light go out. The cry of anguish that escaped her lips, the way she gripped her chest and screamed is something I will never forget as long as I live." The tears begin flowing down her cheeks now. Her voice hitching as she gets closer to the climax of her tale.

"A few nights later, as if going through life in a daze, while you slept peacefully in the little bed upstairs, she was extinguished. I think she –"

"Wait. Wait! Extinguished? Was she...a vampire?"

The look on her face is indecipherable, I can't figure out if she left that part out on purpose and slipped up, or if she genuinely forgot.

"Oh, um, yes. Near your first birthday, your father turned her. They wanted to be together forever. It was the only way."

I am stunned speechless by this. It makes sense, why wouldn't they? But never, in nearly 30 years of being told the same lie over and over again, had Grand-mere even hinted at the possibility that my mother was a vampire. The new wave of revulsion over her carefully crafted lies washes over me. Bash grips my hands tightly, rubbing small circles across my thumb, soothing me slightly.

"The lies never end, I swear."

"It wasn't intentional, Elina. She was my daughter, and that is how I think of her, not as a vampire, not as a Queen, as my daughter."

"Why didn't you tell me? Why lie?"

The circles on my hand get firmer and more distracting. Sebastien is trying to ground me, keep me from losing my new vampire temper.

"I didn't want to. You forgot about him. You were so young. You were so sad. I wanted to make you happy. I was angry. Every bit of happiness and warmth were sucked from the world. I wanted to protect you." She looks at me, so much regret etched in the lines of her face, tears filling her again. "Please forgive me, don't take more from me."

Shaking my head, I stand. "I need to think about all of this. This was...a lot. Please grand-mere, I need some time. I'm sorry." I move to leave, bringing Bash with me, by the hands we still have clasped.

"Wait, wait. I have something to give you." Pulling an envelope from the pocket of her nightdress, she hands it to me. Turning it over and opening it, I withdraw a photograph.

A beautiful woman, green eyes shining and happy, wrapped in the arms of a tall, auburn haired man, on the very balcony I had my first dinner with Nicolas, twinkling lights and all. She is wearing a flowing white wedding gown, a bouquet of blood red roses clutched in her hand, Ezekiel in his black tuxedo with a matching red rose tucked into his pocket. Their binding ceremony. Maman's arm is wrapped in a bandage, the evidence of their blood oath to each other. The happiness I see shining from them is almost enough to bring me to my knees.

I sob escapes me, causing Bash to wrap his arms around me. Resting his chin atop my head, he whispers, "I'm so sorry, baby. They were so happy. You deserved them. I'm so sorry."

CHAPTER 39
BASH

Trailing behind Elina, her hand wrapped around mine, I glance back to see Celeste's heartbroken face sitting where we left her. Closing the door behind me, I tug on Elina's arm to stop her progress.

Standing in the moonlight, staring at the sad face of the woman I love more than anything else in existence, I ask her, "Are you okay?" I ask the worst, deliberately, not as a platitude but as a genuine question. I need to know before we go any further.

The answer is important. The revelations that took place inside her grandmother's house, her mother's house, are earth shattering. Knowing that her mother loved her father enough to bond with him was one thing, but having the entire foundation of her life shaken by the knowledge that they were madly in love enough to hold this kingdom together, and for her mother to turn for him, will have a profound impact.

Her face crumbles and her shoulders shake under the weight of my stare and questions. I want to know a lot more than how she is, like how will this affect us. But for now, her safety and comfort are paramount over myself.

"I- I don't know, Sebastien. What I heard in there, and learned about myself and my parents?" She tilts her head back and gazes at the moon. "It changes everything, but also...nothing at the same time. I am a different person than I was a few weeks ago because of choices my parents made for me. My life would have been so different if I had had them in it." Lowering her head, her gaze finds mine. She releases my hand. *There it is.*

"But I didnt. Because of your family." Turning, she walks away.

Everything has come full-circle. A moment I have been dreading since I learned the truth. I worked so hard, I earned her love but there are some things I can't take back. My family was responsible for the destruction of hers, and my love for her can't change that.

The more I think of it, the more complicit, or even responsible I feel. I wanted her to give me her heart willingly, and she did. Now, I am terrified of losing her for something I did before I even knew she existed.

She needs to know the whole story about *Guerra de Sang.* That I was in the house the night her father was extinguished. I didn't deliver the killing blow but I was there—I know far more about it than she will ever find out from any other source. But how much could she want to know about that night? I need to find out who killed her mother, too. If for no reason other than to understand.

Taking off running, I make it back to the chapel and into my mother's office in minutes. Leaving Elina, wherever she is, hurts but I can't force myself on her, she needs some space.

And I need some answers.

"Mother?" I call out as I approach her door.

"Come in, Bash." She smiles up at me from where she lounges on a chaise in the corner, near the window, reading by the light of the moon. "What brings you to visit so soon after your reunion?" Looking around me, she seems surprised to find I am alone.

"I have some questions for you. Do you have a few minutes?"

"Of course." She sets her book aside, granting me her full attention.

"*Guerra de Sang.* Tonight, we found out that her mother was a vampire, and they were a family. A king, queen, and a little princess. The night we invaded, Ezekiel was killed. Do you know who snuffed him out?" I watch her, critically, to see what she thinks of this line of questioning. I get nothing.

"I'm actually surprised it took you so long to ask, but I understand, you've been distracted." Leaning forward to rest her elbows on her knees, she steeples her fingers, looking thoughtful. "I do know. Are you ready to know? You'll have to tell her if she asks."

"I know." I hang my head.

"Sit, my *Stellino*. The night Ezekiel died and we sacked the city, Marcus remained behind, sending an army and his generals. They included Darius, Victor, Lucian, you, of course, and me. Only one of us was given the order to kill Ezekiel. Lucian takes his responsibility as executioner for Marcus very seriously." She lets the hit land. Of course it was Lucian. It's always Lucian. Marcus keeps Lucian at arms length from the family, my cousin, but from a further branch. He makes him do all the dirty work, like he did with Talia. I want to pity Lucian for his lot in life, but considering how insufferable he's been the last twenty odd years, I just can't find it in me.

Lucian is easily the most monstrous of us all, but I don't know if Marcus turned him into this, or if he simply recognized the monster inside before the rest of us had a chance. I am grateful that it wasn't my mother, or even my close family— seeing Elina grapple with these feelings, while in the presence of the man who killed her father, would be too much for either of us to bear.

"Lucian. I should have guessed, really. And her mother? Nora was queen, and a vampire. There is no way she wasn't recognized so who extinguished her? She was killed days after Ezekiel."

She thinks, an introspective look on her face. "I do not think it was us. After the raid, and Ezekiel's death, everyone else in the compound was also extinguished. We all assumed the queen was amongst the dead. No one had escaped, only those loyal to us remained after a few days. There were no reports." She stands up suddenly and goes behind her desk, switching her computer on. "Where did you say it happened? Vampires who were killed in the days and weeks following the raid had to be recorded so we knew the true toll."

"It was, I think, three days later." I watch her type away. "It happened right in the area of the Vampyre Boutique, some-where between Bourbon and Chartres most likely. She worked there and was killed on her way home." More typing. She studies the screen and looks up at me.

"I do not see anything. No reported vampire executions within a block or 2 of there. I don't think we executed her for her part."

"Then who–?" I sink back into the armchair I've occupied. Laying my head on the backrest, I rack my brain trying to figure this out. More of a mystery. "If we are sure it wasn't any of us, then I don't have any ideas."

Fuck. More frustration to the point of exhaustion. I want to be able to answer the questions Elina has. If I don't know who extinguished her mother, I can't tell her, but knowing that it wasn't a Malvani vampire makes it an easier pill to swallow I guess.

We may have to work on this mystery together if she lets me.

"Thank you, Mother." I give her a kiss on both cheeks and go back out the way I came, determined to find Elina.

Heading out into the night, I try and think of where Elina might hide if she was trying to escape. A few places immediately come to mind; the riverbank, a rooftop, the Velvet Tomb, and the cemetery.

Deciding to begin at The City of the Dead, I take off in that direction. She may want to visit the mother in question for some solace.

Approaching her quietly from behind, I see her kneeling in front of a small brass plaque stamped to the tomb door;

Nora Girard
Devoted Mother

That's all it says. No other information; no indication of her role, how old she was, or anything else. It only highlights her most important contribution—Elina. Watching her shoulders shake in grief, she looks weighed down by tonight's revelation.

"Maman, I finally know everything. Grand-mere finally told me. Tonight, I allow myself to be swallowed by the grief of knowing you were so happy. You had everything; a family, a man who worshipped you, a baby who adored you. And it was stolen away."

I feel grief claw at my chest as she drowns in hers. *What have we done?*

"What do I do, mommy?" A sob tears from her chest as she pounds a single fist onto the ground. "I love him more than life itself, so much that I was willing to give life up for him. Like you." Her voice breaks. "What if he's the reason you're in this tomb? What if he killed Papa? How would I ever get over it? I need him like I need air, like I need blood." Laying on the ground then, she curls into a tight ball and cries, huge wracking sobs, her body trembling with the force of her emotions.

I move backwards, away from her, giving her a moment to breathe. To calm down. I don't deserve her attention, not yet, but I will get her to understand. I want to cry as well, at the consequences of these long forgotten decisions. Decisions that set in motion a thousand small events and altered entire families, entire cities.

Finally, she stands and brushes off her knees. I move a little further away so she understands I was watchful but not intrusive. I want her to feel my presence before she sees me, I am here to support her, not smother her.

"Come out, Sebastien. I can smell you on the wind," she says, her voice low but steady. Completely different than when she was kneeling in front of her mother.

"Hello, *Tesoro*. Can we talk?" I reach out to see if she will take my hand, gauging where we stand

She answers by grasping my fingers, allowing me to envelope her hand in mine. "I'm sorry to interrupt, but I just came from Mother and I was hoping we could talk about what happened tonight. Maybe I can help fill in some blanks."

Squeezing my hand, she simply answers, "Ok," before sitting gently on the concrete pad a nearby tomb is resting on.

ELINA

H olding tightly onto Bash's hand, like it's my anchor
in this sea I find myself adrift in, I lean against the
cool marble of the tomb. This has been the longest
night of my life. I'm tired—I did not think that was something that I would experience anymore but these last few
weeks have been a lot.

"Sebastien, did you kill Ezekiel?" I blurt out, bluntly, before
he has time to begin his own tale. I want to get right to the
matter, really.

Shaking his head, he replies, "No, *Tesoro*, I did not. I know
who did, but it wasn't me."

"Who was it?" I feel relieved it wasn't him. I don't know
what I would have done if he truly was responsible for my
father's death.

"My cousin, Lucian," he answers, sadness in his voice. "He
is my uncle's executioner. He does all the unsavory things no
one else wants to do."

"The one who tortured Talia?" He told me all about Talia's
involvement and subsequent questioning after the rescue.

"The same."

"I think I know Lucian—we had a regular at the Tomb with that name." I recall the many times he sat at my bar, brooding and angry. I wonder if it was his work that made him that way. "He has grey eyes, like yours, but his hair is black, I think. Either that, or super dark brown. He would always hire Lillith. That him?"

"Yes, that's probably him. So, that's who carried out the order to take Ezekiel out so Marcus could fill his place."

"Ok." I breathe out heavily. "Ok." I'm grateful the man I love is not guilty of a crime he didn't know he was committing. A quiet rage simmers low in my belly that my father, before I was even old enough to remember him, was stolen so someone else could step into his shoes. No doubt, if they knew of me, they would have killed me as a child. I shake my head to clear the thoughts, it isn't as though the French, my own family, had not treated me similarly, and they are my flesh and blood.

"What about maman?"

I watch his profile in the moonlight as he sits beside me. There is not a twitch or flinch. "That I do not know. I spoke with my mother and we checked the records. We were required by decree to record the extinguishing of any vampires within the city in the days after the massacre, and there is no record of anyone from our side killing her. I don't know what that means though. Who else would it have been, you know?"

A face, a cruel face twisted in excited pleasure at seeing people suffer, flashes before me. The face that haunts my dreams and my waking hours—the man who is still out there, capable of hurting all of us.

"Nicolas. I think maybe it was Nicolas."

"But why though? She was his queen." He watches me, confusion written on his face.

"You weren't there, Bash. Fuck, you can't fathom this man.

I can't even *describe* him." I shake my head to try and clear the soulless eyes from my memory. "One minute, he was kind, charming. In seconds, a switch would flip and he would kill someone, or order me to be tortured for the tiniest *made up* infraction. And he wanted to be King. My mother was in his way. He only wanted me to secure his claim to my father's seat. The seat your uncle now holds. I think, when he realized you and I were going to do the binding, he panicked and tried to get me so that he could control me and use my name. He hated that I was a hybrid. He may have hated my mother more because she was human."

Grabbing the back of my head, he crushes me to his chest, holding me so tight, it would have hurt if I was still a fragile human. His body is shaking slightly. Letting go suddenly, he stands and walks to the other side of the cemetery. I jump up to follow him, unsure of what is happening. When he reaches the stone block perimeter fence, he unleashes his fury against the stones. One solid punch sends a crack up the entire wall, causing bits of stone to tumble to the ground. He lets out a pained cry from deep in his chest before landing another blow.

I feel my hair move slightly in a breeze before realizing Jack is standing next to me. I startle.

"Sorry darlin'. Didn't mean to scare you. What's happened to him? I felt his anger all the way across town."

Wide-eyed, I stare at him. "Felt his anger?"

"Yeah, it's part of the sire bond, he sired me so I can feel him," tapping the side of his head, "up here."

"Oh, can Sarah feel him too?"

"She can. But he's been my best friend for 200 years; I'm a little more aware, I would guess. I wanted to make sure he was ok."

"Oh, I was talking to him about Nicolas, at the house. I have a theory that he had something to do with my mother's murder." I wonder how much of Bash's moods he can feel. Like, all of them? I don't have a sire so I have no one to be tied to. I wonder if Bash and Vespera are connected?

"Ah. Yeah, he's pretty torn up about the whole thing. And a little mad at himself that it took so long to find you. It's his instinct to protect you, even when you can protect yourself."

At that moment, Bash must hear us talking and he growls at Jack as he spins in our direction, abandoning his destruction.

Jack puts his hands up, placatingly. "Easy brother, I was worried about you."

"I'm fine, Jack. We have to find him." His knuckles and shirt are splattered with blood, but the skin is unbroken. I approach him slowly, making sure he is done with his display. Taking his hand and raising it to my mouth, I slowly lick the blood away, looking into his eyes as I go.

"And that's my cue." Jack smirks, knowingly, before disappearing with a rustle.

A deep chuckle emanates from Bash's chest. Picking me up, he wraps my legs around his waist. I feel his body tight against mine and kiss him. Pulling his tongue into my mouth, I suck on it gently, my fangs sliding out of my gums. Kissing my way down his jaw, I suck lightly against his pulse point.

"Bite me, *Tesoro*. I want to feel your teeth." So I do, easing my fangs gently into the delicate skin covering his jugular, I pull hard on the blood flowing across my lips. He moans huskily in my ear, his dick hardening against my pelvis as he holds me wrapped around him.

Releasing his neck, I lick my lips and plant a kiss on his mouth, sharing the leftover blood with him.

"That was pretty hot, *l'immortal*," I tell him, a huge grin plastered on my face. "Don't hurt yourself because of that psychopath. We will find him, and he will have to face what he's done."

"Let's go, little troublemaker." He takes off at a quick pace, me still clinging to him and laughing the whole way.

"Hey, so, Jack mentioned something," I say, a little shyly, walking beside him a short time later.

"Oh yeah, I can only imagine." He rolls his eyes at me, making me laugh.

"He said he felt your anger across the city..."

"Yeah, we are bonded, through the sire bond. You will have a similar bond to me after we do Legame di Sangue."

"Ok, but...how much can he feel?"

I know his eyes are searching my face as I try to appear uninterested in the answer. Suddenly, he doubles over in laughter, clutching his stomach like I've said the funniest thing he's ever heard.

"You're wondering if he can feel when we..." He lifts his eyebrows at me.

If I were capable of blushing as a vampire, my entire face would be flushed. "I mean, yeah, kind of. *Stop laughing at me!*"

Still chuckling, he nudges my shoulder. "Yes, baby, he can. But he can block it out. And he can't really feel it physically, more like a rush of emotions. I can feel him too. It's like— happiness. He only knows I'm really happy, or maybe pleased. But he can't read my mind or anything."

"And Sarah too? What about your mother? You don't have a sire."

"Yes, to Sarah, and that one was hard to add to my brain once she turned because you were missing. But Ethan was not. And he spent a pretty fair amount of time trying to cheer her up."

"Ew, Bash!" More laughter. I join in this time.

"But no, not Vespera. She's not really my sire. It's weird, I guess, because it would make sense but no. It feels natural to me, like an extension of myself, so I don't pay a lot of attention to it. But if Jack or Sarah were to be hurt, my nature, as their sire, would compel me to find them and make sure they're ok. The same way Jack felt compelled to hunt me down a few minutes ago. When you were missing, I was in bad shape, baby. Jack stuck pretty close to me, making sure I was ok. He walked the city from sundown to sunrise every single night, until he smelled you in that sewer drain. He was as obsessed as I was, but not only for me. For you too."

"Why? Why would Jack care so much about me?"

"I don't know exactly. He loves you. He loves you for my sake, but somewhere along the way, he loved you all on his own too." My heart warms at his words. Knowing that we are building a life, a family gives me a sense of belonging I've never had. It's always been grand-mere and I, plus Sarah.

"What happens when we do the ceremony?"

"From what I have been told, it should be relatively similar —you'll be in my head, bound to me. We will have a stronger connection than I do with Sarah and Jack though. The binding, it's soul deep. It's a different sort of connection. We won't only be able to feel each other, we will be able to find each other. Like I said, no one will ever take you from me again." Grabbing his hand we walk in silence for a while.

"When can we do it?"

"Whenever you're ready, *Tesoro Mio*. Anytime."

Less than twenty-four hours later, I am in a small room in the chapel with Sarah, Vespera, Grand-mere, and Bash's four cousins. Sarah is holding up a stunning black wedding dress and I am ready to pledge myself and my future to this man. I marvel at the timeless workmanship of the stitches, beadwork, and lace. I had never really thought much about what I would get married in, I never even seriously considered the possibility that I *would* get married. Now, I am preparing to take a vow that will tie me to Sebastien for all of eternity.

My hair is pinned up at my temples, clips that look like delicate black moths braided and looped through the curls that cascade down my back. Gia and Lessa take turns working on my makeup, meticulously applying heavy black eyeliner and creating a decadent smokey eye with just a hint of blue shimmer. Knee high stockings with red beading down the back and black sky-high stilettos adorn my legs.

"To the future Corvo Queen!" Everyone raises their glass, clinking them delicately. A tiara studded with black diamonds and onyx is set upon my head.

"How did you manage to pull this together so quickly?" I ask the room.

"We knew, when you came home, that this was your destiny. You're one of us now," Vespera tells me, moving a lock of hair behind my ear.

"Bash told us that you like black and Sarah helped design the dress. We hired a seamstress and had it ready for you. We never doubted that you were coming back," Minnie adds.

I look over at Grand-mere and see tears shining in her eyes. We aren't all fixed yet—there are still a lot of cracks—but she has been the only person to ever hold me up and support me, and I need her here today.

Kneeling in front of the chair I'm seated in, Sarah looks up at me. "Let's get you into your dress, sister. I'm so freaking happy I could cry. I can't believe we are going to be a family now." Throwing her arms around me for a quick hug before she stands, she whispers, "Bash is perfect for you and I am so happy that you're finally choosing you."

Standing, I step into the dress.

Walking into the cathedral, with the women of our family, feels surreal. The large space is filled with people—everyone I've met while becoming such a central part of this family, and the Blood Ravens, are here to watch Bash and I bind our souls together for eternity. The council is seated together to one side, the allies Bash told me he won during my captivity once again intermingled with the rest of the *governaturno* of Ville de Sang.

Darius and Victor stand behind Bash, and Jack stands by his side. The look of love and longing in Bash's face floors me and I have to hold on to Celeste's arm in order to continue my forward progress and resist the urge to run straight to him.

It's not a typical wedding, in that there isn't an aisle I walk down and bridesmaids and groomsmen. All of these people, except Marcus, are here as our witnesses—the official witnesses to the binding. Bash is dressed in his signature head-to-toe black, looking slightly more refined than normal in a pair of tuxedo pants, obviously custom as they hug every lean line and muscle of his legs, a tailored shirt that hides his tattoos but shows off the taut muscles of his abdomen and biceps, and a buttoned vest over it. A blood red tie and a rose in his pocket are the only color on him. I can see the pride reflected in his face and my heart swells. I am in the right place, at the right time.

Bash's cousins take seats nearby, relaxing to watch our vows. As I approach Bash and Marcus, Sarah takes her spot next to me, Vespera and Celeste stand behind me. The shimmering black of their dresses coordinate perfectly with Bash's uncles, our family looking every bit the night kingdom we are. Creatures who dwell in darkness and live by the light of the moon.

There are no overhead lights on, the only light in the cathedral being provided by the silvery glow coming in through the windows, casting an eerie quality across the entire place.

Raising my head to take in the men standing opposite me, Jack gives me a sassy wink before I slide my eyes to Sebastien. As the bells toll midnight, Marcus clears his throat.

"Elina. Sebastien. Welcome to your *Legame di Sangue*. This is a sacred rite that you must both enter into willingly. This is a rite that can not be taken from you and lasts for eternity. Even if, at some point, you find yourself without your partner, the bond remains." Bash takes my hands in his and squeezes, I return the gesture, a large smile on my face.

He mouths, silently, "Are you sure?"

I give an emphatic nod of my head.

"Tonight, you will vow to love and protect one another forever, even until your own death. You will be bound, not only soul to soul, heart to heart, but also body to body. Are you ready?"

"Yes," we answer in unison.

"Who are your witnesses?"

I was told what to expect during the ceremony and know that the witnesses will answer, not us.

"We are." The room answers together, in perfect synchronization, in a way only vampires could achieve.

"Please repeat after me—

In the presence of la luna and these witnesses,
I freely enter into this vow.

333

With this vow, I bind my soul to yours.
With this blood, I bind my life to yours.
With this kiss, I bind my body to yours.
I pledge the shelter of my soul
I pledge the eternity of my life
I pledge the protection of my body
Tonight, I spill my blood in willing sacrifice that
I will love you.

Repeating after Marcus, together, like we practiced, when we reach the end we both add "*In eterno*."

Standing side-by-side, we extend our forearms to Marcus. From a hidden pocket in his coat, he produces a dagger, the blade gleaming in the light of the moon. Engraved on it are the words, "*Un cuore, un'anima, un'eternità*". One heart, one soul, one eternity. My breathing becomes labored as I try and control the emotions welling up inside me.

First grabbing Bash's arm, Marcus orders, "I, Sebastien Enrique Malvani, vow," which Bash repeats as Marcus draws the blade from elbow to wrist, the blood immediately pooling and spilling onto the floor.

Repeating the same with me "I, Elianore Celeste Girard, vow," before making a smooth cut, almost identical to the one I endured while imprisoned, down the entire inside of my arm.

Bash grabs my arm, looping his under it and entwines his fingers with mine. I can feel his blood flowing into my body from the point we are joined. I can feel his heart pushing the blood into me, the way mine is. The flesh begins slowly knitting back together, severing the flowing blood little by little until it's just our bare arms pressed together, coated in each other's blood.

My heart suddenly beats faster, feeling more whole and complete. And inside my head, there is an extra thread of happiness. The greatest joy and pleasure I have ever felt, pushing into me from Bash's blood flowing through my body. I send a wave of happiness back to see if he can feel it. The tips of his lips tilt up and he gives me a squeeze in acknowledgement.

This is the single greatest moment of my life. I thought I knew what it felt like to be happy, but I had no idea what it could truly feel like. I feel the contentment and perfection that was radiating from my mother and father's faces at their binding ceremony. Throwing my arms around Bash, I smash my lips to his as he lifts my feet off the ground and holds me close, deepening our kiss as the room erupts in whistles and claps.

CHAPTER 41

BASH

The moment Elina took up residence in my head was euphoric beyond measure. The thread of her life weaving its way into my consciousness was the most *right* I have felt in almost 500 years. Knowing that she felt me too, sending me waves of joy, was something I always hoped I would experience, but never knew if I would. I would have taken the vow eventually, if only to continue my family line and meet my obligations, but it wouldn't have been like this.

Now that the ceremony is over, it's time for the party. Getting Celeste bundled into the back of the suv with Jack so she gets home safely, I wander back into the cattedrale to watch the magic. The room is almost instantly transformed into a club-like space, multi-colored lights strobing from the balconies, and people dancing to the music in the middle of the cleared church. Alcohol and blood flow freely from fountains stationed around the room. Humans lining the edges of the room, waiting to be of service to any vampires, either their blood or their bodies.

I warned Elina about the party when we first discussed the ceremony, and I warned her, again, last night when she asked me if we could do the binding today.

"Ok, if we can do it whenever, I want to do it now. Tonight," she replies earnestly.

"Well, I think tomorrow. There are some preparations to be made, plus there is the party to plan."

"Party?" she asks me with an inquisitive lift of her brow.

"Yes, the party. Remember when I explained the Legame di Sangue? Back in the letters. The party after the ceremony—the orgy?"

Her eyes widen comically. *"I, uh, had forgotten that. Do I have to be in an orgy?"* she asks incredulously.

Laughing and gathering her in my arms, I reassure her, *"No, Tesoro, you don't have to. But you could. If you wanted. It wouldn't matter to me. You will be bound to me and the only thing the bond wants is your happiness…if you're happy with another man between your thighs…well…I shall endeavor to work harder to please you, but I wouldn't stop you."*

She slaps my arm. *"I will not be orgy-ing"*

Despite my warning, I am concerned she doesn't fully grasp what is going to be happening here tonight.

Watching her sway to the music in her wedding gown fills me with emotion. My cousins did spectacularly with her dress. It's entirely black including the tulle and lace. The full ball gown skirt fans out around her, what seems like a thousand layers of cloth making her look like a princess of the night. The top is a form fitting, lace up corset, similar to the one she was wearing when I saw her for the very first time, and it looks as stunning now as it did then. The onyx and diamond tiara on her head, with its delicate filigree, fits her perfectly, and I wish I could see her this happy and gorgeous every single day.

The demons of our collective pasts still haunt us, but tonight, she is the shining star in the night sky as she commands the attention of everyone in the room. Everyone revolves around her like she is the sun and we are her servants. Aura approaches her where she dances, whispering in her ear. She giggles freely and allows Aura to pull her away.

"Where are you going, *Tesoro*?" I yell after them and they look back at me, laughing loudly. Seeing her so free, and hearing her joy, is like finding a piece of my soul that was missing. But feeling the pure bliss radiating out of her, pulsing in my brain, is transcendent.

Watching the way she disappeared, I wait for her to reappear. I feel Jack before I notice he has walked up behind me.

"Sebastien, my friend, my brother, my sire. Fuck, this is amazing." He wraps his arm around my neck, pulling me against him. "I'm so happy for you. Who would have thought those months ago, when you told me about her, that this is where we would end up. You did it, man." Just as he finishes his sentence, I look back the way Elina went and am stunned to speechlessness.

Jack whistles next to me, laughing under his breath. "Not only am I so happy for you, but you're one lucky son of bitch."

"Shut up." I huff out a laugh at his comments. Elina has reemerged into the party, and if she was the sun before, now she is the moon. Her ballgown has transformed into a short black mini dress with a flaring skirt that shows her thigh high stockings, embroidered with red beads down the back, a garter belt around her thigh made of black lace with black diamond drips, clipped to the stockings. Her gorgeous wedding corset is now tightened, creating a luscious amount of cleavage, and a large red garnet hangs between her breasts. I feel like she switched my brain off when she entered the room, and, based on the hush that has fallen in the party, I am not the only one who feels that way. Appreciative looks rain down on her from men and women, all of them hoping to have an opportunity to get close to her tonight.

Smiling widely, she walks my way on her stiletto heels, confidence pouring off her. She has always been gorgeous, and her confidence is something I have loved about her since the moment I watched her in that bathroom mirror while she adjusted her clothing and fluffed her curls. Tonight, she knows that she is stunning and is relishing in the attention being on her. She deserves to be the object of every affection.

"Hey, handsome," she croons as she approaches.

"Hey, baby," Jack responds from beside me. Elbowing him, I laugh. She shifts her beaming smile to his face, crinkling her nose at him. "You sure clean up nice." He puts on his most seductive smile, for emphasis.

"Hey, Jack." She leans down, planting a chaste kiss against his smiling mouth. "Don't want to disappoint you, but I've only got eyes for one man tonight," she adds, beaming at him.

"Well, if you get some space on your dance card, hold it for me, darlin." Standing, he sweeps her into his arms and spins her around, giggles filling the space around them. Setting her on her tottering heels, he kisses her cheeks and makes his way into the party, likely hunting for some entertainment of his own for the night..

"So, Bash," she straddles my lap, wrapping her legs around me, "I remembered something else from the letter about the party. Blood sharing?"

Reaching up, I move a loose curl behind her ear, looking into her eyes. "Curious, *Tesoro*?"

"Yes," she draws the word out sassily.

Taking her arm in my hand, I bring it to my mouth, tilting my head to expose my throat. "Then by all means, let's do it, beautiful."

Pushing my fangs through my gums, I lick the delicate skin of her wrist before biting gently, feeling the lightning that is her blood, flood my body. Her fangs break through the thin skin of my neck at the same time.

Blood sharing is an intensely intimate moment—the same sort of intimacy that exists in siring. I can feel her elation as she draws life from me. My veins feel like they are full of fire, thunder crackling through me. I'm energized by the blood of my wife, my mate. I grow hard beneath her in my lap. She moves her hips in time with her pulling draws on my neck, moaning against my flesh. Throwing her head back, blood coats her tongue, lips, and cheeks. It runs down her chin, joining the garnet nestled there. I release her arm and move my hands to her hips.

If I thought her outfit change was hot, she is infinitely sexier now, with my blood coating her skin. I lean forward, thrusting my hips up, rubbing my cock against her, and suck on her neck, tasting my blood. I lavish her neck and chest with kisses, licking her clean. Looking around us, I see that other couples have followed our lead, using our display as inspiration to cover themselves in each other's blood, taking turns licking and sucking. The atmosphere in the room becomes charged with lust.

Couples, and groups of up to four or five, strip their clothing off—there are no limits, no conscious coupling, men, women, multiple men, multiple women, skin everywhere. Vampires are inherently hedonistic, and the celebratory feelings in the air turn to sensuality very quickly.

Even the elders partake. Marcus is engaged in a group session with two other men, reveling in each other in a rare display for the Re, and each of my uncles are with human women.

It's raw, it's real, it's incredibly erotic and stimulating.

Elina continues her gyrations in my lap, moaning as she pushes herself closer to the edge, using me as a tool. Reaching down, I slide her panties out of the way and slide a finger inside her as she rubs her clit against me. Her movements become more erratic as I caress her from the inside. Raising her slightly, I slide a second, then a third finger into her.

"You're soaking wet for me, baby, do you want to come? We are in a room full of people. So dirty, so perfect," I whisper, rubbing against her clit with the palm of my hand while I fuck her with my fingers. Kissing her deeply, her tongue moving with mine as she starts to shake, her pussy tightening around my fingers. Her hips move in rough circles, her breath panting out of her—faster, quicker, louder. She cries out as she tips over the edge, her orgasm over taking her, yelling my name into the room, she draws the gaze of the vampires around us. She falls on me and bites me as she comes, biting me deeply and drawing the blood out, enhancing her orgasm, nerve endings firing.

Kissing any part of her I can reach, I murmur, "Such a good girl, that's my girl." She collapses on my chest breathing heavily. Wiping her hair off her face, I gently kiss her mouth. "I love you so much."

A few hours later, Elina and I are laughing, surrounded by everyone we love. Sarah and Ethan are wrapped around each other, love shining in their eyes. Jack and a human woman, Katie, sit nearby. It's a family that I am building for myself, filling all the missing parts and pieces of me.

Tonight, we won't consider what happens next, and the

fact that there is a new monster out there somewhere and none of us know what that will mean. Tonight, we enjoy our loved ones. Tomorrow, Sarah and I have worked on a little surprise for Elina.

"Jack, get us some refills!" Elina calls out.

"Yes, my queen." He bows low, pulling laughter from the group.

"So, Katie," Elina says, as soon as Jack has wandered away. "I didn't realize Jack brought a date. How long have you guys been," waving a hand, "seeing each other?"

"Oh, uh, it's relatively new. We met before that whole thing with you happened. He was with me the night that Bash called him away. He didn't reappear for a few weeks, but he explained everything." Katie frowns a little as she speaks. I had no idea he was seeing someone or that he was with her.

Elina's face is sympathetic, she carries some guilt about the whole thing even though none of it is her fault.

"Woah, what's happened? I was gone, maybe, 30 seconds," Jack asks, taking in the suddenly more serious atmosphere.

"Elina was asking Katie when you met. For all the shit you gave me about not telling you stuff when you showed up at my apartment, you were with Katie when I called you away and you didn't even tell me," I say to him.

"Well, of course I didn't say anything. No offense, baby-doll." He looks in Katie's direction briefly before looking back at me. "You're my sire. If you called me out of my bed, while I'm buried in my mate, I will still show up. Once I saw you, there was no way I could leave again. Besides," he grabs Elina's hand, "I needed to be there. I needed to find her."

I can barely bring myself to acknowledge how much his words mean to me. Knowing that, not only does Elina have me, she has the protection of Jack by her side. If anything ever happened to me, Jack would be there, would protect her and support her.

Reaching out, I wrap my arm around his neck, bringing him to me. "I love you, brother."

"Yeah, yeah, shut up." He shakes his head, turning to look at Katie, and she looks a little unhappy, pursing her lips at Jack. "I'm sorry. Bash would do the same for me."

CHAPTER 42
ELINA

The night after our binding, I sit up as the sun releases me, to find the bed empty. Tilting my head, I listen to the apartment around me, searching for my husband. Tugging gently on the thread that is our bond, I know he's close by.

"Out here, *Tesoro*," he calls from the living room. He must have felt my pull.

Climbing out of bed, I pull on a long, oversized t-shirt with, 'Team No Sun, No Garlic, No Problem', across the front that almost reaches my knees, and walk out into the room, finding Sarah and Ethan already there. They are all speaking in hushed whispers.

"You know, if I wanted to eavesdrop I could so, just know, I'm being polite. What's the secret?" I ask as I sit at the end of the couch, Bash immediately pulling a foot into his lap.

"We have a surprise for you tonight, so you have to get dressed," Sarah says from her perch at the counter.

Suspiciously eyeing them, I ask, "What kind of surprise?"

"Get dressed," Bash answers, before leaning in. "I can help you, if you want." His voice is husky in my ear.

Jumping up, I run from the room, giggling, Bash chasing me. I can practically hear the eye roll from our friends as they laugh at our departure.

An hour later, thoroughly satisfied, I emerge in a little black dress, my curls floating around me, my heavy boots on my feet.

"I'm ready," I tell the assembled group. Sarah and Ethan are wearing coordinating outfits—her in a short, green jumper that looks radiant with her red hair, and Ethan in a lighter green button down and grey slacks. They really are a beautiful couple.

Sebastien is wearing tight, black jeans that frame his muscular thighs perfectly, and a deep grey, bespoke dress shirt, with a skinny black tie tied loosely around his neck, and his shirt sleeves rolled to his elbows, showcasing his strong, veiny forearms and swirling tattoos. He wears equally heavy, black boots. Taking him in, I feel desire course through my veins. He inhales deeply, shooting me a knowing look, and I duck my head, embarrassed. If he can smell me, no doubt the others can too.

Approaching me, he wraps his arms around my waist, leaning to my ear and whispering, "You smell *delicious*, baby." Kissing the side of my neck quickly, chills run down my body before he lets go.

Clapping, Sarah beckons us to follow. "Let's go, Lovebirds, you're making me sick," she says before sticking her tongue out at us.

Approaching the Velvet Tomb, I see the line of vampires waiting to get in. Waving to a few friends, Bash sweeps us both directly to the door. Taylor, the bouncer, ushers us inside. The bar is packed, wall-to-wall, with all my friends, both human and vampire. There is a large banner over the bar that says, "Congratulations", and everyone starts clapping as we enter.

"Bash, what's going on?" I ask.

"Well, since a vampire bonding ceremony isn't exactly safe for humans, we wanted you to have a little human party. You have other friends, mainly from this bar, who want to celebrate with you."

I want to sit down and cry, my emotions overflowing into the room. Sarah rushes over, grabbing my hand and hauling me to the bar where Rian is pouring drinks.

She pulls me in for a hug, holding me tightly. Her shoulders shake a little with emotion.

"Elina, I'm so damn happy for you. You deserve to finally have something for you, that's yours. But *dammit,* you and Sarah both leaving at the same time is killing me!"

"I'm sorry, but I love you!" I tell her as I laugh.

Making our way through the room, I talk to everyone I know, accepting hugs and congratulations. It's all I could have wanted and I am so grateful to have a mate, and a family, that see me, truly see me, and knew that this was something I needed. I'm sad for Amelie. I wish she were here so I could tell her I'm sorry. Everything is so different now.

"Excuse me," Jack's voice cuts through the noise in the room, and I find him standing on the stage, microphone in hand. "Thank you for coming tonight. As you know, my best friend married the love of his life yesterday. In over 200 years, I have never seen him look at anyone the way he looks at Elina. The first time he told me about her, I thought he had lost his mind. Dear Elina, do you know that he told me about you after having only made eye contact with you? That he was falling for a woman who LOOKED at him! The man fell head over heels instantly.

"I've seen what love can do to a person, to a man. It can soften a monster and it can turn a brooding, cold-hearted prince into the sort of man who would burn the world to keep one single woman safe. Sebastien, you have transformed from a storm, dark and unpredictable, into a shelter, for your Queen, and your family. Elina, you fought like hell to stay true to yourself, and you never ceased being a light in this city, even when they locked you away. You emerged stronger, darker, and fiercer. The two of you give me hope for the future.

"I want all of you to know, on this night, I pledge myself to you, Elina Girard Malvani, that I will offer you my service and my protection for as long as I live. I vow to do whatever it takes to keep you safe. To my future Queen!" He raises his glass before he drops to his knees in supplication. Every vampire in the room turns in our direction and goes to their knees.

Looking down, I see Bash kneeling before me, my hands in his.

"Elina, *Tesoro*, never in nearly 500 years have I laid eyes on a creature as beautiful, as *perfect,* as you. You are the sun that moves across the sky, I orbit you as the center of my universe. You are the moon that guides my way. La Luna rules above us and she lives within you. I am eternally grateful that you gave me the chance to earn your love, and I endeavor to spend the rest of eternity proving, everyday, that I deserve you. Tonight, I kneel before you, because it is the place that I feel worthy of you. You saw a monster, the monster from your nightmares, and you stayed, you made me a better man, made me want to be a good man. Because of you, I have something that's mine, not taken, not conquered. Chosen, I chose you the very first night, and I am grateful you chose me back. *In eterno, Tesoro.* In darkness and in light, in war and in peace, I am yours."

Pulling Bash to his feet, I throw my arms around his waist,

holding tightly. "You deserve me just the way you are. I love you, *in eterno.*"

Clapping and whistling fills the space as I am wrapped in Bash's arms. Smiling, I look around at everyone gathered around to celebrate us. This is my future. I won't let anyone take it away from me.

EPILOGUE

F all turned to winter, and winter turned to spring. Our
love as a family grew stronger, and we grew closer
everyday. Jack became a third member in our household, holding us up and together through the months that
follow my kidnapping. The fact that we know Nic is still out
there somewhere haunts me. I do everything I can to focus on
now, but fear lives just outside of my reach, hanging over us.

I had a lot of healing to do, being immortal doesn't get rid
of PTSD, it seems. I made the decision to reclaim the Hotel
Royal, not only for myself, but for my parents. I deserved to
have them and they deserved their happily ever after, but due
to circumstances beyond my control, it didn't work out that
way. Nicolas may have tainted the old mansion with his cruel
and torturous ways, but now, after months of work, Hotel
Royal is ours.

Our home is laid out like a square, with the center being
the large courtyard where the vampires threw parties. Our
wing of the house looks out over Royal Street, and the library
with the corner windows is at the end of the hall. Jack's wing

looks over Phillip Street. The guest wing is next, followed by offices and lounges in the rooms that don't have balconies or street views.

Tearing out every bit of the disgusting decor and torture chambers, we redecorated offices, parlors, and bedrooms. Turned the old concrete room, where my blood dripped into the sewer, into a lounge for visitors. It is a room I never go in, and that's ok.

Jack took over Nicolas's old rooms where he had a sex dungeon. Jack kept that, a huge bedroom with a palatial sized bed—Jack kept the bed too—and a private office, the one where we met after Nicholas revealed my father to me. Jack removed the old freaky paintings and sculptures, and bathed all the rooms in light, mimicking the sun filled days he doesn't get to experience. It is a place that brings joy to my heart when I visit him.

Bash and I remodeled the wing where my bedroom was previously, creating large apartments for us that consist of a large gothic inspired bedroom, with a black four poster bed with intricate carvings, deep green linens and pillows, and the lush canopy over the top is green and black sheer fabric, embroidered with dark flowers in royal blue, purple, and red. There are deep carpets in varying colors of the night; shimmery silver, bloody crimson, and blackcurrant. A large sofa in midnight blue velvet sits in front of the fireplace that used to be in my old bedroom. It seems counterproductive, I suppose, but that room was the only place I felt safe in this house.

In a connecting room is a large space painted a neutral gray, with no other furnishings or adornments. We will, hopefully, use this room one day, for a family we create ourselves— a family created out of the love between us. I hope, whenever it happens, they're a miniature version of Bash, with deep brown hair that falls over dark grey eyes.

The room with the balcony, where I shared a meal with Nicolas the first time—where my parents stood overlooking their kingdom—is my private office, a place where I can retreat into myself and reflect on the world we are sculpting together.

Sarah and Ethan have occupied some of the rooms in the guest wing. They are blissfully happy, and planning their own wedding in the Summer. They will make their vows in the courtyard, and we are going all out for the occasion. They will never have children of their own, and I hope that is enough for Sarah. It certainly is for now.

Instead of the princely chair that sat in the courtyard, now, it's all comfortable chairs and couches. Hightop tables pepper the space, and a dining table sits in the center, large enough for everyone to gather. We don't eat there, but we talk, have meetings, and the council sometimes sits with us. Bash is the heir, and in the last few months, Marcus has begun heavily grooming him for his future role. It seems he was waiting for Sebastien to forsake his bachelor ways and join the ranks of the settled, mated men.

We used the Velvet Tomb sunshine room as inspiration for the courtyard. We may never see the sun again, for ourselves, but sitting in the courtyard in the evenings, we can create our own day and bask in it for hours.

"Elina?" I hear Jack call out as I lay in a daybed under the artificial sun, feeling the warmth on my face.

"Yes, Jack? I'm in the courtyard."

"Hey, *Principessa*," he greets me, leaning over and taking a large inhale of my scent at my neck, before planting a kiss on my cheek. I'm not sure what his reasoning is for this unusual behavior, but he started doing it shortly after the bonding ceremony, and I haven't asked him about it. It seems to make him happy, and after everything he's done for me, I leave him to it.

"Hey. What's going on? Where's Katie? I thought I heard her earlier." He and Katie have gotten much closer, and a lot more serious, since my *Legame di Sangue*. I think she is here more often than not. Bash is pleased he has a companion, and Jack walks around like a peacock preening.

"She's...recovering," he responds, winking. I roll my eyes. "Anyway, Bash is looking for you. I was sent to fetch my lady." He throws his arms out in a flourish as he bows low over me.

I let out a laugh and raise an eyebrow at him. "Your lady alright. Where is he?"

"He said, and I quote, 'Begin your search in the library'."

"Oh, a game?" I exclaim jumping up from my sprawled position. His laughter follows me from the room as I run into the house, up the stairs, and into the library.

The first thing I notice is the smell of roses—an out of place smell in the room that usually smells like dusty old paper. Following my nose, I find a dozen roses interspersed on the shelves and a note;

Roses are red
Violets are blue
If you were thirsty
What would you do?

Snorting out a laugh at the silly poem, I think. If I was thirsty, I would go to the kitchen. Grabbing a rose and my note, I sprint out of the library and run down to the kitchen. On the counter is a glass of fresh warm blood and another note. Sipping the blood I read;

I'm not a bed but fantasies bloom
Sprawled on the desk, in this room
Leather and whispers, a chair that spins
Where power starts and work begins
Scribbling pens and trembling thighs
Windows where you can look at the skies

Tapping my chin, I tilt my head. Considering we have christened every room in this house, I know it's likely an office, but which one? Bash, myself, and Jack, all have one. I don't have a leather chair, so, I'm going to guess and say Bash's office. Leaving the kitchen, I take my note and head upstairs into our wing. Pushing open the door to Sebastien's office, I look around but don't immediately recognize anything out of place. Rereading my note, I glide over to the floor to ceiling windows, and on the window sill is a note, on top of a black box tied with a ebony ribbon.

Reading the note before satisfying my curiosity about the box, I start;

You've found my mind, now follow my lust
But first, a little trust.
Cover your eyes, let your world go dark
And find your way to where we spark
Where pillows know our hearts best
And our hands are never at rest
No need to knock,

Follow the silence and turn the lock.

Squealing with excitement, I pull the ribbon on the box and slide the lid off. Inside, on a bed of velvet, is a blindfold. A thrill of anticipation runs through me. I know where this one leads. To our bedroom. Padding down the hallway, blindfold in hand, I pause outside the door and affix it over my face. Turning the knob, I walk into the room, my vision completely black. Quietly closing the door, I lock it behind me, and perk my ears to listen for any sound. As Bash said, it is silent. Walking my memorized path to our bed, I climb onto it. Unsure as to what to do now, I sit cross-legged and wait, my hands folded in my lap.

After a few seconds that feel like forever behind my dark blindfold, I feel Bash softly press his lips to mine, whispering, "Lay back, *Tesoro*."

Falling back against the pillows, I feel his hands on my hips, looping into my waistband, drawing my shorts and panties down my legs. I can feel the cool night air caressing my bare skin, and hear the faint rustle of his body as he makes adjustments. I smell the faintest wisp of whiskey and smoke that is Bash. Parting my lips, I exhale an audible breath. Capturing my ankle, he lays a kiss to the inside of my knee before securing a padded cuff around my leg, causing me to inhale sharply.

"Shhh, it's ok, baby, it's me. You're safe here." I relax, focusing on his words. "If you want me to stop, say 'stop' and I will."

Putting my leg back down, he repeats his treatment on the other leg. Once they are both buckled, I realize that the cuffs aren't tying me down, they are holding me apart.

"What-what is this?" I ask, moving my legs experimentally to see what I can do.

"It's a spreader bar, just a little-" I hear a click and my legs are pushed further apart.

I gasp in shock, longing filling me. I can feel my body responding, heat building in my belly. As if reading my mind, Bash runs a single finger through my wetness, whispering reverently, "That's my girl. So ready for me." I whimper in response, which elicits a chuckle that sends shockwaves through me.

Feeling his weight on top of me, I realize I can feel all of his skin also. I let out a giggle, thinking about him standing in our bedroom completely naked, waiting for me to solve his riddle.

"What's so funny, *Tesoro*?" he asks, biting my breast.

Shaking my head, my mirth instantly turns to need. "Noth–nothing. It's nothing"

"You'll tell me later," he says matter-of-factly, latching his lips to mine before sitting up.

Pushing on my thighs until my widely spread legs are in the air, he flicks his tongue against my clit before sucking hard on me. My back bows off the bed, a moan escaping my lips. Resting my thighs on his shoulders, he wraps one arm around my abdomen, holding my hips in place, and his other hand snaking under my body while he is rubs one finger in circles around my opening. Tracing my body with aching care, he pays attention to every inch of me, heightening my need with every expert stroke of his tongue.

His probing finger finally slipping inside my soaking pussy, I pulse around him with greedy need. Buried between my thighs, relentless and possessive, he pushes me closer and closer to the edge until I am keening with want, begging for release.

"Please, Bash, please!"

"What, baby? Tell me what you want?"

"I want to come!" I cry out, almost sobbing from the edge where he has kept me suspended at knife point for far too long.

"Your wish is my command, baby." Withdrawing his fingers and tongue, he extricates himself from my legs. I can't watch what he's doing and I am so lost with wanting to orgasm that I am floating in bliss above my body, my skin tingling.

Suddenly, my body is twisted by my ankles, flipping me onto my stomach. I cry out as my overheated, overstimulated flesh makes contact with the blanket below me. Gripping my hips hard, Bash lifts me to my knees before plunging three fingers into my dripping body causing me to convulse with pleasure, crying out for him. Pulling his fingers from me, I hear him licking them clean. It is the most erotic thing I think I've ever heard.

I feel the head of his hard cock slide through my sex, coating himself in my wetness. In one solid thrust, he is inside me, all the way to his pelvis. He pushes into me so fully, I can feel him hitting bottom and I hiss out a mix of pleasure and pain.

"Fuck," he whispers to the skin between my shoulder blades, before he begins thrusting into me hard and fast. I quiver beneath him, my body begging for release from this torture of standing on the edge. With him fucking me this hard, all I can do is hold on.

Moving his hand between my thighs, he rubs hard circles against me while his thrusts never slow. My body sings with pleasure, craving to fall over the edge warming me. As his pounding becomes more erratic, his ministrations become smaller, tighter, harder causing my nerve endings to fire rapidly as I begin my descent over the cliff. I shake, tremble, scream out in pleasure. My upper body collapses, absolutely shattered under him.

His breath comes out in pants, him grinding against me as he holds my hips aloft.

His body goes rigid. "Fuck, baby. Elina, *fuck*." His gasped exclamations are followed by him exploding in a whispered huff of air as he comes, falling across my back as we both press against the mattress. Wrapping his arm around my stomach, his body melded to mine, he withdraws, both of us hissing from the overstimulation of the movement.

He lays sweet kisses into my hair as he pulls my blindfold off.

Later that week, sitting on the banks of the Mississippi with my mate beside me, I gaze out over the water. The freedom of an infinite life stretched out before me, I look over my shoulder at the imposing boundary. Bash was willing to burn Ville de Sang to free me from the clutches of a madman if that's what it took. Refusing to allow fear of Nicolas to control me, I have retaken my life, my future, and I will not be afraid.

Glancing over at his contented face and relaxed body, I frown. I realized I am willing to do a lot more than that to free my people from the prison my new family has created for them. Before, I didn't have the power to help anyone, not even myself. But now?

I smile.

FOX KELLY

The End.

Casa del Malvani

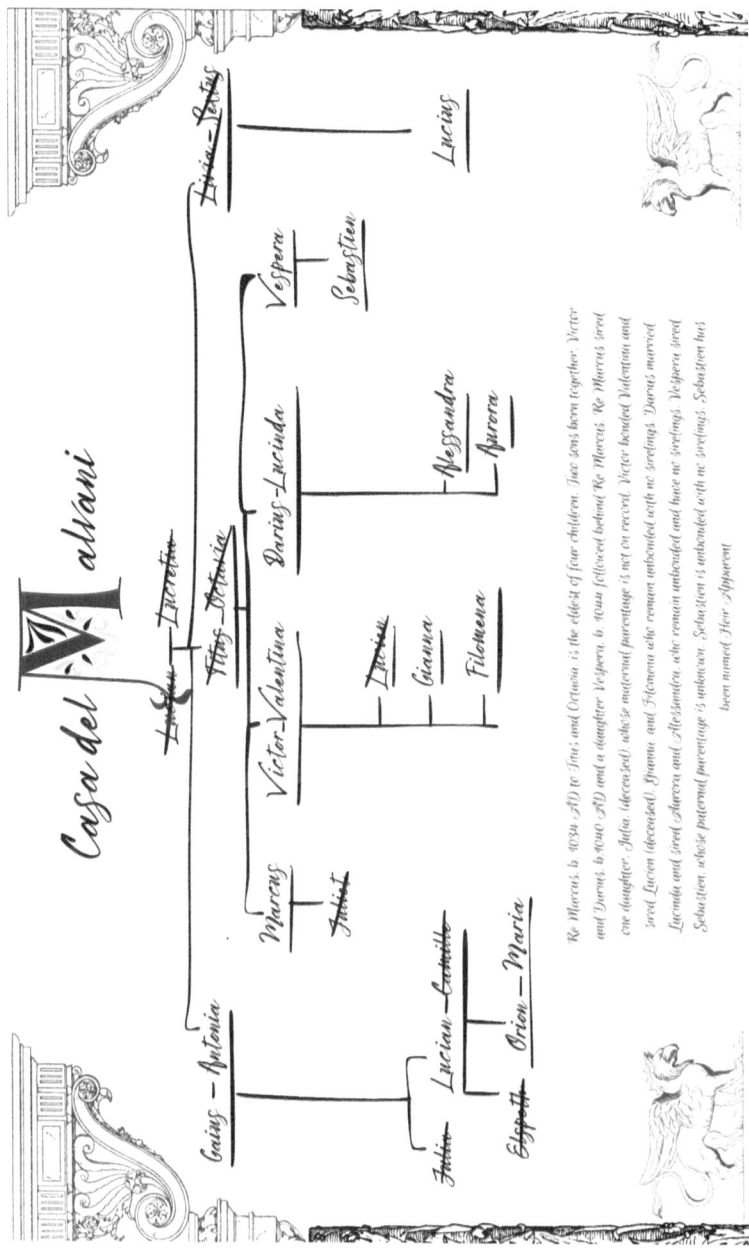

Re Marcus (b. 1034 AD) to Fina, and Octavia is the eldest of four children. Fina's sons born together Victor and Darius (b. 1040 AD) and a daughter Vespera, b. 1044 followed behind. Re Marcus' Re Marcus' sired one daughter Julia (deceased) who'se maternal parentage is not on record. Victor bonded Valentina and sired Lucien (deceased). Gianna and Filomena who remain unbonded with no sirelings. Darius married Lucinda and sired Aurora and Alessandra who remain unbonded and have no sirelings. Vespera sired Sebastien whose paternal parentage is unknown. Sebastien is unbonded with no sirelings. Sebastien has been named Heir Apparent.

ACKNOWLEDGMENTS

Strap in- I'm about to declare my undying love and devotion to everyone who helped bring this project to life.

Heather–First, I love you! Thank you for standing between me and the cliff I was prepared to dive off of everyday trying to get this book into the world. I couldn't ask for a better friend and supporter.

Kathy– Thank you for sticking with me and reading this even though its totally not your genre AT ALL. Your advice was invaluable and honestly, Bash is much better for it. Thank you a million times.

Mr. Fox Kelly– I'm not sure you'll ever read this but the support you offer me constantly keeps me moving forward and I would not be who I am, where I am, if I didn't have you every single day. I love you and I am so grateful to have you standing behind me.

Son– I know you didn't love listening to me ramble on and on but having your perspective helped make my story better, thank you.

Editor– Eisha Malik, Prompted Writings– Thank you for improving my story and getting all those commas in there.

Cover Designer–Lyndsey D. Graphics– Thank you for all the revisions and sticking with me through my vision.

My alpha readers– I appreciate you taking the time to read the rough (and I do mean ROUGH) version of this book. I hope you're proud of where we ended up.

About the Author

Fox Kelly is an emerging author of romance, paranormal and contemporary books. This is Fox's first book. (This did say I write action travel guides...which is an odd choice since the book is about people trapped in a city. Thanks Vellum).

Fox Kelly is a writer/mom/project manager/kid taxi driver from Ohio. Fox has been reading since childhood, and dreaming big dreams even longer. In her spare time (away from my grown-up job), Fox writes. And reads. And writes some more. And sometimes watches vampire television.

Fox's upcoming projects include a contemporary romance set in Montana, a dark romance set in North Carolina, and a novella set in the world of Ville de Sang. Fox writes what comes into her brain so you get what you get.

Stay in touch with Fox Kelly by visiting foxkelly.com, subscribing to my newsletter, and following me on socials.